About

Maisey Yates knew she [...] she knew what it was s[...] she was pregnant with [...] very first Mills & Boon [...] time she'd reached the happily ever after, she had fallen in love. Maisey lives with her supportive, handsome, wonderful, diaper-changing husband and three small children, across the street from her parents and the home she grew up in, in the wilds of southern Oregon.

Penny Jordan, one of Mills & Boon's most popular authors, sadly passed away on December 31st, 2011. She leaves an outstanding legacy, having sold over 100 million books around the world. Penny wrote a total of 187 novels for Mills & Boon, including the phenomenally successful *A Perfect Family*, *To Love, Honour and Betray*, *The Perfect Sinner* and *Power Play*, which hit the *New York Times* bestseller list. Loved for her distinctive voice, she was successful in part because she continually broke boundaries and evolved her writing to keep up with readers' changing tastes. *Publishers Weekly* said about Jordan, "Women everywhere will find pieces of themselves in Jordan's characters." It is perhaps this gift for sympathetic characterization that helps to explain her enduring appeal.

Sharon Kendrick started story-telling at the age of eleven and has never really stopped. She likes to write fast-paced, feel-good romances with heroes who are so sexy they'll make your toes curl! Born in west London, she now lives in the beautiful city of Winchester – where she can see the cathedral from her window (but only if she stands on tip-toe). Visit Sharon at www.sharonkendrick.com.

Scandals

COLLECTION

June 2018

July 2018

August 2018

September 2018

October 2018

November 2018

Scandals of the Crown

MAISEY YATES

PENNY JORDAN

SHARON KENDRICK

MILLS & BOON

Published in Great Britain 2018
by Mills & Boon, an imprint of HarperCollins*Publishers*
1 London Bridge Street, London, SE1 9GF

Scandals of the Crown © 2018 Harlequin Books S.A.

The Life She Left Behind © 2012 Harlequin Books S.A
Special thanks and acknowledgement are given to Maisey Yates for her contribution to *The Santina Crown* series

The Price of Royal Duty © 2012 Harlequin Books S.A
Special thanks and acknowledgement are given to Penny Jordan for her contribution to *The Santina Crown* series

The Sheikh's Heir © 2012 Harlequin Books S.A
Special thanks and acknowledgement are given to Sharon Kendrick for her contribution to *The Santina Crown* series

ISBN: 978-0-263-26721-1

06-2018

MIX
Paper from
responsible sources
FSC™ C007454

This book is produced from independently certified FSC™ paper to ensure responsible forest management.

For more information visit: www.harpercollins.co.uk/green

Printed and bound in Spain
by CPI, Barcelona

THE LIFE SHE
LEFT BEHIND

MAISEY YATES

CHAPTER ONE

It had finally happened. Sheikh Taj Ahmad, ruler of Rahat, had lost his mind completely. She was there, standing in the shadows on the otherwise vacant balcony that extended over the back portion of the ballroom. In an instant all the well-dressed, beautiful women that surrounded him faded away. He could see nothing but Angelina Carpenter.

So many times she had featured in his dreams, and yet, she had never quite looked like this. Hair pulled back into a ponytail, skinny jeans hugging her curves. This was a formal event, the engagement party for Prince Alessandro Santina. And famed oil heiress Angelina Carpenter was wearing jeans and a T-shirt.

The entire party had possessed an air of the surreal from the moment it had started. The presence of the loud, tacky Jackson family, the prince's future in-laws, with their penchant for drama had turned the royal setting on its head from the beginning.

The tension was only heightened by the attendance of Alessandro's ex-fiancée, who looked beautiful and brittle, ready to crack at any moment.

But none of that mattered now. He couldn't see it

anymore. He could hardly remember the reason he'd come tonight. There was nothing but Angelina now.

She turned her head, her eyes clashing with his, in spite of the distance and every person between them. She froze, up in her hiding place there on the balcony, her beautiful lips parting.

He could see her intake of breath, see her hold it, and he held his in answer. Or possibly because breathing had simply become too difficult.

"Taj," the woman to his right, the one who had been attempting to climb him all evening, purred his name, her fingers curving into his bicep, "would you go and fetch me a drink?"

He turned to look at her, breaking the spell Angelina had held him under. The room came back, conversation rising in volume. His unwanted companion's red lips were pursed into a pout. His stomach clenched. With annoyance, not desire.

"I do not fetch," he said, breaking out of the woman's grasp, redirecting his attention to the balcony.

Angelina was gone.

Had she really been an illusion? A dream? A waking one this time, sent to tempt and torment him with the memory of what he could not have?

It wasn't possible. Angelina, in his dreams, was always the polished heiress. Never undone, not even in his more erotic dreams, when he pictured holding her in his arms, their naked limbs entwined. Even then she was the soul of high-gloss perfection.

This woman, with her strawberry hair pulled back into something as juvenile and unsophisticated as a ponytail, was not the Angelina of his fantasies.

That could only mean she was real.

Cold pin pricks dotted over his back, a clammy sweat on his forehead, as he wove through the ballroom, headed to the back doors. Unless there were secret passageways in the Santina palace, and it was possible, she would have to pass by the ballroom when she went down the stairs.

He moved quickly through the crowd, paying no attention to the people who tried to greet him. He hardly heard them, hardly understood them. The low din of conversation and the strains of music simply faded.

He pushed the doors open and cursed when he saw the empty corridor. Perhaps it had been an illusion. Another round of torture at the hands of Angelina Carpenter. Three years since he'd seen her and still she tormented him.

He heard a sound to his left and he followed it, feeling a fool on an even more foolish errand. But he could not stop himself. Not now.

His heart thundered and he rounded the corner and into another stretch of hallway, just in time to see long strawberry hair disappearing around the next corner.

And he ran.

IT COULDN'T BE HIM. No, it very well could be him, and that was the problem. The very scary, very bad, very heart pounding-hand-shaking problem.

Angelina leaned against the wall in the vacant corridor and closed her eyes, tried to catch her breath. Taj.

Flashes. Pictures. The happiest moments of her life flashed behind her eyes. Taj when she'd met him for the first time, his warm smile. His attempt at wearing a cowboy hat and adapting to the Western style of horseback riding. And the evening they'd spent in the main barn at her father's ranch, the night she'd fallen in love with him.

She fought hard against the pain that was threatening to overwhelm her. So much of her life, of what had happened in the past three years, was tied to Taj. All of it, really. Because without Taj, without her father's deception, she never would have run away from Texas. Never would have ended up in Italy, taking care of Princess Carlotta's son, Luca.

Without Taj, she would never have known what it felt like to love someone, and find out how much it hurt when they didn't love you back.

A muttered curse in Arabic brought her head up, and her gaze collided with Taj's coal colored eyes. He looked the same. Dark and commanding. His black hair cropped short, no sign of the slight curl at his neck that she'd loved to twirl around her fingers.

It was the same Taj, yet different somehow. Leaner. Harder.

The impact he had on her hadn't changed, either. Her heart was pounding, her body shaking, a surge of adrenaline making her blood run hotter, faster.

He was the man who haunted her dreams. The reason she woke up in a cold sweat, aching and unsatisfied. The reason no man had appealed to her in the least since she'd left home.

He exhaled a breath and for the first time since spotting him from the balcony, she drew breath in.

"It is you." He sounded like a man addressing a ghost. He looked about like that, too.

She tried to smile. "And it's you."

"I was invited to help celebrate this occasion. What

escapes me is why you're here. No one has heard from you in three years."

"How do you…how do you know that?"

"I keep in touch," he said, his voice cold as stone and just as hard.

She bet he did. Her father had one of the things that Sheikh Taj prized above all else. Oil. Their money was slick with it, and they had been ready to make an alliance. She imagined they had made it, even without her as the glue to hold it together.

Without her as the sacrificial virgin.

"You and my father always did have a lot in common," she said, her tone sharp and lofty. Rich, considering she was standing in front of him in jeans and a ratty ponytail while he was in a custom made suit.

"Not as much as you might think," he said.

"I don't have time to wonder what that means. I have to get back."

"To?"

"Luca. He's asleep he…"

"You have a lover with you?" he asked, his voice going cold.

She laughed in spite of the situation. "Luca is a child."

He jerked back as though she'd hit him. "Your child?"

"Princess Carlotta's child. I'm his nanny."

A muscle in his jaw jumped. "You traded your life, your future, as my queen to be a nanny?"

"No. I traded being your queen for some self-respect."

She turned and walked away from him, her entire body shaking, regret threatening to climb up from her chest and strangle her.

CHAPTER TWO

She closed the door to her room behind her and leaned against the doorway. She'd lied to escape from him, but hey, who could blame her?

Luca was sleeping in his own room, and he didn't require her care at night. That was one reason she'd felt confident enough to sneak down to the engagement party. To catch a glimpse of the life she no longer lived. Glittering royals, an undercurrent of drama beneath the smooth, refined setting. It was all so familiar.

That had been her three years ago, down among the people with her formal gown and fake smile. An heiress with a comfortable, wealthy life stretching in front of her. But she'd told Taj the truth. She'd traded all that for self-respect. For a chance to control her own life and find out what she could be other than a pawn.

A hard knock vibrated the door behind her and she turned sharply, her hand over her mouth. He'd followed her. She shouldn't be surprised.

The worst thing was, she wanted to open the door. Her hand was already on the knob. Just like three years ago, what she truly wanted, was to be with him.

But then, she hadn't wanted marriage without love. And Taj hadn't loved her. He'd wanted to acquire her, along with a significant merger with her father's oil company.

Of course, she hadn't known that. She'd thought the young, Arabic leader had been smitten with her. That he'd looked at her and seen something special. That he'd been as crazy about her as she'd been about him. She'd been so young then. So naive. Love had seemed an easy, wondrous find. It had seemed the be-all and end-all.

She'd learned since that that wasn't true.

If love was so powerful, so important, then the moment her love for Taj had died, all of her thoughts of him would have dissolved and blown away like desert sand. They hadn't. He still plagued her sleep. He was still the man her body desired.

The absence of love hadn't changed that. It was a sobering realization, just how much Taj still mattered. How much power he still possessed. That he could make her run. She gritted her teeth. No. She didn't run. At least, she wouldn't run now. Wouldn't give him that satisfaction, that level of importance.

She took a breath and her hand turned the door handle before she'd fully processed the action, and she found herself staring into Taj's obsidian eyes.

"Don't run from me again," he bit out.

"Again? Don't flatter yourself. I was never running from you. I was running *to* independence. I'm not a frightened child. I don't run from things." She crossed her arms beneath her chest.

"Liar. In the hall just now, you were very much running from me. From the attraction that still exists between us."

"Attraction? Have you been drinking tonight?"

"I don't drink. You know that. And yes, attraction. It

has always been there, or have you forgotten the night we spent in your father's barn?"

"You make it sound like we…" His gaze dropped to her lips. "We kissed. That's all." And they'd cuddled up together, looking at the night sky through a hole in the roof, her hand on his chest, her mouth spilling out all of her stupid dreams for the future. Dreams she'd believed he'd shared in. But while she'd been counting stars, he'd been counting money. The money he would make when he married her.

"There are simple kisses, Angelina, and then there are the kinds of kisses we shared that night. And they are not the same thing."

No, they weren't. But the only reason they'd been different was because she'd been barely twenty and had fancied herself in love. They'd felt new and precious, and more exciting than anything else ever had.

"We just kissed, Taj."

"And if we kissed again? You think you would feel…?"

"Nothing," she whispered. "I would feel nothing."

He leaned in and her breath caught. She didn't back away from him. She couldn't. "Is that so? You have not thought of me since you left? Not once?"

Always.

"No."

"You lie again," he said, his voice rough, his eyes glittering in challenge.

If he was trying to intimidate her, it wouldn't work. Her eyes were open now, to the world, to the people around her. People she'd thought loved her.

She was not a child anymore. And she would not act like one. Wouldn't allow him to walk into her life and devastate it or think even for a moment that he could.

She wouldn't allow him to have all the control. No. She had control now. She had power.

She put her hands on his face, his stubble rough beneath her palms. Leaning in, she pressed her lips to his. They were hot and hard, immobile. Her stomach tightened, a fierce rush of need flowing through her, the kind of need she hadn't felt since the last time Taj had held her in his arms.

He didn't move and she angled her head, sliding her tongue against the seam of his lips. That was when he moved, like a man breaking free from chains. He wrapped his arms around her and pulled her to him, deepening the kiss, his tongue moving against hers.

She could feel his heart beneath her hands, raging hard, out of control. Every bit as out of control as she felt.

He took a step and she took a step back, then he took another and she followed. He released her for a moment to shut the door hard behind him, the sound jarring her back to reality.

"What are you doing?"

"You started it, Angel, shouldn't you have the answer?" he asked.

"I don't…" Her pulse thundered in her head and she tried to form a coherent sentence. She had meant to show him she had command now. That she wasn't so easily manipulated. But all of those intentions had been knocked right out of her the moment their lips had touched.

She couldn't prove a point, not while she was so utterly lost in sensation.

He took a step toward her, his expression changing,

softening. He put his hand on her cheek. "You are real. You must be."

"I…of course I am."

"You never said goodbye to me when you left."

"I was angry at you."

The corners of his lips turned down. When he made that face, it was easy to imagine him as a sulky, spoiled child. Nothing about that should be endearing, and yet, she found it was. "I surmised as much. I never did find out why."

"You don't know?"

He shook his head. "I assumed perhaps you had found a better prospect, and yet here you are, a nanny, so I'm certain now that isn't the case."

She laughed. "I did find a better prospect. Independence. Life beyond being your accessory. When I found out my father was promising you my hand in order to cement the merger I… I couldn't stay. I'm not a thing, Taj, and I refused to be traded like I was."

"Angelina…"

"Is this the part where you tell me I misunderstood? That you weren't really going to do it? That you had other motives?" She'd wondered over the years. Wondered if she'd been too quick to run. If she should have stayed and talked to him.

Waiting for the words now was tantamount to torture.

"No. I'm not going to say that. Because I was using you to get the merger. Though, I confess I thought you were complicit in the arrangement."

Only because she'd imagined she'd meant something to him. That when he'd kissed her, there had been feeling in it.

"I wasn't."

"And now what, Angelina? Do I leave you here? Do we never see each other again?"

The idea of Taj turning and walking away, the thought of never seeing him again, made her heart ache. More than that, it reminded her of the ache that had existed since she'd lost him the first time.

He was the man she'd never been able to forget. The one demon from her past left unexorcised. What would it take? What would it take to rid her body of her desire for him? To squeeze those deeply held feelings from her heart? To erase him from her mind.

Her body burned from the kiss. Her heart burned from looking at him.

She hated it. She hated how much he controlled her. Whether he was standing in front of her, or in another country entirely, the man held too much power. It had to end.

He turned away, and her stomach jolted. Leaving, separation, that wouldn't work. It wasn't enough. She knew it. And she was desperate. Desperate to make it go away. Her desire for him was beneath her skin, in her blood.

There was only one way she could think of to bleed herself of it, to pour it out of her.

"Don't go," she said.

He stopped, his shoulders going ridged. "What?"

It wasn't too late to go back. To stop herself from touching him. From confirming what she was certain he suspected. But she didn't want to. She had run from him, from her feelings, her heartbreak, all those years ago. But she hadn't escaped it. It had clung to her, wrapped itself around her heart like a clinging vine.

Distance hadn't killed it. But he was here now. Maybe if she could have him, just once, she could draw a line through that part of her life and call it done.

She took a deep breath, ignoring the trembling in her fingers as she reached out to put her hand on his shoulder. "Stay. Stay with me tonight."

CHAPTER THREE

Taj's original theory, the one in which Angelina was a mirage, was starting to seem likely again. She had felt real beneath his hands, beneath his lips. Her unsteady fingers felt real on his back, but the words she'd just spoken made it all seem like a fantasy.

He turned to face her, his heart raging, his blood hot. "What did you say?"

She bit one of her lips, swollen from his earlier attention. "Stay. I want you to stay."

"And count stars?" he asked, his tone sardonic, his stomach tight with the memory.

She snorted a breath and shook her head, her strawberry colored ponytail swinging with the motion. "No. I'm not a girl who thinks she's in love anymore. I'm a woman. I got everything I could ask for from my relationship with you. Heartbreak. Betrayal. And yet I never got the one thing that might have made it all worth it."

"You want sex," he said, going for direct. Because if direct didn't frighten her, then he wouldn't question her bold proposition.

Her chin tilted up a fraction, her expression hard. "Yes."

"Sweet, romantic, Angelina who wanted to wait until

our wedding night? Who told me just now she ran because she did not want any sort of arranged marriage?" His words were harsher than he intended, much harsher. But he could hardly breathe. His chest was tight, his muscles so tense they were shaking.

He had been waiting for this moment, for her, for what seemed like an eternity. And she was here now, wanting him. He was afraid that if he moved she would vanish into smoke.

"I might have been those things at one time but I've grown up. A lot," she said, her tone hard. Sad. "And I understand that we can't have everything we want in life. But I can have something I want. I can have you."

"You want me?" He needed to hear her say it, and that need was a weakness he didn't want to stop and examine.

"If I didn't, I wouldn't have asked you to stay."

"Why now?"

"You aren't the only one here capable of capitalizing on an opportunity," she said.

He stopped then and looked at her more closely. She had been so young when he'd first met her. And while three years hadn't changed much in terms of physical age, she was different now. Gone was that magical glitter in her green eyes, that sweet and easy smile. She looked tired. She looked hard.

She looked like a woman who had seen too much, rather than one just starting out into the world.

Had he caused that? Or had something happened to her after she'd left Texas? He didn't like to think it had been either of those things.

Back then he had been doing just what she'd said: capitalizing on an opportunity. But he had liked her.

He had treated her well. He'd certainly never meant to hurt her.

He had paid, though; he had paid dividends since she'd walked out of his life. In ways he could not begin to explain.

Just one of the many things affected had been his sex drive. He'd had no desire for a woman, for sex at all, since she'd left. And now that she was here, that had changed. It had changed drastically.

Desire didn't feel like he remembered. Had it always made him feel like he was standing on the edge of a cliff? Had it always stolen his breath and made his body tremble? He didn't think it had. But it was now. He felt perilously close to losing his balance. To losing himself.

"Then that is what I am to you," he said, "an opportunity?"

"An opportunity was all I was to you, sugar." She'd called him that back in Texas. It had sounded sweet then. An endearment. Silly but it had done something to him. Now it seemed more of an insult.

"I am not interested in banter, or arguments," he said. "If you want me, come here and show me."

It was not his way to have a woman make the first move. It never had been. But he had to give the power to Angelina now, mostly because he stood powerless before her. What had happened in the space of the past half hour?

Taj Ahmad, Sheikh of Rahat, ruler of many, transfixed, controlled, by a woman.

But the revelation didn't bring the power to prevent it. He had no strength to stop what was unfolding. And no desire to stop it, either.

She took a step toward him, her eyes darkening, the

emotion in them unknowable to him. And for once, he was grateful to be ignorant of something.

"This time," she said, "you have to kiss me."

If he did, he would be the one laying down his hand. The one giving in. He did not give in. It wasn't in him.

At the moment, his body seemed to disagree. Because he was moving to her. And then he took her in his arms. He relished the feeling for a moment, the sensation of having her breasts pressed against his chest, of her softness. Her strength.

It was little wonder no woman had managed to appeal to him since Angelina. She was like no other woman, and his desire for her had remained piqued but unsatisfied since he'd met her.

He needed satisfaction. He needed to have her. In his arms. In his bed, or her bed, so that he could move on.

Resisting wasn't an option. It wasn't a possibility.

He was lost, in her kiss, her touch. He pushed his hand beneath her shirt and felt her smooth, creamy skin. He pulled his hand away, as though he'd been burned. He felt like he had been. Down to his soul. He couldn't explain it. Didn't want to.

Not when she was arching against him, whispering words of encouragement, her hands moving over his back.

He looked at her face and saw her eyes, closed tight, as though she was afraid to open them.

"Look at me," he growled. Her eyes opened wide. "I would have you know who you're with."

She looked confused. Dazed. "How could you be anyone else?"

With a groan, he claimed her lips again, walking her back to the opulent bed that was in the corner. He laid her down on the soft duvet, and peeled her shirt over her head, revealing snow-white breasts barely covered by a thin web of a lace that was trying to pass for a bra.

His hand shook as he traced the line of the bra with his fingertip. Had a woman ever made him shake before? He did not think so.

For a moment, he feared it would it be over too quickly. A fear he had never experienced in his life. But three years without sex was a long time. And now that he was breaking his fast, it was with the object of his fantasies.

She worked at removing his clothes, while she divested him of his. When his skin finally met hers, he exhaled a breath. One he thought he might have been holding since she walked out of his life.

It was like everything fit. Finally.

He lavished attention on her strawberry tipped breasts, her sighs of pleasure and the feel of her arching against him almost more than he could handle. He gritted his teeth and tried to call on all of his focus. Focus, single-mindedness, he was renowned for those things. Trained up to be a leader, a man with the power to rule a nation.

And yet, with her, he found he did not have the control of a king. He barely had the control of a teenage boy faced with a naked woman for the first time.

She parted her thighs and he settled between them. He paused for a moment and looked down at her face. Her eyes were on him, open, as he had commanded. She put her hands on his face and stroked him lightly. A shudder moved through him, and he realized that he was not the one in control.

Not in the least.

"Please," she whispered against his lips.

He pressed against the entrance of her body, easing in slowly. Her face tensed, a small sound of pain, deep in her throat, stopping him short.

She shook her head. "It's okay." She slid her hands down to his buttocks and urged him on.

Being inside her, fully inside her, was more than he had fantasized about. It went beyond any experience, real or imagined.

She moved against him, meeting his thrusts, pressing kisses to his neck, pushing him higher, faster. But he needed to ensure that she found her pleasure. He had to. Somehow that directive pierced through the fog of his arousal.

He wrapped his fingers around her thigh and draped his over hers, opening her to him. Then he placed his other hand at her breast, teasing her nipple, drawing it tighter. A short sound of pleasure escaped her lips and he continued on, teasing her, tormenting her. Teasing and tormenting himself.

Then she froze beneath him, arching into him, her internal muscles tightening around him as she embraced her orgasm.

He released his control, his blood roaring in his ears as he ran toward the wave that had been ebbing toward him from the moment he set eyes on Angelina in the ballroom. It overwhelmed him, swallowing him, his mind blank as he emptied himself into her body, his limbs shaking, his heart raging.

Afterward he lay with her. Replete. More so than he had ever been in his life.

And then he did something he had never done with a lover. He pulled her into his arms and fell asleep.

WHEN HE WOKE UP, it was light outside. And the bed was cold. He rolled over and put his hand where Angelina should have been. Empty.

He sat up and looked around the room. His clothes were on the floor. Folded. And Angelina's clothes were gone. Everything of hers was gone.

He pulled his pants on quickly and buckled his belt, shrugging his shirt on, buttoning it as he walked down the corridors of the palace.

Some people might have felt embarrassed doing the walk of shame through a palace. But he didn't do embarrassment. He didn't do uncertainty, either.

And last night had left him very certain of the fact that Angelina belonged with him.

He stopped a member of the household staff who was walking quickly through the corridor. "Do you know where Angelina Carpenter is?"

The woman gave him a hard look. "Princess Carlotta's nanny?"

He supposed he deserved the look. As he was across the palace from where he was meant to be staying, half dressed, his hair likely standing on end. The sheikh looking for the nanny.

He did not care. "Yes."

"I believe she left this morning. Princess Carlotta wanted her son to go back to Italy as soon as possible and Angelina naturally accompanied him."

"Grazi," he said through his teeth.

The woman nodded and turned away. Taj's stomach tightened. Angelina had left. She had left him. She was gone. Again.

He knew where to find her now, of course. He could go after her. He wanted to.

Taj tightened his hand into a fist, gritting his teeth, ignoring the stabbing pain in his chest. He would not be made a fool of. Not again.

He'd had her. He'd had her virginity. And now he would go on. He would not go after her.

He ignored the sour feeling in his stomach and walked down the corridor, making his way out of the grand palace without pausing to greet anyone.

He vowed he would not think of her. Not again. Too much of his life had been wasted on Angelina Carpenter.

No more.

CHAPTER FOUR

She felt awful. More awful than usual. And she'd pretty much felt awful for the past two months, since she'd left Taj lying in her bed and packed her bags as quietly as possible. So feeling worse really was something.

At least she knew why now. Those two pink lines didn't lie.

Misery washed through her. She'd made a mistake. A big one. And now there was nothing left to do but try to call Taj and tell him. It was her responsibility. Did sheikhs have listed phone numbers? She wasn't certain.

She put her head in her hands for a moment, then straightened from her near-fetal position on the bed and took her phone from her nightstand. Dissolving into a puddle wasn't happening.

The past two months hadn't been great. She'd missed Taj. Missed him desperately. But the facts hadn't changed. He didn't love her. And she was perilously close to loving him again.

She'd tried to throw herself into taking care of Luca. Getting him adjusted to his new life in Santa Christobel with Carlotta and her fiancé, Rodriguez. That had helped. When they'd arrived, she'd been called on a lot while the new royal couple had been learning to deal with one another.

And Rodriguez had been scared to death of Luca at first.

But things were changing now. They needed her less and less.

And now she'd found out that she had a child who needed her even more than her little charge. Her own child. And Taj needed to know.

She let out a low whine and surfed through the contacts on her phone. She found the number for Rodriguez's personal secretary, a number she had just in case there was an emergency and for some reason neither Rodriguez nor Carlotta could be reached.

She hit Send.

"Hi. This is Angelina."

"Is everything all right with Luca?"

"Everything's fine. He's with his parents today I... I was wondering if you knew how to get a hold of the palace in Rahat.'"

"Taj?"

Taj's stomach tightened, his heart beating hard. It was Angelina. He knew it with certainty. Not because he recognized her voice, though he did, but because only she made his body react in the way it was reacting now. It was a near supernatural connection. One he would have scoffed at had he not felt it personally.

"Angelina?"

"Yes. I'm... I need to talk to you."

He tightened his hold on the phone. "You are talking to me. What is it?"

"I... I shouldn't have just left that morning. I'm sorry."

"It isn't as though I have wasted much time thinking about it." A lie. He had thought of nothing else. No demons had been exorcised that night. It had not brought back his desire for other women. If anything, he was less interested than he'd been before. Angelina seemed to fill him, surround him.

Angelina Carpenter was an addiction he couldn't seem to kick.

"I'm certain you haven't," she returned, her voice sounding muted. "But whether or not you've thought of me at all…well, that doesn't really matter. I'm not calling to confess my undying love."

"Of course not." He ignored the fierce seizing in his chest.

"I'm pregnant."

He dropped the phone. It crashed onto the marble floor and he prayed fervently that he had not lost the call as he bent to pick it back up. "You're what?" he asked, his tone rough.

"I'm pregnant." The silence hung thick between them, the only sound in the room the beating of his heart, his harsh intake of breath. "You're the father, by the way. That's why I called."

"I know I'm the father," he bit out. "What do you suppose I think of you?"

"It wouldn't be an insult, I suppose. How many lovers have you had since we parted?"

"None," he snapped.

"Oh." She sounded shocked. Subdued.

"You must come here."

"I figured as much. I'll have to tell Carlotta and… and Luca." She sounded sad about that. Sad to be coming to him? Or sad to leave her charge?

"We have to get married," he said.

"I figured that, too."

"You sound very calm." It maddened him that she could be so calm. So unaffected. As though the world had not just tilted on its axis. As though she had not just agreed to marry him.

As though she was not carrying his child.

"I think there are those in the medical profession who call it shock," she said, some of the fire he recognized returning to her tone.

"I see." He looked out his office window, out into his lushly landscaped courtyard. It reflected nothing of the desert beyond it. None of the hot, red sand that stretched as far as any man could see in every direction. "I will send for you. Tonight."

THE HEAT OF Texas hadn't prepared her for the arid, invasive climate of Rahat. Stepping out of the air-conditioned car that had been sent to the airport and into the elements had been a shock. It wasn't heat that seared her skin, it was fear that seared her skin and reached down her throat, pulling out every drop of moisture, scorching her lungs.

The sky was bleached white, the sand red, nothing green or living visible anywhere. And the only thing more forbidding than the environment was the man who seemed to rise from it. Standing in front of the gates to the castle, heat waves blurring her view of him, but not disguising who he was.

Taj was waiting for her. His arms crossed over his broad chest, his expression stoic.

She took a step away from the car and looked back at

the driver, who told her in fluent English that her bags would be sent in and up to her room.

Her room. At least she would have her own room. She didn't think she could handle the forced intimacy of sharing one with Taj. Not now.

"Salaam," he said, moving away from the gates and coming to greet her, his strides long and certain. He looked so at home here. He looked like a part of the desert. And she had never felt more alone.

"Hello, Sheikh," she said, inclining her head, feeling the weight of his title fully for the first time with his grand palace in the background.

She'd known he was a sheikh. That he was the ruler of a country. And yet, when she'd met him it had been in Texas. They'd made out in a barn and laughed and talked. He had seemed approachable. Accessible.

He seemed nothing of the sort now.

"Taj," he said. He took her chin between his thumb and forefinger and tilted her face up to him. "You must call me Taj."

"Taj," she repeated.

"You are well?"

"As well as can be expected."

A shadow passed over his handsome face, his eyes darkening. "Good." He looked up at the sky, shielding his face with his hand. "Come, Angel, we need to get you in from this heat."

She turned and followed him into the palace. It took her a few moments to realize he'd called her Angel.

CHAPTER FIVE

"Is everything up to your standards?" Taj studied Angelina's sullen face at dinner. She looked pale. She looked unhappy. She looked like a woman about to face capital punishment rather than one who had been moved into a palace and offered a position as queen.

Although, maybe offered was the wrong word.

"Everything is lovely," she said, his focus on her dinner plate.

"And yet you sound like a petulant child who has been denied a pony for Christmas."

Her head snapped up, her green eyes glittering. "Do you think so?"

"I know so."

"Quite the pronouncement. Especially coming from a man who's never been denied anything."

He shrugged. "It's true, I had seven of my own Arabian horses by the time I was six. They were not considered ponies." He studied the glass of *sharbat* in front of him. "But you're wrong."

His stomach burned as she glared at him, the green turning arctic, the corners of her lush lips curved down. "Is that so?"

"I have been denied things I've desired greatly," he

said, thinking of the years he'd gone without her, of the months after she'd left him. Of the feeling of arousal, relief and utter fear he'd felt when she'd called him again.

"Have you?" she said, scraping her empty plate with her fork.

"You have no idea, do you?"

"I don't play guessing games, Sheikh, so you might as well cut to the chase."

"Taj. You will call me Taj. And I'm not trying to play a game. Do you think I gave no thought to you over the past three years?"

She tilted her chin up. "I can hardly say."

"I did. I thought of you every night. Every time a woman looked my direction. I thought of the one woman I truly desired. And how she had been denied to me."

Her lips thinned, her body going stiff. "Now who sounds like the petulant child, Taj?"

He leaned back in his chair, arousal and annoyance battling each other. "I have been accused of being petulant, it's true. But I am royal and it's my right."

"Indeed!" she snapped.

"Yes. Indeed. But one thing I am not and you should know this, Angel, is a child."

Crimson color flooded her cheeks and she stood. He stood as well, anger more in play than any sense of good manners. "I can't deal with you right now."

She turned to go and he caught her arm. "Then when will we deal with each other?" He leaned in and caught her scent. Vanilla soap and something beneath it, something clean and unique to Angelina. "When?" he asked again, loosening his hold on her but keeping his hand on her soft skin, his thumb stroking her. "On our wedding night? When our child is born?"

She shook her head. "I...no. But not now."

He leaned in and kissed her, a challenge. To her strength. Her defiance. To the fact that she seemed so utterly composed and distant while he felt like his desire was a living thing, burning him alive from the inside out.

She kissed him back. Her lips clinging to his, her body arching to his. Then, as suddenly as she acquiesced, she broke away, her eyes wide, her chest rising and falling on short, choppy breaths.

"I'm not in the mood for that, either," she said.

"Your body, and your manner, would suggest otherwise, my Angel," he said, his need threatening to strangle him.

"My body isn't running the show. My mind is."

"Was that true a couple of months ago?"

A false smile curved her lips. "I think we both know it wasn't. Call it temporary insanity, sugar." That name again. She used it to put distance between them. He would not allow it.

"With permanent consequences," he said.

Lust leached from him as he looked down at her flat stomach. A sense of surreal awe filling him. She was carrying his baby. Their baby.

He'd thought about children, in terms of heirs and fulfilled duty. But he'd never thought about what it would really mean to create a child. To have a baby that was part of him, part of its mother. Part of Angelina.

If they had a daughter, would she have her mother's red hair? Or would his Middle Eastern heritage dominate? He'd never given time to such thoughts before. And now he seemed to be bogged down by them.

"You're pregnant," he said, releasing his hold on her

completely and taking a step back. It was no longer desire that was trying to strangle him.

She swallowed visibly. "Yes. That is why I'm here."

"But…you're having a baby."

"That's what pregnant means," she said, crossing her arms beneath her breasts.

"How do you feel?"

"I'm a wreck, actually, Taj, but thank you for asking."

He frowned. "What has wrecked you?"

"I feel like the world's biggest idiot. I slept with a guy, that's you, with no protection and there's no excuse for that. None."

"It was my responsibility. I failed. You were…you were a virgin," he said.

"So? I didn't live under a rock. I know how things work. I know about being responsible and I wasn't."

"Desire gets the best of people sometimes." It had certainly gotten the best of him. For the past three years it had gotten the best of him.

She shook her head. "I suppose that's true. Because there is no other explanation for it."

She turned to walk out of the room and he felt something large, indefinable, squeezing his chest. "Do you regret it, Angelina?"

She stopped, her shoulders sagging. "I don't know yet," she said, her voice quiet.

He vowed right then that she would never regret it. Not if he could help it.

CHAPTER SIX

It was only six in the morning and already the temperature was rising. The palace was cool, but stifling, the walls feeling like they were closing in on her. She doubted she would ever get used to this place. She wanted to run. She wanted to hide.

It wasn't an option.

Taj had sent dressers to her room this morning with beautiful silk gowns in bright colors. They were cut into Western styles but bore beautiful Eastern influences. They were fit for the Queen of Rahat, one of the women said.

And they were right. But she wondered if it was the mistresses of Rahat who had worn them before. If they'd been used by other women. The idea made her skin itch. Made her feel violently possessive and jealous in a way she had no right feeling.

She'd run away from being Queen of Rahat once. Now it seemed she was trapped.

"Sheikh Taj is on his way," the other woman said. "You are meeting the press this morning and he would like to make sure you are prepared."

Her stomach sank, a faint impression of nausea wrapping itself around her. "You can tell him that I would rather have bamboo shoots shoved up my fingernails," she muttered.

"Noted."

She turned and saw Taj standing in the doorway. She froze and her two aids bent their heads and scurried out of the room.

"Did you bring bamboo, sugar?" she asked, turning her Texas drawl up a notch.

"I thought perhaps you would prefer tea," he said, lifting a delicate china cup up to chest level. "It's green tea, no caffeine. I thought it might be preferable to torture."

"Tea, yes, a meet-the-press moment, no."

"Our engagement must be announced."

She wrapped her arms around herself in an effort to keep from falling apart. "I haven't even been here for twenty-four hours."

"We'll need to marry before it becomes obvious you're pregnant."

"I forgot you're traditional around here."

"Show me the royal family that disregards such traditions completely. Have they disregarded them in Santina?"

Angelina thought of Princess Carlotta, of the shame the press had put her through for having a child out of wedlock. Even now, years after the fact, it marked her. Marked her entire existence, and the existence of her son. "No."

"Then do not play like Rahat is such an anomaly. We have traditions to uphold, certain expectations we must meet. You will become accustomed to it."

"I'm not sure I can," she said, her voice hardly achieving the volume of a whisper.

When he responded, his tone was surprisingly gentle. "What other option is there, Angelina?"

She could leave. She could go into hiding. Hope that he never found her. She could take her child away from his father; she could steal her child's birthright. Deny it the chance to be royalty, the first born of a king.

Yes, she could do that. But it would be wrong. It would be selfish. If Taj were a bad man, if he were incapable of being a good father, of loving their child, then maybe it would be excusable. But the fact was, he was just as likely to be a good parent as she was.

The look on his face after dinner last night, when his eyes had fallen to his stomach, had nearly brought her to her knees. There had been tenderness there, a longing that had made her chest ache in response.

No, she could not take Taj's child from him. She couldn't take her baby from his father.

And that meant, no matter how much it sucked for her, she had to stick it out.

She met Taj's eyes and her heart tripped and fell over itself. There were certain things that wouldn't be a hardship. Being with Taj…it had been incredible. Unlike anything she'd ever experienced before.

He had been as amazing as she'd imagined. No, even more amazing.

But she was afraid of what he made her feel, too. Afraid of getting involved with him again. Afraid of loving him again.

He was arrogant and entitled, with strong and proud tendencies when he was angry. Loving him should take effort. Yet, she found it was a lot harder to stop herself from loving him. And that was just stupid.

"There is no other option," she said.

"You knew that from the beginning."

She nodded. "Yes. I did." From the moment she'd seen the positive test, she'd known. It was either hide the truth from him forever, or embrace life as his queen. "But…where did these dresses come from?" If she really was going to be his wife she would take a stand here at least. She wasn't wearing cast-off gowns from cast-off women.

His face hardened, for a moment he looked like he'd been carved from stone. "They have been here. Just as this room has been here. Awaiting its queen."

"What?"

"They are yours. I had them prepared when you accepted my proposal."

"And you…kept them?"

He tilted his chin upward, the gesture making him look haughty. Defiant. "I was to marry one day with or without you. Clothes are altered easily enough, why should I replace them."

"Why indeed?" she struck back. "If the woman in question does not matter, if she's only part and parcel to a business agreement then why does it matter what she might want? Who she is?"

"It matters," he said, his voice rough.

She took a step back, her stomach curling in. "Oh. I… I…"

He appraised her for a moment, his dark eyes searching. "It will not be so bad to be my wife, will it?"

She didn't know what to say. Words stuck in her throat. Words in denial and in agreement.

His expression hardened. "Well then, let us prepare to speak to the media."

She had a feeling she'd done the wrong thing. But

she could not find the words to placate him. Because they would be a lie.

It would be hard to be married to him. Hard to guard her heart against feelings she didn't want but wasn't certain she could deny.

"You were exquisite," Taj said as he closed the limo door and encased them in the air-conditioning.

"I hardly spoke." She felt horrible. Her head was pounding, and she was still shaking from having to sit there in front of so many people.

"And in Rahat, that will be considered a bonus."

"Oh, I do hope you're joking," she said, treating him to her deadliest glare. In addition to the headache, she was hot, starving and in no mood to take garbage off anyone. Least of all Taj.

He shrugged, as if shaking off her anger. "I was. Sort of. But the way the more traditional citizens of my country think is not necessarily the way I think."

"And how *do* you think, Sheikh Taj Ahmad, because I think I'm entitled to know that seeing as I'm about to leg-shackle myself to you for the rest of our lives."

Something flashed in his dark eyes. Amusement mixed with something deeper. Deadlier. "A leg shackle doesn't do anything for me fantasy-wise. Handcuffs, perhaps."

"I am in no mood," she said, keeping her sharp glare trained on him.

"My apologies," he said, his voice stiff. "I expect a wife to meet my needs. To provide me with heirs."

"What?" she asked, leaning forward in her seat. "Meet your needs? What does that mean?"

"I expect for her to share my bed, to accompany me

to events, to have my children. That's straightforward enough."

"That's…sexist enough," she said.

"How? It has nothing to do with you being a woman, and everything to do with being the wife of a sheikh. I have particular duties as ruler, and you have particular duties as the spouse of a ruler."

"So if I was sheikh…"

"You very likely wouldn't be called sheikh."

She let out an exasperated breath. "Fine. If I were sheikha," she said, drawing out the syllables, "then you would be expected to fulfill my sexual needs and hang on my arm at events?"

"That sounds fair," he said, a frown marring his features. "I take it you are not thrilled with my expectations?"

"Does it matter?" she asked, feeling panic start to rise in her breast. "Does any of it matter? I'm stuck. You have the power here. You and I both know that."

"I am not a tyrant, neither am I a dictator. I get no pleasure from beating you into submission. What do you expect from a husband?"

Love. If there was love, so many other things could be forgiven. But without it…what was there? "I… I would like to be considered as a person, not an ornament. I don't want my life to begin and end with my husband's needs. I want him to consider mine. I want a husband who will love his children and take an interest in them." *A husband who loves me.* His brows were drawn together, his expression contemplative. "It is not how things are done."

"What isn't?"

"There are…certain things expected of the Sheikh

of Rahat, things I learned as a child and…they did not include caring for children or…many of the other things you mentioned. My duty is to my people."

"But if you can't love the people in your household, how can you expect to care for those you rule?"

"Ruling requires distance and a firm hand."

Something inside her deflated and sank down to her toes. "It's the love that you have trouble with."

"I did not learn it."

The way he said it, so authoritative and so final, told her he never intended to try.

CHAPTER SEVEN

Angelina pulled her thin robe more tightly around herself and stepped out into the gardens, the cobblestones, cooled by the night air, felt good on her feet. Calming. Soothing.

She followed one of the paths that led into the center of the lavishly kept landscape, her thoughts turning over that afternoon's conversation with Taj. Taj didn't know how to love. He hadn't learned how.

A shame since *she* loved *him*. She was certain of that now. That she loved him. That she had loved for him for years, and that no matter how bad their first parting had been, the good memories would always be stronger.

"What brings you out here?"

Angelina whirled around to find the voice in the darkness and nearly ran into Taj. "What are you doing out here?"

"I asked first. Come now, I am sheikh and I am accustomed to being answered." He said it with no irony. Nothing but the absolute certainty of a man who only knew how to get his way.

She shifted her weight to one leg and put her hand on her hip. "You'll have to be disappointed then, sugar."

He narrowed his eyes, clearly annoyed. Good. "Then I'll settle for giving you my reasons. I couldn't sleep."

She shrugged. "Oh, funny. I could. That's why I'm out here. You're just seeing my astral projection. I'm sound asleep in the house."

"You have such a mouth on you," he said. "I am not complaining. I've benefitted hugely from your use of that mouth."

It was her turn to be annoyed. "A gentleman wouldn't bring such things up."

"I'm not a gentleman," he said, his tone rough.

"Ah…no of course not. You're a sheikh."

"Sit," he said, gesturing to the fountain.

She crossed her arms and tilted her head. "Come on now, Taj, you should know me better than that."

He kept his dark eyes trained on her, his face shadowed in the dim light of the garden. He moved to the edge of the fountain and sat down, then touched the place beside him. "Please, sit with me."

The change was so abrupt, so unlike him, that it made her chest feel tight. It made her feel like maybe he did know her. Like he might at least try to be the right man for her, instead of just asking her to be the right woman for him.

She turned and sat down beside him, her hands in her lap. "What is it, Taj?"

"I might ask you the same question since you're wandering the gardens at night."

"And so are you."

"I thought…" He frowned. "I was certain I heard you, but I know that isn't possible. My rooms are on the other end of the palace. But… I was certain I did."

His brow was furrowed, his forehead lined with concentration.

His admission made her stomach tighten, made her
chest feel full. "I'm all right, I just…"

"You aren't," he said, turning and cupping her cheek,
his thumb sliding lightly over her cheekbone, the movement sending a shiver through her body.

"I will be," she said, not sure if that was the truth
or not. "Your family has ruled Rahat for…for generations, right?"

"A thousand years."

"You believe in…in fate and destiny, I'll bet." She
looked down at her hands, still folded in her lap.

"Yes."

"So tell me, did I ever have a chance of escaping
this?" She looked up, around the courtyard. "Or was I
always meant to be Queen of Rahat, the mother of your
heirs, no matter what? Is our fate written in stone or do
we have…do we have any control?"

He frowned. "Angelina…" He looked away from her,
appearing to change tactic. "We both had a choice that
night in Santina. We chose to follow our desire."

He touched her again, his fingers sifting through
her hair. And she could feel the unsteadiness in his
hand. "But did we have a choice in that?" she asked,
her voice a whisper.

He slid his hand down to her face and she looked at
him. She saw heat in his eyes, lust, but there was something deeper. A longing that went further than the need
for physical satisfaction. She knew that longing. It went
so deep, felt so essential, it was painful. She wondered
if he truly felt it. For her, as she did for him.

"There is always a choice, Angel," he said, leaning

in, firm, hot lips touching hers, shocking in the cool night air. "What choice will you make now?"

"I…" Her lower lip trembled and she caught it between her teeth, the tremor working its way through her body. She released her lip. "I choose you," she said.

His breath rushed from his body, a low growl behind it. He wrapped his arms around her and pulled her to him. He kissed her and she nearly sighed with relief. It had been too long.

Everything. All of it had gone on far too long. Taj was the only man she'd ever loved. Being away from him had been like functioning with a piece of herself missing. She'd done it, she'd done what she had to do to try to be strong. But she would be lying if she didn't admit to herself that being in his arms felt so much better than keeping her pride ever had.

And that was frightening.

"Wait," she said, pulling away from him, her heart thundering. Pride would have a place here, and she would see it had a victory.

"What?" he asked, pressing his forehead against hers, his breath sporadic.

"How do you see me?"

"What does that mean, Angel?"

"What am I to you? Am I the woman you are chained to? Am I the woman who got away that you seized the chance to capture again? A salve for your wounded ego?" She put her hands on either side of his face. "What am I to you?"

He hesitated, and in that moment of hesitation, she saw the man she'd known first. The man who had romanced her in Texas, rather than the autocratic ruler. "You are…the woman who has haunted my dreams these past years. When I saw you at Alessandro's engagement party I thought you were a mirage. I didn't trust myself. I had seen you too many times before, only to get close and discover it wasn't really you. You are my most hated delusion and my deepest desire." The words sounded pulled from him, as though each one carried a heavy weight. A high price. "Does that answer your question?"

She felt a tear slide down her cheek and she brushed it away. "I… I imagined you never thought about me again after I left."

He laughed, a short, bitter sound. "There was a time when I thought of little else."

"That surprises me."

"Why? Did you forget?"

She didn't want to give him honesty, but there was no way around it. Not when his words were so naked and raw, so obviously true. "Of course I didn't forget. I uprooted my whole life. I left my country. The money, the lifestyle I was used to having, to try to escape the situation I found myself in."

"To escape me."

"To escape marrying a man who saw me as nothing more than a possession. To escape a father who saw me as a bargaining chip. To find out who I was away from the manipulation of others. Don't flatter yourself by making it so personal."

He tightened his hold on her, his gaze intense. "You think it's not?"

She shook her head.

"You are a liar," he said, leaning in, his lips skimming her cheek. "I think the things you feel toward me are very personal."

Why did he do this to her? Why did she have such a hard time resisting him? She didn't even want to resist. She tilted her head and kissed him, her eyes closed tight. She pulled her head back, her breathing shallow.

"What am I to you, Angelina Carpenter?" he asked, tracing the line of her lips with his finger.

"You are—" she cleared her throat and tried to disguise the quiver in her voice "—you are a mystery to me, as is my attraction to you. That's why I keep coming back to fate."

For a moment, he looked stunned. Then in one fluid movement he picked her up from her position on the fountain and stood, striding across the courtyard. She looped her arms around his neck and held on.

"That's a good enough answer for me," he said, stopping in front of a divan that was shrouded in palms. He set her down on the velvet surface and pulled his shirt over his head, coming to sit down beside her. "Is it enough for you?"

She nodded, unsure she could make her voice work.

"Good," he whispered, lowering his head and kissing her.

She slid her hands to his chest, reveled in the feeling of his muscles beneath her palms. He was everything she'd ever fantasized about. He was… Taj. And even though so much of what she wanted from him was going unmet, she knew that for now, for this moment, she would give everything.

One moment to lay herself bare, in a physical sense, to hold nothing back, before she retreated behind her emotional protection. She couldn't love him for their whole marriage, not without his love. It would destroy her.

But she would do it right now. Unreservedly.

While his guard was down. While he was unprotected, too.

He pulled off her robe, then her flimsy top. The cold air hit her bare breasts and she gasped. Taj laughed and bent his head, drawing a tightened nipple into his mouth. She clutched his shoulders, his name on her lips, her body on fire with need for him. All of him.

She pushed her pants down her thighs and kicked them off while Taj worked to free himself of his own clothes. When his skin pressed against hers, she sighed in relief. How did he feel so essential? How did being with him make her feel like something that had been missing all her life was present in a profound way?

He lowered his head and kissed her neck as he settled between her thighs, sliding into her slowly. A short sigh of pleasure escaped her lips and he caught it with his, the kiss deep and sensual, working with his thrusts.

She kept her eyes open, locked with his as she rocked against him, driving them both higher until they reached the peak together. He held her against him, his heart thundering, his skin slicked with sweat.

She felt empowered by it. By the fact that she'd affected him. By the fact that she wasn't in it alone. She'd wondered if it had all been in her head. For so long she'd wondered that. If she'd been the only one who'd felt anything. If he'd had to close his eyes and think of Rahat when he kissed her back in Texas.

But she knew now, knew it with even greater certainty than she had that night in Santina. She knew that while he might not love her, he desired her. That it was the kind of desire that went beyond simple lust and set out to drive a person crazy.

She knew, because she felt it, too. Because she recognized that what she felt lived in him, too.

She could hold on to that. She could forget about the love thing and pretend that lust was all that mattered. She closed her eyes tight and tried to cling to the lie.

CHAPTER EIGHT

"The wedding will take place in two weeks." Taj walked into Angelina's quarters and a hard slug of arousal hit him in the gut.

They'd stayed out in the garden until the sky had started turning pink at the horizon line, bleeding up into the inky blackness, washing it clean. He'd held her until he was certain they would be missed, and possibly discovered, naked on the divan, covered only in her robe.

Then he'd sent her back to her room, and he'd gone back to his. And his body had burned. He'd ended up in an ice cold shower, gritting his teeth as the water hit his skin like a thousand needles and his erection ached, finding absolutely no relief.

He'd ended up shivering *and* horny.

What was it about her? How was it she'd managed to burrow her way under his skin all those years ago? It was as though she lived in him. A strange thought. A foolish thought, and yet it seemed the only explanation for what he felt when he was around her.

Angelina looked at him, her lush lips shaped into a perfect O. "What? Why so soon?"

He looked pointedly at her stomach.

"Oh," she said. "Well, I won't start showing for a

while. I mean, I knew you wanted to marry quickly but…two weeks? In the States I would have a hard time getting a wedding cake on two weeks' notice!"

"You underestimate the power of money."

"No. I don't. Trust me. My family is practically made of money."

"Then you underestimate the power of the sheikh of Rahat. I will have my staff see to the wedding feast. The ceremony will be held here at the palace. Small by royal standards but it cannot be helped."

Her smooth brow crinkled as she drew her eyebrows together. "Oh, yes. It can't be helped because I'm disgraced. Can't have people thinking I'm pregnant, it would reflect badly on me. Not on you, of course, but then, isn't that the way of it?"

Anger curled his stomach. Anger at whom… Angelina, his country and its traditions, or himself, he wasn't sure. Possibly all three. "If you had married me three years ago you could have had the finest wedding imaginable," he said through clenched teeth. "A parade through the city. A handmade wedding gown. Thousands of attendants ready to pay homage to the new queen."

If she had married him three years ago he would have spared so many sleepless nights, so much longing.

At least he had her now. She would have to stay with him. She would be his wife and the mother of his child. She could not leave him now. That brought a slight sense of a relief, took away some of the pressure in his chest.

"Oh, yes, that's what I need, Taj. A bigger wedding. That's the problem. It simply won't be grand enough if I'm not brought into the church on…on…camel back." She stood, her pale cheeks flushing a dark rose. "How did you know that was the most essential thing to me? I should have married you three years ago, if not for the wedding, so my wardrobe would be more current."

He stepped back, the heat in his stomach spreading now, a blaze of anger streaking along his veins. "Is that what you want? More gowns? I will give them to you. I can give you anything. Everything. I am Sheikh. I can provide you with things no other man can."

"Oh, is that so," she said, hands on her shapely hips. "Well, I believe that, sugar, I do. But there are men who could provide me with things you will never be able to give me."

"I think not," he said, striding forward and wrapping his arms around her, pulling her against him. Her eyes widened and he gentled his hold, his heart hammering. "I think not," he said again, his voice softer.

He moved his thumb over her bottom lip and a shiver of desire racked his body. "The need I feel for you is as much a part of me as my blood," he said. "And I am certain you feel the same."

She pulled back. "That's sex. So maybe we have good sex, and maybe we both want more of it. But sex isn't everything."

"You say that, but you are wrong. You have some... misconstrued idea that marriage is about love, I imagine. A modern concept that I have no patience for. Suitability, chemistry, that is what matters. Not some vague idea of a feeling that has no guarantee of existing let alone lasting. This," he said, putting his hand on her chest, feeling her heart beating rapidly beneath his palm, "this is real. What I make you feel."

"Go away, Taj."

Dismissed. No one dismissed him. No one left him. And Angelina seemed to do both of those things freely.

"For now," he said, taking a step back, ignoring the ugly twisting in his chest that was threatening to cut off his air supply. "But remember this, Angelina. You are pregnant with my heir, and you will be my wife. There is no running from this."

He said it as much to remind him as her. She couldn't leave him. Not now.

A good thing. Because if she did…he did not know how he would live with himself.

CHAPTER NINE

"She is getting sicker, Sheikh." Hana, one of the maids trusted with Angelina's care, stood before him, wringing her hands. "She is not keeping any food down. Not all day."

"Do you think she needs a doctor?" he asked.

Hana shrugged. "The doctor has been. He says as long as she does not lose too much weight...he says her sickness is normal. Bad, but to be expected."

Hana was one of the few on staff who was aware of the fact that Angelina was pregnant, but as she was attending her, Taj had felt it important.

"There is nothing that can be done?"

"She was given medication for motion sickness, which helps some women. Though she's reluctant to take it. It makes her nervous."

"Stubborn woman," he said, running his fingers through his hair. "Is she asleep now?"

"Yes."

"I will go to her. Keep everyone away from her end of the palace. I do not want her disturbed. Today, she is in my care."

He stalked across the palace, his footsteps echoing

on the marble floor, staff scurrying aside when they saw him coming.

His heart was pounding heavily by the time he reached the entrance to her quarters. He moved through her rooms, the elegant seating area, her sunroom, to her sleeping chamber. He paused at the door, a strange unease filling him.

He'd never cared for anyone in his life. Not on a personal level. On a grand scale, he cared for his people. But he sent others to do his bidding. He signed papers, he waved from vehicles. It was his administrative staff who assigned the execution of tasks.

He was aware, for the first time, of how different ordering care and giving it were.

He pushed the gilded door open and saw Angelina. She was in bed, the covers drawn up beneath her chin, her hair damp, sticking to her forehead.

"You are too hot," he said, striding across the room, sitting on the edge of the bed and putting his hand on her forehead.

She stirred, opened her eyes, the expression in them confused and sleepy. "I… I'm not. I just… I threw up again and it makes me sweaty. What are you doing here?"

A good question. He felt completely and totally out of his depth. A foreign experience. "I heard you were unwell."

"I'm morning sick," she said, as if that explained everything.

"It is three in the afternoon."

"Morning sickness isn't always confined to morning, I've discovered. But other than feeling like death warmed over, the doctor says I'm fine. The baby is fine."

"You do not look fine," he said. "You look like a ghost."

"I'm not one, though. Promise." She put her hand on his cheek, his skin warm against his.

"What do you need?"

"What?"

He stood. "What do you need? I will order... I will get it for you." He didn't know why, but it seemed important. There were other things he had planned on doing today, but this seemed essential. It seemed like the most essential thing he could do with his time.

"I don't... I don't know. I..."

He looked around the room and saw a bowl sitting on the vanity with a white washcloth draped over the side. The bowl was filled with water. He touched his fingers to the surface and found it cold.

"One moment," he said. He went into her opulent bathroom and refilled the bowl with warm water, bringing it back into her room.

He dipped the cloth in the water, wringing out the excess before returning to her bed.

He pushed her damp hair from her forehead, resting his palm against her skin for a moment before replacing it with the cloth.

She sighed, her eyes meeting his. "Thank you. I felt disgusting."

"Did you?"

"Sweaty." She arched slightly. "My shirt is sticking to me."

He frowned. "Do you need a bath?"

"I wanted one. I was afraid I would pass out."

He hesitated to ask the next question, because intimacy between them, even the basest intimacy of greeting one another in the corridors, had been cut off since their argument two days earlier. But he had to ask. "Can I stay with you? Can...can I help you?"

"I...yes."

Angelina watched Taj disappear into the bathroom. She had no idea what had caused his sudden desire to take care of her. Concern for her? For the baby?

Of course he was worried about the baby. It was his heir.

She bit the inside of her cheek. That wasn't really a fair thought. Taj wasn't a terrible person, and he'd never acted cold and detached in regards to the baby. It was her he seemed to feel nothing for.

Well, nothing beyond lust and possession. He wanted her, but that wasn't the same as caring. A man could want riches, but it came from greed. From the need to possess. Not from caring.

She was nothing more than an acquisition to him. Like a new car. A lucrative business deal.

He returned a moment later. He had taken his shirt off, his muscular torso bare and beautiful to her, even in her current state. He bent and scooped her from the bed. She looped her arms around his neck and allowed him to carry her into the bathroom, where he set her gently in front of the newly filled tub.

"Do you need help?" he asked.

"With...with my clothes?" Her heart beat unevenly. "No."

He turned his back, the muscles shifting, enticing. Somehow, her appreciation of his body transcending her nausea. Almost.

She wobbled slightly as she stepped out of her pajama pants then pulled her top over her head. She got into the tub, the water coming over her breasts, the bubbles helping preserve her modesty. As if she really cared. As if Taj hadn't already seen it all.

"I'm in," she said.

He turned, the tension in his body obvious, his jaw tight. He knelt down on the floor beside the tub and she rested her head against the back of the tub. She felt Taj's hand on her neck, his strong fingers slowly kneading away the ache in her muscles. She hadn't realized how tense she'd gotten.

But then, heartbreak and constant vomiting could do that to a girl.

He put his other hand on her shoulder, working at the knots there. She released a breath, trying to ignore the other kind of tension that was flooding through her while the muscle tension receded.

This was what she craved from him. This caring. This touch that went beyond a need for sex and satisfaction. A touch that gave.

She wanted to stay with him like this forever. And she also wished he'd never shown her this part of himself. Never shown her this fleeting glimpse of how it could be if he loved her.

If only things could be different.

She closed her eyes, and felt a tear roll down her cheek. "I wish things were different."

CHAPTER TEN

I wish things were different. Her words echoed in him. Mocked him. Tore at his insides. He replayed them over and over as he helped her from the tub, drying her, trying to keep his body disinterested, as he carried her to bed and tucked her back in.

As he walked out into her sitting room and collapsed onto the sofa, his hands were shaking as he forked his fingers through his hair.

She was unhappy. He had known it. Had seen the unease in her from the moment she'd arrived in Rahat and he had not cared. Because he had her. That was all that had mattered to him. That she couldn't leave him again. That he would be able to keep her.

Keep her? As if she was an exotic pet or a rare collectible? His stomach rebelled at the thought.

She was a woman. The only person he had ever…

It hit him then, like a punch to his jaw.

He loved her. She was the only person he had ever loved. He had, from the moment he'd met her. And what had he done? He had set out to buy her, like an item. Like anything else he hoped to acquire in his life. Because currency, power, that was what he understood, not feelings.

Three years later he understood. Why he had not wanted another woman since he'd met Angelina. Why it had felt so essential to hold her to him when he'd finally found her again.

But at what cost? He had only thought of himself. Had only thought of what it meant to him to have her.

How had he not realized it was a prison sentence to her?

He would rather go through life alone than subject her to it. Than to force her to be with him when she had no desire to be his wife.

She never had.

Fate. She had blamed fate for forcing them together when he had been the one forcing things all along.

She wanted things to be different. And they would be.

"TAJ?" ANGELINA CREPT out of her darkened bedroom and into her sitting area. Taj was sitting on her couch, still shirtless, the lights off. He appeared oblivious to the fact that the sun had gone down. He was just sitting, looking at his hands.

"Taj," she said again, moving to sit beside him. "Is everything all right?"

He looked at her, his face lost in shadow. "You are here, and you are safe. How could anything be wrong?"

There was something off about his tone. Something dark in his voice. Gritty.

"I just thought..."

"How do you feel?" he asked.

"I'm fine. Better. Actually I feel ready to eat, which is a first for a few days. Either the hormone induced nausea is over, or it's the eye of the storm."

"I hope it's over," he said, his tone still flat.

"What's wrong?"

"You asked me, Angelina, if fate had forced us together."

"I… I remember that." She wanted to touch him, but something stopped her.

His gaze was distant. "I have the answer now. There is no such thing as fate. Only sheikhs who think they are God. I will not play at a profession so far above myself. Not anymore."

"What do you mean by that?"

"We will not marry."

Angelina felt like the floor tilted sideways. "What?"

"You ask far too many questions," he said, standing. "I have made myself, my wishes, very clear. We will not marry at the end of the week. We will not marry."

"And…where will I go?" she asked, not caring about his anti-question mandate. Because she had questions. Lots and lots of questions. And giving voice to them, needing the answers to them, was the only thing keeping her heart from splintering. "What about our child?"

"I will see our child. I will support our child in every way possible. But I am not holding you here."

"What changed?"

"I cannot lock us in a situation that would be unendurable for us both." He turned his back on her, and she felt a sharp stab hit her in the chest. "You may stay here in the palace as long as it suits you. I will not have you move under the present circumstances. It is your choice where you go when you feel able to leave. If you choose to stay in Rahat, a home will be provided for you."

"And if I choose to leave the country?" she asked,

ice coating her words, her body, her heart, offering protection. Shock providing insulation against the pain.

"Visitation will need to be arranged," he said, his eyes black holes in the darkness of the room. "I will be there when my child is born, make no mistake. You will not shut me out."

She felt like she was breaking inside. Slowly cracking apart.

But she wouldn't beg. She wouldn't show him. Already, she loved him while he felt...what did he feel? He had been so kind earlier and now this. Now he could cast her off as quickly as he'd brought her into his world.

Already he had too much power. She wouldn't let him know it.

"I promise, Taj." She tilted her chin up, called on every bit of strength inside of her and used it. "If you want to see our child, anytime, day or night, you will be able to. I will never keep them from you."

"Good."

"Can you please go?"

He nodded once. "I'm on my way out."

He walked out of the sitting room and she heard the double doors to her segment of rooms close behind him.

Only then did she allow tears to fall.

CHAPTER ELEVEN

On the day that would have been her wedding day Angelina took one last look at her suite of rooms in the Rahatan palace, and closed the double doors behind her.

She didn't know where she would go. She'd given up her house in Italy to follow Princess Carlotta to her new home in Santa Christobel, and she'd given up her position there to come and marry Taj.

She could go back to Texas. That thought only brought intense regret.

She looked out the window at the sun-washed desert and wondered if she would ever feel home anywhere else. Anywhere besides this place that had seemed an alien planet when she'd first arrived.

She moved through the corridor and tried to ignore the way the staff moved around her. The way they ignored her presence. She supposed she was written off now. Cast off by their sheikh, cast off by them.

Taj. Oh, Taj. Her heart bled his name with each beat.

It was hot outside. It was always hot there. She should be glad to leave the miserable heat. She would be happier if she had any idea of where she would end up. Anywhere beyond the lovely, modern hotel in the center of the capital city.

That was her next stop. It would do for now.

She closed her eyes and looked to the sun, letting it warm her face. She ignored the limousine that had pulled up to the front of the palace courtyard, waiting for her. Waiting to take her away.

"Angel?"

She turned sharply, her eyes opening. "Taj?"

He was standing at the entrance to the gardens. She hadn't seen him in the days since he'd broken things off with her. She'd assumed he'd gone to one of his other homes. It was what she'd been told.

"I didn't think you were here."

"I wasn't," he said, his voice rough. "I was trying to keep away until you'd left."

"Am I so repulsive to you?" she asked, her voice crisp, masking the wound his words left in her heart.

He closed the distance between them, his strides long and fast. "Are you repulsive to me?" he asked, his expression stark. Open. "You can't ask me that? Do you realize that for the three years since I first met you I have wanted no one else? That I've had no lovers because the memory of your kiss was enough to keep me from being aroused by any other woman?"

"Lust." The word came out a whisper. She couldn't believe it. That he hadn't wanted anyone else. That he hadn't had anyone else. It didn't seem possible. "Lust is all that is. It isn't enough."

"Lust is cheap, Angel. If it were lust I could have satisfied it with any number of women in any number of ways. That's not what it is."

"Then why are you making me go?" she asked, her voice breaking, her pride forgotten for the moment.

"Because I will not hold you prisoner. I will not bend

your will to fit with mine. I will not make you miserable to ensure my own happiness. Not anymore."

"I… I don't understand."

"I saw you, in your father's home, so beautiful. So perfect. And I wanted you. I sought out to buy you like I would anything else I coveted. Because nothing in my life had ever been denied me. I simply asked, or wrote a check, and it was mine. I thought you would be no different. But you left me. And I thought I would forget. But I couldn't. When I saw you again, standing in the balcony at the palace in Santina, I thought only of satisfying my desire for you. Of having you. Possessing you. Exactly like the first time."

Angelina crossed her arms beneath her breasts, tightening her hold on herself. She would stand upright. She would not dissolve. "And now what? You've decided you want to return me?"

"Then I had you. And you left," he said, continuing as if she hadn't spoken. "I swore I wouldn't chase you. I swore to forget you. Still I could not. And when you told me you were having my baby…the chance at last to tie you to me forever. To bring peace to my world. I was happy. Happy because you could not leave me. Because this time you had to stay."

He shook his head, a sudden flash of disgust curling his lip. "But something changed. I found myself wanting to give to you. And as I did, I realized how much your happiness meant. How much more it meant than my own. How could I be happy when you were so miserable? How could I hold you prisoner and call you mine?"

"But…but… Does my father have anything to do with this…has he?"

"Nothing," he said, his voice fierce. "I rejected his

offer of a partnership after I lost you. It was I who rejected it, not him. Because I couldn't face having a connection to you without having you."

"You said you kept in touch."

His expression turned bleak. "I called sometimes. To see if there had been word of you."

"You did?"

"I love you," he said. "I love you more than I love myself, and I don't think I have ever felt that way. I'm certain I haven't. I want... I want your happiness so much more than I want my own. So you must promise me, Angelina, that you will be happy. And then I will let you go with a smile."

Angelina's breath caught, her hands shaking. "You... love me?"

"Yes," he said.

She shook her head, tears stinging her eyes. "I... I can't do what you asked just now. I can't go and be happy."

"What do you need?" he asked, his eyes shining. "What do you need and I will give it to you."

"You," she whispered, wrapping her arms around his neck and burying her face. "I need you."

One of his arms curved around her waist and he lowered his head, pressing his forehead against her shoulder. "Why did you wish so badly for things to be different, then?"

"Because you didn't love me. I wanted your love and knowing I couldn't have that...that's why I was sad."

He raised his head, his eyes meeting hers. "I did love you. I didn't know what to call it. And I did not love you in the right way. I know with certainty that I've loved you since the first moment I saw you. But now I'm ready to love you right."

"What changed?" she asked.

"I did. I think it's because of you. No, I know it is. You have changed me. You have humbled me. And I needed it, badly."

"I love you, Taj. I loved you then. But I couldn't stand the thought of marrying you just because you wanted to strengthen your nation's economy. I wanted to be more to you than that."

"You are," he said. "Though I could not have said it then. I was foolish."

"Maybe we both were."

"Maybe we will be again," he said.

"But we love each other. And that's why we'll stay together."

"You'll stay with me then? Be my wife?"

"Yes," she said, pressing a kiss to his lips, her heart swelling with emotion, tears sliding down her cheeks.

He kissed her deeper, tightening his hold on her.

"I'll get a procession of camels, right, sugar?" she whispered, nipping his earlobe.

He chuckled. "Nothing is too grand for you."

"On second thought, I don't need the camels."

"You don't?"

She shook her head, raised her hand and traced a line of moisture on his cheek. "No. I only need you."

* * * * *

ABOUT THE AUTHOR

Maisey Yates knew she wanted to be a writer even before she knew what it was she wanted to write.

At her very first job she was fortunate enough to meet her very own tall, dark and handsome hero, who happened to be her boss, and promptly married him and started a family. It wasn't until she was pregnant with her second child that she found her very first Harlequin Presents® book in a local thrift store—by the time she'd reached the happily ever after, she had fallen in love. She devoured as many as she could get her hands on after that, and she knew that these were the books she wanted to write!

She started submitting, and nearly two years later, while pregnant with her third child, she received The Call from her editor. At the age of twenty-three, she sold her first manuscript to the Harlequin Presents line, and she was very glad that the good news didn't send her into labor!

She still can't quite believe she's blessed enough to see her name on, not just any book, but on her favorite books.

Maisey lives with her supportive, handsome, wonderful, diaper-changing husband and three small children, across the street from her parents and the home she grew up in, in the wilds of southern Oregon. She enjoys the contrast of living in a place where you might wake up to find a bear on your back porch, then walk into the home office to write stories that take place in exotic, urban locales.

Visit Maisey's website at www.maiseyyates.com.

THE PRICE OF
ROYAL DUTY

PENNY JORDAN

CHAPTER ONE

'Ash.' Sophia Santina, youngest daughter of the King and Queen of the island of Santina, breathed the name silently to herself, almost reverentially. Just the feel of the nearly silent breath that whispered his name and caressed her throat was enough to raise erotic pinpricks of desire within her flesh. Ash. How the whispering of his name was enough to unleash within her an aching echo of the tumultuous teenage desires he had once aroused in her. The very air was electric with the reckless sensual excitement that wantonly flooded her, even though she had sworn she would not, positively not, allow herself to experience it.

She had known, of course, that he had been invited to her eldest brother's engagement party here at the castle that was their family home, but knowing that and actually seeing him with that strikingly sensual maleness of his that she remembered so well were two very different things.

She would have recognised him anywhere, just as she had done now merely from her brief glimpse of the back view of him as he walked into the ballroom and then turned to refuse a glass of champagne. Just the turn of his head, just the thick dark sheen of his hair and the way it curled into the nape of his neck, was enough to conjure up old memories. Memories of longing recklessly for the right to bury her fingers in its softness, curl them around its strands and then urge his mouth down to her own. A shudder of sensual awareness jolted through her. Some things never changed. A certain kind of need, a certain kind of desire, a certain kind of love.

First love? Surely only a fool believed that first love was an only love, and she prided herself on not being that. No, Ash had killed that tremulous, tender love when he had rejected her, telling her that she was a child still who was putting herself in danger by offering herself to a man of his age, that she was fortunate that his own sense of honour and the repugnance he felt at the very thought of taking what she offered meant that she was protected from him taking advantage of her naivety. Telling her that even if she had been older he would not have wanted her because he was wholly committed to someone else.

She had promised herself then that in future her love would only be given to a man who was worthy of it and who valued it and her. A man who loved her as much as she did him. And because of that promise to herself, she needed Ash's help now, no matter how much her pride reacted angrily against that need.

Putting down her virtually untouched drink, she started to walk towards him.

Standing in the packed ballroom in the castle on the Mediterranean island of Santina, the official residence and home of the royal family of Santina, Ashok Achari, Maharaja of Nailpur, frowned as his grim, obsidian gaze swept the scene in front of him. Beyond the open doors to the stunningly elegant ballroom with its crystal chandeliers and antique mirrors stood footmen wearing the livery of the royal family. An impressive dress-uniformed group of the king's own personal guard had been standing motionless in front of the castle in honour of the occasion and the guests. As a fellow royal, Ash had seen them salute him as the limousine that had picked him up from the airport had swept up to the main entrance. It was plain that no expense was being spared to celebrate the engagement of the king's eldest son and heir.

His fellow guests milled around him, and laughter and the sound of conversation filled the air.

Ash had gone to school with the groom-to-be, Alex, and they were still close friends. Even so, he hadn't wanted to attend this engagement party as he had more pressing matters to deal with at home, but duty was important to Ash—far more so than any personal desires—and duty had compelled him to accept.

He had, though, ordered his pilot to have his private jet standing ready to fly him back to Mumbai where he had an important business meeting in the morning.

A sixth sense had him turning round just as an exquisitely beautiful petite brunette came hurrying towards him.

Sophia.

A woman now, not the girl she had been the last time he had seen her in person. Where he had remembered a girl trembling on the brink of womanhood, innocent and eager, in need of protection from herself, he was now being confronted by a woman who clearly knew all about her sexuality and its power and how to both use it and take pleasure from it. That his body had recorded and registered that information in the time it had taken him to exhale and breathe again pointed to a weakness within himself of which he had previously been unaware.

The shock of his instant male awareness of Sophia as a woman had caught him totally off guard and Ash did not like that. That kind of thing was not something he permitted himself to do. It smacked too much of a hidden repressed need and Ash did not allow himself to have hidden repressed needs—needs that could make him vulnerable. Besides, the very idea of him being vulnerable to Sophia was laughable. She wasn't his type. No? So why then was his body reacting to her as though it had never seen a woman before?

A momentary lapse. He was a man, she was a woman, and his bed had been empty since he had dismissed his last mistress. If he was aroused by the sight of Sophia then it was probably completely natural. After all, from the luxuriant tumble of long, dark brown waves via the stunning beauty of her delicately shaped face with its dark eyes and soft full lips to the voluptuous curves of her sensationally sensually shaped body, Sophia Santina was an instant, irresistible magnet for male attention— and his own body was reacting just like any other heterosexual man's would. Wasn't it?

Yes. He would be a fool if he allowed that reaction more importance than it merited. To be caught off guard by a surge of physical desire so strong that he was glad of the packed floor of the ballroom and the darkness of his dinner suit to conceal the evidence of his reaction to her was an alien experience for him and added aggravation to what he was already experiencing. He had no desire whatsoever to be aroused by any woman right now, never mind Sophia Santina.

But he couldn't deny the fact that he was. Not with that arousal already straining at the expensive fabric of his suit, despite the ferocity of the mental control with which he was attempting to prevent it.

She was still coming towards him and in another handful of seconds she would be flinging herself into his arms, just as she had done as a young girl. And if she did that... His body beat out a raw demanding pulsing clarion call of lust. Ash cursed inwardly. He was a man who prided himself on his control of his appetites, especially when it came to sex.

It meant nothing that Sophia was sexually desirable and—if one believed the gossip press—sexually available, as well, should a man chance to catch her attention. Desiring her wasn't on his agenda for where he planned to take his life and it never would be.

Apart from anything else, as he had already reminded himself, Sophia simply wasn't his type. Following the death of his wife, the women with whom he had shared his bed had all been elegant long-limbed women skilled in the arts of sexual pleasure, with cool logical minds in whose lives emotions did not play a part. Women who, when the game ended, gracefully accepted the generous gift he gave them and left his bed as discreetly as they had entered it.

Sophia was not like that. Sophia, as he well knew from watching her grow up, was an intense melding of passionate emotions. A man who took her to bed would need... His body reacted again, causing him to have to shift his weight from one leg to the other in an attempt to ensure that that reaction was disguised. There was no question of him taking Sophia to his bed. Not now, not ever.

'Ash,' Sophia said again, automatically stepping forward to embrace him, her eyes widening when he immediately encircled her wrist with his right hand to fend her off while stepping back from her in rejection.

How could she have been so stupid? There was, after all, a history of rejection between them, or rather of Ash rejecting her, and now she had put herself on the back foot by allowing him to feel that he needed to push her away. In her anxiety to plead for his help she had acted foolishly. She must be more mentally alert, she warned herself.

Yes, an inner voice argued defensively, but all she had been doing was greeting him as she would greet anyone she knew well, not coming on to him. She opened her mouth ready to make a feisty protest and berate him for misinterpreting her gesture and then closed it again, as she controlled her emotions. This was not the time to antagonise him, no matter how strongly she felt that she was being misjudged. And now that she was so close to him, she could see what she hadn't seen before: the change in him that was clearly written in the steely uncompromising coldness of his expression.

Against her will, sadness locked her throat. The Ash she remembered had been a warm, outgoing young man who had laughed a lot and enjoyed life. What had happened to change him and turn him into the cynical, almost-brooding man in front of her now? Did she really need to ask herself that? He had lost his wife, a wife whom he had loved.

Her sadness grew, compassion for the Ash she remembered filling her. That Ash had been a young man whose innate kindness—especially to the young sister of a school friend on those holiday visits he had made to the island—had made that girl feel for the first time in her life that someone understood her, and valued her. His kindness and his understanding had meant so much to her, and it was her memory of those things that had brought her to his side now and not the abrupt sea change in their relationship as she had turned from a girl to a woman, and his rejection of her because of it.

Those qualities though had been stripped from the man in front of her now, Sophia recognised with a sudden painful jolt of her heart into her ribs. This Ash possessed a dark and brooding air that she didn't remember, along with a cold remoteness, as though somehow a dark cloud had darkened the warmth of the personality of the young man she remembered.

Something deep within her ached for what he had been. Immediately, Sophia clamped down on that feeling. She must not allow herself to be vulnerable to him emotionally. She must not feel anything for him. Not even when she had once patterned her ideal of what she thought desirable in a man on Ash himself? That had been a foolish mistake and one for which she had paid through the heartbreak that only the young and idealistic can know. The reality was that right now she should be feeling glad that he had changed and that there was therefore no danger of her being foolish enough to…

To what? To still feel something for him?

That was impossible.

But what if her responsiveness to him both physically and emotionally was burned into her DNA? *Burned into it?* Sophia winced. *Burned* was the correct word and she still had the scars to prove that. But those scars protected her now. She would never make the same mistake again. She was immune to Ash now and she intended to remain immune. She wasn't sixteen any more, after all.

Before, she had been filled with a young, romantic teenager's need to taste the apple the serpent had offered to Eve, and she had turned to Ash to help her assuage that need. That had been a terrible mistake for which she had paid in tears of shame and anguish.

Now she had to think past that, to that innocent time when she had merely seen Ash as her saviour, the one person she could turn to, to help her, the person who had, after all, saved her very life on more than one occasion. It was that Ash she desperately wanted to talk to right now, the words she would use to elicit the help she needed from him honed and practised. Now though she was beginning to recognise that somehow she couldn't just simply turn back and open the gate into the garden of innocence whose pathways Ash had walked with her when she had been a child.

She must not give up hope. She could not, Sophia reminded herself. But she must be careful. Careful and aware of what she needed to achieve for her own survival. This was just one meeting. One ordeal she had to go through to gain something she desperately needed. After tonight she would never have to see Ash again and she would be safe, from her own past and from the future her father planned for her.

She took a deep breath, and informed him with cool self-control, 'You can let go of me now, Ash. I promise you I won't touch you.'

Not touch him. Little did she know that his body, his flesh, his manhood, was screaming out to be touched by her. Inside his head, to his own self-disgust and anger, Ash could all too easily mentally visualise—right here, right now, in this packed and very public place—the need his flesh felt for him to place her hand over the hard aching pulse of his sex. No wonder she had the reputation she did if this was the effect she could have on his body. On his body, but not on him. That could not be permitted. Abruptly he released her wrist.

The very speed with which Ash released her proved to Sophia what her heart had already told her, namely that as far as he was concerned any physical contact between them was as taboo now as it had been when she had been sixteen.

And yet, as she had just reminded herself, Ash had once been kind to her. Very kind, indeed. The truth was that he had been her hero, her one place of safety and comfort.

Perhaps that was why, despite the dismissal and that brooding air of withdrawal about him, somehow, instinctively, if foolishly, she still felt as though Ash was the one person in her world to whom she could turn for help, should she need it. Or perhaps it was because she was desperate and there was no one else. And right now she certainly needed help. And needed it very much, indeed.

However, his grim manner had put a barrier between them so that now she was forced to recognise how misplaced her confidence in his kindness had been. And how much the change she could see in him complicated a plan which had seemed so simple when she had lain alone in her bed helplessly searching for a way to escape her fate.

She could easily have told the old Ash, the Ash she

remembered, what the problem was and just as easily have begged him to play the role she needed him to for the course of this evening. But this Ash, who looked at her with a gaze that held no affection for their shared past, but which instead seemed to look broodingly into a past that excluded her, diminished the hope she had brought with her to tonight's party.

But he *had* helped her in the past, she reminded herself. And not just helped her. He had saved her from death—not just once but twice. As she needed him to save her again now from another kind of death. The death that came from being sacrificed in a marriage to a man she had never met but whose reputation told her that he was everything she could never want in a husband.

Somehow she must find a way of breaking through the barriers between them, because without Ash's understanding, without his aid, her plan simply could not succeed.

And if he rejected her—again?

She must not think of that. She must be honest with him. She must beg him for his help. Taking another deep breath, she began, 'Ash, there's something I want to ask you.'

'If it's which of your current string of young men you should take to your bed next then I'm afraid I don't give that kind of advice. And anyway, you seem very skilled at picking the one that will gain you the most print inches and the largest photographs in the world's celebrity press.'

It was an emotionally brutal rebuttal and rejection, and that hurt. She knew she had her detractors but somehow she had not been prepared for Ash to be one of them. Because she wanted him to remember her as the innocent girl he had protected?

What if she did? It was only because she needed him to remember that relationship. As for that sharp sting-ing pain his words had brought her, that was nothing. She was not going to allow it any power. Even so, she couldn't stop herself from defending her actions. 'So I go public with my…relationships and you keep yours private.' She gave a small shrug, intending it to be dis-missive.

'Which of us, I wonder, would an unbiased bystander consider to be the more honest?'

She had her own reasons for not just allowing but positively encouraging the world at large to think of her as a young woman who relished her hedonistically sexual lifestyle and who indeed revelled in it. After all, wasn't the best way to disguise and protect something precious to camouflage it, to hide it from view in plain sight?

Sophia daring to call his morals into question was something Ash's pride could not tolerate, especially when… Especially when, what? Especially when he had once taken on the responsibility of protecting her from the consequences of her emerging sexual needs because of those morals? Or especially when he was al-ready having to deal with the private fallout he was fac-ing inside himself from his still-active, and very much unwanted, physical sexual reaction to her?

His voice as hard and unforgiving as his expression, he told her curtly, 'But I'm afraid that such discussions aren't of any appeal to me, Sophia, no matter how much idle chatter and currency they might find amongst your friends. Now if you'll excuse me, I must go and thank your parents for this evening, as I have to be back in Mumbai tomorrow morning, and I'm flying out just after midnight.'

He was leaving so soon? That was something else she hadn't expected or prepared herself for. The window of opportunity that was her planned escape was closing down by the minute. Panic had started to build up inside her, a panic that had her blurting out emotionally, 'Ash, once you were different, kinder. Kind to me…my saviour… You saved my life.' Only desperation could be making her behave like this, betray herself like this. 'I know from the charities in which you are involved and the help you give to your people how philanthropic and good you are to those in need. Right now, Ash, I need…' She stopped, her breath locking in her throat. 'I've never been able to say to you how sorry I was about the death of your wife. I know how much she and your marriage meant to you.'

He was withdrawing from her, she could sense it, almost feel it in the chilling of the air between them. She had learned young how to judge other people's emotions and to be wary of antagonising them. She shouldn't have mentioned his late wife. So why had she? No reason. She had just wanted…

There was a flicker of something in those dark eyes, a tightening of the flesh that clung with such powerful sensuality to the bone structure of regal facial features with a lineage that went back across the centuries to a time when his warrior ancestors had roamed and ruled the desert plains of India. She knew she had angered him.

He was angry with her. For what? Mentioning his wife? Sophia knew how much he had loved the Indian princess he had married but it was several years now since her death and she was sure his bed hadn't remained empty during those years. Bedding someone was one thing, but as Sophia knew, loving them was another thing entirely.

However, if he thought he was going to frighten her off with his forbidding manner towards her, he was wrong. He no doubt remembered her as the young girl who was very easily hurt by any hint that she might have offended the man she hero-worshipped so intensely, but she wasn't that young girl any more, and when it came to being hurt and surviving that hurt… well, she could easily lay claim to having qualified for a master's degree in that particular emotional journey.

Ash could feel the tension invading his body. Sophia had dared to mention his marriage. He allowed no one to do that. It was a taboo subject.

'I do not discuss either my late wife or our marriage with anyone.'

The words delivered in a harsh blistering tone only confirmed what Sophia already felt she knew, and that was how much Ash still loved his dead wife.

She must not think about that, though. She must think instead about her own need for his help.

From the minute she had learned he was coming to the engagement party, she had seen him as her salvation and her only hope of rescue from a situation she simply could not bear. She must not falter now, no matter how vulnerable she felt inside.

Sophia had gone silent. Ash turned to look at her. She was trying to appear confident but he could see the apprehension beneath. It was a protective device she had often employed as a child. A child who as the youngest of the family, and a girl, was often overlooked. Somehow against his will, he found his anger receding.

Ash's penetrating gaze was assessing her with hawklike scrutiny, Sophia recognised, and yet there was something in his expression that had softened, as though the bones of his face had subtly moved so that she could see again the Ash whose memory she cherished, beneath the harshness that time had overlaid on those bones—something that resurrected her desperate hope.

There was no time to waste, she decided. She must be brave and strong, and trust in her own judgement, her own belief in him.

'My father wants to marry me to off to some Spanish prince he's found.'

What was that sensation that uncurled inside him and attacked with the deadly speed of a poisonous snake, causing his heart to lurch inside his chest? Nothing. Nothing at all.

'So your father wishes to arrange a dynastic and diplomatic marriage for you.'

Ash shrugged dismissively, but Sophia stopped him. 'It would be a forced marriage, and I would be the one forced into it.'

Her words might have been those of the passionate, emotional, sensitive young girl he remembered. How fierce she had been then in her defence of people's personal freedoms, her conviction that everyone had the right to dictate the pathway of their own lives. It was no real wonder given how often she and her father had clashed, as they were obviously doing now.

'Don't you think you're being a tad dramatic?' he asked her in a wry voice. 'You aren't a naive girl any more, Sophia. Royalty marries royalty, that is the way of our kind. Marriages are arranged, heirs conceived and born, and that is how we fulfil our duty to our forebears and our people.'

This was not how she had imagined he would react when she had lain sleepless at night, longing for his arrival, aching for his help, needing his support.

'I'm not being dramatic,' she defended herself. 'Surely I should have some rights as a person, a human being, some say in my own fate, instead of having my future decided for me by my father?'

'I'm sure he only has your best interests at heart.'

Ash just did not want to get involved in this. Why should he? He was a busy man about to enter the final negotiations on a contract, the success of which would secure the future of his people for generations to come.

'No. No,' she denied immediately. 'He doesn't have my best interests at heart. All he is interested in is securing a royal marriage for a daughter of the house of Santina. He told me that himself when I begged him to reconsider, that he had had to promise this Spanish prince that I would be an obedient and dutiful wife, a wife who would not try to interfere in his own preferred lifestyle of bed hopping amongst his many mistresses.

'When I told him that I didn't want to marry this prince, he said that I was ungrateful and ignoring my royal duty. He said that I would grow accustomed to my husband. Accustomed. To endure marriage to a man who has simply agreed to marry me because he wants an heir, and to whom my father has virtually auctioned me off in exchange for a royal alliance. How could that ever be having my best interests at heart?'

'I should have thought such a marriage would suit

you, Sophia. After all, it's well documented that your own chosen lifestyle involves something very similar, when it comes to bed hopping.'

A body blow indeed and one that drove the blood from Sophia's face and doubled the pain in her heart. It shouldn't matter what Ash thought of her. That was not part of her plan. But still his denunciation of her hurt and it wasn't one she could defend herself against. Not without telling him far more than she wanted him to know.

'Then you thought wrong,' was all she could permit herself to say. 'That is not the kind of marriage I want. I can't bear the thought of this marriage.' Her panic and fear was there in her voice; even she could hear it herself, so how much more obvious must it be to Ash?

She must try to stay calm. Not even to Ash could she truly explain the distaste, the loathing, the fear, she had of being forced by law to give herself in a marriage bed in the most intimate way possible when… No, that was one secret that she must keep no matter what, just as she had already kept it for so long.

Not even to Ash? Definitely not to Ash. Now she *was* letting her emotions get muddled instead of focusing on the practicalities of her situation.

Steadying her breathing she told Ash as calmly as she could, 'When I marry I want to know and respect my husband and our marriage. I want to love him and be loved by him. I want us to bring our children up in the safe secure circle of that love.' That, after all, was the truth.

And it was a truth that Ash heard and couldn't refute. He frowned. Against his will he was forced to acknowledge that there was something in her voice that touched old nerves, revived old memories. Revived them? Since when had they really needed reviving? He had never forgotten, could never forget.

'Please, Ash, I'm begging you for your help.'

CHAPTER TWO

THOSE words—the same words with which she had cried out to him once before—sliced through his self-control, cutting the cords that held fast the doors to the past.

Once before Sophia had begged him for something.

She'd been just past her sixteenth birthday the last time he'd seen her. He could still remember the shock he had felt at seeing her all grown-up. One minute—or so it had seemed—she had been a child, but somehow six months later she had been trembling on the brink of what would become her womanhood, a girl still for all her burgeoning physical maturity, a girl with tears tracking down her cheeks, her huge dark brown eyes drowning in tears. Then she had still been an innocent: naive, unknowing, virginal and vulnerable. He had been determined that it would not be through him that any of those things were taken from her, no matter how hard she begged him to do so.

What had happened to her during those intervening years to turn her into the wanton sensualist she was now? Why should he care? The sixteen-year-old towards whom he had felt so protective belonged to another life, another Ash.

Even then she'd been sensationally beautiful, with

everything about her already hinting at the sensuality to come. Then she had had the promise of a sweet, almost ready-to-ripen peach, yet still a girl compared to his adult-male maturity, and his natural sense of responsibility and moral probity had naturally reacted to that. He had known that he had a duty towards her to protect her not just from herself but from that shock of awareness within himself of the fact that she was becoming a desirable woman.

Ash discovered that there was suddenly a sour taste in his mouth. For himself. For that brief ripping through his moral code, caused by the shocking sexual awareness he'd had of her when he had seen the change in her. Desires he never should have had for that girl given the protective role he had previously played in her life and the fact that he had been about to be married.

Desires he still had for her? He swallowed hard against that question. She was a woman, and available. He was a man, but he could not allow himself to want her. He *would* not allow it. After all, he had nothing left within him to give to a woman like Sophia, who so obviously brought emotional passion to her relationships along with her sexual desire. A grim wryness filled him. So he was back in his old role towards her, was he, protecting her from his own desire?

'Ash, please.' The panic in Sophia's voice made Ash frown. Twice before he had heard her say his name in that same tone of mingled fear and need and now somehow his body reacted to that memory, instinctively halting him in his tracks.

'Sophia…'

'Please, Ash. I need you. There isn't anyone else I can turn to.'

'No? What about one of those young men who share your bed?' His challenge was harsh and acerbic.

This was getting dangerous, Sophia recognised. The conversation was going now in a direction she most certainly did not want.

'That's just sex. What I need from you is help.'

Just sex? Ash could almost taste the ferocity of the atavistic emotions surging through him.

Across the years that separated him from those other occasions inside his head he could see the sixteen-year-old she had been, pleading with him for something it was impossible for him to give her. He could almost smell the hot summer fragrance of the small grassy bank on which they'd been sitting. Inside his head he could see a clear image of her in her thin cotton dress. It had shown quite clearly the perfect shape of her high rounded breasts with their eager thrusting nipples pushing against the fabric, just as she had pushed against his chest with small fists when she had begged him to take her and show her what it was to be a woman—and the icy cold shock to his system it had given him to realise that his awareness of her was darkened by the sexual desire. He had wanted to walk away from her there and then, to put an end to the danger he could sense, but before he could do anything she had continued emotionally, 'I'm the only girl in my class who's still a virgin, and I hate it. The other girls laugh at me because of it. They say that I'm a baby and...'

He could still remember the duality of the feelings her confession had brought him. Firstly, a desire to protect her and defend her, but beneath that, shockingly and shamefully, a slow awareness of the sweet pleasure there would be for the man to whom she would ultimately give herself for the first time. He had reminded himself that he was too old for her, and that she was too young for him. To even think about doing as she asked would be an abuse of their relationship that could never be allowed, but still there had been, inside his head, that treacherous thought that were she two years or so older and he two years or more younger... He would what? Bed her and then leave her—dishonour her—for the marriage that had been arranged for him since childhood? Never.

And so he had put temptation aside and told her as though it was no concern to him, 'I'm sure there are any number of boys your own age who would be delighted to relieve you of your virginity.'

'I don't want it to be them, I want it to be you,' she insisted, her eyes dark and stormy with the heat of her need.

Only he knew how tempted he'd been to wish away some of the years that separated them and to give in and take her. Just the smell of her sun-warmed skin had sent him half maddened with aching, longing to lie her down and lick and kiss his way over every inch of her delectable, hotly eager body until he reached those dark flaunting nipples. Inside his head he had already been suckling on them, drawing cries of tormented delight from her whilst his hand covered the wet heat of her sex and his fingers teased an open eager passage.

The secret betrayal of his thoughts and his body had felt to him as much of a betrayal of his duty to protect her as it was of the duty that lay on him towards his future bride and their marriage.

He had been angry. With himself more than with Sophia but it had been on her he had vented his anger, telling her savagely, 'It can't be me. You already know that, Sophia. I'm engaged to be married.'

'An arranged marriage,' she had reminded him. 'Not a love match.'

Something in the truth of her words had turned a knife in his heart as sharp and destructive as one of the fine jewelled daggers favoured by his ancestors, cruelly sharp knives that could rip out the heart of a man and still leave that heart beating and the man breathing. For a while.

'My marriage is my concern, and as for it not being a love match, it will be my duty and my pleasure to learn to love my wife and to teach her to love me. My very great pleasure.'

His words had been cruel. He had seen that in the look in her eyes. He had taken a step towards her, Ash remembered, and then he had stopped as she dashed away the tears she hadn't been able to control. A child's tears, and if he had been cruel then it had been to protect that child.

And now as then, Ash wanted to turn and walk away from her, but somehow he couldn't, just as he couldn't drag his gaze from her or stop his body reacting to her. His own weakness lashed at him, biting deep into his pride. But still he looked, still he let his senses fill with the pleasure of her.

Her dark curls caressed the bare shoulders revealed by her figure-hugging goddess-style amber-gold silk dress with its diamante waistband, her velvet-soft eyes sparkling, her lips warm and invitingly parted. They would taste of sensuality and promise, and her low-cut gown would be no barrier to the man who was determined to enjoy exploring the soft warmth of her naked breasts. But that man would never be him. Sophia was the sister of one of his closest friends; she was passionate and emotional. To bed her would bring complications into his life that he didn't want. And why would he need to bed her when he had so many other willing women to choose from who understood that sex was all he required from them? Sex and nothing more.

Oblivious to the turmoil of Ash's most private thoughts, Sophia looked over at the table where her parents were seated with some of their guests. As always it was her father who was commanding everyone's attention whilst her mother looked on, her blonde head inclined towards him, her whole manner one of calm, controlled formality. Just as her father demanded. Just as the husband he had chosen for her would demand of her. She was not her mother. Her own nature was far more turbulent and intense. Still focusing on the table, she told Ash with fierce desperation, 'My father thinks he can argue me into giving way. But I won't.'

Ash could hear the desperation in her voice. Against his will he found himself thinking that she reminded him of a beautiful butterfly beating her wings against the iron bars of a cage that imprisoned her, her desperate attempt to find freedom destined only to leave her crushed and broken. Unexpectedly, for all the gossip about her hedonistic lifestyle, there was still an innocence and vulnerability about her. Against his better judgement he realised that he felt sorry for her, but he knew her father and he knew that King Eduardo would not give up his plans easily. He was as traditional and old-fashioned a father as he was a king, ruling his family and his country with the firm belief that they were his to command and control and that their duty was to obey him in all things. He did feel sorry for her, he allowed himself to acknowledge. Yes, but it was not his business and there was nothing he could do, other than offer her a reminder of the reality of what being royal meant.

'As your father's daughter you must always have known that ultimately he would arrange a marriage for you to someone he considers to be suitable?'

Just for a minute Sophia was tempted to drop her guard and admit to him that the kind of marriage of which she had always dreamed and for which she had always yearned was one based on mutual love, not dynastic necessity. But she knew that if she did that she might easily betray to him what she did not want him to know. She had her pride after all, and she certainly wasn't going to have him feeling sorry for her because she wanted...

What? Love from the one man she knew would never give it to her? No. She might have wanted that once as a foolish sixteen-year-old but she did not want Ash now.

But she did want to marry a man she was in love with, a man who loved her back, and she was prepared to wait until she found it.

Only when she stood before her chosen bridegroom, ready to give herself to him in the sacred intimacy of marriage, would she finally be free of the scorching pain of Ash's rejection.

But as yet she had not found that man or that love, and it certainly wasn't for a lack of trying.

Watching her, he saw a bleakness in her eyes, and Ash felt himself filled with an unexpected compassion for her. She had been such a sweet child, so loving and giving, so sweet in her hero-worship of him. She had looked up to him as though he was a god. Childish adoration from a girl who had desperately wanted her father's love and been denied it, that was all. He was not a god and she was no longer a child. He owed her nothing. Right?

She was not a child any more, he reminded himself. She had stopped being a child to him that fateful afternoon when she had begged him to take her virginity.

Who was the man who had taken it and her? Could she even remember his name? Given what the gossip columns had to say about her, Ash doubted it.

Sophia swallowed, knowing that she had to make one last attempt to secure his help. 'Ash, all I want from you, all I want you to do, is behave towards me tonight as though you want me—not just to share your bed, but potentially as the wife everyone knows you must ultimately take in order to give Nailpur an heir. You are such a matrimonial prize that my father is bound to drop the Spanish prince if he thinks that there is any chance he can marry me to you. You have everything my father admires—royal blood, status and wealth.'

For once Ash was lost for words. When Sophia had said that she needed his help it had never occurred to him that she meant she wanted help of that nature for the kind of plan she had just outlined to him. She had a shrewd brain, he acknowledged. She was completely right in her assessment of her father.

'Ash. I *need* you to rescue me and be my prince in shining armour just like you used to rescue me when I was little,' Sophia continued in a voice made husky with impassioned need. 'Do you remember that time I nearly drowned when I followed you, Alex and Hassan along that rocky cliff face?'

Against his will Ash could feel the tug her words were having on his heartstrings. 'That was a long time ago,' was all he permitted himself to say.

'I still remember it,' Sophia told him softly. 'I was nine years old, and when I slipped into that deep pool you jumped in and rescued me. Alex laughed at me but you carried me back to safety. You made me feel safe and protected.' Yes, he had then, she thought, but later... later he had hurt her so badly that even now... No. She mustn't think about that tonight. She must only think of her plan, the plan she had been working on from the minute she had learned that Ash was coming to the engagement party and she had seen a possible way out of the trap that was closing round her.

Ash frowned. There it was again, that echo of vulnerability in her voice, that admission that was like a private memory, a private awareness shared only between the two of them, as though he was the only one she could allow to see beneath her shell.

Sophia let some of her pent-up breath ease out of her lungs, the release unwittingly causing her breasts to swell softly over the top of her gown.

They were fuller than they had been when she was sixteen, and even more tempting in their allure, Ash recognised, irritated with himself that he should be so aware of them. His memory supplied him with an intimate mental image of the dark crowning of her nipples, erect and hard, pushing against the fabric of the dress she had been wearing, showing him how much she desired him. That had been then, Ash reminded himself, and now he was old enough and cynical enough to know one woman's body was much like another, and that physical desire once slaked soon evaporated, leaving him bored with the woman he had previously wanted.

Imploringly, Sophia reached out and placed her hand on Ash's arm. Immediately his body reacted.

In an attempt to distract himself he tried to focus on her hand and not his own feelings. He looked down at where Sophia's small hand lay against the sleeve of his expensively tailored, dark coloured Italian linen suit. Her nails were buffed to a natural sheen, and against his will his mind recorded for him the way he would feel if she were to rake those nails against his back in the intensity of her ecstasy. Sweat dampened his chest beneath his shirt from the heat pounding through his body.

'Our father is allowing Alex to choose his own bride, so why should I have to submit to having my husband chosen for me?' Her brother's engagement had come as a complete surprise to her, and to Carlotta, the sibling to whom she was the closest. 'You loved Nasreen. Why shouldn't I be loved and love in return within my own marriage?'

The passion with which she spoke confirmed what he had already told himself about the emotional intensity she would bring to her sexual relationships. Such emotions had no place in his life any more, and he was determined that they never would. And if he could have her without those emotions? If they could enjoy each other now as the sexually experienced adults they both were? The rush of fierce male urgency that surged though his body gave him its own answer. But then there had never been any doubt about his awareness of her as a woman from the minute he had turned round tonight and seen her coming towards him.

In fact, if he was honest, Ash couldn't remember ever before having such an immediate and insistent ache of hunger for a woman to the extent that it came between him and the cool logic of the business affairs to which he gave priority these days.

He had to distance himself from her.

'My marriage is my business,' he told her curtly, as he fought against his reaction to the thought of taking her to bed.

She had done it again, Sophia recognised. She had trespassed into a private place where she was not welcome. Because he still loved Nasreen?

That pain she could feel in the region of her heart was simply caused by the fact that if her father succeeded in marrying her off to this prince, she would never know what it felt like to be loved in that way. It wasn't for any other reason—such as her wishing that it was Ash who loved her. Certainly not. She wasn't sixteen any more. And neither was she going to let the subject drop. To her family she was the rebellious 'difficult' one, the one who was always challenging the status quo and pushing their father, the one who bit harder than anyone else. That was her reputation and she wasn't going to abandon it now just because Ash was looking at her in that forbidding, icily cold way.

Nasreen. Ash wished that Sophia hadn't mentioned her name, but she had.

He had vowed that he would love the bride who had been chosen for him, and that their marriage would be one of mutual, total faithfulness to each other. Loving the woman who had been promised to him in marriage from childhood had been a matter of great pride and honour to him, and a duty that he had taken seriously.

Orphaned as a young boy, he'd been brought up by an elderly nurse, whose stories about the great love affair between his great-grandfather and his English bride had built a responsibility within him to love and cherish the young maharani who would one day be his bride. Love mattered more than anything else, his nurse had told him. He must love his bride and she would love him back, with that love making up for the loneliness he had known as an orphan. After listening to his nurse he had believed when he married he would love his bride as completely and faithfully as his famous warrior ancestor had loved his.

Had that belief sprung from arrogance or naivety? He didn't know. His mouth twisted in a grim expression of bitter self-contempt.

He only knew that the harsh reality of his marriage and the death of his wife—a death for which he believed that, in part at least, he had to carry a burden of blame—meant that he would never, ever again allow emotion into any intimate relationship he had with a woman. Never again would he mix sex and love. Never. Sex was a pleasure and a need, but it was just sex. He could allow himself to want a woman but he could not allow himself to love her.

CHAPTER THREE

ASH must still love Nasreen very much indeed to react to the mere mention of her as he had just done, Sophia decided.

How she hungered to be loved like that, wholly and completely, as herself and not for her royal blood. One day, one day she would find that love, Sophia assured herself fiercely, just so long as she remained free to look for it, and wasn't forced into a marriage she didn't want. Her passionate nature, like molten lava compressed for too long beneath unforgiving stone, pushed against the unspoken rules of never betraying any real feelings in the Santina family. Before she could stop herself she had burst out, in self-betrayal, 'My parents don't believe that love matters. Duty to our family name is all that counts. Especially to my father.'

The pain in her voice caught Ash's attention. He knew her history so well that he could easily recognise the real reason for the way her voice had trembled over those telling words...*my father*.

What was happening to him? He had a thousand more important things on which he ought to be focusing. The negotiations he had been involved in to turn the empty, decaying palaces which had once belonged to minor, now long-dead members of his extended family into elegant hotel and spa facilities were at a vitally important stage, as was the exhibition of royal artifacts being mounted by his charity to raise money to help educate the poor of India. These should be at the forefront of his mind, not this wayward passionate and far too desirable young woman standing in front of him.

He needed to bring their conversation to an end.

'I'm sure that your father only wants what's best for you,' he told her as he had done before. He knew that his words were bland and meaningless but why should he try to comfort and reassure her? Why should he care what happened to her? He didn't, Ash assured himself.

Best for her? Wasn't that what he had said to her all those years ago before he had walked away from her? That refusing the plea she had made to him was 'best for her' when what he had meant was that it was best for him.

'The best for me?'

Ash could see the bitterness and the despair in her eyes as she shook her head in rejection of his words.

'No!' The second vigorous shake of her head that accompanied her denial had the dark cloud of her soft curls and waves sliding sensuously over her bare shoulders, reminding him... Reminding him of what? Of how much his body was still aching for her?

'What my father wants is what he thinks is the best for him and for the Santina family. And as far as he's concerned I've always been an unwanted and unexpected addition to the family.' The softness of her mouth twisted painfully as she challenged him. 'You know that's true, Ash. You know the gossip about...about my birth as well as I do.'

It was true. He had been a boy, invited back for the school holidays with Alex after Alex's mother had realised that he was an orphan with no family with which to spend the long holidays from their British boarding school; Sophia herself had barely started school when he had first heard the rumours that the king might not be her father.

'You have the Santina looks,' was all he felt able to say to her now.

'That is what my mother said when I asked her if it was true that the English architect everyone gossiped about might be my father, but doesn't it tell you something that never once whilst I was growing up did anyone ever suggest I should have a DNA test?'

'What it tells me is that both your parents were so sure that you are their child that a DNA test wasn't necessary.'

'That's what Carlotta says,' Sophia admitted, 'but then with an illegitimate child of her own and her refusal to say who the father is, she would say that, wouldn't she?' Normally Sophia wouldn't have been so outspoken about Carlotta's situation. The birth of Carlotta's son, Luca, had meant that she, too, was out of favour with the king. They both felt they were outsiders and this had bonded them together, despite the fact that Carlotta had a twin sister.

'And Carlotta has always been very sensible.'

Sophia gave him a wry look. 'You call having a child out of wedlock by a man who she won't name and, according to our father, bringing disgrace on the family sensible?'

A child—a son—only he knew how atavistically he

longed for fatherhood, Ash acknowledged as he felt the familiar strike of sharply savage pain burning into him.

He had assumed when he and Nasreen had married that she would be as keen to start their family as he had been. Initially, when she had told him that she wanted to delay it because she wanted to have time alone with him he had been charmed and captivated. But then he had learned from Nasreen's own lips the real reason why she did not want to have a child—ever—and that had led to the first of many rows between them.

To outsiders, his desire for children would be seen as the natural desire of a man in his situation to have an heir to follow him. There was an element of that there, of course—he had a duty to his inheritance, after all— but his need went deeper and was far more intensely personal than that. The loneliness he had felt as a child had made him long for a family of his own in a way that had nothing to do with being royal, and it was a need he could not turn away from or deny. One day he would marry again—it would be a marriage of practicality and not emotion, but the children that came from that marriage he would love, because that love would come naturally and not have to be forced, or pretended. As he had done with Nasreen. The bitterness of his failure to love Nasreen still brought him guilt.

'It isn't what one would have expected of Carlotta,' he acknowledged.

'No, Carlotta was always the good one. Not like me. I suppose if anyone outside the family had to choose one of us to do something disgraceful to our father they would choose me.' Sophia pulled a face. 'Oh, don't bother denying it. We both know that it's true. If it had happened to me I'd do exactly what Carlotta has done and insist on keeping my baby. No matter who tried to take it away from me.' Her face softened as she added, 'Little Luca is so gorgeous that sometimes I almost wish he was mine.' There was genuine warmth and tenderness in her voice. 'Not that my father would ever tolerate such a lapse from what's expected from me. It would be the last straw, I expect, and he'd probably completely disown me.'

'I doubt that your father would be trying to arrange a suitable marriage for you if he himself wasn't convinced that you are his child, especially not to a fellow royal.'

His statement was intended to reassure her, as well as bring their conversation to a halt, but instead of doing that, it had Sophia firing up again and telling him fiercely, 'If you think that then you don't know my father at all. It isn't for my benefit that he wants this marriage. It's for his own. For the Santina name. That's all that matters to him. Not us. Just the reputation of the Royal House of Santina. It's always been the same, all the time we were growing up. All he ever said to us was that we must remember who and what we are. He rules us as he rules the kingdom, because he believes it is his right to do so. Our feelings, our needs, don't matter. In fact, as far as he is concerned we ought not to have feelings at all, and that applies especially to me. He doesn't understand me, he never has. You could help me, Ash. It wouldn't take very much. As I've already told you my father would drop the Spanish prince like a hot potato if he thought he had any chance at all of marrying me off to you.'

'I doubt very much that your father would switch his

allegiance, son-in-law-wise, on the strength of seeing us together for a handful of hours at a party.'

'Yes, he would,' Sophia told him succinctly. 'And I'll prove it to you if you help me.'

Sophia's problems were nothing to him, Ash reminded himself. He was simply here as a friend of her eldest brother. The fact that he had felt a certain amount of protective compassion for Sophia as a young girl didn't mean anything now. After all, then he had been an idealistic young man looking forward to a future filled with love and happiness, or so he'd thought. Now he was a realist—an embittered hard-hearted realist, some might say—who knew that such dreams were exactly that. Wasn't the truth that it was his view now that an arranged marriage worked better, lasted longer and fitted the purpose it was designed for—the production of an heir and the continuation of a family name—than so-called love? Wouldn't his own second marriage be exactly that? After all, one only had to look at Sophia's parents to see the strength of such a union. Whether or not the rumours about Queen Zoe and the young architect were true, their marriage remained solid, as did their shared dedication to preserving the Santina family name. If Sophia thought that her father would ever sacrifice that to allow her to make a marriage of her own choice then in his opinion she was wrong. Besides, she was grown-up now, and could take care of herself. And he didn't want to muddy the waters of diplomatic relations with a poorly timed flirtation.

'I don't see the point in us discussing this any further, Sophia.' He pushed back the sleeve of his dinner jacket to look at his watch.

He had extraordinarily sexy hands and wrists, Sophia

acknowledged, and the warm tone of his skin only emphasised that. For months after he had rejected her she had soothed herself to sleep at night imagining those hands on her body in a caress that was warm and loving, as well as sensually erotic. The pain of the sudden sense of loss that swept her locked her breath in her throat.

'I have to leave soon,' Ash told her. 'If you spoke to your father about your feelings I am sure that he will give you more time to get to know the man he has chosen for you.'

The fierce shrug of her slender, tanned shoulders in a gesture of denial and despair caused the strapless top of her dress to slip downwards, so that the shadow of the areole of her nipples was clearly visible to him. Desire hot and feral shot through him. What was the matter with him? It was as though his body was taking delight in deliberately disobeying the orders he had given it, as though his own flesh was actively delighting in punishing him by making him…want her?

Anger gushed through him. With a figure like hers she must surely have known the risks of wearing a dress like that.

'If you don't want everyone here to see what I can see right now I suggest you do something about your dress,' he warned her curtly. 'Unless, of course, you do want every man in the room to see what only a lover should be permitted to enjoy.'

Not understanding what Ash was saying, Sophia stared at him in confusion and then took a step towards him, gasping as she stepped on the hem of the front of her dress and felt it slide down her body.

Instantly Ash moved towards her, shielding her from

everyone else's sight, his hands on her upper arms so that no one could see what she now knew must be clearly visible.

She had sunbathed topless as and when appropriate in front of any number of people, so why right now did she feel so embarrassed and self-conscious, her hands trembling as she tried to tug up the front of her dress, succeeding only in dislodging it even more. She choked, 'You'll have to help me—I need you to reach round and unfasten the hook and eye at the back so that I can adjust the front.'

He wanted to refuse but how could he without letting her guess the effect she was having on him, as though he was a callow youth who had never seen a woman's naked breasts before.

It was just as well the elegant ballroom was so busy, Ash acknowledged as he reached around behind Sophia almost as though he was about to take her into his arms, deftly unfastening the hook and eye and then lowering the zip.

'That's too much,' Sophia protested, her face burning as she felt the top of her dress fall away. Not, thankfully, that anyone could see that. Not with her virtually pressed up against Ash in the way that she was, his arms around her.

'Pull the top up, then I can fasten the zip,' he ordered her.

'I can't, you're holding me too close,' Sophia complained.

Exhaling impatiently, Ash started to step back only to have her grab hold of his arm and tell him frantically, 'No. Don't move, everyone will see.'

'I thought that almost everyone already had,' Ash felt

bound to tell her grimly, and then frowned as he saw the speed with which she tried to conceal her expression from him and the hint of tears that had dampened her eyes. She was genuinely embarrassed, he recognised as she tried desperately to stay close to him and at the same time tug up the top of her dress.

'Here, let me help.'

He had only meant to put the top of her dress back in place but somehow his hand was cupping the side of her breast, his fingertips accidentally grazing her nipple.

Fiery flames of male hunger burned at his self-control. Because his bed had been empty for too long, that was all, whilst an involuntary shudder of sensual awareness openly seized Sophia's body.

Silently they looked at each other, and then looked away, neither of them willing to speak.

Why on earth had that happened? Sophia asked herself, still shocked by her reaction to him. She didn't still want him. How could she when she had outgrown her foolish youthful feelings for him? It had been an involuntary reaction of her body to the unexpected intimacy of a male touch, she assured herself. And that male touch could have been any male touch? Yes, of course. Of course.

Silently Ash reached behind Sophia, his expression grim as he refastened her dress, and then stepped back.

He was on the point of walking away from her, his work done and his self-control shot to hell, when he saw that King Eduardo was beckoning them over. Impossible for him to ignore that royal command. Ash sighed and told Sophia, 'I think your father wants us to join him.'

As they had reached the king and queen, champagne was being handed round in anticipation of a toast. Sophia's intense focus on how to get around her father's insistence on this ridiculous arranged marriage had momentarily made her forget that this was her oldest brother's engagement party. His fiancée Allegra's father, Bobby Jackson, got to his feet, albeit rather unsteadily, and made a rambling speech of congratulation to the newly engaged couple. When it finally came to an end, they all dutifully toasted the happy couple, but an uneasy rumble of chatter spread around the ballroom in reaction to Bobby's graceless public display.

'Ash, how lovely to see you,' Queen Zoe welcomed him, the diamonds in the tiara she was wearing sparkling in the light from one of the room's many chandeliers. Sophia's mother was clearly covering her embarrassment with polite small talk.

Deprived of Ash's presence at her side as her mother engaged him in conversation, Sophia had to fight hard not to feel alone and abandoned, emotions that were all too familiar to her growing up, despite the fact that then, as now, she had been surrounded by her siblings. The trouble was that she had never felt truly accepted or loved by them. Because she had never felt accepted or loved by her father? That was why it was so important to her to marry someone whom she loved and who loved her, someone who would share her determination to raise the children they would have in a loving home in which those children would know how much they were loved. That was her secret and deepest desire.

As her father began his toast to the happy couple, Sophia turned to look longingly towards Ash. Only a metre or so separated them but it might as well have been a mile. Listening to her father's speech he had his back to Sophia, and she rubbed her arms in a small sad gesture of self-comfort.

Her father was still talking, and looking straight at her, Sophia realised, as he announced, 'And Alessandro's engagement is only the first Santina engagement we are to celebrate. I am delighted to be able to tell you all that my youngest daughter Sophia's fiancé is shortly to arrive in the kingdom.'

The shock of what her father had said descended on Sophia like an icy wall, numbing her, reducing her to dumb, frozen shock, unable to speak or move as she was jostled by the throng of press photographers who had all been focusing on her brother and Allegra but who were now all around her, instead, their cameras flashing.

As swiftly as it had engulfed her, the numbness receded, leaving her with the reality of the full horror of her situation. Inside she felt as though she was shaking from head to foot, as she was gripped by a rising tide of nausea and furious helpless despair. This couldn't be happening. Her father couldn't have trapped her into an engagement without giving her any warning. But he had, and now she had no way of arguing him out of his plans. She felt so weak and helpless, so lost and alone. Instinctively she looked towards Ash but there were too many photographers in the way. Her father, on the other hand, she could see, and the cold warning look in his eyes told her what he expected of her.

Reporters and photographers surrounded her, pushing mikes and lenses in her face as they demanded a response to her father's announcement.

'I...'

'My daughter is delighted to be engaged,' the king answered for her. 'Aren't you, Sophia?'

Shock and a lifetime of always giving in to her father's will couldn't be ignored or overcome no matter how much she wanted to do so. As though someone else was speaking the words Sophia bowed her head submissively and responded, 'Yes.'

From the queen's side Ash watched and listened to what was happening with a mixture of feelings, the least wanted of which was the sudden savage stab of antagonism he had felt towards the unknown prince to whom Sophia was now officially engaged.

'Such a relief that Sophia has finally seen sense and realised that her father knows what's best,' Queen Zoe murmured to Ash. 'All this gossip about her in the press has made the king very angry. Marriage will do her good. The king believes that the prince shares his traditional values and beliefs on the role of a royal consort and royal children, and will soon have Sophia realising where her duty lies.'

'Sophia…' Sophia felt a small tug on her arm, and she turned from the throng of reporters to see the concerned face of her sister Carlotta.

'I can't believe what Father has done. He knows I don't want to be engaged. I can't stay here, Carlotta,' she told her sister. 'Not now. I'm going to my room.'

By the time she reached the relative sanctuary of her room Sophia's thoughts were in such turmoil that she was trembling from head to foot as though the force of them couldn't be contained within her body. How foolish and naive she had been to think that her father would allow her the freedom of trying to change his mind. That had obviously never been an option. Her father must have known all along that he intended to announce her engagement without her real consent. Now her plan to parade Ash in front of her father, in the hope that the king could be deceived into thinking that there could be a match between her and Ash, seemed so juvenile and ridiculous—the pointless hope of someone who didn't recognise or understand reality. Angry, helpless, frustrated tears blurred her vision. All the things she had done to avoid marriage until she found the right man had been a complete waste of time. She might as well have remained here in her room at the palace as a good and dutiful daughter who never did anything to challenge the status quo.

How was she going to endure what would now be her future? She couldn't, she wouldn't, Sophia decided on the wave of panic and pain that welled up inside her, and she certainly wasn't going to stay here and let her father marry her off. She'd run away and leave the island, cut herself off from her family, before she'd allow herself to be forced into this marriage. Her heart was hammering even faster at the enormity of what she was thinking.

Without allowing herself to think through what she was doing she ran to her wardrobe and started pulling clothes out of it and putting them into a case—something that normally one of the maids would do for her—tears running down her face whilst she did so.

Panting and out of breath she froze when her phone beeped with a text. It was from Carlotta asking if she was OK. About to reply to it, Sophia checked. She didn't want to involve her sister in what she was going to do.

Now all she had to do was get changed and go to the airport. Then within a few hours she would be on her way to London where she had school friends who she hoped would offer her a temporary sanctuary from her father and from her unwanted marriage.

They would help her, wouldn't they? She did have friends. Did she? Who? Those good-time, fun-loving crowds whose lives consisted of moving from party to party?

She'd make new friends. Get herself a job. Anything, just as long as she didn't have to marry the man her father had chosen for her.

She pulled a dress out of her wardrobe and quickly put it on, grabbing a jacket to go over it, mentally checking through what she would need.

Her passport, she had that; some money, she had that. Of course, the national airline would let her board any plane she chose, and with luck it would be morning before anyone realised she had gone, by which time it would be too late for her father to stop her from leaving. By morning she would be on her way to start her new life. A life where she would be in control, and no one else.

'The last flight's gone?'

'Yes, Your Highness. Several hours ago. We had to cancel most of our flights because of the number of private jets the airport has had to accommodate. The first flight to London will be tomorrow morning. I think several journalists are booked on to it.'

Sophia gave a small shudder at the thought of travelling with a curious press pack.

She was well and truly trapped on the island, just as she was going to be trapped in her unwanted marriage.

'Maybe one of the party guests could offer you a

seat?' the young girl manning the enquiries desk suggested with a smile.

'No. I don't think…' Sophia began, only to stop as she remembered Ash telling her that he was going to have to leave the party before it ended because he needed to get back to India. Her heart thumping, she asked the girl as casually as she could, 'Do you happen to know if the Maharaja of Nailpur's plane has left yet?'

The girl consulted a list out of Sophia's view and then told her, 'It's scheduled for take-off in twenty minutes, Your Highness. His plane is waiting at the royal departure gate right now, but the maharaja is flying back to Mumbai and not London.'

Nodding her head Sophia turned away and reached for her suitcase. Ash would help her now, surely? He knew how she felt. He had seen how unfair her father was being. There *was* no one else she could turn to. She wasn't going to ask much of him, just a lift in his plane to Mumbai, that was all. From there she could get a flight to London. Despite the glamorous lifestyle she lived, Sophia was very good with her allowance and did have some savings. Enough certainly to pay for a flight to London from Mumbai, and once there… Once there she would worry then about what she would do. Right now she needed to get on Ash's plane and make sure that he allowed her to leave the island with him.

If the security guards on duty at the doors to the private royal departure and arrivals gate were surprised to see her on her own and wheeling her own suitcase they didn't show it, bowing briefly to her as she walked past them. Their presence and the bow they had given her brought home to her the reality of what she was about to do and how her family and especially her father would view her behaviour. There could be no going back once she had broken the unwritten rules of the Santina family by defying the king. For a moment she hesitated. And then an image of her standing in church beside the stranger her father wanted her to marry filled her head, galvanising her. Her heart had begun to thump wildly just in case someone at the palace had discovered her absence and had realised that she might try to leave the island. The thought of the ignominy of being dragged back to the palace to face her father and his wrath was all Sophia needed to carry her out of the airport building and into the April night air.

In front of her, down the length of the red carpet that had been put out to welcome their guests, she could see the steps to the executive jet with Ash's royal crest emblazoned on its side.

There was no one around to stop her as she climbed the steps to the plane, dragging her case with her. Sophia wasn't used to carrying her own luggage, just as she wasn't used to packing her own things. The case was heavy and she was slightly out of breath by the time she had managed to drag it behind her and into the empty body of the executive jet.

The main cabin of the plane was elegant but business-like compared with some of the private jets on which she had travelled before. It was clear to her that Ash used his plane as an extension of his office when he travelled, but then, unlike some of the men who formed part of the smart set with whom Sophia partied, Ash was primarily a businessman, despite his title. At the far end of the cabin there was another door. Sophia went to it and opened it. Beyond it lay a bedroom fitted with a large double bed; a door next to the bed opened into a bathroom. The grey-and-white decor of the main cabin was repeated throughout.

The bedroom area of the plane was in darkness and through the window Sophia could see Ash striding down the red carpet towards the plane accompanied by a uniformed steward. Her heart skipped a beat, tension filling her. She wanted to rush to meet him and beg him for help but he was frowning and looked impatient. Sophia looked towards the bathroom. What if she simply hid herself in there and waited until they had taken off before she revealed her presence to him? That way he would have no choice other than to help her.

The bathroom was compact with a good-size shower and the usual facilities. Most of the spare floor space was taken up by her case so she had to perch on it after she had pulled the door to and taken the precaution of locking it. Presumably there was another lavatory off the main cabin of the jet for staff, so she should be safe in here until they had taken off.

As soon as the jet's door was locked behind him, enclosing him in its cabin, Ash removed his jacket and sat down at his desk, reaching for his laptop. He had work to do ahead of the meeting he was returning to Mumbai to attend. He had planned to speak with Sophia before he had left the ballroom. His deep-rooted sense of responsibility demanded that he at least tell her that her marriage need not be as bad as she obviously felt it would be, but he hadn't been able to find her. And if he had found her? If she had pleaded with him yet again for his help? He pushed the laptop away and stood. He had no idea where it had come from, this persistent unwanted ache of what he refused to call anything but mere male lust, but he did know that neither it nor Sophia herself could have any place in his life.

In her hiding place Sophia felt the plane start to move down the runway and then gather speed, before lifting into the sky. She had done it. She had left the island and it was too late to change her mind now. In the morning her family would know she had gone, and her father... Her father would be furious with her, but if he wouldn't listen to her and let her tell him how she felt then she had no other way of showing him just how much she did not want this marriage.

The plane levelled off. Sophia opened the bathroom door. The bedroom was still in darkness. She looked towards the door to the main cabin and the light showing underneath it. She went towards it and then stopped. She felt so vulnerable and alone. If she went to Ash now she was afraid that she might... That she might what? Throw herself at him and beg him to hold her, to comfort her, to keep her safe? That was ridiculous and it just showed how unlike her real self she was behaving to even think such a thing. It would be better though, wouldn't it, for her to wait a little longer before she did see Ash in order to give herself time to feel less vulnerable.

Ash didn't much care for the new temporary steward who had been taken on while his usual man, Jamail, had gone home to look after his sick mother. The man hovered too much and too closely. There was something in his eyes that Ash didn't like, although he told himself that he was probably being unfair to him as he shook his head, refusing the drink the steward had offered. He looked at his watch. Just gone 1:00 a.m. It was a six-hour flight to Mumbai at least and, with the time difference, it meant it would be 9:30 a.m. before they landed. He had arranged for his meeting to take place in his office in his penthouse apartment in the city, to save time and also to allow him to leave for Nailpur—the Rajasthan state of which he was the ruler and from which he derived his title—the following day to attend to his business there.

A new message from Hassan caught his eye. In it his old friend was complaining that they hadn't had a chance to catch up at the engagement party.

It was true that Alex, Hassan and Ash didn't get much opportunity to catch up with one another in person. They all had busy lives. Ruefully, he emailed back—Perhaps you should get engaged yourself, and throw another party—and then went back to concentrating on the key points he wanted to discuss with the consortium that was going to renovate one of Nailpur's smaller palaces and turn it into an exclusive luxury hotel.

Whilst he personally did not need the money this venture would bring in, the people of Nailpur did. Ash sat back again in his chair as he contemplated the problems he and the highly trained young managers he had hired were having persuading the people of the benefits of growing their crops in a more modern and cost-effective way. For the hotel and the other plans he had to bring tourists and money into the area, which needed to become more self-sufficient. They had the land and the climate with which to grow much of the food visitors would require, but the local farmers were afraid of committing to the new methods of agriculture Ash wanted to introduce. In order to get round that he was encouraging their sons—and daughters—to go to agricultural colleges so that hopefully they would come back and persuade their families to adapt to modern ideas.

The door that led to the small kitchen beyond which lay the flight deck opened and the steward came out asking Ash if he would like anything to eat or drink.

In the bedroom, sitting on the edge of the bed in the dim glow from the brilliantly star-lit sky outside—she hadn't dared switch on the light in case it alerted Ash to the fact that she was here before she was ready to face him—Sophia took a deep breath. She couldn't hide herself away in here forever. She got up, heading for the door into the main cabin, then stopped as she heard voices and realised that Ash was talking to someone.

She couldn't go in there now. She'd have to wait until he was alone. She went back to the bed and sat down on it, stifling a yawn as she did so. It had been a long and exhausting day and the bed looked very tempting. Too tempting to resist, Sophia admitted as she had to stifle another yawn.

Two minutes later, having automatically removed her shoes and her dress, she was tucked up beneath the beautifully welcoming and expensive sheets, her eyes already closing.

CHAPTER FOUR

FOUR o'clock. Another couple of hours or so and they'd be touching down in Mumbai. He might as well get some sleep, Ash acknowledged as he closed down his laptop and then made his way to the jet's bedroom, not bothering to turn on the light as he headed for the bathroom where he stripped off his clothes and then stepped into the shower. Emerging from it he dried himself and then pulled on one of the two thick towelling robes that hung on the inside of the bathroom door.

This time he did switch on the bedroom light and then froze in disbelief as he saw what—or rather who—it revealed.

'Sophia! What the…'

The angry sound of Ash's voice brought Sophia out of her shallow sleep to struggle into a sitting position as she clutched the bedclothes around her naked upper body, and wished that her heart was not hammering so fast.

'I'm sorry, Ash,' she apologised immediately. 'I was going to come and tell you that I was here but you were talking to someone and then I was so tired that I must have fallen asleep.'

This was the last thing he needed right now, Ash

thought. In the intimacy of the cabin he could smell the scent of her skin, lush and warm, subtly demanding that his male senses respond to it as nature had designed them to do.

'You've done this deliberately, haven't you?' he accused her. 'Even though I told you that I couldn't help you. I don't like having my hand forced, Sophia.'

Sophia bristled. How dare he accuse her of that kind of subterfuge and deceit. 'You're wrong,' she snapped. 'I'm not trying to force your hand. I came to the airport thinking I'd be able to get a scheduled flight to London but all the normal flights were cancelled because of the number of guests arriving for the party on their own private jets. When the girl at the airport said that yours would be the first to leave I just—'

'You just got on board? Have you any idea of the diplomatic reverberations your behaviour is going to cause? And not just with your father. How do you think your husband-to-be is going to react to the news that you've disappeared with another man within hours of your engagement to him being announced?'

'He will never be my husband. Never. I wish this was any plane but yours, Ash, I really do, but I had no choice. I will not let my father sacrifice me for his dynastic ambitions. All I want is to get to London. I've got my passport. After your plane puts down in Mumbai you need never have anything to do with me again. In fact, I don't want you to. I thought you were someone special, Ash, a true hero, and someone I could turn to, but you aren't. Stupid of me when I already knew the danger of putting my faith in you and then being rejected as a result.'

He knew immediately what she was alluding to and her criticism stung.

'You offered me your virginity and I refused it for your own sake as much as anything else. You were sixteen. To have taken your innocence from you would have been dishonourable.'

They shouldn't be having this conversation. It took him too close to a dangerous place he didn't want to be.

'All I want from you is a lift to Mumbai,' Sophia told him. 'No one need know that I left the island with you.'

'You're damned right they don't because the truth is that you did not leave *with* me. And why London?'

'I've got friends there.'

She was avoiding looking at him, causing Ash to demand curtly, 'Friends, or a man? A lover who—'

'No!' Sophia denied truthfully. Please don't let Ash ask her if she was really sure those so-called friends would welcome her and help her, she prayed, because the honest answer was that she didn't know.

Now that the shock of being woken up by Ash's angry voice was abating, another and far more dangerous awareness was spreading quickly through her body and that was the realisation that under that robe he had tied so carelessly Ash was probably completely naked. Why should that either concern or disturb her? She didn't want him any more.

And yet she couldn't remove her gaze from where the robe gaped as he paced the cabin floor with angry strides. She could see the shadow where the dark line of hair that bisected his body started to broaden out after it had crossed the taut plain of his belly. Once and only once she had attempted to trace that line, but then she had only got as far as the waistband of the jeans he had been wearing. Now… She was suddenly finding it very difficult to swallow, Sophia realised, and even more difficult to drag her gaze away from Ash's body.

'By rights I ought to instruct my captain to turn this plane round and—'

'No!' So great was her panic that Sophia didn't stop to think as she launched herself towards Ash, reaching out to grasp his arm, her eyes brilliant with fear and pleading as she looked up into his, totally oblivious to the fact that her anxious movement towards him had dragged down the bedding that had been protecting her nudity.

Her breasts were everything he had known they would be, Ash thought, her waist every bit as narrow and her hips every bit as lusciously curved. The tiny bikini pants she was wearing were somehow more a provocation highlighting her sex than a means of covering it. Deep down inside him a truth that refused to be ignored was surging through him. Whether he liked it or not, he wanted her.

In the soft light of the room her skin glowed, her tan contrasting with the white bedding, the lush sensual promise of her body emphasised by the almost monastic and starkness of the decor. Until now he hadn't realised just how much the clinical decor reflected the emotional emptiness of his life. Now, though, the sight of Sophia's near-naked body with its ripe readiness for sex had the effect on him of tightening an already-too-coiled spring of needs and desires that had tormented him all evening.

The plane dropped several feet, catching Sophia off guard as she struggled to pull up the sheet to cover her nakedness, her breath escaping from her lungs in a soft gasp as the movement of the plane threw her towards the edge of the bed.

Instinctively Ash reached out to stop her from falling. Instinctively, and disastrously, because it was her naked body he was now holding and his own was reacting to that fact. He had to let her go. He had to leave this cabin, but instead he was moving closer to her.

This couldn't be happening. It must not be happening, Sophia told herself. But it was too late. It was happening, and somehow it seemed that her treacherous body wanted it to happen even though that should have been impossible.

He shouldn't be doing this. He didn't want to be doing this, Ash told himself, but he was, the lean darkness of his hand cupping one of her breasts whilst his lips feathered tiny tormenting kisses around the nipple of the other.

She wanted to deny him, to stop him, to tell him that this must not happen, but like a sealed jar of sweetly potent honey-infused wine exposed to the sun's heat, the seal on her emotions and needs melted beneath his touch, leaving the sweet wine of her own desire to spill hotly through her veins.

Where did it come from, this instinct that was pure and intense? After all, she had no past experience of this kind of intimacy, no matter what others might think. But now, it had her reaching out to clasp Ash's head between her hands to hold him to her breast whilst her body arched, her head thrown back in an agonised delirium of a desire she wanted to reject but couldn't. A wild febrile urgency possessed her.

Her nipples, sensitised by his touch, and the shockingly fierce tug of his mouth, were sending almost violent spasms of erotic raw need to every part of her body, but most of all to the trembling aching heart of her sex. The pulse that sprung up there was growing more insistent, more urgent, more demanding, with every touch of Ash's hands and mouth. It was as though, deep within her, the womanhood she had told herself she had guarded so assiduously for the man who would love her and take away the pain Ash's rejection had caused her was pushing against the bonds of her virginity, swelling and softening, pulsing with its female need for the man arousing it so intensely.

Ash groaned. She was everything he had never allowed himself to imagine that she would be and more. Now, with the iron denial he had been trying all evening to forge around his desire for her to seal himself off from it, broken apart by the strength of that desire, he had no need to imagine what it would be like to give in to the lure of her, because he was already doing it.

She smelled of vanilla and almonds, her flesh dew-damp from her own arousal, the dark crowns of her nipples hard eager tellers of female need. He parted her thighs with his hand, caressing their sensitive inner flesh, his own body responding to her shudder of reaction and soft moan of impatient need. He was hard and ready, the head of his erection swollen and taut. Her briefs had bows at the sides which he unfastened with a tug. Her sex was bare to his gaze and touch, her Brazilian wax revealing its delicate shape. He was just reaching out to part its neatly folded outer lips when there was a knock on the cabin door and it started to open.

There was barely time for him to thrust the sheet over Sophia's nakedness and conceal his own body with the robe he was still wearing before the steward was in the room, his eyes widening as he apologised and started to back out, telling him that the captain wanted him to know that strong head winds meant that their flight would be delayed by fifteen minutes or so.

An icy cold revulsion every bit as all-consuming as his desire had been earlier gripped him. How could he have behaved as he had?

'You'd better get dressed,' he told Sophia without looking at her as he started to move away from her. They dressed in silence before moving out into the cabin.

What on earth had possessed her? Sophia felt sick with shock and disbelief, unable to say a word.

Eventually the captain announced that they were coming in to land. Ash hadn't spoken to her once since they had left the bedroom, and Sophia hadn't wanted him to. She was still in shock and bitterly angry with herself for her own behaviour.

His curt warning, 'Seat belt,' broke the silence between them, and had her fumbling with the straps, the colour crawling up under her skin as she caught the look that the hovering steward was giving her. He might not have seen her naked body thanks to Ash's prompt action but he knew exactly what had been happening; his look told her that.

In the past when men had given her that lustful knowing look she had been protected from it by the truth that only she knew—namely that no man had ever touched her intimately or shared her bed—but now thanks to her own betrayal of herself she had no defence against it. And there was no one to protect her from the pride-savaging pain of that. No one. For the rest of her life now she would know and remember how she had let herself down by succumbing to a…a need she had believed she had conquered years ago, Sophia acknowledged as the plane came in to land.

It would be a long flight to London, and she hoped that she wouldn't have to wait too long at the airport before beginning it.

She looked at her watch. At home people would be waking up, and her maid would be discovering that her room was empty and that her bed hadn't been slept in. Her stomach churned, but now more than ever she knew that she could not marry the Spanish prince her father had chosen for her.

Ash was unfastening his seat belt and standing. Automatically Sophia did the same.

'My case…' she began when Ash headed towards the door that the steward was just beginning to open for them.

'Leave it,' Ash told her curtly as he indicated that she was to precede him to the now-open door. 'The steward will attend to it.'

'But I want to get on the first flight I can…' Sophia began, only to come to an abrupt halt, her face paling as she looked out of the door of the plane and saw the camera crews and photographers jostling for position at the bottom of the steps. Paparazzi.

Obviously irritated by the fact that she wasn't moving Ash came up behind her and then stopped himself, cursing under his breath as he saw the press waiting for them below.

'I suppose this was your idea. Run away in secret and then let the world know what you've done,' he told her angrily.

'No. It's got nothing to do with me,' Sophia defended herself, but she could see from the look Ash was giving her that he didn't believe her.

There no escape for them, Ash recognised. To retreat back into the plane now would only increase the gathered press's hunger for their photographs. They had no option other than to try to outface them.

'Come on.' He took a firm hold of her arm.

No matter how much she might long to persuade herself that Ash's hold on her arm was protective it just wasn't possible, Sophia acknowledged miserably. Not after she had seen the anger in his eyes.

As they neared the bottom of the steps the waiting reporters started firing a barrage of far-too-intimate questions at them, demanding, 'Is it true that the two of you are an item and that you've left a fiancé behind on Santina?'

'Have you any comment to make on the fact that you've spent the night together?'

'Does King Eduardo know that the two of you are together?'

'Are you together, or is the princess going to go back to her fiancé?'

'Did you enjoy your in-flight entertainment, Your Highness?'

The last comment given with a knowing leer as a camera was lifted to catch her expression was too much for Sophia's control. She turned towards Ash, instinctively seeking his protection as she clung to his arm and turned her face into his chest.

'Thanks, darling,' the photographer called out. 'Great shot.'

'So I was right. You did engineer this,' Ash accused Sophia in a savage undertone. 'Have you no sense of dignity or shame? What do you think it's going to do to your own reputation, never mind your father's and your fiancé's, when this…this circus of predators splash their photographs all over the world? Or don't you care?'

'I didn't do anything.' Sophia tried to defend herself, her voice catching on a small hiccup of misery. She was trembling as much with the hurt of Ash not believing her as with the anxiety caused by the unexpected and unwanted presence of the press. She was, of course, used to being besieged by the press; she was even used to them asking her very intimate questions about her personal life and the men she dated, but then she had had the protection of knowing that no matter what they chose to believe and publish none of it was true. Now, though, things were different. Now she had been seen with Ash in a very intimate situation, indeed. 'Why would I? I don't want my father to know that I'm here. I don't want him to know anything until I'm safely in London.'

'Well, no one else could have organised it.' Ash only began to frown as out of the corner of his eye he saw the steward sidling up to one of the reporters who handed him a fat envelope, whilst the steward glanced furtively over his shoulder.

It looked very much as though Sophia was telling the truth, Ash had to admit, but there was no time to question the steward now or, in fact, to do anything that would draw further press attention to them, he decided.

'This way,' he instructed Sophia, still holding her arm as he pushed his way through the crowd, almost dragging her with him as he headed for the waiting limousine.

'What's this for?' Sophia demanded when she saw it. 'I need to be in the airport sorting out my flight to London.'

'And I need to be in my office for a very important meeting,' Ash countered, 'which is where we're going right now, unless of course you want me to leave you to be eaten alive by the press. We can sort out your onward flight later.'

The thought of being abandoned by Ash to deal with the ever-hungry-for-gossip paparazzi had Sophia getting into the waiting limousine without another word of protest.

The car was soon speeding through the city streets. Sophia had never visited Mumbai or India before, although she'd always wanted to—and not just because the subcontinent was Ash's home. She was genuinely interested in what she could see beyond the car windows and couldn't help turning to Ash and murmuring, 'Everything's so colourful and vibrant. It makes everywhere else I've been seem pale and uninteresting.'

They'd come to a halt in the traffic and out of nowhere a boy appeared with a bucket of water and proceeded to clean the car's front windows, despite the driver's dismissive wave for him to stop.

A tender smile softened Sophia's face. Thin and wiry, the boy gave her a wide smile, his brown eyes sparkling when he realised that Sophia was watching him, and quickly came round to her side of the car.

Watching her as she dug into her handbag, Ash felt something he didn't want to acknowledge catching on his emotions.

Nasreen had thoroughly disliked the poor of India, and had made no attempt to conceal her contempt for them.

'Here you are.' He dug into his own pocket for some change, knowing that she would not have any Indian currency.

The car had started to move again.

'Oh, make him stop, Ash, so that I can give the boy the money,' Sophia begged, giving Ash a smile nearly as warm as the one she had given the boy when he did as she asked.

It would be unbelievably easy for a man to be seduced by the warmth of such a smile, Ash acknowledged. And by Sophia herself, as well? He shrugged as the question arose, knowing full well as he did so just how much his body was still aching from the denial he had imposed on it.

They were out of the centre of the city now and travelling on a road along a sea-facing promenade. On the other side of the road Sophia was surprised to see that the buildings had a distinctly art-deco flavour to them, but before she could ask Ash about this they were climbing along another road into what Sophia could see was a very exclusive-looking residential area filled with expensive modern apartment blocks.

Sophia wasn't totally surprised when the limousine came to a halt outside one building that looked even more expensive than the rest.

'My case,' she reminded Ash, avoiding the hand he held out to her to help her from the car. She simply did not dare to touch him, not with every bit of her still aching with longing for him.

'The driver will have it sent up to the apartment,'

Ash told her. He looked at his watch, mindful of his appointment. It shouldn't take too long for him to organise a suitable flight to London for Sophia. He could, of course, have left her to fend for herself but that wasn't Ash's way. He had been brought up with a strong sense of responsibility towards his heritage and a duty to those who depended on him. That was part of the role into which he had been born as maharaja.

When he had children, a son, an heir—as he must— he would make sure that whilst that child understood the duties that went with the privilege and the wealth he would inherit, he would not be burdened by them. A child needed to be allowed to be a child. And between parent and child there needed to be love, as well as mutual respect. As an orphan he had missed out on that love, but even having parents did not guarantee it. Sophia was the proof of that.

Sophia. There he was allowing himself to feel sympathetic towards her again. His footsteps ringing out on the cool marble of the floor to the foyer of the apartment building, Ash paused to turn round to look at her.

Her dark hair was softly tousled, her face free of makeup, her eyes dark and luminous with curiosity as she studied her surroundings. Her lips parted slightly.

To his chagrin, desire, raw and fierce, and definitely unwanted, kicked through him, causing him to turn away from her as he told her curtly, 'The lift is this way.'

Reluctantly Sophia followed Ash. She'd have preferred it if he'd simply left her at the airport to make her own arrangements to board the first available flight for London. The lift, like the building itself, was very modern in glass and steel, and Sophia wasn't surprised when she followed Ash into his apartment to discover a

large open-plan living space with a whole wall of glass
and a terrace beyond it, both with panoramic views. Nor
did the decor of cool whites, charcoal greys and strong
matt black surprise her, either. It was all so very masculine. Like Ash himself? A dangerous twist of sensation ached low down in her body.

'Sit down. I'll organise some breakfast.'

'I'm not hungry,' Sophia refused. 'All I want is to
get to London. I wanted you to leave me at the airport
and not bring me here—' She broke off as her mobile
chirruped the arrival of a message, her body tensing.
They'd know at home by now that she wasn't there.

Ash had left her and she was on her own in the room.
She reached for her phone, seeing immediately that the
text she'd received was from Carlotta.

OMG, Sophia, her sister had written, what were
you thinking? You being caught in bed with Ash is
all over the internet. And I mean all over. There are
reporters here and they're grilling Father about you
joining the mile-high club with Ash. He didn't answer
them, of course. He just stormed out the room. He's
really angry, Soph. And humiliated. I hope it was
worth it. In my experience, though, it never is.

Quickly Sophia deleted the message, her fingers
trembling and her heart pounding.

In the kitchen of Ash's apartment the television was on
showing a bulletin from a local English-speaking news
channel. The sight of his own face on the screen had
Ash stopping to watch.

A reporter was explaining that following the press
discovery of Ash and Sophia together on his jet an announcement had just been put out by a spokesperson for

the Santina royal family to say that, regrettably, when Princess Sophia had informed her father that he was about to be asked for her hand in marriage, he had been unaware of her whirlwind love affair with the Maharaja of Nailpur and had assumed that she was referring to another royal suitor.

The matter had now been clarified however, and the king was pleased to announce that Princess Sophia was engaged to be married to the maharaja.

Leaving the kitchen abruptly Ash returned to the living room of the apartment, reaching for the control to reveal the concealed TV screen.

'I've found a flight with a seat on it but it doesn't leave until this evening,' Sophia told him. She'd have preferred an earlier flight and it went against her pride to have to accept Ash's hospitality for longer than she wanted.

'Watch this,' he commanded grimly, ignoring her words as he switched on the TV which was running a weather bulletin.

'What—?' Sophia began, but Ash shook his head.

'Wait,' he said tersely.

For what felt like a small eternity Sophia stood in silence in front of the TV screen, not daring to move because of Ash's grim manner, and then she heard the news reader's announcement.

'There is sad news to report for Mumbai's match-makers because today the King of Santina has announced that his daughter the Princess Sophia is to marry the Maharaja of Nailpur.'

With a growing sense of disbelief and horror Sophia watched and listened as the news item Ash had seen earlier was repeated.

Only when it had finished did she turn to Ash and tell him shakily, 'You'll have to speak to him, Ash, and tell him—'

'I shall certainly have to speak to him, and the sooner, the better, but he obviously felt he had no other choice,' said Ash coldly. 'There's only one person responsible for this situation, Sophia, and that person is you. You put yourself on my plane.'

There was nothing she could say to refute that, no matter how much she might wish to. Ash was opening his smartphone. He looked so grimly angry that for the first time in her life Sophia felt that she was facing a man who was even more formidable than her father. Far more formidable, in fact. This was Ash the maharaja, Ash the leader and the ruler of his people. This was an Ash who instinctively she knew would stop at nothing to defend the probity and honour of his royal role, and a quake of very real apprehension made her tremble inwardly.

The speed with which his call was put through to King Eduardo told Ash that the king had been expecting it. Indeed it was Ash's opinion that the royal spokesperson had given the statement he had specifically to ensure that Ash did contact the king.

'Ash.' The older man's voice was harsh and Ash suspected the use of his own first name intended to make him a supplicant for the king's forgiveness rather than an equal.

'Highness.' Ash still responded formally, though. 'There has obviously been a misunderstanding.'

'A misunderstanding?' Anger grated through the king's voice. 'There's no misunderstanding about the fact that you have publicly shamed this family and Sophia's fiancé.'

'I understand your anger, Your Highness, but I can assure you that nothing happened that either you or Sophia's fiancé need be concerned about.' Ash spoke crisply whilst Sophia listened, white-faced and feeling far more distressed than she wanted to admit to.

Was it because of that, because of what he could see in her agonised expression, that he told her father in a more conciliatory tone, 'The truth is that Sophia was overwhelmed by the unexpectedness of your announcement of her engagement. In a moment of panic she boarded my plane unbeknownst to me, intending to make her way to London. An impulsive, ill-thought-out action, I acknowledge, but without any intention of causing anyone embarrassment.'

'And you discussed this together in bed on board your plane, did you? Do you take me for a complete fool? Sophia may not want to get married but she has no choice. And that's her own fault. She's never out of the gossip columns, with her name linked to a different man every week, and now this.'

Her father was speaking so loudly and angrily that Sophia could hear what he was saying. Her face burned, and she might be hurting inside but she wasn't going to defend herself. Her father didn't understand her, he never had.

'Well, there's only one thing to be done now,' said King Eduardo. 'You must marry her yourself, and as quickly as possible. Unless and until you do, she will no longer be considered a member of this family. If you don't marry her then I shall disown and disinherit her. She's brought more than enough shame and trouble on this family. The only way she can redeem herself now and put a stop to this appalling gossip is by marriage to you.'

There was a sharp click as the king ended their call without giving Ash the opportunity to reply.

CHAPTER FIVE

THE king had put him in a completely untenable position and Ash could see from Sophia's expression that she had heard what her father had said. For himself he could feel the ferocity of the opposing emotional claims at war within him. His pride baulked at the thought of anyone, even a fellow royal, dictating to him what he had to do. Yet his own sense of duty to his heritage, to his friendship with Sophia's brother, and in a sense to Sophia herself, to save her from the disgrace and humiliation she would suffer if he refused to marry her, told him what he must do.

'My father doesn't mean what he just said,' Sophia told Ash unsteadily. Her father's statement had shocked her, but what had shocked her even more was the swift pain it gave her to have to contrast her youthful dreams of what marriage to Ash would be like and the harsh reality of what was happening now. Then she had dreamed romantically of a relationship filled with love and happiness. The bitter taste of the ashes of those foolish dreams clogged her throat. 'We can't marry, Ash.'

'We don't have any choice,' Ash responded brutally.

'I want to marry for love.'

'You lost the right to make that choice when you hid yourself away on my plane.'

His words hurt, but hadn't she told herself all those years ago that she would never allow Ash to hurt her again, and that she would be completely immune to him? Immune to him? Just as she had been in the cabin of his plane. It should be her face that was burning but instead to her chagrin it was her body that was engulfed by heat at the memory her thoughts had brought her.

'I lost it the minute I was born,' she countered tartly, but Ash made no response.

Looking at him and seeing the resolution etched into his hard expression, the apprehension she had felt earlier turned into a much stronger fear. Just as those unwanted shocking moments on the plane had shown her a side of herself and the power of her own sensuality that had overwhelmed her, what was happening now was showing her a side to Ash that as a child and then a teenager she had never considered. As she had recognised earlier, the man in front of her was Ash the royal prince, the leader of his people, a man who would allow nothing to stand in his way of doing what he thought was right for the responsibility he owed to his people. Right now, she suspected, that included her, hence that icy trickle of fear that had just run down her spine.

A fear that was reinforced when Ash told her coldly, 'I am in the middle of some very important business negotiations with people to whom the morals of those with whom they do deals are very important. If I don't marry you my reputation as a man of honour will be damaged. I cannot allow that to happen. I have a duty to my ancestors—and more importantly, to my people. Their future, the education of their children and their childrens' futures depend to a large extent on me bringing more money into our local economy and keeping it there to provide better opportunities for them. All that will be prejudiced if it becomes known, as it most assuredly will, that your father has insisted that I marry you and I have refused. That is the way it is amongst people of our inherited status and blood, Sophia. You know that as well as I do.'

Every word he said confirmed what she had already recognised. Now she knew exactly what his priorities were and they certainly weren't her feelings.

Ash turned away from Sophia and looked out of the window.

This was the last situation he wanted, but he had no choice. The honour of his name had to come before his own personal feelings. And he had to marry someone. In the eyes of the outer world, their outer world, his marriage to Sophia would be seen as a businesslike and wholly acceptable decision. He had to have an heir. He had always known that. An heir created with Sophia in a dutiful coming together for that purpose? For an unguarded second he remembered how it had been between them on board his plane. He tried to close down on that memory but it was too late. Without looking at her he heard himself telling her more openly than his need to control his reactions liked, 'We may both know that a marriage between us is not what either of us would have chosen, but since we have no choice, at least on the evidence of last night, we will share a mutually pleasurable sex life. And as I am sure you will know from your own experience, good sex enhances the lives of those who share that good sex.'

Good sex? Experience? Was this what her dreams of a marriage grounded in true love had been reduced to?

A buzz on the outer door to the apartment halted him momentarily to say, 'This will be my appointment. Once it is over I shall set in motion the arrangements for our marriage. Under the circumstances, the sooner and the more quietly it takes place, the better. From your father's point of view and our own, presenting the world with a fait accompli will bring an end to the current gossip and speculation far more speedily than a press announcement that we are to get married in the future. Once we are wed we will retire to Nailpur. I have business to attend to there, and the privacy it will give us will allow at least some of the gossip to die down. When you return to society you will do so as my wife.'

'And the mother of your child?' Sophia asked him, dry-mouthed.

'Yes. If life chooses to bless us with your speedy conception.' He paused and then gave her a look that stripped her pride bare as he told her, 'Let there be no doubt about one thing, though, Sophia, and that is that from now on you will behave in a way that befits a married woman, who is faithful to her marriage vows and her husband.'

'A marriage that is empty of love, and to a husband I have not chosen for myself?'

'It is as a direct result of your own behaviour that we are now in this situation,' Ash stated coldly. 'And as for love, it is the last thing I will be looking for in our marriage—or outside it. For the sake of the children I hope this marriage will be one they can respect and one which does not dishonour either them or their family name.'

So much pride, so much importance placed on duty, and no place left for love. But he had loved Nasreen. And buried his heart and his capacity to love with her?

Why should she care? She had her pride, too, and it certainly would not allow her to want Ash's love. Before she could comment on the flat cold statement he had just delivered, there was a brief knock on the door and a member of Ash's staff entered.

'Highness, I am sorry to disturb you but Mr Alwar Singh is here with his accountant and solicitor.'

'Thank you, Kamir.' Nodding his head, Ash went towards the open door, saying as he did so, 'Mr Singh, please come in,' and extending his hand to the smartly suited middle-age man who was shown into the room. He was followed by an elegant dark haired woman dressed in a beautiful salwar kameez, and another business-suited man.

'I am sorry to have kept you waiting. Please allow me to introduce you to my fiancée and wife-to-be, Princess Sophia of Santina, before we begin our meeting.' Ash turned towards Sophia, smiling at her as he did. But Sophia could see that the smile did not quite reach his eyes. Formality and the business of protocol and good manners were no strangers to her, and it was easy for her to step forward to accept the good wishes of Mr Singh and his companions.

She knew why Ash had introduced her as he had, of course. He had just made their marriage to each other official and placed it in the public domain, and now there was no going back from that declaration.

'Kamir, please ask the kitchen staff to serve tea in

my office,' he instructed the waiting staff member before turning to her and saying politely, 'Please excuse us, Sophia.'

'We shall try not to keep you apart for too long,' Mr Singh told her with a smile as the group departed.

She was alone in the clinical vastness of the now-silent room. Alone with her sick dread of the emptiness of the future that lay ahead of her and her despair at the loss of the goal she had promised herself she would one day achieve.

Her glance fell on her mobile and she remembered her sister's message. Numbly she picked up her phone and quickly texted Carlotta. Am to marry Ash. And then she switched her phone off. She had too much on her mind to dare to allow herself the interruption and complication of other people's views and input into the situation, even someone as close to her as Carlotta.

The door opened. She looked up quickly, her heart racing, only it wasn't Ash; it was a staff member who had come to ask her if she would care for tea or coffee.

'Coffee, please.' She thanked him, and went back to her lonely thoughts.

In his office, even though he was doing his best to focus completely and only on what Alwar Singh had to say to him about their proposed business venture, Ash knew that in reality his thoughts and his concentration were divided. He was committed now publicly, as well as privately. Sophia would be his wife. His body responded with a surge of male heat. He wasn't going to make the same mistake again, though. This marriage would be based on practicality and the need for him to have an heir. There would be no love involved. And no question of Sophia continuing with her present hedonistic lifestyle.

Alwar Singh's accountant was running through some of the figures that would be involved in the transformation of the currently derelict palace into a world-class hotel.

'You will, of course, have a forty percent share in the hotel.'

'Fifty percent,' Ash checked her firmly. 'That was our original agreement.'

'It is Mr Singh who will be putting in most of the money and bearing the larger part of the risk.'

'Not so,' Ash contradicted her. 'As Maharaja of Nailpur I have a responsibility towards my people and towards the cultural inheritance left to me by my ancestors. If the unique historical value of the palace is damaged in any way by its conversion to a hotel, something irreplaceable will be destroyed, not just for the present but for the future. That is my share of the risk.'

After the meeting had concluded, his visitors left and Ash turned his concentration to the matter of making the necessary legal and practical arrangements for his marriage.

In the drawing room of the apartment, Sophia threw aside the English language newspaper she had been attempting to read. Freed from the powerful determination of Ash's presence her own independence was beginning to reassert itself. Her independence or her fear? What did she have to fear? She would only need to fear marriage to Ash if she was still vulnerable to him through her emotions, through the love she had once had for him, and that wasn't the case. It was simply her desire to control her own life and to make her own decisions that was filling her with this increasing sense of urgency and need to escape. And why shouldn't she escape? Why shouldn't she prove to herself that she could be strong enough to claim her right to her freedom of choice. She already knew that there was no point in trying to make Ash understand how she felt. Her feelings didn't matter to him.

The staff member who had brought her coffee had returned and was removing the tray. Before she could change her mind, Sophia told him, 'I'd like my case, please.'

The man nodded his head and withdrew.

She was running away again, she knew, but Ash had made it plain that he intended to marry her, leaving her no alternative.

Ash had just finished putting in place the arrangements he had needed to make when one of his staff came into the office.

'The Princess Sophia, she has asked for her suitcase, Highness,' he told Ash.

Sophia swung round when the door opened, her heart banging into her ribs when she saw that it wasn't the man with her suitcase who had come in but Ash himself. One look at his face told her that he knew what she planned to do.

Sophia took a deep breath. Very well, she would just have to make it clear to him that she wasn't going to give up her freedom.

'I don't want to marry you, Ash,' she told him. 'I don't think it's the right thing for either of us.'

Ash could feel the fierce surge of his anger slamming into him.

'You are supposed to be an adult, Sophia, but you are behaving like a child—a child so selfish and self-obsessed that she thinks only of herself.'

His accusation appalled her.

'If you refuse to marry me now after I have introduced you publicly as my fiancée, the damage that will do not just to my role as the leader of my people but to those people themselves will be impossible to repair. Here in India we place great store by certain values—honour, duty, responsibility and the respect we have for our forebears, and what we owe to them in terms of the way we live our own lives.

'You are the one who is responsible for the situation we are in, and you have a duty to that responsibility.'

He was right. What he was saying was true, Sophia recognised. With his coldly angry words he had drawn for her a picture of herself that she didn't like, and that filled her with shame.

She gave a small jerky acknowledgement of her head, and told him shakily, 'Very well.'

She looked so alone and vulnerable, so in need of someone to protect her. Against his will the desire to comfort her invaded him, compelling him to take a step towards her. Abruptly he stopped himself. He had to think of his people and his duty. He had to put them first.

'You give me your word that you agree that this marriage between us must take place?' he pressed her.

'Yes,' Sophia agreed. Her mouth was so dry that the word was a papery rustle of sound.

'Good. Normally it takes thirty days after one registers one's wish to marry in a civil ceremony before that marriage can take place, but in our case that requirement has been waived and our civil marriage will take place tomorrow.'

Tomorrow? Sophia's heart jerked against her ribs.

'I have informed your father of our plans. We have agreed that in lieu of the formal marriage ceremony we might have been expected to have, a post-wedding reception will be held later on in the year, either in Nailpur or Santina.'

Ash reached into his pocket for the box he had picked up on his way back to the room, telling Sophia as he handed it to her, 'I have this for you. The ring is a family heirloom and may need to be altered.'

Sophia stared at the imposing-looking velvet-covered box with a crest embossed on it. Taking it from him, and determined not to let him see how much it hurt her that he wasn't even attempting to make the romantic gesture of opening the box and placing the ring on her finger himself, it was all she could do to pretend to be enthusiastic. But as she opened the box she gasped at what she knew was the largest and most flawless diamond she had ever seen. Pear shaped and on a thin platinum band it had to be priceless. A family heirloom, he had called it. Did that mean…?

'Was this your first wife's engagement ring?' she asked him, her voice and her body both stiff with the distaste of being second best.

Guilt and anger dug into Ash's insides like red-hot wire. 'No. It belonged to my great-grandmother.'

He had never offered Nasreen his great-grandmother's ring, a ring given to her by his great-grandfather as a symbol of their love. Nasreen had told him that she longed to wear the enormous emerald ring that was part of another suite of jewellery, and against his better judgement he had allowed her to have it. Against his better judgement because it was a formal piece meant to be worn with the rest of the set.

Somehow it seemed right that Sophia should have the ring that had been a gift of love. His own thoughts made him frown.

Thankful that she wasn't going to be wearing Nasreen's ring, Sophia removed the ring from its box and slipped it on to her own ring finger, surprised to discover that it fitted her perfectly.

It fitted her and suited her, Ash recognised, as he looked down at where his great-grandmother's ring shone on Sophia's finger as though it had found its rightful place.

'Alex texted me to ask what is going on,' he told her, changing the subject. 'Your father obviously told him that we are getting married. I should warn you that I've told him that meeting up again at his engagement party made us both realise that we had feelings for each other that we couldn't ignore.'

'Alex thinks that we're in love?'

'It seemed preferable to telling him the truth. He and I may be old friends, but you are still his sister. I felt it was wiser all round to allow him to think that our marriage is based on a mutual desire to be together, which brings me to another point. Having told him that, I think that in public it will be for the best if we behave as though we want to be together. I have no wish for our marriage to become the subject of any ongoing gossip and speculation, and given that your father publicly announced your engagement to another man, the press are bound to be curious. The discovery that our feelings for each other are stronger than mere friendship will provide the necessary explanation. And that goes for anything you might say to your family.'

'But if my father has told them that he has insisted that you marry me...'

'He hasn't, and he agrees with me that the sudden discovery of our love for each other will provide an acceptable excuse for him to give to the prince. In the eyes of the world this marriage will work, Sophia. Make no mistake. I am determined about that.'

It was over, done. Now, standing here in this anonymous public building that was the marriage registry Ash had chosen, in the eyes of the law she had become his wife. It had been a civil ceremony so plain and direct that against all her expectations she had found in the exchange of the words that had committed them to each other a meaningful simplicity that had touched her emotions. Instead of feeling deprived because she was not having the exotic glamour of a three-day-long traditional Indian wedding, or the pomp and ceremony of being married in the cathedral on Santina, during the ceremony she had thought of all those couples who had made the simple commitment they were making out of love for each other. And that was the cause of the sharp up-rush of pain she felt? Yes, of course it was. What else could it be? It certainly wasn't because she was still foolish enough to dream of being loved by Ash.

They had signed the registry, their signatures had been witnessed, and Ash had told her that her father intended to break the news to their family that their marriage had now taken place later that evening.

'Carlotta will say that I should have waited.'

'And you will tell her that our love for each other meant that we couldn't.'

To step out into the colourful bustle of the busy street as Ash's wife felt almost surreal. There had been no couture wedding gown for her, just a simple white linen dress, its colour drawing a look from Ash that had told her how little a claim she had to its virginal purity.

It was too late now for her to change her mind. They were married. Desperate to distract herself from the anxiety and the feelings of being unloved and totally alone in the world that were beginning to engulf her, Sophia looked around at her surroundings once their car had pulled away from the registry office. It would be impossible not to be excited and entranced by the verve and colour that was India, or to have one's heart captivated by it, she acknowledged. She desperately wanted to share with Ash her wonderment and belief that she would very quickly grow to love her new home, and to ask him questions about the city and of course about his home of Nailpur, but she had to remember that this was a dynastic marriage of convenience. Ash did not want any kind of emotional bonding or sharing between them. All Ash wanted from her was her sexual fidelity and an heir.

'We need to get back to the apartment,' Ash told Sophia. 'We're flying to Nailpur in a couple of hours.'

A new text beeped into Sophia's phone. From her mother this time and not Carlotta. Darling, your father and I are so pleased about you and Ash. I remember how you used to adore him when you were young. Be happy.

Be happy? That was impossible.

Another text had arrived, this one from Carlotta, demanding, Are you sure you're doing the right thing?

Hitting Reply, Sophia wrote defiantly through the emotion threatening to close up her throat. It's a dream come true. Have loved Ash forever and couldn't be happier.

Couldn't be happier, she had told Carlotta, but wasn't the truth that she couldn't have been more unhappy?

Ash stared out of the window. He had done the right thing, the only thing given the circumstances, in subjecting his decision to exactly the same logical tests he would have subjected a vitally important business deal, given the development of a situation that meant that decisive action had to be taken and quickly. Yes, he might have had to make the best of a bad job as it were, but his decision had passed those tests.

So why did he have a niggling feeling that there was something important that he had failed to consider? Why did he feel this wary sense of some kind of danger from which he should retreat? Ash knew the cause of his disquiet perfectly well. It could be traced back to those minutes in bed with Sophia on the plane when he had come so close to relinquishing his self-control. Of almost glorying in succumbing to his own need to abandon that self-control for the sake of the pleasure he had known it would give him to take her without it. That would have been an act as reckless in its way and with potentially as far-reaching effects further down the line as if he had had full sex without using any protection. If he had given in to that need, if he had allowed his desire for Sophia to breach his self-control then... But he had not. The steward's timely interruption had seen to that, and now that he was aware of that possible weakness within him he was in a far better position to deal with it. And he *would* deal with it.

CHAPTER SIX

THEY flew out of Mumbai, its crowded streets swarming with busy life and brilliant with the vibrant colours of its fabrics and decoration that Sophia had already come to feel somehow warmed against the coldness of the loss of her dreams and the harshness of reality that was chilling her heart. It was just after night had fallen, so that below them, the city was a brilliant spangle of multicoloured lights against the darkness of the night sky.

Ash glanced towards Sophia as she sat still strapped in her seat, and looking out of the jet's cabin window. He heard her indrawn breath and saw that they were flying over Marine Drive with its plethora of lights.

'They call it the Queen's Necklace,' he told her.

Sophia nodded her head. After all those teenage dreams of becoming Ash's wife, the mundane reality of the two of them together with nothing of any importance to say to each other was certainly not what her fevered longings had once imagined. But then conversation of any kind hadn't featured in those teenage longings, Sophia was forced to acknowledge, other than a passionate 'I love you' murmured in between the unrestrained passion of Ash's kisses and caresses.

'Nailpur isn't Mumbai,' Ash felt obliged to warn Sophia as they left the city behind and headed west.

'No, I know,' Sophia answered him. 'I loved what I saw of Mumbai but I'm really looking forward to seeing Nailpur and Rajasthan. I read somewhere that the name translates as the Land of Kings. My father would certainly approve of that.'

'Nailpur isn't Jaipur, nor is it any of the other well-known and well-established tourist destinations of Rajasthan. Nailpur is a poor state, its people uneducated, its palaces crumbling. It is my duty to lift my people from that poverty. The days when the maharaja class could live a life of luxury whilst their people endured poverty are not something that can be tolerated any more. And just as it is my duty to lift my people from that poverty so it is also my duty to live amongst them. Your duty as my wife and the mother of my children will be to live with me. So if you were hoping to live in Mumbai—'

'I am not.' Sophia stopped him, too cast down to feel like telling him that as a girl she had read everything she could about Rajasthan in general and Nailpur in particular simply because then she had seen it as a part of him and she had wanted to know everything she could about him.

He couldn't allow this marriage to turn out like his first, Ash thought. No matter what either of them felt, this marriage would endure and not just for the sake of his pride. Only a son brought up to understand and value their family history and the history of their people could truly take his place when the time came.

A royal bride with royal blood was something that his people with their conventional outlook on life, and their belief in the old feudal codes of family and marriage, would expect. He knew that. He had always known it.

A royal bride whose royalty would satisfy the traditional desires of his people.

And a woman whose sensuality would satisfy the desire she aroused in him in a way that his first marriage had denied him?

As always, whenever he thought about the failure and disappointment of his first marriage, guilt gripped him. Must the whole of his life be shadowed by the mistakes he had made then? Nasreen had died because of those mistakes, Ash reminded himself.

The truth was that he had married expecting to give and find love within that marriage and when he had found that love could not be forced by either of them he had retreated from Nasreen. He had allowed her to live her own life because of his own anger and disappointment, because of the blow to his pride of the reality of their marriage, and his discovery that no amount of willpower on his part could ignite the love he had been so arrogantly sure they would share. Because of that Nasreen had died. He could never allow himself to forget that.

Where Sophia was concerned things were different. There could and would be no emotional complications. It was safer that way.

The plane had started to lose height, and below them in the silvery light from the moon and the stars Sophia could see acres of plastic tunnelling of the kind used to grow crops. Turning to Ash, who had been working on his computer throughout the flight, she said curiously, 'I thought this area was too dry for crops and that was why the people were poor and nomadic?'

'It is, but the experts I commissioned discovered an underground river that we've been able to tap into via bore holes and this has allowed us to begin cultivating crops. The people are used to traditional ways and it isn't always easy persuading them to accept new technology. However, I intend to persist. Our water supply is a precious resource, so in addition to educating the people about modern methods of cultivation we also want to educate them to use this resource wisely. The reason I commissioned experts to look into the possibility of an underground source of water was because I'd seen paintings of my great-great-grandfather's indoor bathing pool—it no longer exists but obviously the water had to come from somewhere, and fortunately my guesswork proved to be correct.'

The seat-belt light flashed. Sophia had been relieved to discover that the steward on this flight was not the same one who had been on their previous flight, and she was even more thankful when the plane came to a standstill and the door was opened to see that there were no photographers waiting for them, merely a small group of officials.

Ash had telephoned ahead to his Royal Council to tell them of his marriage, and duly introduced Sophia to them once they had left the plane. As a royal daughter she was well versed in the formality of such things and Ash could see the looks of relief and approval on the faces of his officials as they welcomed her. She had surprised him with her knowledge about the area, he admitted as they were ushered into the waiting limousine, the crest of his ancestors on its door and on the pennant flag flying from the bonnet. Ritual and the preservation of tradition were very important to his senior officials, many of whom could remember not just his parents but also his grandparents before the terrible monsoon floods in the area in which they had been staying had swept them away to their deaths.

Their car left the modern highway which had sped them from the airport through agricultural land and towards the walled city, whose main gate was flanked by huge stone tigers, similar to those in the car's family crest they were now driving. Sophia held her breath. She wasn't quite sure what she was expecting. She'd read of the fabled cities of Rajasthan but there had been very little information about Nailpur, other than a description of its architecture as being typically Rajput in its beauty and richness.

Now, though, as they emerged from the gate in the wall, despite the fact that it was late at night, Sophia could see how busy the city was, the narrow street barely wide enough for the limousine flanked by impressive-looking stone buildings, their narrow windows shuttered and sightless. Up ahead of them the street opened out into a busy square thronged with people. Motorcyclists, often carrying several passengers, eased their way past camels adorned with colourful tassels and enamelled jewellery, their awkward progress accompanied by the stately elegance of the women who accompanied them, the colours and intricate embroidery of their traditional clothing captivating Sophia as she leaned closer to the car window to see them.

Despite the lateness of the hour, the steps to some of the elegant buildings enclosing the square were filled with merchants selling their wares, rich spices, colourful flowers, a joyful display of enamelled ban-

gles. Instead of saris or salwar kameez, the women in
the square were wearing brilliantly coloured gathered
skirts with tightly fitting blouses, one end of the veils
they were wearing tucked into their waistbands then
taken over the right shoulder to cover their heads.

Sophia looked as entranced as a child, Ash realised
as he glanced at her and saw the way she was leaning towards the window as though anxious not to miss
anything. Nasreen had disliked the traditionalism of
Nailpur. She had rarely worn Indian dress, preferring
Western couture outfits. The sari she had been wearing
when she had died had been the cause of a row between
them. He had asked her to wear it to a formal event to
which they'd been invited earlier in the day in honour
of the women of Nailpur who had so lovingly made
the beautiful sari for her as a wedding gift. Wearing it
had killed her as much as her reckless driving had. He
had made her wear it. He had killed her. The old guilt
sat within him, a cold leaden weight from which there
was no escape even if he had been prepared to allow
himself it.

They crossed the square, their progress the subject
of curious but discreet attention from Ash's subjects,
and then they were going down another narrow cob-
bled roadway, with women sitting outside doorways attending to cooking pots whilst children played around
them. The road widened out, the buildings either side
of it becoming larger and far more intricately adorned
with filigree balconies and impressive doorways, and
then they were in another square and in front of them
was the palace flanked on either side by imposing buildings of a similar stature.

As someone who had grown up in a royal palace, Sophia had not expected to be overwhelmed by Nailpur's, but when they had been welcomed into it by a guard of men in traditional dress with huge Rajasthani turbans, she had been unable to stop herself from turning to Ash and commenting, slightly awed, 'How impressive they look and so very fierce. Far more so than my father's uniformed guard. Their turbans are gorgeous.'

'Rajasthan's warriors are known for their ferocity in battle and their loyalty to their leaders. As for their turbans, their style and colour indicates the wearer's status,' Ash informed Sophia. 'That is why these men—members of what was once the Royal Guard—are wearing scarlet turbans that mirrors the background colour of my family crest.'

'They certainly are magnificent,' Sophia responded, pausing as they reached the top of the cream marble steps inlaid with contrasting bands of dark green onyx to ask him, 'I suppose you wore traditional dress for your marriage to Nasreen?'

'Yes,' Ash answered her in a dismissive tone that warned her it wasn't a subject he wanted to discuss. Nevertheless it was hard for her not to imagine the emotional significance of such a wedding with all its history of tradition and culture and the happiness with which Ash must have committed himself to his bride.

What was the reason for the pain that was stabbing through her? Her ability to suffer pain over the realisation that Ash loved someone else and not her had burned itself out a long time ago. Scars sometimes ached long after the original pain had gone, Sophia reminded herself. It meant nothing other than a reminder not to invite that kind of hurt again.

They were inside the grand reception hall to the palace with its alabaster columns decorated with gold leaf, and its marble floor. Long, low, carved-and-gilded wooden sofas ornamented with beautiful, intricate and richly coloured silk cushions stood in elegant alcoves, prisms of light dancing across the floor from the many hanging lanterns suspended from the ceiling. The scent of jasmine wafted in the air and rose petals floated in the ceremonial gold-embossed bowls of water that were brought in for Ash and Sophia to wash their hands.

A maid dressed in a gold-and-cream salwar kameez was summoned to take Sophia to her room after Ash had informed her that they would be eating within the hour.

Upstairs and along a corridor decorated with what Sophia suspected were priceless works of art, she was escorted into what the maid explained to her in halting English were the private rooms of the palace's maharani.

'There is no seraglio here any more as His Highness's great-grandfather married for love and had only one wife. She closed it down, but it is still our tradition that the maharani has her own apartment.'

Behind the fretted and gilded doorway, with its secret 'windows' that allowed those behind it to look out into the corridor beyond without being seen, lay an elegant hallway ornamented with mirrors and alcoves for the lanterns that reflected in them. A pair of highly decorated wooden doors opened out into a much larger room, its polished wooden floors covered in beautiful woven rugs whilst sofas similar to those she had seen downstairs were dotted around the room.

A huge chandelier illuminated the room's vastness,

throwing out sparkling light into the muted shadows of the large room. At one end of it, shutters opened out onto an enclosed illuminated courtyard garden with stairs going down to it from a balcony, the sound of running water reaching her ears from the rill of water below.

'It is very beautiful,' Sophia told the waiting attendant, who gave her a beaming smile in response before telling her in careful English, 'The bedroom is this way, please.'

The bedroom was more European than she had expected, vaguely thirties in its design, with stunning, delicately crafted lamps and light fittings. It had its own wardrobe-lined dressing room and bathroom.

The maid cleared her throat, sounding slightly anxious. 'Please, I take you now to eat with the maharaja.' Sophia stopped exploring her new domain further. She would have liked to have had a shower and changed her clothes before having dinner with Ash but there obviously wasn't going to be time. As she followed the attendant through a maze of corridors she reflected that she needed to contact her family to have the contents of her own wardrobes at home sent over to her.

The girl stopped outside a door secured by two of the turbaned guards who both bowed low to her and then pulled open the double doors.

As she stepped into the room Sophia blinked in the brilliance of the reflected light that filled the room. Every surface within it, or so it seemed, was decorated with a mosaic of glittering metalwork inlaid with pieces of mirror that reflected the light from the suspended lanterns, whilst Ash sat waiting for her on a richly embroidered cushion in front of a low table loaded with a variety of small, tempting-looking dishes.

When Ash saw Sophia gazing around her he explained, 'These mosaic-mirrored rooms were once considered to be a status symbol amongst the Rajput rulers. They are called sheesh mahals, which roughly translates as "halls of mirrors."'

Two waiters stood ready to serve them but Ash dismissed them, telling Sophia after they had gone, 'I prefer to dispense with formality when I can.'

Sophia nodded her head as she took her place on her own cushion. 'I agree, although my father tends to prefer pomp and ceremony.'

'With those who work here dependent on their wages it would be unfair to let them go, but I suspect they find my preference for independence and privacy somewhat bewildering. A need for personal privacy isn't the Indian family way, but it is my way.'

Was he warning her off expecting any intimacy with him other than the intimacy that would be necessary in order for her to conceive?

'The dishes in front of you are a traditional Rajasthani thali,' Ash informed her, 'and mostly vegetarian, although you will find that laal maas and safed maas, which are spicy mutton dishes, are very popular and an important speciality of the Rajput community.'

'It all looks delicious,' Sophia told him truthfully. She loved spicy food and had no hesitation in helping herself to the dishes on offer, although a certain apprehension was inhibiting her appetite. Just for food or for the intimacies of marriage, as well?

It was late when they had finally finished eating; a word from Ash to the staff who had come to clear away the remains of their meal resulted in the appearance of the maid who had attended Sophia earlier. As she turned to follow the waiting girl, Ash leaned towards her and told her quietly, 'I will come to you in an hour if that is acceptable to you?'

Her heart started thumping heavily, her mouth going dry. There was no logical reason for her to be surprised. She knew why Ash had married her after all.

'Yes. Yes,' she managed to agree, stumbling slightly over the words, conscious of how gauche she must seem and even more conscious of how much difference there must be between her wedding night with Ash and the wedding night he had shared with Nasreen. Then, no doubt, Ash would have taken advantage of the intimacy provided by the soft cushions to pull his bride closer to him and perhaps feed her morsels of food while he whispered to her how much he loved her....

She must not think like this. It weakened her and made her vulnerable and for no good purpose. The past was the past and she wasn't an idealistic sixteen-year-old any more. It wasn't being denied Ash's love she grieved for, Sophia assured herself. It was the love she had so much longed to find with the man who would love her as Ash never had and never would. She grieved for what she would never know because of what she'd had to do.

Maybe in marrying as she had, putting duty before her own needs, she was proving to be more of a Santina than she had previously realised, Sophia admitted as she followed the maid, whose name she discovered was Parveen, back to her own apartment.

A silk nightdress was already laid out ready for her on her bed, and in the bathroom steam rose gently from the large, sunken, rectangular, mosaic-decorated bathing pool. Rose petals floated on the surface of the scented water.

'Thank you, Parveen. I can manage on my own now.' Sophia dismissed the maid.

An hour Ash had said. It had probably taken them a good ten minutes and more to walk back to her apartment, along the narrow twisting labyrinth of corridors, which Parveen explained had originally been designed to confuse enemy invaders.

In her bedroom Sophia undressed quickly, her hands all fingers and thumbs as her nervousness increased.

As tempting as the warm and fragrant water of her bath was, she didn't dare linger in it just in case Ash arrived whilst she was still there. Clambering from it naked and dripping wet whilst he watched her was hardly going to add to her confidence.

Once she had dried herself she made her way back to the bedroom and looked at the silk nightdress. Ignoring it she wrapped herself in a towelling robe, instead. Maybe the knowledge that she was naked beneath its folds would ignite the same desire in Ash for her that knowing he was naked under his robe had ignited in her for him on the plane.

She could hear footsteps crossing the room beyond the bedroom. Her stomach tensed into tight knots of anxiety. Ash was bound to compare her to his first wife and no doubt find her wanting. Why had she done this? Because she had had no other choice, Sophia reminded herself as the richly painted wooden doors were opened and Ash walked into the bedroom.

He was wearing some kind of beautifully embroidered gold silk robe, its beauty instead of feminising him somehow actually intensifying his masculinity. His head was bare and the shadows of the room threw the sharp angle of his cheekbones into relief whilst concealing the expression in his eyes from her.

He had closed the doors. The room was so quiet Sophia could hear the sound of her own breathing.

'If we are fortunate you will conceive quickly, which will spare us both the necessity of an ongoing intimacy that neither of us really wants.'

He had to make it clear to her that he had not married her out of any desire for her, Ash told himself as he caught the sound of Sophia's indrawn breath. For Sophia's benefit or for his own? Wasn't it true that he had not been able to subdue the ache of need she had already aroused in him despite all his attempts to do so? And wasn't it equally true that right now simply the sight of her and the knowledge of what was to come was accelerating the intensity of that need at a speed that he couldn't control?

But he must control it. He must remember what this marriage was and why he had entered it.

He started to unfasten the closures to his robe—a traditional garment that had been laid out for him by his valet, and beneath which he was naked. Unable to take her gaze off him, Sophia watched with her heart in her mouth as he removed the ornate robe and then came towards her.

He was all male muscle and sinewy strength, long limbed and lean, his body possessed of all the classical male beauty of a Greek statue. She could see the scar on his thigh that she knew must be from a fall he'd had during a polo match that Alex had once mentioned to her. How she had hoarded all those little bits of knowledge about him, how she had clung to them as her own precious pieces of him, and how her sixteen-year-old self had hated herself for her weakness in doing so when he had turned his back on her to go to another woman. These were dangerous thoughts, taking her back to a time and place when all she had wanted was to give herself to Ash. Her heart started to race, the sudden surging ache deep inside her a growing wash of liquid heat that caressed her desire every bit as fiercely as she had once dreamed of Ash caressing her body. A small sound of female need strained against the taut muscles of her throat that were denying it a voice.

There was no need for her to question whether or not Ash was ready to consummate their marriage; she could see for herself that he was. Her heart was beating so fast she felt as though it might burst with her need to reach out and stroke her fingertips along the hard length of his erection in eager virginal exploration and delight.

A man—another man who was not him and who did not know that it was merely a practised gesture—would not be able to help having his male vanity aroused by the look that Sophia was giving him, Ash acknowledged. He fought against what it was doing to him, even though he knew it was a look she must have given innumerable men before him. Not that he had any right to expect a past sexual exclusivity from her, and nor did he do so. They were both adults with their own individual sexual histories. Histories, yes, but he would not tolerate infidelity from her now that they were married.

It was that thought, the thought of another man touching her now that she was his wife, that took him to her side, to untie her robe and push it from her shoulders, his hands sculpting the soft warm flesh of her body with a feather-light touch. So much lush sensuality was almost too much, Ash thought; it could overwhelm a man until he was trapped in his own desire to possess her. But that would not happen to him, he assured himself, and yet within him there was an urge, a need, to bury his face in the rich dark cloud of her hair, to breathe in the scent of her and then to change that delicate fragrance to something stronger and more elemental as he aroused her. He wanted to stroke his hands all over her, to draw the rigid peaks of her nipples between his fingers until she gasped with the urgency his touch aroused; he wanted to dip into the soft wetness of her sex and taste the juices of her desire for him, and only for him. He wanted... He wanted to possess her as no man had ever possessed her before, Ash recognised, that knowledge thundering through his mind.

He was a man, she was a woman. He had married her so that he could conceive a child with her. It was only because of that that he felt this intense desire to fill her senses and her body. Nothing more than that. It was time he did what he had come to her to do and stop listening to unwanted and illogical thoughts.

For all her lush curves, she was delicately boned and softly light in his arms as he lifted her and carried her to the bed.

His hands tightened on the narrowness of her waist as he laid her on the bed. He reached out and cupped her breast. Her flesh was silky soft and warm, her nipple immediately rising to his palm in stiff supplication.

He rolled her nipple between his forefinger and thumb, seeing her stomach go concave as she sucked in her breath and trembled.

She certainly knew all the pretty little tricks of making her partner feel desired. Well, two could play at that game. He curled the tip of his tongue round her other nipple and then teased it with darting strokes of deliberate arousal. Her whole body trembled, her thighs softening in instinctive invitation. He released her breast to stroke his hand down over her belly and then tease the vulnerable inside of her thigh with the gentle stroke of his knuckles.

Any minute now he was going to possess her. Her body knew that and wanted it, Sophia admitted, but her senses, her emotions, hungered for an intimacy that went beyond mere physical pleasure, no matter how skilled the giver of that pleasure was. She was lost, caught up in the powerful demands of a need that had its roots in the very deepest part of her sexual psyche. A longing she couldn't hope to control forced its way past everything she had told herself this act between them must be in order for her to retain her pride. She wanted, craved, ached for more than Ash's skilled touch against her flesh. She wanted the potency and the passion of his kisses.

Ash started to move between her thighs. As though the words were sprung from some trap deep within her, she heard herself begging him, 'Kiss me, Ash. Kiss *me.*' Reaching for him, sliding her hands into his hair, she pulled his face down towards her own, opening her mouth against his as the fiery hunger of her need spilled through her.

So much passion, too much passion. He should resist, pull back, but the sweetness of Sophia's taste, the quick eager flicking movements of her tongue tip against his lips as though it was a hummingbird unable to survive without the nectar of his kiss, pulled him down, down into a place where his own senses couldn't deny the savagely sensual urge she was creating within him to take her mouth and crush it beneath his own until they were one breath.

Wasn't that dangerous? Because he was afraid that if he kissed her he… He what? He wouldn't be able to stop? No, of course not. Could he prove that to himself? Of course he could.

'If kisses are what you want then kisses are what you will have,' he told her against her mouth as her lips trembled beneath his and the sweet boldness of her daring became an inferno of pulsating need that possessed every inch of her body.

Ash was leaning over her, his hands tangling in her hair as he kissed the side of her throat slowly and gently, and then nibbled on her ear, his thumb stroking the sensitive secret place just behind it.

A soft sound of delight bubbled in Sophia's throat, her eyes wide open and dark with an arousal she made no attempt to hide as she looked at him.

She was the most sensual woman he had ever touched. Everything about her was a hot sweet tide of melting female desire that begged him to complete her. No woman had ever looked at him with such open need, turned to him with such confidence in his ability to satisfy that need. No woman had ever unleashed within him an answering torrent of unstoppable longing for her.

He shouldn't have kissed her. But he had and now he couldn't stop.

He cupped her head to hold her still beneath him and then plundered her mouth in a kiss that stamped her with his possession as surely as though he had penetrated her and filled her body with his sex, until her own sensuality stormed through her, demanding her submission to its needs and to him.

Sophia couldn't contain her own aroused need and delight. Her hands were on Ash's forearms, her fingers curling round them, her body arching up to his in a blatant offer that, driven by his own compelling need, Ash was incapable of refusing.

As the white-hot power of her unleashed passion poured through her, Sophia felt the first surging movement of Ash's body within her own. A fiercely wild sense of joy gripped her. She moved with him, eager for his full possession.

Ash thrust deeper into her and then stopped, in stunned shock and disbelief, as his body fought against what his brain was telling him, the effort it took him to leash his need causing his body to throb with unsatisfied desire. There was a barrier in his way that shouldn't have been there, the barrier of virginity. His brain recognised that. His body, though, ached and pulsed, his flesh demanding that he allowed it to complete what it had started and satisfy its need. But he couldn't. Not now. Not until he knew what was going on.

Lying beneath him Sophia was filled with the urgency of her own unappeased need. He couldn't stop now. Not now when she needed and wanted him so much. Lost in her own desire Sophia had forgotten all about her virginity, but now with Ash pulling back from her and her body still crying out for him she realised what was happening. She had to stop him leaving her. She had to. Female determination filled her as she deliberately tightened her muscles around him.

'You want me to conceive,' she reminded him. 'That's why we're doing this.'

It was true but more than that the movement of her body against his was destroying his attempt at self-control. Ash could feel it slipping, draining away from him as desire for her roared over him. He moved within her, intending to pull back, but somehow his body surged forward and once it had and she was moving with him, making those soft urgent cries of pleasure and need, it was impossible for him to stop what was happening. The barrier parted, the look on Sophia's face as she cried out one of satisfaction and delight rather than one of pain.

Now she had what she had wanted for so long. Now he was hers. Truly hers in the most intimate way possible. Now he had taken what she had always wanted to give him and her body was responding to his possession with the pleasure she had always known it would, wave after wave of it, each one bearing her higher, making her want to take him deeper and deeper within her as she wrapped her legs around him and held him to her more eagerly with each urgent thrust of his possession.

The climax was swift and intense—for both of them—leaving Sophia gasping and shuddering with the intensity of her pleasure as Ash watched her and cursed himself in silence whilst the red mist of his desire for her evaporated to leave him gripped by anger and guilt.

Nothing about his coming together with Sophia had been as he had expected or as he had prepared for. He had expected the sex to be good, but controlled, a coming together of two experienced people who knew the value of sexual pleasure but who would remain free of any emotional involvement in that pleasure. It would be strictly physical, and strictly controlled, but somehow Sophia had got under his skin, and under his self-control. Because Sophia had welcomed him where Nasreen had rejected him, telling him on their wedding night that his love was the last thing she wanted? Telling him that her love had already been given to someone else and that that someone was a married man with whom she had been having a secret affair. An affair which she had no intention of ending and which she fully expected Ash to tolerate and their marriage to cover. It was the way of such things she had told him with a dismissive shrug.

It was the anger he had felt when she had revealed the truth to him that had destroyed not just his physical desire for her but, and far more hard for him to bear, his duty to feel any desire to love her. He had thought that sense of duty so strong and so much an intrinsic part of himself. He had taken pride in it and yet with a handful of words Nasreen had shown him its pitiful weakness. His heart had chilled to her. He hadn't been able to forgive either her or himself for what his reaction to her had shown him about himself.

He had, in effect, turned his back on her, giving in to his own pride and his own feelings about the destruction of his plans for their lives together. And because of that she had died. If he had thought less about the pride he had taken in telling himself that he would love her because it was his duty to do so and instead set his personal standards lower, they could possibly have worked something out—a discreet arrangement of a marriage in which they produced an heir but privately went their own ways. If he had tried harder, been more realistic, maybe they could have salvaged something and then perhaps she would not have died. Instead, he had allowed his emotions to take control.

He deserved the burden of guilt he had to carry. It was his punishment for the pride he had taken in believing that he could create love, not just within Nasreen but within himself, when that power did not belong to him. He had no right to take pleasure in the response that Sophia had given him, and even less to feel that primitive surge of male possessive pleasure to know that he was the one to have brought her to what had obviously been her first experience of the intensity of her own capacity for sensual pleasure.

He could not allow himself to savour that achievement. Instead, he must punish himself for even allowing himself to think of it. And as for his own pleasure? The result of too much abstinence. Nothing more. He could not permit himself to feel anything more.

The darkly bitter emotions that burned inside him turned outwards seeking an escape. He looked to where Sophia lay on the bed, her gaze still awed, her body still sensually satisfied and soft with the aftermath of her climax.

If he went to her now, held her now, kept her close to him and told her of all the many ways in which their coming together had been so very different from anything he had known before, if he told her that she was different from any other woman he had known before... He was already turning towards her, already... Already what? Prepared to break a vow he knew he had to keep if he was to ensure that this marriage worked for the good of his people.

From somewhere he found the will to turn the weakness within him that he didn't want into the anger he needed. Like Nasreen, Sophia, too, had deceived him, leaving him to discover a truth that vitally affected their marriage on their wedding night—even if his discovery that she had been a virgin was the complete opposite of Nasreen's revelations to him. And he was grateful to have that reason to feed his anger because he was afraid that without it he might be in danger of giving in to those feelings he had already had to fight back once. Feelings of tenderness and care, feelings that… Feelings that meant nothing, were nothing, and which he would stifle and destroy, because that was the way it had to be.

Without looking at Sophia he told her coldly, 'I want an explanation.'

The abrupt coldness of Ash's voice and demeanour after the sweet hot pleasure of the sensuality they had just shared shocked Sophia back to reality.

What had happened to her? How and why had she reacted to him in the way that she had, given everything she had believed she knew about herself and her desires for her own emotional future? It didn't make sense that she should have wanted Ash so immediately, so passionately and so intensely, that it seemed as though her body had been waiting for this and for him. At least, it didn't make sense, of course, unless that was exactly what had happened, and why she had responded to him the way she had. A cold chill of fear trickled down her spine. That was not true. It couldn't be true. She refused to let it be true. So why had it happened?

She didn't know. All she could think, all she could allow herself to believe, was that there had been a moment—a handful of several long delicately spun-out golden moments—during which she had felt as though she had touched heaven and held a rainbow of unimaginable delight in her hands. But that had not been reality. That had been a mirage, an imaginary fantasy, that could not and did not exist, and the last dying echoes of the foolish dreams she had once had.

It meant nothing, and for her pride's sake, for the sake of the future, she must now learn to forget about it.

'For my virginity?' she responded in as cool a voice as she could manage. She must not allow herself, never mind Ash, to feel that their coming together had touched her emotions, because it hadn't. As she had just analysed, for herself that reaction had simply been a long-ago echo of something that no longer existed.

'Yes, of course for your virginity.'

She still looked slightly dazed, her eyes huge and dark, her mouth flushed a deep rose pink, but for all the signs of her pleasured sensuality, there was also a vulnerability about her, as though she was in need of... Comfort? Tenderness? These were things he could not give her. White teeth snapping together, he pulled on his robe and went across to the table where the maid had left her a bottle of water in a bucket of ice. He removed and opened it, pouring two glasses, one of which he brought over to her. Water, most precious gift of all to those born into a desert race, because it was the gift of life.

Sophia willed her hand not to tremble as she took the glass Ash held out to her. The water slid coolly down her throat, both reviving her and giving her new strength. Ash watched as a drop of condensation on the glass fell onto her chest and ran down the valley between her breasts. He wanted to look away but somehow he couldn't. He wanted, he discovered, to reach out and stop its descent with his finger and then lick it from her skin with his tongue. He wanted... He wanted nothing other than a marriage of duty and mutual respect through which he could dedicate himself to his people and his responsibility to them.

Sophia pulled the sheet up around her naked body. Ash turned away, an unfamiliar feeling slicing into his gut. She was rejecting him? Why should that bring him such an immediate and intense desire to go to her and hold her, to feel her responding to him again as she had done earlier instead of retreating from him? He didn't know. But he felt as though he didn't know anything any more, and for a man who liked being in control of his life that was intolerable.

He turned back to Sophia. The evidence of the intensity of what had happened between them was plain to see. It was there in the tousle of her dark hair, the flush on her cheeks and the sensual exhaustion in her eyes. She looked like a woman who had been made love to and whose body had shared enthusiastically in that experience. Or did he just see that because it was what he wanted to see?

'It's a bit too late for that now,' he told her brusquely, gesturing to the sheet with which she had so modestly covered herself, 'and I still want an explanation.'

'It isn't a crime to be a virgin, is it?' Sophia shrugged as casually as she could. Despite everything, she recognised that a part of her, that part that still belonged to her sixteen-year-old self, wanted desperately to celebrate the ability of her body to give and receive pleasure, and to know that the wonderment and joy it had given her was shared by the man who had partnered her in it. But of course, to Ash what had happened between them was nothing special. How could it be? She knew that. The euphoria she had felt had gone and all that was left was the chilly reality of what she had lost—not her virginity, but her dreams and her hopes of being truly loved.

'No,' Ash agreed, 'but you have to admit that when a woman goes to as much trouble as you have done to give the world the impression that you are sexually experienced and available, it is bound to raise the question of just why you did so.' Sophia could hear the anger and the bitterness in Ash's voice. 'And I want an answer, Sophia.'

'You already have that answer,' she told him proudly. 'I gave it to you when I told you that I wanted to marry for love. When you rejected me, Ash, I promised myself that I would only give myself to a man who loved me as much as I loved him. That is why I didn't want my father forcing me into an arranged marriage. I wanted to find a man who would love me for myself, and as myself, not as the daughter of the King of Santina.' Sophia paused. Just speaking like this was activating so many feelings she desperately wanted to deny. The temptation not to say any more was great, but something deeper and more demanding was driving her on as though seeking a form of catharsis for her.

'When you reminded me of my responsibility for my actions, for boarding your plane, I realised that I would never reach that goal. But I still have no regrets that I made such a goal my priority. When you rejected me, Ash, when you told me that you didn't want me because you loved your bride-to-be, I was so very envious of her that I promised myself one day I would meet someone who would love me like that and who I could love like that in return. I promised myself then that I would wait for that person. I promised myself that he would be my first and my only lover.'

Why was he allowing her words to cut so deeply into his conscience? The reality was that he had done the honourable thing in doing what she referred to as 'rejecting' her. To have taken her innocence would have been a gross abuse of her and of his own values, even if he had not already been committed to marriage to Nasreen. He had done the right thing, the only thing it had been possible for him to do. He had, in his arrogance, his blind belief that he could order his own emotions and those of Nasreen, given a naive sixteen-year-old the belief that if one waited long enough and believed hard enough that love must appear.

Wasn't he already carrying a heavy enough burden of guilt? Did he have to force himself to carry even more? Was there never to be any peace for him, or any salvation? All he had done was try to emulate the happiness of his great-grandparents' marriage.

A surge of something so intense that it physically hurt him to breathe seared through him—a sense of great loss and regret, sharpened with guilt.

Deliberately not looking into his face in case she gave away more than she wanted to, Sophia continued. 'I knew, though, that if men knew I was a virgin they'd try to get me into bed, as some kind of challenge, so I decided that the best way to hold them at bay was to pretend that I had had loads of lovers. That was why I didn't want my father to force me into a marriage without love.'

Ash had drained his own glass and had gone back to the table to pour himself a second one. Wrenched by guilt, he tried to defend himself to himself with a caustic, 'And do you intend to continue looking for this once-in-a-lifetime love despite the fact that you are now married to me?'

Why was he doing this? Why did the thought of her turning to another man fill him with such a savagery of emotion that it ran like fire through his veins? Because of the disaster that had been his first marriage. Not because of any other reason.

'No,' Sophia denied.

Her voice was filled with so much calm conviction that Ash knew she meant what she was saying. She might claim that she wanted to reject her royal status and upbringing, but right now, no matter how much she herself might deny it should he tax her with it, she was every inch the royal princess bound by her own awareness of the demands placed on her to fulfil her birth role. It was impossible for him not to admit to the respect he felt for her.

Unaware of his thoughts Sophia confirmed her right to that respect when she told him firmly, 'I'm not a child, Ash. When I agreed to marry you I knew what I was committing myself to. It's called growing up. The reality is that I was wrong to think I could persuade my father not to force me into a marriage of which he approved. I recognised that when I heard what he said to you when you telephoned him, just as I also recognised that if I had to have a marriage that would please my father then I would rather it was to you than someone I don't know. Those of us with royal blood aren't always free to follow our own dreams. We have a duty to fulfil the role for which we ourselves were created by our own parents.

'If my virginity disappointed you then I'm sorry, but I am as committed to this marriage and to my own fidelity to you within it as I would have been had our marriage been a love match.' That was certainly true. 'I never want any of my children to have to wonder if my husband is their father. Never.'

Ash closed his eyes. Just for a moment, listening to her, he had thought…felt…wanted… *What?* Nothing, he assured himself grimly. Nothing at all. Unable to trust himself to look at Sophia he picked up his robe and put it on before turning and walking away from her.

Ash had gone. She was on her own. And she wished that he was here with her. Wasn't that natural after the intimacy they had just shared? The *intimacy?* Didn't she mean the sex? Ash had made the lines that would govern their marriage clear enough to her and she had accepted them. Wallowing in self-pity now was as pointless as looking back at dreams that would only ever be just that.

So what was she going to do with the rest of her life? What was she going to hang her future on? What goals was she now going to set for herself?

It wasn't her fault that she'd never been allowed a proper working role as part of the Santina royal family other than that of appearing at formal functions as 'our youngest daughter.' Given the chance, she'd have loved to have had an opportunity to get her teeth into a far more demanding role. She'd once persuaded her mother to allow her to visit a local school and what she'd seen there had filled her with enthusiasm for doing something to help the more needy in their own society, but her father had thoroughly disapproved of the idea. Now, as Ash's maharani, she naturally had duties that went with that role. Could that be her salvation? Good works instead of love? Love came in many different forms, Sophia reminded herself firmly. Loving Ash's people because they would now be her people and finding ways to help them would benefit her as much as it would hopefully benefit them. Even so, as she contemplated her future, a small shiver of sadness and loss ran across her heart.

In his own room Ash couldn't sleep. The shock not just of discovering that Sophia was a virgin but also of her admission of what her private dreams had been was still sinking in. Now, when it was far too late, he berated himself angrily for not paying more attention to the instinct that had said to him over and over again that there was a vulnerability about her, despite everything he had thought he had known. Why hadn't he thought more deeply about that? Asked more questions, listened to his instincts? Because he hadn't wanted to. Because the demands on him of the past, and Nasreen, overshadowed the present. He had a duty never to forget Nasreen and the guilt he felt about her, didn't he?

It was too late now to wish that he had taken the time to understand Sophia better. They were married, the marriage had been consummated and they both had no choice now other than to make the best of the situation. She had wanted to marry for love, she had said. Well, if she had mentioned that earlier he could have told her that sometimes marrying for love was the worst thing you could do, especially when the other person didn't think of 'love' in the same terms that you did.

He slipped out of his robe and headed for his bed, not sure whether it had been the action of removing it that had brought to mind the way Sophia had looked at him when she had seen his naked body, but knowing that whatever had caused it he wished it hadn't. Being reminded of that right now simply wasn't something he could summon the strength to deal with.

What he'd discovered earlier about Sophia had turned everything he had thought he had known on its head. Lying sleepless in a bed that suddenly felt far too empty, he couldn't hold on to the barriers he wanted to erect against his own emotions. Guilt, pain, a sense of over-whelming loss—he could feel them all.

Moonlight edging in through the unshuttered windows stroked across the faces and bodies of the two people who slept alone and separated. Sophia's hand was on the pillow adjacent to her own as though in her sleep she was reaching for something—or someone. Ash's dreams were vivid with unwanted memories unleashed to torment him. He was a bridegroom approaching his bride on their wedding night. Regret and guilt slowed his progress to where she stood waiting for him, her head bowed, her face veiled. With every step he took towards her the sense of doom filling him grew stronger, but somehow he forced himself to go on. When he reached her he took hold of her veil, pushing it back off her face as she lifted her head.

The sight of Sophia's glowing face looking back him, her eyes warm with desire, her lips soft and parted, filled his heart with an intense relief and joy. He took hold of her, drawing her closer to him, his lips seeking hers as he murmured emotionally, 'Sophia…'

Abruptly Ash woke up, the clarity of his dream still

with him, his heart pounding and thudding into his chest wall. What was happening to him?

Nothing. *Nothing.* And to prove it he would stay away from Sophia's bed until he knew he could take her in it without any shred of emotion threatening his hard-won resolve. This was a marriage of necessity, a marriage that would work because of the duty they both owed to it and to each other. It must not be prejudiced by emotion or by any desire with him that was prompted by any kind of emotion. Once they knew whether or not Sophia had conceived, that would be the time for him to return to her bed. And the ache within him that was burning so fiercely even now must be overcome, because to allow himself to want her was to allow himself to become vulnerable, and he could not permit that.

CHAPTER SEVEN

THEY had been married almost three weeks, and not once since that first night had Ash even touched her, never mind taken her to bed again. Did she want him to? Sophia closed her eyes. It made her feel so humiliated to have to admit how badly her body ached for more of the pleasure he had given it. All those years when she had been able to turn down attempts to seduce her without feeling she was missing out on anything had not prepared her for feeling like this: of lying awake and raw with need in the emptiness of her bed; of feeling her body surge with fierce tight longing just at the sight of Ash's bare throat or arm; of wanting what he had already given her so badly that she had to fight against her need for him. Of course, she had expected to feel like that about the man she loved, but she did not love Ash, he did not love her, and it left a sour and bitter taste in her mouth to know how shamefully she wanted him.

Ash had told her himself that he felt they should wait to see if she had conceived before they had sex again. His uncompromising words had stunned her. He had made it sound as though he didn't want to have sex with her. His words had been a stinging reminder that for him sex with her was merely a duty. That had hurt. In fact, it had hurt so much that even now when her body's evidence said she was not pregnant, she had not said anything about it to Ash. Because she was afraid that now he was married to her, and despite everything he had said to her about duty, he had discovered that the comparison between her and Nasreen was such that he simply could not bear to touch her.

Nasreen. She didn't want to allow the other woman to take up residence in her thoughts and undermine her but somehow she couldn't help it. If Ash could make her feel like that without loving her then how must Nasreen have felt? How much had she delighted in the pleasure they must have shared. As a new husband, Ash would not have stayed away from her bed. The hot surge of jealousy burned her pride. She couldn't allow herself to be jealous of Nasreen. She must focus instead on her own life. So why was she constantly breaking the rules she had made for herself by questioning Parveen about Ash's first wife?

When she had broken the protocol with which she had been brought up and questioned Parveen, the maid had been reluctant to satisfy her curiosity at first, but gradually Sophia had coaxed her into confiding in her. Nasreen had not been well liked by those who staffed the palace, which she rarely visited, preferring to be in Mumbai with her own family, she had been told.

'When a woman marries, her husband's family becomes her family, but the maharani was very close to her family,' Parveen had said.

'But Ash, the maharaja, loved her?' Sophia had asked.

'Yes, the maharaja had loved her very much,' Parveen had replied reluctantly after a small pause, before offering, 'but a man may love more than one wife. For the wife who gives a man his first son there will always be a special place in his heart,' she had added.

And if that wasn't a hint then she didn't know what was, Sophia thought tiredly. Yes, Ash needed an heir. But she had her needs, as well, and right now her pride needed evidence that her husband valued her enough not to humiliate her by rejecting her sexually, because of the intense way she had responded to him.

Today at least she had something with which she could occupy her time and her thoughts.

She was visiting a school in a small village not far from the city, as part of her role as maharani, accompanied by the wife of one of Ash's most important advisers. Aashna, a teacher herself before her marriage, had become Sophia's unofficial lady-in-waiting for such events.

'You may feel shocked by the poverty of the village,' Aashna warned Sophia. 'India is not Europe, and although Ash is doing his best to modernise and educate our children, this will take time. The first generation of young graduates who have benefitted from the schemes he put in place when he came to his maturity are only now returning to Nailpur to help their families. Many of them were agricultural students. Ensuring that we grow enough to feed our people and the tourists that Ash hopes will bring investment to the area will be a vitally important part of our growth towards prosperity.

'We also have doctors graduating to staff our new hospital which will be opened later in the year. Ash has already done much for the people but there is more to do, especially with the young mothers from the tribes.

Their husbands are not always willing to allow them to take advantage of modern health care. The traditional nomadic lifestyle is an important part of our identity and heritage, but it brings its own challenges.'

Listening to her Sophia felt both a huge sense of pride in Ash and all that he was doing and an equally intense desire to be contributing something towards benefitting his people herself.

'The maharani's interest in the new education programme is most gratifying, Highness. My wife is accompanying her today to visit one of the newly opened schools.'

As he signed the final batch of official papers, Ash looked up at his most senior adviser, the words, 'And which school would that be?' spoken before he could stop himself.

'It is the village school at the oasis of the White Dove where some of the children of the nomads are also schooled.'

Nodding his head Ash watched as the older man left the room. It was three weeks since he had married Sophia. Apart from that first all-consuming night, they had spent every subsequent one apart, and most of the days, too. Because he was afraid of what might happen if he went to her? Because he feared the desires, the needs, the emotions she had somehow managed to stir up in him?

It was the shock of discovering that she had been a virgin that had thrown him off guard, that was all. Nothing more than that. He had never intended their marriage to be the kind in which his only contact with his wife was the occasional necessary visit to her bed.

They were partners in the business of being royal, after all, and as his wife, Sophia had a role to play amongst his people. A role which she was already playing without any help from him and playing very well if his most senior aide was to be believed.

Going over to the door Ash opened it and summoned an assistant, telling him, 'Have my car brought round. There won't be any need for an official escort.'

Squatting down on the dusty floor of the single-storey, single-room school, so that she was at the same level as the children, Sophia drew them out of their shyness, communicating with them in their hesitant, newly learned English, watching the excitement and enthusiasm for what they were learning burning in their dark eyes. Their uniform was provided for them by the state, and once she had broken the ice they couldn't wait to tell her how much they loved their new school, their young voices full of praise for the maharaja, whom it was plain they worshipped.

Their innocence and joy caught at Sophia's heart, the sight of their dark eyes and hair causing her womb to contract a little with the knowledge that Ash's children would have that colouring. Ash's children, her children, their children. It would be to them that she would give the outpouring of her love that Ash did not want. They would not grow up as she had done, feeling unwanted and too overwhelmed by the distance that existed between her and her parents to dare unburden herself to them and trust them with her fears.

Engrossed in her own thoughts and the solemnity of the young boy showing her his computer skills, Sophia was oblivious to the silence that had gripped the rest of the room or the fact that behind her the adults were bowing low and moving back in shy awe as they watched their maharaja stride towards his bride. It was only when the boy with her looked up, his eyes widening before he prostrated himself, that she looked round to see Ash looming over her, looking every inch the ruler that he was, even though he was in western dress.

Ash was extending his hand to her, and Sophia was far too aware of the need for royal protocol to be observed in public to refuse to take it. It must be because she had been kneeling down for so long that she felt so dizzy, she decided as she got to her feet.

It was Ash who cordially thanked the teachers for permitting them to intrude on the children's lessons and Ash, too, who shook hands with everyone before exiting the room, leaving her to follow behind him.

Outside, the pungent smell of camel dung stung Sophia's nose. The animals were tethered close to their owners, as the brightly dressed tribeswomen waited patiently for their children to finish their schooling for the day. The nomad women's jewellery jangled musically as they made their low bows to Ash, their odhni modestly pulled across their faces to conceal them, the ends fluttering in the dusty breeze.

'The maharani will travel back with me,' Ash told her waiting escort, turning to Sophia herself to tell her, 'There is something I wish to discuss with you.'

'There is something I want to talk to you about, as well,' Sophia responded.

Once they were together inside the car, though, heading back to the palace, the darkened windows of the limousine somehow made the interior of the vehicle more secluded and intimate. Sophia didn't feel quite as confident about broaching with Ash the possibility of taking for herself a more proactive role in his modernisation plans as she had done when she had listened to Aashna on their outward journey. She couldn't forget how her father had rejected her request to do something on Santina, and how that had made her feel.

Ash looked out of the darkened car window. The sight of Sophia crouching on the floor surrounded by the village children, communicating with them and so plainly loving being with them, had touched a nerve. Only once had he been able to persuade Nasreen to visit one of his schools with him. She had complained that the children were dirty and had refused to have anything to do with them. Ash could still remember the confused, hurt looks he had seen on their faces and those of their mothers. He had sworn that he would never allow that to happen again. Sophia came from a different culture to his own and if anything he would have expected her to be even less inclined to have anything to do with the children than Nasreen. Instead, though… Instead she had reached out to them in such a way that he had seen how happily they had responded to her.

Abruptly he told her, 'My most senior adviser has suggested that it might be appropriate for you to have a formal role to play. I was wondering how you'd feel about getting more involved in the new-schools programme.'

Immediately Sophia turned towards him, her face alight with delight and excitement. 'Oh, Ash, I'd love that. In fact, I was going to ask you if I could become involved. I…I love children.' A small look away from him and a sudden surge of colour into her face told Ash as clearly as though she had spoken the words out loud that she was thinking of their children, of the children he would give her and the children she would conceive for him. The sudden urgency in his body, the slamming thud of his heart and the ache of fierce desire burning in him would have told him exactly what was happening in his own imagination if he hadn't already known.

'I was going to ask you if there was a role that I could play, something that might perhaps relieve you of some of the burden of your own royal duties.'

'There's also the new hospital plan for women and children,' Ash answered her. 'The women, especially those from the nomad tribes, are more likely to be open with you about their medical needs than they are with me. Their culture forbids them contact with men outside their own family circle. In time I want to bring them more into the modern world, but that is complicated and can't be rushed.'

'No,' Sophia agreed. 'Such things have to be handled sensitively. I could perhaps have lessons in their language—just to learn a few words, you know, to break the ice....'

Suddenly the atmosphere in the car had eased, and Sophia felt able to talk easily to him just as she had done when she was younger. 'I want to fulfil my role as your wife, your maharani, as fully as I can,' she told Ash enthusiastically and truthfully. They drove in under the gate which had now become so familiar to her, their car leaving the dust of the open road behind them as the sights and busyness of the walled city closed round them.

'Since you have said nothing to the contrary I take it that...'

Guessing what he was going to say Sophia interrupted him to confirm, 'Yes. That is to say, no, I am not pregnant.'

Tonight. Tonight he would allow himself to go to her, Ash decided. He wouldn't be giving in to an unwanted need within himself if he did. It was, after all, his duty to ensure that he had an heir. Sophia was his. That he should choose to take her to bed to create that heir meant nothing, and did not break his vow to remain emotionally distant from her. Didn't it? Then why was his heart thudding in such a heavy and impatient manner? Why was his body already aching with its need for her? Physical desire, that was all. Physical desire for her and nothing more.

Sophia would have liked Ash to stay with her after their return to the palace but he had business matters to attend to, and as Parveen told her with some excitement, 'many boxes' had arrived from Santina. They were now awaiting her inspection in her bedroom.

Ordering tea and the small sweet biscuits that were a local delicacy and to which she was half afraid she was becoming dangerously addicted, Sophia made her way to her apartment, where the boxes were waiting in her dressing room.

When she opened the first one there was a large rectangular package on top of her clothes with her father's personal seal on it.

Frowning slightly, Sophia removed it and broke the seal, remembering as she did so how as a small child she had been entranced by the 'magic' of stamping her father's seal in hot wax and then applying it to a piece of paper. She had been happy then, before she had realised that there were doubts about her parentage.

Inside the package was a handwritten letter from her father. His letter would no doubt be a reminder of how she should conduct herself and how angry she had made him, Sophia reflected. She was tempted not to read it but she had been brought up with an observance to duty that prevented her from doing that.

Sitting down she opened the letter and began to read it. To her astonishment, rather than being critical of her and angry, her father's words were relatively warm and approving.

'My dear daughter,' he had written, 'I write to tell you how delighted I am by your marriage. It is an excellent marriage and one that pleases me a great deal. To have the ties first established via the friendship Alessandro and Ash shared as schoolboys further cemented by your marriage to him can only strengthen the bond between our two states. Such bonds play an important role in the minds of rulers, which is why I have always stressed to all of my children the importance of the right kind of marriages.

'If I have been overstrict with you then it is because I have been concerned for you. However, I know that in Ash's care you will be well protected.

'I know, too, that our two states can look forward to forging even stronger bonds via their shared business, as well as their shared personal interests.'

The letter was signed with her father's familiar bold and flourishing signature.

The words blurred in front of her as she read them again through the tears she couldn't hold back. *My dear daughter,* her father had called her, even if his letter had turned quickly to the more material advantages he hoped her marriage would bring to Santina.

Such small things really, a kind letter from her father, and an acknowledgement earlier in the day from Ash that he trusted her enough to give her a personal role to play with his people. Neither of them could compare with the great love that had once been her goal, but in their way both of them offered her some comfort and some hope for the future.

A young maid arrived with her tea and biscuits. Smiling at the girl as she quietly left the room, Sophia sat down to drink the tea she had poured for her. When she'd finished, she put down her cup and then stood, ready to sort through the boxes of clothes that had been sent to her from her home.

Two hours later, she and Parveen had opened all but three of them and filled virtually all her wardrobes and cupboard space with the exception of the small row of wardrobes along the dressing room's shortest wall.

'What's left in these last three boxes can go in there, Parveen,' Sophia told the maid, indicating the remaining wardrobes.

Immediately her maid looked apprehensive and uncomfortable as she, too, looked at the narrow run of wardrobes, but made no attempt to go and open them.

'What is it? What's wrong?' she asked her. After a brief struggle where it seemed to Sophia that Parveen wasn't going to answer her, eventually she managed to blurt out quickly, her head down as though she didn't want to look directly at Sophia, 'So sorry, Maharani Sophia, but the clothes of the Maharani Nasreen are in there.'

Nasreen's clothes were still here all these years after

her death. Shock, anger, distaste—Sophia felt them all.
A cold shiver ran over her skin, soon followed by an
overwhelming feeling she didn't want to name.

Ash obviously loved his first wife so much that he
couldn't even bear to dispose of her clothes. They were
still stored here in the room that was now *hers*. Nasreen
still had Ash's love; she had his devotion, his loyalty.
She had probably been inside his head on their wedding night, and it was probably because of his love for
her that he had not been able to bring himself to return
to that bed. Well, she might have to put up with all of
that, but she was not going to put up with Nasreen's
clothes in what were now her wardrobes, Sophia decided wrathfully.

'Very well, Parveen,' she told the maid, adding, 'you
can go now, I will deal with the rest of my own clothes
myself.'

The girl looked relieved to be dismissed, Sophia saw.

As soon as Parveen had gone and she was alone in
the dressing room, Sophia went over to the short length
of wardrobe doors. Standing in front of them, she took
a deep breath and then before she could change her
mind she yanked open one of the two pairs of double
doors. The draft of air caused by the speed with which
she had opened the doors caused the delicate silks inside the wardrobe to move sinuously together almost
as though someone was actually wearing them. Sophia
closed her eyes. The heavy scent escaping from the
wardrobe was making her feel slightly sick and dizzy
but as desperately as she wanted to close them and to
shut away the sight of the delicate garments so different to her own clothes, once worn by the wife Ash had
loved, she couldn't.

Her mood suddenly changed, her earlier fierce, righteous wrath giving way to something more self-destructive and painful. Just seeing the clothes of the woman Ash loved touched those scars within her she knew she must not allow to be reopened. But it was too late. Like serpents escaping from a carelessly sealed basket, the old pain was back.

Reaching out she touched the clothes—red and gold ceremonial saris, sugar-almond-coloured salwar kameez in soft pinks, blues and turquoises. What would she look like dressed in these clothes of another woman? The woman Ash loved. It was as though a terrible compulsion that she couldn't resist had possessed her.

Unable to stop herself she reached into the wardrobe and removed a pale blue salwar kameez set. Like someone in the grip of a dream—or under hypnosis—she walked into the bedroom with it. She was shaking from head to foot. She knew that what she was doing was wrong—for Nasreen, for Ash and for herself—but somehow she just couldn't stop herself, and it made her feel sickened and ashamed of her need to see how Nasreen would have looked. Because Ash had wanted Nasreen, desired her as he did not desire Sophia?

No. She did not care about that, but she had her pride and she and Ash must have a child, a son who would one day continue the royal line. That was how it was for them. And besides… Besides, didn't she herself long for the promise of a new life to love, a child—children—to whom she could give the love she already knew instinctively she would have for them? Quickly she started to undress, despising herself for what she was doing and yet unable to stop herself.

* * *

Walking in the private gardens into which his apartment opened, Ash asked himself why the surroundings which normally gave him so much pleasure and solace, this evening made him feel so alone. Was it because their enjoyment, like the enjoyment of the act of love, should be a shared pleasure? His muscles tightened, his body heavy with desire. Sophia. Just thinking about her was enough to send that desire spilling urgently through him.

Every night since their first as a married couple the memory of the way she had looked at his body had tormented him as he tried to find sleep. He wanted to see that look in her eyes again. He wanted to touch her, hold her, lose himself in her as he blotted out the past while together they created their own shared future in the shape of their child. He wanted. He wanted her.... A tormented groan broke from the rigid tension of his throat. He turned back towards the palace, his stride quickening with impatience, just as his body was quickening with his need.

In her bedroom Sophia stared at the stranger looking back at her from the full-length mirror, a stranger wearing another woman's clothes and smelling of another woman's scent.... The salwar kameez was slightly loose on her own narrow waist and Nasreen must have been a shade taller than her because the fabric was pooling slightly on the floor around her bare feet. The fine silk shimmered as she walked, subtly hinting at the body that lay beneath it, the diamante beading decorating the scarf with which she had covered her head shimmering as she moved.

Experimentally, Sophia draped the scarf over her

lower face, and watched her image in the full-length mirror in front of her. Was this what Ash longed for whenever he had to look at her? Another woman, the woman he truly loved?

He shouldn't be doing this but he couldn't help or stop himself, Ash admitted, too impatient to use the public twisting labyrinth of corridors that led to Sophia's apartments, using instead the passage that his great-grandfather had had installed when the royal apartments had been remodelled so that he and Ash's great-grandmother could come and go to each other without the knowledge of the servants or the need for formality.

The hidden door in the wall of the entrance hall to Sophia's apartment, disguised to look like a painting, opened easily to his touch. He might not normally use the passage but that did not mean that it was not kept clean and in order by his household.

Ash pushed open the door to Sophia's bedroom. And then froze as he stared at the back view of the woman in front of him, not wanting to believe the evidence of his own eyes.

Nasreen. Even though he knew it couldn't be, a surge of the darkest feelings he thought he had ever experienced eviscerated his guts. His first wife had no place here. Just as she had, in reality, no place in his heart? Just as he now had no right to want to forget that his marriage to her had ever taken place? His own thoughts fell into the darkness of his guilt, trapping him ever deeper in its grip.

The woman moved, and instantly he knew.

Sophia.

Only Sophia with that incredible body of hers could move and walk like that.

Anger. A huge rolling wall of it powered through him. Anger against Nasreen for betraying the duty they had owed each other, anger against Sophia for her intrusion into that place within his conscience where even he could not bear to go, and most of all anger against himself. An anger that came out of nowhere, like a desert storm obliterating reality, destroying the landscape within himself, leaving him alone and defenceless against its power and what it had created. In three strides he was at Sophia's side, reaching for her to turn her round, to face him as he demanded, 'Take it off. Take if off *now* unless you want me to tear it from you.'

CHAPTER EIGHT

THE shock of Ash's presence as a witness to something she could only ever want to be private, never mind the fury she could see and feel in him, had Sophia dropping the corner of the scarf, guilt darkening her eyes and burning up under her skin.

What a dreadful thing to happen. It was bad enough that she had been caught by anyone trying on Nasreen's clothes, but that it should be Ash who had found her just at the moment when she herself had tasted the acid agony of shame in what she was doing heaped a humiliation on her that she knew was deserved. No wonder Ash was so very, very angry with her. What she had done was surely a violation of something precious and a privacy that should never have been breached by anyone.

She wanted to apologise to Ash. She wanted to tell him that she had only realised too late what an unforgivable thing she was doing in letting her curiosity and envy of Nasreen get the better of her, but Ash was so angry he wouldn't even let her speak.

The sight of Sophia in Nasreen's clothes made Ash feel as though raw flesh had been ripped from his body, the anger, the shame, the bitterness he felt infusing that guilt with true darkness. He had no right to blame Nasreen and the memory of their marriage for making him feel like this. And no right to feel that he was being cheated of something that deep down inside he ached for, though he knew he had no right to ache for it. Someone or something? He had come here tonight to be with Sophia after far too many long days—and even longer nights—of battling his own inner demons as he fought to allow himself a logical reason for appeasing the need he knew she aroused in him. That might be a need he had no right to allow himself, but tonight, with the future of his name to the forefront of his mind, he had assured himself that being with Sophia, having sex with her, was permissible under the rules he had laid down for himself after Nasreen's death.

Now with the anger boiling inside him, at what unforgivably his senses were now seeing as an unwanted intrusion of Nasreen, and the past into the intimacy he ached to share with Sophia, his guilt could only increase. He had no right even to have such feelings, never mind seek to satisfy them. He had no right to want Sophia. He had no right to anything other than the burden of the guilt he must never, ever forget. And by rights now he should turn round and walk away as a punishment to himself, not returning to Sophia until he had stripped from himself every vestige of personal desire and need for her.

The movement of Sophia's body as she tried to pull away from his hold on her wrist disturbed the air around her, releasing into it the sickeningly familiar odour of Nasreen's scent. He could still remember how it had hung between them on their wedding night after he had realised that he could never love her. Heavy and over-sweet, it clung now to the air, draining it of oxygen, cloying and all-pervading, filling him with revulsion.

'Take it off. All of it,' he demanded again, his voice harsh with the emotional weight of years of guilt, anger and despair added to the even more burdensome weight of his desire for Sophia herself.

Ash released her abruptly, the revulsion he felt for her behaviour written plainly on his face. He couldn't bear to touch her and he couldn't even bear to be in the same room with her. She couldn't blame him for that. What she had done had been unforgivable, but it was too late now to wish that she had been stronger and that she had resisted temptation. If she had... Ash had plainly come to her intending to take her to bed. Against all logic her body reacted to that knowledge with a surge of fierce longing. Longing for a man who'd had sex with her once and then hadn't come near her for three weeks? Sex with a man who had shown her body what sensual pleasure could be, the only man—thanks to the vows she had made—who would ever have sex with her. She was a normal, modern healthily functioning woman, so wasn't it only natural that her body should want to know again that sensual pleasure? Without love? Without respect? Without Ash wanting anything from her other than an heir?

Where was her pride? This was not the right time for them to come together as prospective parents-to-be. She must remember that she was a Santina. She must remember the role to which she was now committed. She wanted Ash to leave so that she could rid herself of Nasreen's clothes and her shame in private. She made to walk past him. She was trembling from head to foot, desperate now to remove the silk garments.

Thinking that Sophia was ignoring him, half maddened by his own unbearable feelings, Ash reached for Sophia again, dragging her towards him as though the very sight of her in Nasreen's clothes maddened him beyond all sanity, tearing the scarf from her, and then, to Sophia's shock, reaching for the neck of the tunic and starting to rip it apart.

'No, Ash,' Sophia pleaded with him. He would hate himself later for the destruction of Nasreen's beautiful outfit, she knew, and he would hate her even more for being the cause of that destruction. He wasn't listening to her, though, wasn't paying her any attention at all, as she struggled in his hold. He refused to let her go, his knuckles pale against his skin with the pressure of his grip as he wrenched the delicate silk apart. The awful tearing sound of the fabric made Sophia cry out in protest, and as though that one small sound somehow penetrated the red mist of his fury Ash turned his back to her and ordered her, again, 'Take it off. Now. All of it.'

From out of nowhere Sophia felt a surge of white-hot anger of her own rise up inside her to meet Ash's fury. It burned along her veins swiftly, reaching the unstable powder keg of her jangling emotions.

'You want me to take it off. Fine, then I will!' she yelled furiously at Ash as she pulled and tugged at the clothes that she now loathed so much because of all they represented, as though they were shackles that bound and imprisoned her, flinging the garments down on the floor as she removed them. Her face was flushed, her temper was up and her dark brown eyes burned with her emotions. Within seconds the floor around her was strewn with discarded garments as she hurled them away from her, and Sophia herself was left standing virtually naked in nothing but her own tiny briefs, out of breath, her chest heaving, the full force of her fury leaving Ash momentarily lost for words. She was. She was… She was magnificent, he found himself admitting, magnificent. Her anger had somehow cleansed her completely of the taint of Nasreen which had so appalled him, just as her feisty removal of her own clothes had left her revealed to him as exactly what and who she was. Herself. Magnificent. And right now he wanted her so badly that the force of that wanting was ripping him apart inside.

'Satisfied now, are you?' Sophia challenged into the silence that had fallen between them, but Ash's unmoving silence had definitely brought its heat down a few degrees.

'Satisfied?' Why was he having difficulty framing the word? Why was his body giving him a thousand messages about just what would bring him satisfaction right now, when it and he knew that he couldn't give in to those illogical needs? And yet… His desire still roiled and thundered inside him, refusing to be subdued.

He took a step towards Sophia and then another, his actions shocking her because she had expected him to leave.

'No, I am not satisfied,' she heard him telling her. 'And I shall not be satisfied until you have conceived our child.'

Then she was in his arms, and he was kissing her, angrily, savagely, humiliatingly, and yet she couldn't find the willpower to resist him. Something within her own anger had ignited a force inside her that was overwhelming all her deep-rooted senses of self-preservation. There was a wildness in the air and in her body, a deep hot fiercely female urgent need that refused to listen to reason and insisted instead that it must and would be appeased. That need was carrying her with it, taking her as passionately as it was telling her that she wanted Ash to take her, as herself, as a woman whose desire was so powerful that it was impossible for him to resist or deny his need to match it. With such thoughts, such hungers, swirling around inside her it was impossible for Sophia to hold on to reality or sanity, especially not when Ash was kissing her with such scorching intensity. Or rather, he was kissing the woman he really wished were here with such scorching intensity, Sophia warned herself.

Under his dark mastery of her senses, and the spell it cast on them, she still couldn't stop herself from responding to him, even though she knew that inside Ash's head the woman on whom he was pouring out his passionate need was cast in Nasreen's image and not her own. All that mattered was the white-hot heat his kiss and his touch were creating inside her. Her body knew him now and knew the power and delight of the pleasure he could give it. Her body had no conscience and no pride, all it knew was that the touch on it was a touch that sent coded messages of past and future pleasure surging along its most intimate pathways, condemning to oblivion anything that might have tried to stand in its way. It was pointless for her to try to tell herself that the fiercely possessive hunger of Ash's touch belonged in reality to another woman. Foolishly her body wasn't willing to listen, not when Ash's obvious desire for it was laying out in front of her a positive banquet of intimate delight. From the curl of his hand in her hair as he pushed it back from her neck so that he could kiss its slender stem, to the strength of that hand on her as he smoothed his thumb over her skin, trapping the betraying rash of goose bumps that gave away her sensual vulnerability to him, every touch aroused a storm of sensual longing and delight.

He should stop, and right now. Every rational and responsible thought in his head told him that; Ash struggled to obey those voices but when he tried to pull away from her Sophia moved closer to him.

Ash was going to leave her but he mustn't. He couldn't. Not when the female hunger and need he had aroused was such an intense longing ache inside her. Sophia wrapped her arms around his neck, pressing small, eager, pleading kisses of her own against the dark sensuality of his throat, shivering with pleasure as she tasted the salty male tang of him on her lips, that taste feeding her appetite for more. His shirt was unfastened at the neck allowing her to slide her hand against the lower buttons and unfasten them, which in turn allowed her to kiss her way along the hard jutting angle of his shoulder.

No. No. A thousand times, no. He might be voicing that denial inside his head but somehow he couldn't bring himself to say those words out loud, Ash realised as his flesh burned raw with the hunger that Sophia's kisses were igniting. How long had it been since a woman had affected him like this, made him hunger and ache like this?

A groan of torment—for past guilts and present longings—tortured his throat. Sophia's kisses, the soft sweetly passionate kisses of a woman to whom the deepest dark mysteries of the raw heat of sexual intimacy were still unknown, filled him with a need to take her and show her how he longed to be touched, how intimately and possessively he wanted to be taken and owned by her feminine desire.

He had never known a need like this, never allowed himself to imagine it could exist. Now he wanted to lie naked beneath Sophia's learning touch, to give himself up completely to her tender exploration, give himself over to her innocent possession. Then when she had had her fill, he wanted to turn things around and show her, teach her, give her the full power of his male desire until their mutual possession of each other took them beyond time and space.

It was too late. Things had gone too far. He couldn't pull back now. He couldn't give her up now. Ash felt Sophia's hand tremble as she battled with his shirt buttons.

The feeling of Ash's chest lifting as he drew in a deep breath and then trapped her hand against his body filled Sophia with despair. He didn't want her touching him. He was going to stop her. But to her shock and disbelief when he lifted her hand from his shirt, instead of releasing it, he placed it flat against the hardness of his erection. For a handful of seconds Sophia allowed herself the erotic joy of knowing him so intimately, of feeling the life force of his maleness beneath her hand, of letting that hand curl against the breadth of his arousal. She felt slightly dizzy, giddy with the swift rush of the responsive desire that was pounding through her own lower body, setting up a rhythm she could feel pulsing into the very heart of her sex.

'Ash…'

His name on her lips was a soft sound of agonised

need, her breath rushing his skin. In the dimly lit bedroom her skin gleamed a soft gold, the almost pagan sight of her naked breasts full and taut, their nipples swollen and dark, wrenching away the remnants of Ash's self-control. In between possessively intimate and erotic kisses he undressed himself, watching with raw male pride when Sophia shuddered softly at the sight of his own naked body, her eyes slipping helplessly to his sex, her small tremble of longing mingled with uncertainty answering a need in him as old as time itself.

'Touch me,' he commanded her softly. 'Touch me and know me.'

There was something almost hypnotic about Ash's voice, or was it her own desire that was hypnotising her, Sophia wondered helplessly as she went towards Ash. Letting him take her hand and draw her down onto the bed with him where he put her hand back on his body, he told her again, 'Touch me.'

Just the sound of the words was enough to send quivers of eager desire darting through her as she bent towards him. The feel of his hard hot flesh beneath her uncertain fingers was both alien and yet somehow in some way already known, as though in her dreams she had touched him like this a thousand plus times before. Each touch, each discovery, each sound of pleasure wrenched from Ash's locked throat felt like a marker put in place on a territory that she had been destined to call her own.

Growing braver, she leaned over and brushed her lips against the taut plain of Ash's flat muscular stomach, hot wilful pleasure possessing her when the slide of his hand into her hair and the raw gasp her touch drew from him told her that despite his stillness his body ached as much as her own.

A few more kisses, scattered daringly against the hair-roughened tautness of his thigh, a tentative caress of the hot tension of his erection, an awareness of the damp heat and the ache between her own thighs, and the coil of need within her had become a full-blown ravening demand.

Inside her head, images formed: the temptation to straddle Ash where he lay and let her body demand the upward thrust of his body into her own and the satisfaction it yearned for, a relentless unceasing hunger that grew with every breath she took.

How long before his self-control broke—how many seconds, how many heartbeats. How much could one man bear and not give in to such an intensity of need? Like a dam breaking, Ash felt his self-control give way. Reaching for Sophia he pulled her down against him, kissing her throat, her jaw, her mouth, taking the sobbed breath of pleasure she exhaled as he covered her breasts with his hands, kneading their soft warmth, letting his thumbs and fingertips mimic the intimate movement of his tongue within the soft damp heat of her mouth,

When he made to lift her on top of him she moved eagerly, almost knowingly, to his guidance, one fierce tremor of her body and the flash of desire in her eyes her response to his removal of her briefs. Her sex was open and naked to his gaze and his touch and it was impossible for Ash to withstand the temptation to caress its soft inviting warmth, his touch drawing a wild shudder of pleasure from Sophia married to a sweetly agonised cry of female longing. The need to pull her down on top of him and pleasure her aroused flesh with his lips and his tongue had Ash sliding his hands along her thighs before he could stop himself, his hunger for the intimate taste of her overwhelming him, as much as Sophia's moan of shocked delight overwhelmed her.

How could she endure such pleasure? How could her body hold back the tide of longing that swept her or the convulsive tremors of preorgasmic sensitivity it unleashed? A fine dew of aching arousal bathed her skin. Her nails raked Ash's skin as he lowered her onto his body, a small mewling sound escaping her lips in her exquisite agony of relief as her muscles welcomed the full hard thrust of him within their embrace, her body rising and falling in concert with his as passion gripped them both.

Without thinking about what he was doing as they lay together in the aftermath of their shared ecstasy, Ash instinctively ran his hand down Sophia's still-damp back, and let it come to rest on the curve of her hip. It was only a small gesture, a natural one, he suspected, for a man who had just shared so much pleasure with his partner, and who wanted to draw that partner closer for the intimacy that came after such intensely satisfying sex, but it was not one with which he was familiar, not one he had ever been tempted to indulge in ever before. Abruptly he withdrew his hand and moved back from her. Moved back but did not leave the bed. They were husband and wife; he was not a machine, and he was certainly not without respect for Sophia or her role in his life. She had just given herself to their marriage, to their commitment to each other to create the next generation, not just with her natural sensuality but also with generosity. He owed her something at least for that.

And that was why he was staying? For Sophia's sake? For the sake of their marriage, for the sake of the duty they had both agreed they would share. For them he would stay, but he would not allow himself the emotional pleasure of drawing her back into his arms to hold her there whilst her heartbeat stilled and he breathed in the warm Sophia-scent of her skin. No, he would not allow himself that, because he did not deserve it.

It was over, and despite the—to her, at least—intense intimacy and closeness of what they had just shared, Ash was already withdrawing from her, still sharing her bed but not touching her, not showing her any tenderness, not saying a word about what to her had been an experience of true unimaginable wonder and delight. And he had wanted what had happened between them; he had wanted it badly. She might not be experienced but no woman could misunderstand the messages his body had given to hers.

To hers?

The sharp sound of Sophia's indrawn breath with its raw note of pain had Ash frowning, his voice harsh as he demanded, 'What's wrong?' Their lovemaking had been intense and passionate and she had given herself fiercely over to it; if he had accidentally caused her discomfort, that was the last thing he had wanted to happen.

'Do you really need to ask?' Sophia challenged him. 'It wasn't me you took to bed tonight, was it, Ash? It was Nasreen. That's my fault for wearing her clothes. I don't know why I did that. It was wrong. I know you still love her.'

Sophia thought he would do something like that? She thought that he could have the kind of powerful, all-consuming sex they had just had and want anyone but her in his arms? Something—a force, a need, a tidal wave of something he could not suppress—rose up inside him.

'No,' he told her. 'I do not still love Nasreen.'

He paused as though his words had somehow caused a seismic movement within himself over which he had no control, and which had now set in motion an unstoppable force within him—a shift in the weight of his burden and its pressure on the dam behind which he had sealed it away. Like an unstoppable landslide it plunged down on that dam, smashing it apart, tearing at its foundations, words he had never expected to hear himself utter in the privacy of his own thoughts, never mind to anyone else, bursting past its barriers in an unchecked torrent, dragged from the depths by the sheer force of the reaction Sophia's accusation had aroused within him.

'The truth is that I never loved Nasreen.'

Shock, disbelief, confusion—Sophia felt them all, but on some deeper level and with the new maturity the short weeks of their marriage had brought her, she could hear the starkness of the truth in Ash's voice. Those words were dragged from him against his wish or control, the first time she had ever seen any break in that control when it came to his silence on the subject of his first wife. The first time he had allowed her to see what lay behind that silence, and what she could see was a man in torment.

Now that he had started to speak, to his own shock Ash discovered that he couldn't stop, the words tumbling from him one after the other, as though desperate to finally be heard.

'I should have loved her. It was my duty to love her.'
His voice was raw with the burden of past pain. 'It was
my duty to make our marriage as filled with love for
each other as my great-grandparents' marriage was.
As a boy growing up, orphaned, with only my nurse's
stories of that love to show me what adult love could
be, I believed that it was enough for me merely to want
to love my chosen bride. I was both naive and arrogant.
I made promises to myself for our marriage that I was
unable to keep. Over the course of our wedding celebra-
tions when I looked at my bride, despite her undoubted
beauty, despite the fact that our marriage was one arranged for us with our best interests at heart, when I
listened to her, when I saw how different our goals in
life were, when I dismissed her as shallow and empty-
headed, selfish and greedy, unkind to those who served
her, and not worthy of the great love I had promised myself I would have for her, I showed that I was the one
who was not worthy, not worthy of my duty, not worthy
of the gift of love shared by my great-grandparents.'

The words were pouring from him with an uncon-
trollable force now, increasingly desperate to escape
and be heard, desperate to escape his desire to have
them silenced, as though a part of him had yearned for
this escape, this stripping down of himself to the bare
bones at the root of his angry contempt for himself, so
that his failings could finally be seen in the clear light
of day. As though somehow he had been waiting for this
moment and this one woman to lay bare his dreadful
weakness and shame, because only she would understand, because only she…

'I should never have married her.'

'You had no choice,' Sophia felt bound to point out.

'I had the choice of choosing another path once I realised that my original goals for our marriage were not achievable. I could and should have chosen then to forge our marriage along different lines, practical royal lines.'

Like their marriage, he meant, Sophia thought. That pain inside her meant nothing. She was as resolved to make their practical marriage work as he was. In fact, she preferred not loving him because not loving him meant that she could not suffer the pain of not being loved back.

'I didn't do that, though. I allowed myself to be directed by my own emotions, by my anger at myself for all that our marriage could never be instead of focusing on what it could be.

'Nasreen was far more practical in that regard. She told me on our wedding night that for her our marriage was merely a diplomatic dynastic union and that her heart along with her body had been given forever to another man.'

Ash heard the shocked indrawn gasp of Sophia's breath.

'She told you that she loved someone else?'

'You pity me? There is no need. The truth is that I was relieved to discover that I would not have to bear the burden of a love from her that I already knew I could not return. However, since I was not prepared to countenance a continuation of their relationship and Nasreen was equally determined that it would continue despite the fact that he was married, there were frequent quarrels and much ill feeling between us. Nasreen's plan for her married life was that she would live the life of a wealthy titled young woman in Mumbai, socialising with her friends. I, on the other hand, wanted her to spend more time here in Nailpur as my maharani, helping me to improve the quality of the lives of my people.

'The night she died we had quarrelled even more than usual. I had gone to Mumbai and brought her back with me against her will to attend a formal court event. I had even insisted that she wear a sari that had been embroidered for her by some of the tribeswomen as a wedding gift.

'Nasreen had objected to all of this. She had further told me that she had no intention of conceiving a child any time soon because being pregnant would stop her from living the life she wanted to live, and that I would have to wait until she was ready.

'I was furious with her, and told her that I would not allow her to return to Mumbai. Whilst I was engaged in a business meeting she left the palace in the sports car she insisted on keeping here because she said that driving it was the only freedom she could have outside of the city. By the time I was alerted to the fact that she had gone, intending to return to Mumbai, it was too late to stop her. And too late to save her.'

Instinctively Sophia reached out towards him in a gesture of sympathy and compassion. How could the touch of such a cool, healing hand on his own burn him with such intense pain? It was his guilt that was responsible for that pain, Ash told himself, that and the knowledge that he did not deserve Sophia's compassion, because he did not deserve anything other than to endure the burden of his terrible guilt. That was the payment he had to make for his arrogance and his pride.

She wasn't hurt by Ash's immediate avoidance of her touch, Sophia assured herself. What she was doing now was simply fulfilling part of her role as his consort. She may not love him as she had done as a teenager, but that did not mean that she could not feel for him, and be touched by this unexpected vulnerability he was showing her.

The promise of the comfort of Sophia's touch had been withdrawn from him. He deserved that loss, Ash berated himself inwardly. He deserved to suffer. He deserved to be punished for setting himself against Nasreen and not finding a way for them to make their marriage work, just because his pride had not been able to tolerate finding any success in their marriage once he had realised he could not love her. He had said too much to Sophia, expressed things he had always sworn to keep to himself, and yet even now, somehow, he could not stop allowing the words he knew damaged him from being said. It was as though he was being driven by a compulsion that wouldn't let him go, a need to reveal to Sophia the very worst of himself in the aftermath of a shared intimacy that had taken him to a place he had never imagined he might find. Because he needed to punish himself for that experience? Because he needed to hear the words out loud to remind himself of exactly what he had done? Ash didn't know. He only knew that he needed to reveal the true horror of what had happened, and that he was culpable.

The deep breath he took tasted acidic in his lungs. Unable to look at Sophia he continued, 'Nasreen must have had the top of the convertible down, because when they found her they discovered that she had been strangled by the scarf of her sari—the sari I insisted she had to wear—as it caught in the wheels of the car.'

Tears burned the backs of Sophia's eyes. Poor

Nasreen and poor Ash, too. What a dreadful, dreadful
tragedy. No wonder it had marked Ash so strongly. But
Sophia still felt that he was being too hard on himself.
That, of course, was typical of the man he was and typical, too, in its way of the younger Ash she remembered,
the Ash who believed in doing the right thing and in
being honourable, the Ash who had had his idealistic
dreams.

'I may not have been able to behave as a man of honour in my duty to love Nasreen,' he continued bleakly,
'but I can and will fulfil my duty to bear my guilt for
her death.'

Sophia's heart ached for him. His revelations had
shocked her, but more shocking, and far more dangerous, was her awareness of how keenly her own emotions had been touched by his pain.

The danger of that feeling was brought home to her
within seconds when Ash told her grimly, 'It was because of my failure to find within myself the love I
should have had for Nasreen that this marriage, our
marriage, and indeed any second marriage I might have
made, is based on practicalities. Emotions are dangerous when they take control of our lives.'

Sophia could agree with that. She knew even now
just how dangerous her emotions had been to her when
she had loved him so passionately as a girl.

'There is something else I must say. Tonight has
again proved to us both, I hope, that we are sexually
compatible. That will help to strengthen our marriage.
I have also to say how much I appreciate the commitment you are making to my people in your role as maharani. You have an instinctive way with the women
and the children. I have watched how they respond to

you. It is through you I believe that I will be able to put into effect my plans to improve the education of the poorest amongst the people. I am grateful to you for that, Sophia.'

How truly he was humbling himself, Sophia recognised as she savoured the sweetness of his unexpected praise.

'I am enjoying what I am doing.' It was the truth and she was happy to say so. 'I want to feel that I am making a contribution to the children's future and that I have a useful role to play here in Nailpur, Ash, aside, of course, from that of giving you an heir. Perhaps there is more Santina in me than I ever thought. I don't know. But I do know that my royal role here as your consort is one that I value. The education of the next generation is vitally important and everything I can do to help with that I want to do. I dare say there are plenty of other royal princesses who could have fulfilled the role as well, if not better, than me but—'

'No.' Ash stopped her, cutting across her immediately. 'No. I cannot think of anyone who would make a better maharani than you, Sophia, or who would make a better and more loving mother to our children.'

It was the truth, Ash recognised.

'And there is no one who will make them a more honourable father.' Sophia returned the compliment.

An honourable father, she reflected later, after Ash had left her, but would he be a loving one? Her own father was honourable, but children needed love. There was no doubt that Ash had been badly affected by his marriage to Nasreen, and she could understand why. Remembering the idealistic young man he had been it was easy for her to see how dreadful it would have been for him to be forced to admit that he could not love the bride he had so confidently believed he would love because it was his duty, his destiny, almost, to do so. To have those ideals smashed by his own emotional inability to give Nasreen love would have destroyed the deepest of his core beliefs about himself. She knew how that felt in her own way. She had suffered a terrible loss of sense of self when she had understood the meaning of the gossip about her mother's relationship with the English architect she had admired so much.

But Ash had praised her as his maharani. He had shown her a desire that she could now accept belonged to their relationship. She had responded to that desire; she had welcomed it. These were the foundations on which she must now build her new life, and those foundations would no longer be overshadowed or undermined by her own previous false beliefs about his relationship with Nasreen. There had been a cleansing of that wound, and this was an opportunity for a fresh start between them. Just as long as she remembered and respected the fact that that relationship would be without love.

But that was what she, too, wanted. She didn't want to love Ash all over again and she wasn't going to do so.

CHAPTER NINE

THE sound of Sophia's laughter, warm and spirited, but soft with underlying tenderness, filled the private courtyard she had made her own, and had Ash hurrying towards her, eager to bring her up to date with the results of the soil tests he had just received with a view to enhancing the variety of crops the land could grow. The breaking down of his self-imposed barriers when it came to talking openly to Sophia about his first marriage had brought profound changes to his life, changes which all had their roots in his relationship with Sophia. Maturity had brought a confidence to the natural warmth of her nature, and the courtyard garden had become an oasis to which others seemed naturally drawn when it was occupied by his wife, as they brought her their concerns and their hopes.

As he himself did?

It was only natural that as a husband he should turn to his wife to discuss those issues that affected them both so closely, especially when they were also responsible for the welfare of his people. There was no law that said such discussions had to be held in the solemnity of a grand council chamber rather than discussed in the relaxed atmosphere Sophia had created so skilfully.

As he approached her the sound of the running water of the fountain fell soothingly on his senses, but it was Sophia herself who was responsible for the swift uplift of his heart and the need he felt to smile.

The sound of Sophia's voice had his heart lifting. Because he knew he had made the right decision in marrying her, and because their marriage was working. There was a new atmosphere in the palace. The effects of their shared purposefulness with regard to the people, and the harmony between them, was reflected in the smiles and manner of those who lived close to them. He had much for which to be grateful. He had made the right decision. That decision had been based on logic without emotion just as the passionate intimacy he and Sophia shared in their bed together at night was based on a mutual natural physical desire that was also without the dangerous, potentially damaging effect of emotion. And yet if he was so sure that the decisions he had made were the correct ones, why did he so often feel the sharp sting of anxiety when he thought of Sophia? Why could he not relax until he had heard her laughter and seen her smile with their reassurance for him that she was content with their marriage? Those were emotional reactions after all.

He was simply concerned that she should not overdo things, that was all. She had thrown herself into the new role she had taken on with so much enthusiasm and diligence that it was only natural that he should be concerned.

Sophia tried to still the frantic, giddy, dizzy race of her heartbeat as Ash came towards her. It was just her body's way of reminding her of the pleasure he gave it; it meant nothing else. It happened every time she saw him and she should be used to it by now after these past busy weeks of them working together for the future of his people, even if on this particular occasion there was a legitimate reason for her to feel happy to see him.

She didn't give any indication to him of that, though, when he made an appreciative sound at the sight of the tea tray. She dismissed the maid to pour the tea for him herself, saying with a smile, 'I ordered it when I heard you'd got back from your meeting. How did it go?'

'Even better than I had hoped,' Ash told her, accepting the cup she handed to him. Their fingers touched, Sophia's skin flushing sensually as Ash maintained the contact in a silent promise of the way they would spend the night. The sex between them was a bonus in their marriage that benefited them both, Sophia acknowledged. A bonus which if she was right had already produced a bonus of its own. A happy smile curved her mouth.

'The soil tests have shown that we will be able to grow a much wider variety of crops than even I had hoped for. If all goes well within the next few years the people will not only be self-sufficient in growing their own food, they will also have spare to sell.'

'I'm so pleased, Ash,' Sophia told him truthfully. 'You've worked so hard on this project.'

'No harder than you are working on your projects, Sophia.'

Now was her chance to tell him, Sophia decided. With a relationship like theirs, emotional displays were not the way of things, she knew, but it was impossible for her to keep the small breathless catch out of her voice as she bent her head to tell him meaningfully, 'It seems that we are having the good fortune to progress with all our projects at the moment, Ash, although I cannot be entirely certain until Dr Kumar can confirm my hopes.'

When Ash put down his teacup to look at her, Sophia told him simply, 'I think I'm pregnant.'

She'd known he would be pleased. It was what he'd married her for, after all. But the naked delight and joy that lit up his face caught at her heart, every bit as much as the way he got to his feet and came to her, saying her name in a voice that trembled slightly as he took hold of both her hands in his; it made her heart turn over inside her chest all over again. She had suspected for several days that she could be pregnant. She had known that Ash would be pleased if she was—she had known that she would be delighted herself—but this unexpected and unlooked-for tender act of husbandly intimacy could only be affecting her with such intensity because of the pregnancy hormones that had been released into her system, she assured herself as she battled against the need to cling to him and be held by him, held close in his arms as those arms bound both her and their child to him.

'I shall send for Dr Kumar immediately,' Ash told her. The news Sophia had just given him was so welcome and wanted that that was why he felt the way he did, elated, delighted and yet at the same time anxious for Sophia, proud of her and very, very protective of her. It was because their child was so important that he felt like this. So much of the future depended on them producing an heir, after all.

'It's still very early days,' Sophia felt bound to warn him.

'Then you must be even more careful not to overdo

things. It would be more restful for you if you could curtail your duties here and perhaps go to Mumbai where you could rest more, but with the rainy season starting there...'

Ash was pacing the courtyard now, plainly concerned. A small smile softened Sophia's mouth. Wasn't this the universal reaction of new fathers-to-be to the creation of that new life they wanted so much and which they instinctively wanted to protect?

'I have no desire at all to go to Mumbai, Ash,' she told him. 'I can rest perfectly well here if I need to rest, which I most certainly do not at the moment. I want to be here. This is our home and it will be our child's home, and as for me overdoing things—Ash, I am a healthy young woman and pregnancy is a perfectly natural function.'

'I don't want you—'

'You don't want me taking any unnecessary risks for your child. I know that, and I promise you that I shan't, but you mustn't try to wrap me in cotton wool.'

'I just want—'

'To protect your child.'

To protect *you,* he wanted to say, but Ash knew as the thought formed that it was not one he was permitted. By his own rules. Rules he had put in place to protect their marriage and now their child.

She was in danger of feeling far too emotional, Sophia recognised, and that she could not and would not do. The best way to deal with such a situation as she was now learning was to concentrate instead on something practical, something achievable, something that did not involve her mourning what she could never have. So she changed the subject to say practically, 'It was a good idea of yours to suggest that we donate Nasreen's clothes to charity. We've had the most lovely letters from the various charities I contacted saying how grateful they are to receive such a donation in Nasreen's name.'

He didn't want to talk about Nasreen or her clothes or even the charities they were benefiting, Ash thought. He wanted to talk about them, about their child, about their future. But a newly pregnant Sophia must be protected and indulged, he decided, although he was unable to stop himself from pointing out, 'Your idea to create scholarships in her memory was very generous, Sophia. By rights they should be in your name because Nasreen would certainly never have thought of doing anything so generous.'

'I am happy to be generous on her behalf,' Sophia assured him.

The truth was that she wanted peace for Ash more than she wanted to do something for Nasreen, especially now that she was carrying their child. And after all, wasn't it only natural that as that child's mother she wanted him or her to have the full commitment of his or her father without any darkness from the past overshadowing him? What she could not and would never ask Ash for, for her own benefit, she could and would, Sophia was beginning to realise very determinedly, work towards asking for their child. That was the nature of motherhood, was it not?

And the growing longing she was experiencing to feel emotionally closer to Ash, was that only because of her instinctive desire to secure a father's love for her child? Why not? As a child herself she had known what it was to feel she had cause to doubt her father's love for her and she certainly didn't want that for her child. Wasn't it only natural that she should be particularly anxious to ensure that her own child was loved by Ash? It was for their child that she wanted them to be close, not for herself. Ash, she felt, had been too hurt, too damaged, by what he saw as a failure within himself to ever come anywhere near risking breaking the vow he had made to keep their marriage emotion-free for its own safety. She would be a fool to allow herself to pin any dreams on that changing.

And did she want it to change?

The very fact that she couldn't let herself answer her own question was a warning she needed to heed, Sophia told herself.

The gel that had been placed on her tummy by the radiographer in charge of the expensive new scanning equipment in Nailpur's new hospital's maternity wing felt cold, and Sophia gave a small gasp that had Ash looking sharply at her. She had been surprised but pleased when he had insisted on coming with her for her scan, but his protective concern wasn't for her, she reminded herself. It was for their child, his child and heir. Not for her the tenderness of a husband who reached for her hand whilst the scan was in progress, sharing the special magic of the moment with her as it united them emotionally. Instead, Ash was standing slightly to one side of her, so that it was towards him and not her that the radiographer looked when she announced a little breathlessly, 'Highness, the maharani is carrying twins—boy twins.'

There was no logical reason why the scent of Ash's skin, as he leaned across her to look at the images on the screen being pointed out by the radiographer, should fill her with such an intense surge of emotional longing for the right to reach out and take hold of his hand and to have him look at *her* with the same mix of awe and disbelieving male pride in his gaze she could see he had for his sons. But she couldn't deny the fact that it did. This should have been a special moment for them as parents but instead she felt as though she didn't matter as herself, her only value in the room that was now rapidly filling up with medical personnel including the royal physician was as that of the woman who was carrying Nailpur's precious heirs.

It made no difference either telling herself that she not only should have expected this but that as a royal princess in a convenient marriage she should also have been prepared for it. Her heart bumped heavily into her ribs. She was delighted to be pregnant, of course she was, but she also felt very alone just at a time when surely she most needed to feel valued and… And what? Cherished? Adored? *Loved?*

Her heart thumped again but no one else in the room including Ash himself seemed to notice or care. If only Ash would just look at her, just share this special time with her in some small private way, it would make all the difference, but instead he had his back to her as he talked with Dr Kumar. Could a man who could ignore his wife at such a special time give the sons he was so proud of creating right now the love that they would need, a true father's love? The kind of love she herself had craved and been denied by her own father? Was it natural for a woman who had every reason to be on top of the world to feel so vulnerable and anxious, instead?

Ash didn't dare allow himself to look at Sophia. That

feeling he had of wanting to reach out to her and take hold of her hand instead of having to stand by and simply watch as the radiographer prepared her for the scan had unsettled him. It ran so counter to everything he expected from himself with regard to their relationship. It spoke of feelings he had no right to have. And then if that hadn't been enough for him to have to deal with, there was his reaction to the news that they were to have twin sons. The surge of joy he had felt was natural and allowable. A man in his position would naturally feel such joy after all, but that other feeling…that surge of protective anxiety for Sophia herself? That was because he was concerned for her as the mother of his sons, that was all.

The medical staff were finally turning towards her, all beaming faces and delight for her, although it was to Ash that they spoke in answer to his brusque question about the risks attached to a twin pregnancy, as they reassured him that there was no cause for any concern, and that both babies were of similar, healthy weight and measurements.

On the face of it they could have been any couple confronted with the news that where they had expected confirmation of the conception of one child they were now having the double pleasure and excitement of realising that there were going to be two, Sophia acknowledged. She tried determinedly not to allow her own feelings of vulnerability to spoil what she wanted to be a happy moment for them both, even if she had to accept that it wasn't going to be a moment that united them as a couple, as well as parents-to-be. It was just an upsurge of pregnancy hormones that was making her feel so vulnerable and so in need of Ash's emotional support, a clever device invented by mother nature to ensure that a pregnant woman did everything she could to keep the father of the child she was carrying as close to her as she could. After all, in prehistoric times the survival of both her and her child would have depended on the willingness and the ability of the father to keep them safe and fed. It made her feel better to be able to give herself this rational explanation for feelings that had made her feel so vulnerable. And it stopped her wanting that physical and emotional closeness to Ash that had so caught her off guard, didn't it?

She had her babies to think about now, not just herself. She was still learning what it meant to be Ash's wife and to live by the rules he had imposed on their marriage, and the truth was that living by those rules didn't come naturally or easily to someone who had always wanted to marry for love. Motherhood, on the other hand, and her feelings of maternal love and protection for the babies she was carrying, was as instinctive and as natural to her as breathing. Just like wanting to reach for Ash's hand when she had had her scan. But that was forbidden.

How many other things would be forbidden under the complex barriers Ash had erected against love? Would those barriers come between him and his sons? Would they, too, be denied emotional intimacy with their father? Sophia gave a small shiver despite the sunny warmth of the airy room. She must not look for problems. She must be positive and she must be strong—for the sake of their babies.

'There is no doubt that your people will welcome the arrival of your sons, Highness,' the royal physician was saying.

Sons. Another unexpected pang gouged Sophia's sensitive emotions. Had she been carrying daughters, how much of a solace might they have been to her as they grew up, members of her own sex with whom she might have had a special closeness that helped to alleviate the loneliness of being an unloved wife. Sons would be raised as future leaders of their people; sons would align themselves to their father. Sons would pattern themselves on that father. Another chill of dread shivered over her body. That wasn't what she wanted for her sons. She wanted them to grow up knowing what love was and valuing it.

'It is a gift indeed that there should be two children, for us and for them,' said Ash to Dr Kumar.

Sophia was so delicately built despite her lush curves. The thought of her carrying two babies was causing Ash anxieties for which he hadn't been prepared. Of course, it was only natural that he should be concerned for her well-being. He knew all about the loneliness suffered by a child who lost a parent, and it was equally natural therefore that there should be that core of anxiety within him for Sophia's health and safe delivery.

Suddenly, as pleased as he was about the conception of his sons, Ash was also aware of a need to withdraw into himself so that he could put a safe distance between himself and the dangerous intensity of the emotions that were threatening to take control of him.

'I have to go,' Ash told Sophia abruptly, still not looking directly at her. 'I have a meeting I have to attend. Dr Kumar will arrange for you to be driven back to the palace and I shall have a word with him about having a nurse on hand there—'

'No. That's ridiculous and unnecessary.' Sophia

stopped him, whilst the medical staff discreetly disappeared, leaving them alone in the room.

'I'm not sick, Ash, I'm pregnant—and healthily pregnant, too.'

'You are—'

'—carrying your heirs, yes, I know, and I hope that you don't think that I would do anything that would prejudice me carrying them safely to full term.'

Sophia's feisty reaction warned Ash that she wasn't going to allow him to wrap her in cotton wool.

'I simply want to make sure that all three of you receive the best care possible,' Ash defended himself.

All three of them, when he hadn't even cared enough about her to understand how much she had needed some small show of physical affection from him earlier on whilst she had waited to see her scan?

She must not allow herself to become downhearted, Sophia warned herself later as she was driven back to the palace. It had been a shock for both of them to discover that she was carrying twins. Surely the knowledge that they were to become parents was bound to bring them closer? After all, it was what they both wanted.

CHAPTER TEN

It was almost exactly a month since her scan, but far from bringing them closer together those four weeks had, if anything, led to Ash putting an even greater distance between them, Sophia thought as she sat alone in her private courtyard garden in the welcome cool of the evening.

Where the twins were concerned, Ash was scrupulous about keeping a check on their health and her own, but whenever she tried to talk to him on any kind of personal level he retreated from her and changed the subject.

And most humiliating of all for her, as her own need and indeed craving for a loving gentle intimacy with him grew, along with her feelings of emotional insecurity, Ash had rejected her by no longer coming to her bed.

Whilst part of her—the old feisty Sophia—longed to demand to know what had happened to the sexual chemistry he had told her existed between them, the new mother-in-waiting Sophia was far too protective of the future emotional security of the babies she was carrying to want to risk a confrontation that could destroy the increasingly fragile bonds that held them together.

Besides, she seriously thought that Ash's distance from her was the way things were going to be and that nothing she could say or do could change that, and that really scared her. Not for her own sake but for the sake of their sons. It was one thing for Ash to refuse to let her get close to him, but increasingly she was worrying that he might behave in exactly the same way with the twins, locking them out emotionally. Not necessarily deliberately—she knew how pleased he was about them—but because he simply couldn't help himself?

She had grown up with a distant father whom she had felt had rejected every attempt she had made to get close to him. She couldn't bear the thought of that happening to her precious babies. But they would have her, and Ash would be a good and protective father in many other ways. Right now, because her pregnancy was making her feel so emotionally vulnerable, she was achingly conscious of all that she was missing as a woman by not having a husband who loved her, but it was the twins who mattered most, not her. There was no sacrifice of her own personal happiness she was not prepared to make to give them the security of growing up with their parents living together. That didn't mean that she wasn't right to feel concerned that Ash might not be able to stop his attitude towards her from spilling over into his behaviour towards his sons.

In the privacy of his own suite, Ash paced the floor of his office. He had taken to working late into the evening, telling himself that he needed to ensure that all his projects were up to date ahead of the birth of the twins, but he knew that the reality was he worked late because that was the only way he had of blotting out the demons that were stalking him.

It was illogical and…and *unnecessary, unwanted and unacceptable* to him, this almost constant need he had to be with Sophia. And not just to be with her. He wanted… Ash stopped pacing, a dark frown slashing his forehead. He had told himself that it would be no hardship for a man of his level of self-discipline to deny himself Sophia's bed as a precautionary measure to ensure the safety of her pregnancy—after all, as good and passionate as the sex between them had been it was only sex—but the truth was that with every night without her, his desire for her found a thousand different new ways in which to torture him. Just the memory of the scent of her skin, the sound of her breath as it accelerated with the desire he had stoked, the small mewling sounds of increasingly out-of-control pleasure she made when he aroused her, all of those just by themselves were enough to have a need coursing through him that left him feeling as though he had been burned with acid and left raw and close to crying out with the pain of his wounds.

He had lost count of the number of times he had woken in the night thinking he could hear her breathing, conjuring up out of the darkness the sound of her voice as she whispered his name so sweetly when she pleaded with him not just for the pleasure he gave her but also for the right to return that pleasure to him. How could one single woman in the space of a handful of weeks have come to have such a powerful effect on him? He had desired women before. But never as much as he desired Sophia, and certainly never as much as he needed the sweet agony the desire gave him.

That he should feel like this was a warning to him, Ash told himself. A warning and a test. He must surely prove to himself that he could stay away from Sophia's bed—in the first instance for the practical reason of not wanting to endanger her pregnancy in any way, especially as she was carrying twins, but in the second instance so that by the time they were sharing a bed again the need he felt for her would be under his control, not the other way around.

Given all that, why was he right now walking down the corridor that led to Sophia's room?

She knew it wasn't the sensible thing to do. Surely she'd spent far too many hours preparing herself logically for what her life with Ash was going to be like to waste all that effort on some kind of irrational emotional outburst, or even worse, the kind of emotionally demanding behaviour that was bound to make Ash retreat even further from her?

This wasn't about her, Sophia reminded herself as she hurried towards her bedroom door, intent on seeking Ash out to confront him with her growing concern about how his emotional distance from her could impact on their sons if he behaved the same way towards them. She'd been on her way to bed when the emotional firestorm that was now propelling her towards her bedroom door had struck, leaving her to pull a robe on over her cobweb-fine silk nightgown.

Ash reached out for the handle to Sophia's bedroom door. He should not be doing this. An ice-cold river of self-loathing held him immobile whilst also trapping his emotions in its familiar numbing wasteland. Even his heartbeat seemed to have slowed in tune with the emptiness that had now filled the gap left by the rush of longing that had brought him here. His hand fell back to his side just as inside the bedroom Sophia pulled open the door.

The unexpectedness of seeing Ash there, outside her bedroom door, obviously on his way to see her—where else could he be going, after all?—flooded her with so much happiness that she immediately reached out to him, her hand on his arm as she urged him inside her room, her joy showing in the warmth in her voice as she said his name.

Automatically Ash allowed himself to be drawn towards her. Her open delight at seeing him was confusing the ice-cold deadening river of controlled self-loathing inside him. His gaze—the one that only seconds ago under the influence of that deadening flow had, like his other senses, assured him that there was nothing about any aspect of Sophia that could break through the barriers he had so regrettably allowed to weaken in the privacy of his own treacherous thoughts—could see the sweet warmth of the curve of her lips, lips which he already knew were so soft and incredibly responsive to his kisses that just to look at them was enough to have them quivering with longing, and her body softening with desire for him just as right now his was hardening with its desire for her.

He must not think about that. He dragged his gaze from her face and then realised his mistake as it slipped to her body, its burgeoning shape revealed to him through the flimsiness of the nightgown he could see beneath her open robe. Her breasts looked fuller, her belly rounding. His heartbeat had picked up and was now racing, thumping, in fact, with the renewed force of his longing to reach out for her and take hold of her, to discover her newly forming body with his fingertips so that he could learn its promise and rejoice in the gift it was holding.

Ash was here. She had been allowing her silly vulnerability to get the better of her. He was here and soon he would hold her and in the secret darkness of their bed they would share an intimacy that surely she could build on to sustain her. Only now that he was here could she admit to herself the true depth of the sense of loss and abandonment she had felt through his absence from her bed. In fact, she was physically trembling with the intensity of her relief—trembling inside and close to tears caused by that relief, as well. Perhaps there was hope for the future after all. It was obvious that she had misjudged the situation in thinking that Ash didn't want her any more now that she was pregnant. Loving him meant…

Loving him? Loving Ash? Her heart felt as though it had been thrown into a theme park ride and was now racing upward towards the final terrifying drop. When had love crept into the equation? It wasn't a question Sophia was in any state of mind to answer. All she did know was that in one blinding moment of clarity she had been shown the reality of her own feelings. She loved Ash. Hadn't she read somewhere that women were engineered differently than men by nature, to produce a hormone during sex that automatically forged a unique bond by that woman's senses and emotions to the man with whom she had shared the experience?

And wasn't it the truth that she had already been programmed to love Ash by her own past even if she had genuinely believed that he had killed that teenage adoration with his rejection of her?

Love. For her husband and their sons. Surely that was something worth fighting for, something worth striving and hoping for? They were already married, and...

And Ash had sworn never to allow himself to look for love within their marriage.

But he was here. He had come to her.

Here in this room was everything in his world that held real value, Ash found himself thinking. Here was everything he could ever want or need because here was Sophia.

He moved closer to her just as she moved closer to him, an appeal in her eyes that he couldn't misunderstand. His body certainly wasn't misunderstanding it. His body was welcoming that soft look of female need she was giving him.

'Ash.' All Sophia's pent-up emotion trembled through her voice. Ash was so close to her. He was within touching distance of her.

'Ash.' She whispered his name this time, and then felt the warm gust of his breath against her lips as he exhaled in response before bending his head to kiss her.

He wanted her so much. His body was on fire with that need. It had already gone far too long without her, and it hungered for her. As though something inside him had snapped Ash felt his self-control break. Wrapping Sophia in his arms he began to kiss her over and over again, the sensuality of his passion turning her weak with her own response to it as she returned each increasingly deep kiss.

Unable to stop himself, Ash started to caress Sophia's body, the full curves of her breasts with their dark crests so clearly visible beneath the fine silk and so responsive to his touch, causing her to make small sounds of pleasure deep down in her throat. Her head was thrown back against his supporting arm as he brought those sweet moans of pleasure from her. He couldn't wait to take her to bed and complete their lovemaking. His body ached and burned for that intimacy and that release; it dragged out the need racking him so that he could feel it in every nerve ending. He kissed her hungrily, savouring the sweet rich taste of her, the pleasure that lay within the warmth of her mouth, his free hand automatically moving lower over her body and then stilling when it encountered the soft swell of her pregnancy.

Lost beneath the intensity of Ash's kiss and her own response to it, at first Sophia couldn't quite take in what was happening when Ash abruptly stopped kissing her and pushed her away from him, releasing her.

'What is it?' she asked him shakily. 'What's wrong?'

'The twins,' was all Ash could bring himself to say, his voice terse as he half turned away from her to conceal from her his own disgust with himself. How could he have been so lost to all sense of what it meant to be a father to have allowed his desire to drive him towards an action that might have endangered the twins' safety and Sophia's physical comfort? He was disgusted with himself.

'The twins?' was all Sophia could manage to repeat as she tried to cling to the remnants of her dignity, pulling it around herself in much the same way in which she was now drawing her open robe around her body.

After the realisation that she loved Ash, his appearance in her bedroom and then her hopes heightened by what had looked as though it was going to turn into intense lovemaking, his rejection of her now was unbearably painful.

'I don't want…' Ash began, but Sophia was in no mood to let him continue. Where there had been hope and arousal, there was now disappointment, hurt and anger—the hurt anger of a feisty woman who wanted her man but who was being rejected by him.

'You don't want me any more now that I'm pregnant, is that what you were going to say? I'm carrying your sons so you don't have to have sex with me any more, is that it? What about that sexual chemistry between us you spoke of when you were persuading me to marry you, Ash, or did that only exist when you were thinking about me conceiving your heir? Or maybe it's just that you don't find me desirable now that I'm pregnant. But whatever the case, I want you to know that coming here and…and…and doing what you did and then rejecting me isn't the kind of behaviour I expect from a man like you. It's…it's cruel and…and unfair.' Her voice was becoming thick with the tears she was determined not to unleash. Ash was standing with his face averted from her, and not moving at all.

He was ignoring her, blocking her out, distancing himself from her. Because he didn't want her in his life at all, really? Because he never had and he never would?

It was too much for her to endure.

'Did you ever really desire me at all, Ash, or was it just something you forced yourself to pretend?'

'No.' The denial was ripped from Ash's throat before he could silence it, the sheer intensity of the emotions inside him that had broken through physically forcing him to turn round, and look at Sophia. 'Of course I wanted you.' He wanted her now. He wanted to go to her and take hold of her and show her how wrong she was, but he had her to think of, and the twins. He was a husband and a father-to-be now and not just a man burning and driven by his own shameful lusts.

'But you haven't been near me for weeks, and just now...'

'I was thinking of the twins and of you. I didn't want...' It was so hard for him to admit to any kind of emotional vulnerability but his moral need to set the record straight was stronger than his need to protect his defences.

'I didn't want to risk hurting them or...or you. You are so small and you are carrying two babies.'

There was a huge lump in Sophia's throat. She couldn't deny the truth she could hear in Ash's voice. She couldn't argue against such an obviously genuine explanation. But why couldn't he have told her that before?

'I'm a woman, Ash. I'm designed by nature to carry your sons safely. And women do have sex when they're pregnant, you know.'

'I didn't want to take any unnecessary risks.'

Yes, she understood his fears. But why couldn't he have opened up to her and explained what was in his thoughts? He couldn't because Ash didn't deal in emotions.

The warmth she had felt when he had explained why he had stayed away from her had turned to the cold chill of a returning fear that was already worrying her, namely that Ash would not be able to relate emotionally to his sons and that he would keep them at a distance, because he no longer knew how to relate emotionally to others.

Ash saw the pain darkening Sophia's eyes and the sadness shadowing her face. 'What is it? What's wrong?' he asked her.

'I know how much the twins mean to you, Ash, but I'm worried that *they'll* never know, because you will never be able to show them or tell them how much they mean to you. I'm afraid that you'll distance yourself from them in the same way that you distance yourself from me. I know how much that hurts, having a father who doesn't seem to care. That kind of thing can hurt a child so very badly and make them feel so rejected. A child can't rationalise that it might just be that a father does care but can't show those feelings. I want our sons to know the real Ash, the Ash that I knew whilst I was growing up, the kind, understanding, always ready to listen, happy Ash whom I loved so much. I want you to be that Ash for our children, but I'm afraid that they will never know him, because the Ash you feel you have to be now has locked him away and will never let him be free to enjoy his children and to love them.'

Every emotion-filled, spoken-from-the-heart word Sophia offered felt a like a seismic shock deep inside Ash that shook him to the core. He knew with a flash of insight and at the most powerful deepest intense level of himself that Sophia's words had touched a nerve, set in motion a reaction like the clicking open of a series of locks that had opened doors inside him that showed him an inescapable truth. That truth was that he couldn't bear to be the man Sophia had just described to him, the man who whilst loving his children could not reach out to them and so left them to feel that he didn't care, and the husband who wanted and needed his wife so much that he was filled with fear because of those feelings.

'Sophia!' Her name broke from his heart and tore at his lungs, his stride towards her to reach her swift and slightly uncoordinated, his breathing unsteady. A fine tremor gripped his body as he held her hands in his own and told her thickly, 'I promise you that I will be the father you want me to be for our sons, that I will try to be the Ash you remember for them and that they will never, ever have to doubt my love for them.'

'Oh, Ash.'

'And as for me not wanting you...'

He was kissing her so sweetly and tenderly, drawing her close to his body so that she could feel for herself his desire for her, that it was impossible for Sophia not to respond.

'I don't want to hurt you or the babies,' Ash was whispering to her in a voice raw with a desire he wasn't making any attempt to hide.

'You won't,' Sophia assured him. 'We can be careful and make it slow and sweet, and...'

The violent shudder that racked Ash's body told her more than any words how much hers had affected him. But when he carried her to the bed and then carefully undressed her to gaze reverentially at her naked body, it was her turn to tremble with the intensity of her emotions.

Had she really thought that Ash might be turned off by the changes in her body? If so he was showing her now just how wrong she had been, with the warmth of the long, slow, deep kiss he was giving her.

All the new sweetness of the lives they had created together and the love she had now discovered for him were in Sophia's response to Ash. Her lips clung to his, her arms reaching out to hold him, her heart melting with the tide of feeling that swept through her when Ash placed his hand on the rounding shape of her body. There was something so inexpressibly tender and special about such a touch, about the contact between father and child, and the warmth of his caress on her own skin at the same time conveying to her body a sense of care and protection.

But it wasn't just care and protection she wanted from Ash. Her body ached with a hot but gentle sweetness for him and for his lovemaking. And as though he knew exactly how she felt and exactly what she needed and longed for, it seemed somehow to Sophia that with every touch and caress Ash brought a new and deeper meaning to their lovemaking, as though he *wanted* to bring a new and a deeper meaning to that lovemaking.

The kisses he placed on her belly, the sweet slowness of his possession of her as he waited for her to reassure him that she wanted that possession, spoke so clearly of a man who genuinely cared not just for the welfare of his children but for her, as well. And when the final moment of her pleasure came it brought with it for Sophia an upsurge of emotional tears. She loved him so much.

Feeling Sophia's tears dampen his face Ash's first reaction was one of concern that he had, despite the care he had taken, still managed to hurt her, and the shake of her head which she gave in answer to his question had him demanding urgently, 'Then what is it?'

'I'm afraid, Ash,' Sophia admitted, the intimacy of their entwined bodies, the tenderness of the moment and her love for him overwhelming her natural instinct to conceal her feelings from him. 'You see, I've fallen in love with you all over again, and sometimes I just don't know how I'm going to be able to cope with that when I know that you don't want my love.'

Later Ash would remember this second out of time and believe that he had actually physically felt the cracking apart of the wall he had built around his emotions, but right now it was the splashing down of one single tear and then another from his own eyes onto Sophia's damp face that told him all he needed to know. He, who had never been able to cry for any of his own pain or grief, was weeping now for the pain he had caused Sophia, because he loved her, because her pain was worse for him to bear than his own could ever be, and he was the one who had caused that pain.

'I do want your love, Sophia,' he told her. 'I want it and you more than I have ever or could ever want anything or anyone else in my life. I've known that for weeks, although I've been trying to deny it. You say that you are afraid. I have been afraid, too, afraid to admit how much you mean to me, so very afraid that I couldn't even allow myself to admit to that fear. It was easier to pretend that it wasn't happening. Easier to make rules for you to obey than to risk admitting that no rules on earth can overpower true love. I've known what's been happening to me but I've still tried to fight it, to push you away, to punish myself for even thinking about how I feel about you.'

'You really mean it?' Sophia asked him tremulously. 'You really do love me?'

To see his feisty, brave-hearted Sophia so vulnerable because of his cowardice tore at Ash's heart. 'Yes. I really do and I really mean it. I intend to spend the rest of my life proving to you just how precious you are to me. You'll need to help me though, Sophia. I'll make mistakes, and get things wrong. I'll need you to show me how to love you and the babies in the way you deserve to be loved. You'll have to teach me through your own sweet, loving, generous example.'

'I will. I'll show you every day, my darling, darling Ash,' Sophia assured him tenderly as she cupped the side of his face with her hand and kissed him softly.

Tears for her, fallen from the eyes of the man who loved her, had washed the last of the doubt from her heart.

A tiny flutter of movement, followed by another inside her body, had her giving a small gasp and immediately reaching for Ash's hand to place it over her stomach.

'It's your sons, letting us know that they definitely approve of two parents who love each other,' she told Ash. And when he bent his head and kissed first on the place where his hand had been and then cupped her face to kiss her, Sophia knew that when it came to learning how to show his love for them, her husband was going to be a very good pupil, indeed.

EPILOGUE

It was no good, Sophia admitted. Although she'd wanted to have a natural delivery, she'd had to give in, not so much because Dr Kumar and the obstetrician brought in by him from Mumbai had insisted that a planned C-section was the safest way to deliver the twins now that they were getting so big, but because of the very real fear she'd seen in Ash's eyes.

He'd told her that it must be her choice but she'd seen how worried he was, and last night after the medical team had delivered its verdict, she'd woken up to find Ash pacing the floor of the bedroom they now shared, and he'd admitted to her how terrified he was that he might lose her.

'Nasreen died because I didn't care. I'm so afraid that I might lose you because I care so very much.'

He hadn't added 'as a punishment,' but Sophia had known that was what he meant, and immediately she'd known that she couldn't let him suffer the anxiety of her going through a natural birth.

So now here she was at the hospital, and Ash was pacing the floor nervously once again, as the medical personnel went about the business of preparing her for the delivery of their sons.

'It really is the most sensible option,' the obstetrician told her. 'You've got over three weeks to go to your natural delivery date and the twins are so big already that I just would not be happy about that, for their sake, as well as your own.'

Sophia nodded her head, and reached for Ash's hand as he came to stand at her side.

'I love you so much,' he whispered to her, and Sophia felt his hand tighten on hers as the operation began, and first one and then the second of their sons was lifted from Sophia's body and handed to their parents.

For Sophia, seeing the look on Ash's face as he held one and then the other of their babies before giving them to her to hold told her beyond the need for any words just how much love their sons would have from their father. They would bond and form a male trio that at times as the twins grew would exclude her, as a woman, but the bond that she and Ash shared would be so strong that it would hold them together for ever, through the birth of other children hopefully, during the growing up of those children and into those years when they would perhaps become grandparents. A bond of the truest kind of love, given from the heart of a man who'd had to overcome so much to be able to make that gift.

'I promise you I will be the father you want for them, Sophia,' Ash told her tenderly. 'And the loving husband that you so deserve.'

* * * * *

THE SHEIKH'S HEIR

SHARON KENDRICK

To Max Campbell, for ensuring that my iPhone
plays more than one Beatles song.

CHAPTER ONE

WOULD this damned party never end?

In the softly lit anteroom of his friend's palace, Sheikh Hassan Al Abbas let out an irritated breath and turned to the man standing a few deferential paces away from him.

'Do you think there's any chance I could just slip away and leave them to get on with it, Benedict?' he demanded, knowing only too well how his loyal English aide would respond.

There was a pause. 'Your absence would almost certainly be noticed, Your Highness,' answered Benedict carefully. 'Since you are one of the most esteemed guests present. And furthermore it would offend your oldest friend if he knew that you could not be bothered to stay to wish him happiness on the night of his engagement.'

Hassan's fists clenched against the unaccustomed lounge suit which clothed his hard body, hating the strictures of collar and tie. He wished he was wearing soft and silken robes against his naked skin. That he was galloping free on his horse, with the warm desert wind blowing against his face. 'And what if I believed deep in my heart that such a wish would not only be futile but hypocritical?' he iced back. 'That I think Alex is about to make the biggest mistake of his life?'

'It is often difficult for two men to see eye to eye when it comes to the subject of women,' answered Benedict diplomatically. 'Particularly regarding the subject of marriage.'

'It's not just his choice of fiancée I don't agree with!' Hassan said, unable to contain the frustration which had been growing inside him since his oldest friend, Prince Alessandro Santina, had announced that he was to marry Allegra Jackson. 'Though that is bad enough. Even worse is that he has abandoned the woman to whom he has been betrothed since he was born! A woman of noble birth, who would make a far more suitable bride.'

'Perhaps his love is too strong to be—'

'Love?' interrupted Hassan, and now he could feel the bitter lump which had risen in his throat like a ball of nails. A brief yet undeniable pain clenched at his heart. For didn't he know better than anyone that 'love' was nothing but an illusion which could wreck lives with its seductive power?

'Love is nothing more than a fancy name for lust,' he bit out. 'And a ruler cannot allow himself to be guided by the stir of his loins or the beat of his heart. He must put duty before desire.'

'Yes, Highness,' said Benedict obediently.

Hassan shook his head in disbelief, still unwilling to accept that his high-born friend had let his standards dip so low. 'Did you realise that Alex's future father-in-law is some grubby ex-footballer with a long list of wives and mistresses he has been publicly unfaithful to?'

'I had heard something along those lines, Highness.'

'I cannot believe that he is willing to marry into such a disreputable family as these Jacksons! Did you see the way they were behaving at the ball? It turned my stomach to watch them quaffing champagne as if it was water and making fools of themselves on the dance floor.'

'Highness—'

'This woman Allegra cannot possibly become the wife of a Crown Prince!' Angrily, Hassan slammed the flat of his hand against an adjacent table and its delicate frame juddered beneath the contemptuous force. 'She is a tramp—just like her mother and her sisters! Did you witness the spectacle which brought me seeking refuge in here, when the sister with the voice of a crow stormed the stage and attempted to sing?'

'Yes, Highness, I saw her,' said Benedict softly. 'But the Crown Prince has made up his mind that he will marry Miss Jackson, and I doubt whether even you will be able to change it. And should you not now return to the ballroom before your absence is commented upon?'

But Hassan was not listening—at least, not to his aide. He raised a hand for silence, his ears straining for the whispering of a sound. His body tensed. Had he heard something? Someone? Or had the recent harsh months spent in battle meant that he suspected danger lurking everywhere? Yet he could have sworn that the room had been empty when he'd come searching for an escape.

'Did you hear something?' he questioned as he felt the instinctive pricking of his skin.

'No, Highness. I heard nothing.'

There was a brief silence before Hassan nodded, feeling some of the tension ease from his body as he allowed himself to be reassured by his aide. This might be the worst party in living memory, but at least security was tight. 'Then let us return to this mockery of a reception. Let me see whether I can find anyone tolerably attractive enough to dance with.' He gave a sardonic laugh. 'A woman who is the very antithesis of Allegra Jackson and her vulgar family!'

With this, the two men swept from the softly lit room, while from her hiding place behind a carved chest in a corner of the vast chamber, Ella Jackson wished that she could open her mouth and scream with rage and frustration.

How *dare* he?

Waiting for a few moments to check that he really *had* gone, she stretched limbs which were cramped from sitting still for so long. Greedily, she sucked great gulps of air into her lungs because she'd had to keep holding her breath in case she was discovered. For a moment back then, she'd been sure he was going to find her. And something told her that she was lucky not to have been discovered by that arrogant beast of a man who had been so insulting—not just to Allegra and Izzy, but to the entire Jackson family.

The other man had called him 'Highness'—and judging from the way he'd been calling all the shots, he had certainly *sounded* royal. His voice had been deep and faintly accented—not the kind of voice you heard every day. It had also sounded bossy and proud. Could that have been the powerful sheikh everyone had been banging on about? The groom-to-be's oldest friend, who had been expected at tonight's party and anticipated with the same kind of breathless excitement which might have greeted a movie star?

Uncomfortably, Ella rose to her feet. The beads of her elaborate dress were pressing painfully into her skin and her wild tangle of curls was desperately in need of a session with the hairbrush. She would have to do something drastic to repair her appearance before she thought about returning to the general scrum which was her sister Allegra's engagement party to the Crown Prince of the Santina royal family. Even though she would have happily given a month's salary not to have gone back into that ballroom.

Wasn't it ironic that she had slipped away from the party for precisely the same reason as the sheikh? The moment her sister Izzy had staggered onto the stage to sing, Ella's heart had hit her boots and she'd wanted to curl up and die. She loved Izzy. She *did*—but why did she have such a penchant for making a complete fool of herself? Why sing in public when you had absolutely zero talent?

Ella had slunk into this darkened anteroom and instinct had made her crouch down behind the concealing bulk of the chest when she'd heard the sound of approaching footsteps. There had been the sound of the door quietly clicking shut and then someone uttering a short, terse expletive. And that's when she had heard the damning words of the accented man as he had torn her family to shreds.

Yet hadn't he only been speaking the truth? Her father *did* have a long list of women he'd been intimate with. He had two ex-wives at the last count, and one of those he'd married twice. Plus all the mistresses on the side—some of whom were reported in the newspapers and some whom he'd managed to hush up.

Hadn't her own mother's life been blighted by her hopeless longing for a man who seemed to be incapable of any kind of fidelity? Her sweet, foolish mother, who'd never been able to see any fault in her errant husband, which was why she had been his bride twice over. And why she let him treat her like a complete doormat.

If ever Ella had needed to know how *not* to conduct a relationship, she'd never needed to look any further than the example set by her own parents. And hadn't she vowed that she would never, *ever* let a man make a fool of her like that?

She reached down and picked up her handbag, extracting the wide-toothed comb which was the only implement which could ever come close to taming her soft but wayward curls. Dare she risk putting a brighter light on in here?

Why not? The outrageously opinionated sheikh didn't sound as if he was in any danger of coming back. He was probably subjecting some 'tolerably attractive' woman to a dance. Poor her, Ella thought with a genuine trace of sympathy. Imagine dancing with someone who had an ego as big as his—why there would be barely any room left on the dance floor!

She clicked on a light which illuminated the regal splendour of the vast antechamber and hunted around until she found a mirror recessed in one of the alcoves. Stepping back, she surveyed herself with critical eyes.

Her silver-beaded dress was a little on the short side but it was extremely fashionable—and such a look was essential in Ella's line of work. Her rather flashy clients expected her to reflect their values, to make a statement and not fade quietly into the background. As a party planner catering to the nouveau-riche end of the market, Ella had decided to cash in on her family's notoriety by working for the kind of people who had plenty of money, but very little in the way of generally accepted 'taste.'

She'd quickly learnt the rules. But then, she was a quick learner—it came with the territory of being a survivor, of having lived with scandal and notoriety for most of her life. If a glamour-model bride wanted to arrive at her wedding in a dazzling diamante coach, she expected the woman organising the event to dazzle in a similar way. So dazzle Ella did. She'd got that down to a fine art. With her trademark slash of scarlet lipstick accentuating her wide mouth, she wore the on-trend clothes which so impressed her clients. She turned heads when she needed to.

But all that was for show. She kept the real Ella locked away where no one could find her. Or hurt her. Underneath the dazzling exterior, when she was dressed down and chilled out at home, it was a different story. There she could be the person her family had always teased her for being. Bare of makeup, wearing old jeans and a T-shirt—sometimes with paint underneath her fingernails. She wished she was there right now, instead of having to endure the longest evening of her life. A night she would never have believed could happen.

A member of her family was marrying into one of the Mediterranean's oldest and most revered royal families—and the knives were out. Hadn't she just heard for herself, via the arrogant sheikh, how the entire Jackson clan were being judged and found wanting? Weren't the sly eyes of various members of the press watching every move they made, to report with glee how ill-equipped the Jacksons were to mix with the aristocracy?

Well, Ella would show them. She would show them all. Their cruel comments wouldn't get to her because she wouldn't let them. She bit her lip, for once feeling vulnerable about the charges which were always levelled at her and her siblings. She worked hard for her living—she always had done—and yet her Jackson surname made people pigeonhole her. They thought she just lay around all day, drinking champagne and generally whooping it up, and yet nothing could be further from the truth.

Raking the comb through her red-brown curls, she checked for any stray smudges of mascara and then applied a final, defiant coat of scarlet lipstick.

There.

Her dangling earrings were swaying in a sparkling cascade and even her blue eyeshadow had bits of glitter in it. Her shiny armour was firmly in place and she was ready to face the braying masses. Let anyone *dare* try to patronise her!

The sound of music and chatter grew louder as she clattered along the marble corridor in her new shoes.

In glossy black patent, with towering silver heels which were wonderfully flattering to the legs, they were a fashionista's dream and an orthopaedic surgeon's nightmare. But they made her walk tall and stand straight and tonight she needed that more than anything.

The ballroom was crowded and noisy and Ella's eyes skimmed the dance floor. The place was packed. Royals mingled with minor television stars, and one-time Premier League footballers who'd worked with her dad were propping up the bar. She could see various members of her family partying away with enthusiasm. Rather too *much* enthusiasm. Her father was downing a flute of champagne, her mother hovering nearby with an ever-hopeful smile on her face. Which meant that she was worried he was going to get drunk. Or make a pass at someone young enough to be his daughter.

Please don't let him get drunk, thought Ella. And please don't let him make a pass at someone else's girl-friend. Or wife.

There was her sister Izzy dancing, grinding her hips in a way which made Ella turn away with embarrassment. Knowing there was no point in trying to reason with her wayward sibling, she redirected her gaze to the dance floor. Her heart suddenly beginning to pound as her eyes came to rest on a man whose exotic looks marked him out from everyone else.

She blinked. In a room which wasn't exactly short on the glamour quotient, he drew the eye irresistibly. And yet he looked totally out of place among the glittering throng and she couldn't quite work out why. It wasn't just that he was taller than any other man there or that his muscular body was all hard, honed muscle. He looked *hungry*. Like he hadn't eaten a decent meal in months. Ella's gaze roved over his face. A *cruel* face, she thought with a sudden shiver. His black eyes seemed devoid of emotion and his sensual mouth was curved into a cynical smile as he listened to his blonde dance partner as she lifted her chin to chatter to him.

Ella's heart missed a beat. It was him. Instinct told her so. The man who had been so unspeakably rude about her family when she'd been hiding in the anteroom. The man she had silently cursed as being arrogant and judgemental. And yet now that she'd seen him, she couldn't seem to tear her eyes away from him.

His olive skin gleamed, as if he'd been cast from some precious metal, instead of flesh and blood. She watched as a beautiful redhead brushed past him, saw the way he automatically glanced at her bursting décolletage without missing a beat.

He was danger and sexuality mixed into one potent masculine cocktail—the kind of man most people's mothers would warn you to steer clear of. Ella felt a debilitating kick in her belly, as something deep inside her responded to him. As if on some instinctive level, she had discovered something she hadn't even realised she'd been looking for.

He raised his head then and she saw the way he stilled. The way his black eyes narrowed as he moved his gaze around the ballroom until at last it came to alight on her.

Like a hunter, she thought.

Ella felt as if she had been caught in a dark yet

blinding spotlight. She could feel herself flush—a slow heat which started at the top of her head and seemed to work its way right down to her toes. Had he known she'd been staring at him? Look away, she urged herself furiously. *Look away from him right now.* But she couldn't. It was as if he had cast some powerful spell over her which was making it impossible for her to tear her gaze away.

From across the dance floor, his black eyes grew slightly amused as their overlong eye contact was maintained. A pair of ebony brows were raised at her in arrogant question, and when still she did not move, he bent to whisper something into the blonde's ear.

Ella was aware of the woman turning and glaring at her and of the man with the black eyes beginning to walk towards her. *Run*, she urged herself. Get away from here before it's too late.

But she didn't run. She couldn't. It was as if she'd been turned into a tree and was rooted to the spot. Now he was almost upon her, and his physical presence was so overwhelming that she felt the breath dry in her throat. His shadow moved over her as he approached, enveloping her—and suddenly it was as if every other person in the crowded ballroom had ceased to exist.

There was a pause while he let his eyes rove unashamedly over her face and then her body, just as he'd done when the big-breasted redhead had passed him by.

'Have we met somewhere before?' he questioned.

Ella didn't have to hear his deep, accented voice to know that she had been right. It *was* him. The opinionated man who'd been so rude about her family. She'd already decided that he was proud and arrogant, but she hadn't expected this level of charisma. Nor for him to have such an overwhelming effect on her that she could barely think straight. And she needed to think straight. Now was not the time to demonstrate that her tingling body seemed to have taken on a greedy life of its own. All she needed was to remember his unforgettable insults.

'Not until now,' she said, injecting a noncommittal note into her voice and hoping it sounded convincing.

Hassan's eyes flicked over her, interested at the play of emotions on the Madonna-like oval of her face. She had been staring at him as if she'd like to rip his clothes off with her teeth! Not an uncommon reaction from a woman, it was true—and she was pretty enough for him to have given the idea a moment's consideration. But her initial hungry look had been replaced by one of wariness and suspicion. He felt the faint prickle of hostility emanating from her, and *that* was novel enough to arouse his interest.

'Are you sure about that?' he murmured.

She thought how incredibly well he spoke English, despite the sexily accented voice. It seemed to whisper over her skin with its velvet caress, and inexplicably she started wondering what it would be like to have that voice murmur sweet nothings in her ear. 'Positive,' she replied coolly.

'Yet you were staring at me as if you knew me.'

'Aren't you used to women staring at you, then?' she questioned innocently.

'No, never happened to me before,' he drawled sardonically, wondering what was making her blow so hot and cold. He looked at the provocative scarlet gleam of her lips and felt a sudden rush of desire. 'What's your name?'

Ella wished that her breasts would stop tingling and likewise the molten throb of lust deep in her belly. She didn't want to feel like this about a man who had talked about her family in a way which had made them all sound like some sort of *gutter animals*. She stared at him, defying him to contradict her. 'My name is... Cinderella.'

Hassan gave a slow smile. 'Is it now?' So she wanted to play, did she? Well, that was fine by him. He liked games—particularly of the flirty, sexual nature. And particularly with nubile young women with glossy, red lips and firm bodies which had been poured into a shiny silver dress which emphasised their every willowy curve. As a child, the only female role models he'd known had been servants and as an adult he had discovered that women were usually predatory and nearly always beddable.

He felt the sudden beat of anticipation as he looked at her. 'Then I think the fairy tale must have just come true, Cinderella,' he said. 'Because you've just met your prince.'

It was the corniest line Ella had ever heard and yet, somehow, it worked. For some insane reason it made her want to smile—a little I'm-so-pleased-with-myself sort of smile to accompany the embarrassing rise of colour to her cheeks.

But she didn't fall for meaningless chat-up lines, did she? Hadn't she learnt—from the humiliating example set by her own father—that men spent their lives saying things to women that they didn't mean? And hadn't she vowed never to become one of those women who drank up worthless compliments and then let their hearts get broken as a result?

Drawing back her shoulders, she stared at the exotic-looking man, pleased that she'd worn such ridiculously high heels which meant that their eyes were almost on a level. 'So you're a real live prince, are you?'

'Indeed I am.' For a moment, Hassan felt a flicker of impatience, acknowledging his own obstinacy. He didn't like being recognised for his royal blood and yet he found it faintly irritating when his regal status was not alluded to. He wasn't expecting her to curtsey—which was a good thing, since she clearly had no intention of doing so!—but a little deference surely wouldn't have gone amiss? Surely she could have allowed a small amount of awe to creep into an English accent which he found oddly difficult to place. 'In fact, I am a sheikh,' he expanded proudly. 'My name is Hassan, and I am a prince of the desert.'

'Wow!'

Hassan's eyes narrowed. Was that *sarcasm* he had heard tingeing her voice? Surely not. People were always impressed by his sheikhdom, indeed being ravished by a sheikh seemed to be the number-one sexual fantasy among most of the Western women he met. Yet the uncertainty of her response fired his blood into a slow, pulsing heat. The cat-like slant of her blue eyes was very appealing and he felt another kick of lust as he imagined those eyes growing opaque in time to the powerful thrust of his body. He swallowed, for his groin had grown exquisitely hard in conjunction with his thoughts.

'And now I think we are supposed to dance,' he said unevenly. Slowly, he allowed his gaze to travel all the way down her legs to where her feet were encased in a pair of toweringly high stilettos. 'Before you run off as the clock strikes midnight, and leave one of those gravity-defying and very sexy shoes behind.'

Ella's heart hammered. Of course she *knew* the shoes were sexy—you didn't wear heels this high because they were comfortable. But it came as something of a shock to hear him come right out and say so like that. There was something very blatant about his remark. It made her feel...*weird*.... As if she was something she wasn't. As if she'd worn them so that an arrogant sheikh might look at her legs with unashamed appraisal. And she had certainly not done that.

Every instinct she possessed was screaming out to her to get away from him. But even as the adrenalin pumped around her body, wasn't there a contrary instinct urging her to do precisely the opposite? Didn't she have some insane desire for him to take her into his arms and pull her against his powerful body to see whether he felt as good as he looked?

'I'm not really that into dancing,' she said truthfully.

'Ah, but that's because you've never danced with me,' he drawled as he took her by the hand and led her onto the dance floor. 'Once you have, you'll change your mind. You'll become an instant convert, believe me.'

Ella swallowed. What an arrogant boast to make! Now was the moment for her to wrench her hand away from the firm grip of his fingers and walk away from him and these confused emotions she was experiencing.

So why was she letting him lead her to a spot where the overhanging chandeliers spilled their fractured diamond spangles onto the glossy dance floor? Because she liked his touch, that was why. It was that simple and that complex and it was doing strange things to her. Making her feel light-headed and excited. Making her heart race as if she had just endured an hour's hard workout at the gym.

She felt a brief flash of shame but still she didn't move. And she knew she was about to betray her family by dancing with a man who despised them.

Without warning, Hassan took her into his arms and his presence enveloped her, just as his shadow had done earlier. His body felt as warm and as hard as she'd imagined and she moved closer to him, as his hands splayed possessively across her back.

Remember all those things he said about your family, she reminded herself dazedly. About Izzy sounding like a crow and them all being nothing but tramps.

And yet it was difficult to remember the insults when he was holding her in his arms like this. Difficult to do anything other than melt against him.

'You smell beautiful,' he murmured. 'Of summer meadows in the sun.'

With an effort, Ella lifted her head to stare at the proud jut of his jaw. 'What do sheikhs know of summer meadows?'

'Plenty. When I was a boy, I used to come and visit Alex and sometimes we would go to England, to play the polo at which we both excelled. It was there that I learned that the smell of newly mown grass was one of the most seductive smells in the world.' He smiled against her hair. Particularly if there was a nubile and willing female lying in it, with most of her clothes undone.

Ella could now feel the gentle caress of his fingertips on her bare skin and she knew she had to stop this before it went any further. Before his sexy voice and sure touch made her do anything else she regretted. Turning her face up, she flashed him a smile which was completely insincere. 'You must have been amazed to find someone *tolerably attractive* to dance with among all these women here tonight,' she observed. 'Should I be flattered?'

Hassan frowned at the unexpected change of topic, some subtle emphasis in her words nudging at a faint memory. 'Perhaps you should.' He moved his hand to allow his fingers to tangle briefly in the spill of curls which danced around at the base of her waist. 'Though I imagine that flattery is something you're quite used to.'

The easy compliment slipped off his tongue and it helped fuel her indignation. Ella wriggled a little in his arms. 'Are you always this predictable when you talk to women?'

'Predictable? You want me to be a little more original, do you, Cinderella?' he questioned, feeling the provocative thrust of her beaded breasts pressing into his chest. 'But that would be exceedingly difficult with someone who looks like you. What can I tell you that countless men haven't said before? You must be bored with hearing that your eyes are the blue of a summer sky. Or that your hair is so lustrous that if I moved a little closer, I'd swear I'd be able to see my face in its reflection.'

He positioned his head as if he intended to do just that, but instead he found that his eyes were closing and that he was breathing her in and pulling her against his body. And that suddenly he wanted her very much. It had been, he realised achingly, a long time since he'd held a woman in his arms. Particularly a woman who sent out messages as conflicting as this one...

Ella felt his arms tighten around her and was appalled at how much she wanted to sink further into that embrace. To feel the beat of his heart and to listen to those admiring comments which he probably said to every woman and which meant precisely nothing.

'Hassan,' she said, realising how thready her voice sounded. But why wouldn't it sound like that when he had just splayed his hands so proprietarily over her back? She was wearing a dress which left a lot of skin on show. Skin to which he now had access. She felt the almost imperceptible caress of his fingers and she shivered with a strange kind longing. She had to stop this.

'Or the most beautiful pair of lips I've ever seen. Tell me, does that lipstick come off when a man kisses you and does it taste of roses, or berries?'

'Hassan,' she said again, more weakly this time.

'Mmm? I like it when you say my name. Say it again. Say it as if you want to ask me a big, big favour and let me see if I can guess what that favour might be.'

With an effort, she ignored the shockingly erotic

command and pulled away from him so that she could see his reaction. 'What do you think of the bride-to-be?'

A look of displeasure crossed his face as the sensual mood was broken by her unexpected question. For a moment back then, he'd almost forgotten where he was—and he did not care to be reminded. 'I don't think you want to know,' he said, an unmistakable note of finality in his voice warning her that he did not wish to pursue the topic.

'Oh, but I do,' argued Ella. 'I'm fascinated to hear your opinion. I'm sure it'll be really enlightening.'

He drew back. She was enchanting in her own way, but he thought that she was in danger of overstepping the mark. Didn't she realise that if he wanted a subject closed, then it was closed? Immediately. And that persisting with her girlie questionnaire to test out his views on marriage—which was clearly what this was all about—would put a complete dampener on the rest of the evening? Because if he told her the truth—that marriage was not for him—wouldn't her beautiful scarlet lips inevitably crumple with disappointment?

He wanted to dance with her, to feel the softness of her skin and the press of her flesh against his. If she continued to please him, then he might later take her to his bed, but she must quickly learn that his word was law.

'I think that the less said about the bride-to-be, the better, don't you?' he drawled dismissively.

'No, I don't, actually.' Ella saw the spark of warning glittering in the depths of his black eyes and a sudden, heady power infused her. Was he so spoiled that he was used to people just falling in with his wishes every time he snapped his fingers? Yes, he probably was. She recalled the words of his aide. The smarmy way he had tried to talk him round. Ugh! She leaned forward, her voice probably not as low as it should have been but her rage was so profound that she didn't care. 'But then you've probably exhausted the topic since you've already said quite a few nasty things about Allegra, haven't you?'

He stiffened. 'I *beg* your pardon?'

He had relaxed his hold on her and Ella took the opportunity to step away from the distraction of his touch, staring fearlessly into the ebony glitter of his eyes. 'You heard me,' she said. 'But perhaps you're suffering from some sort of short-term memory loss and need me to remind you of the things you said. Shall I do that?'

'What the hell are you talking about?'

Ella began to count the facts off against her fingers. 'Let's see, you think she's highly unsuitable and that Alex shouldn't be marrying her. Didn't you describe her as a "tramp"—just like her mother and sisters? And didn't you say that you considered the whole Jackson family far too "vulgar" ever to be related to the Crown Prince of Santina?'

'Where the hell did you hear all this?' he demanded.

'I notice that you don't deny it!' she accused, her voice growing louder as several of the other dancers turned their heads to see what was going on. She could see the dawning light of recognition in his eyes and she leapt in for the final thrust, a fierce protectiveness sweeping over her as she thought of her wayward family. 'You delivered your damning verdict on people you have never met, didn't you? And then you left to find someone "tolerably attractive" to dance with. And that someone just happened to be me!'

There was a split second of a pause before his eyes narrowed as he looked at her. 'You're one of the Jacksons?' he guessed.

'Oh, bravo, *Sheikh* Hassan! *Prince of the desert!* It took you long enough to work it out, didn't it? Yes, I'm one of the Jacksons!'

Resisting the desire to show her just how speedy his responses could be, he glared at her. 'You were eavesdropping in the anteroom!'

'And if I was?'

'Eavesdropping!' he repeated contemptuously. A slow anger began to build inside him as he met the defiant light in her blue eyes. But in truth, he was furious with himself for not having followed his own instincts. He had *thought* that he'd heard something, and yet he had allowed himself to be convinced otherwise. And wasn't that lazy and dangerous behaviour from a king, especially one who had just left behind a war zone? Was he getting complacent now that he was away from the battlefields?

He lowered his voice to an angry hiss. 'That's exactly the kind of vulgar attitude I would have expected from a family such as yours, and one which completely vindicates my belief about your general unsuitability to be mixing in royal circles. I rest my case.'

It wasn't so much the hateful things he was saying which made Ella's blood boil, but the sanctimonious way he was saying them. As if *he* was in the right and she was in the wrong! As if he was allowed to say what he pleased and there wasn't a thing she could do about it. Her blood was pounding in her veins as she felt her rage rise, and an odd kind of hurt and frustration come bubbling to the surface.

People were staring at them quite openly now, but she didn't care.

'Unsuitability?' she declared. 'I'll show you un-suitability if you want!' Almost without thinking, she grabbed a glass of champagne from a passing wait-ress and tossed it over his dark, mocking face before turning to push her way through the throng of open-mouthed spectators.

CHAPTER TWO

For a moment Hassan was frozen into shocked immobility, scarcely able to believe what had just happened. The impudent minx of a Jackson girl had thrown champagne over him!

Angrily, he wiped both cheeks, aware that people were staring at him, their voices beginning to rise in excited chatter above the brief, stunned silence which had followed their very public row. But he barely paid them any attention. He was too busy watching the tottering sway of 'Cinderella' Jackson's silver-clad bottom as she moved through the ballroom, as swiftly as her ridiculously high heels would allow.

He could see his bodyguard fixing him with a questioning look, as if seeking permission to go after her and give her a crash course in royal protocol. But Hassan gave a decisive shake of his head as a cold realisation crept over him.

How dare she humiliate him in such a way? And in *public*! Why, if a man in his own country had done such a thing, he would have been thrown immediately into the city jail!

His mouth hardening into a grim line, he began to follow her, his long stride quickly covering the distance between them. Now he was close enough to hear the clatter of her high heels on the marble floor and see the gleam of light as it highlighted the curve of her silver-beaded bottom. He saw her glance over her shoulder, her blue eyes widening when she saw him behind her, and a brief sensation of anticipation rippled over his skin as she increased her speed.

Silently, he pursued her, pleased when she briefly hesitated between two corridors—one wide and one narrow. She wouldn't have a clue where she was going, he thought with satisfaction, whereas he knew well the labyrinth network of passageways which comprised the Santina palace. Hadn't he and Alex played hide-and-seek in them often enough when they were children?

She chose the narrower passage and he continued to shadow her, knowing that he could easily have caught up with her there and then but he was enjoying the thrill of the chase too much to want to end it. It was like being back in battle, his senses honed and height-ened as he pursued his quarry.…

Only when the main body of the palace had re-treated and the corridors were bare of servants did he surge forward. She whirled round as he backed her into a corner, her breath coming in short little pants. Her abundant curls were spilling down over the silver dress, one thigh was pushed forward as if to showcase its honed perfection, and he thought that he had never seen a woman look so wild and so wanton.

'Got you,' he said, his voice a triumphant murmur, but he didn't touch her.

Ella stared at him, her heart pounding so hard that it felt as if it was about to leap out of her chest. She was hot and out of breath. Running in these heels had been a stupid thing to try to do because her feet now felt as if they were on fire. What had possessed her to react like that? To dare to chuck a drink over a man who was now towering above her looking like the devil incarnate, a patch of his pristine white shirt clinging wetly to his chest. A man who was different from every other man she'd ever met. Well, she had done it, and now she just had to keep her nerve.

'You don't scare me!' she blurted out, but she wondered how convincing her words were as she met emptiness of his eyes.

'Don't I?' Hassan leaned in a little. 'Then maybe I need to try a little harder. Most people would be pretty scared of my reaction if they'd done what you've just done.' He observed her rapid breathing which was causing the silver beads over her breasts to shimmer in a provocative sway. And suddenly it was difficult to remember just why he was so angry. He swallowed, so unbearably turned on that for a moment he could not speak. 'That was some scene you created back there.'

Ella told herself that she ought to tread carefully. That she was dealing with someone who had danger written all over him. Someone who she, with her laughable lack of experience, didn't have a clue how to deal with. The voice of reason was telling her to try to make it right between them, yet the apology she knew she really ought to make stayed stubbornly unspoken. For how could she forget those harsh things he'd said?

'Who cares about a scene?' she questioned stubbornly.

He met the defiance in her ice-blue eyes. 'Clearly

you don't, but then you don't have any reputation to
wreck, do you?'

Actually, she *did*. She'd worked hard to build her
own business and she survived on the income it provided. But the irony was that causing a scene with the
sheikh was likely to bring new customers flocking to
her, instead of taking their custom elsewhere. The fact
that she was even *mixing* with royals would be great
publicity. A bit of scandal never seemed to affect *her*
client base. Hadn't she noticed a definite growth in
business whenever her father's face was splashed all
over the papers, no matter how dodgy the story? 'And
you do, I suppose?'

'Of course I do!' he snapped. 'I am the ruler of a
desert kingdom and my word is law. In fact, I *make*
the laws.'

'Wow! Mr. Powerful,' she mocked.

Her insolence was turning him on almost as much
as it was infuriating him. He felt a muscle working in
his cheek and an even more insistent throbbing at his
groin. 'And I have people who look up to me who will
not enjoy reading that their king had champagne flung
at him by a brazen English nobody.'

'I should have thought that people would have been
used to your *flings* by now!' she returned, and for one
brief moment she thought she saw the edges of his
lips tilt in the beginning of a smile. But it quickly disappeared and so did her small moment of triumph as
she reminded herself that this man was the enemy.
'Anyway, you should have thought about that before
you started laying into my family.'

'By telling the truth, you mean?'

'It's not—'

'Oh, please, spare me the empty defence!' His eyes took on a look of challenge. 'You're denying that your father is no stranger to the bankruptcy court? Or that your sister's awful singing brought the house down, but not in a good way? Or that the Crown Prince has dumped his long-term girlfriend and fiancée in order to marry your other sister?'

Ella gritted her teeth. 'If only there was another waitress nearby, I'd happily upend *another* drink all over you!'

'Would you now?' He tilted his head to one side and studied her. 'And do you make a habit of resorting to playground tactics?'

'Only if I'm forced to deal with the class bully!' Ella stared at him with growing bewilderment. Why did she feel this overpowering sense of *frustration* which was making her want to pummel her fists against the solid wall of his chest? 'Actually, I've never done anything like that before.'

'No? You just thought you'd make an exception for me, did you?' He stared at her, wanting to crush her rosy lips beneath his. Wanting more than that. Wanting to feel the soft surrender of her body as it gave itself up to the hard dominance of his own. 'I wonder why?'

The arrogant flick of his gaze made her skin grow heated. 'Because you're overbearing, overopinionated and ridiculously traditional? Could that give you some sort of clue? You spout such outdated and macho comments that it's obviously made me react to you in an uncharacteristically primitive way!' Raking her fingers back through the wayward spill of her curls, she glared at him. 'And you obviously haven't got a clue what the modern world is like.'

His eyes narrowed. 'You think that I am a stranger to the modern world?'

Suddenly, Ella wasn't sure what she thought. Not any more. Not when he was staring at her so intently and every cell in her body was responding to that black-eyed scrutiny. Her senses seemed to be short-circuiting her brain, but there was one thing she was certain of. He'd just lumped her in with the rest of her family and he seemed stubbornly unrepentant about doing it. Maybe it was time he discovered how it felt to be treated as if you were simply a stereotype, instead of an individual.

She met the challenge in his eyes with one of her own. 'Yes, I think you're a stranger to the modern world! How can you not be? How can you know how most people live if you're stuck in some remote desert country where you probably travel round by camel and sleep in a tent?'

For a moment Hassan could scarcely believe his ears. *Camel?* It was true that his most recent months had been spent on horseback as he had battled to settle the long-running dispute on the borders of his country. But although much in his life involved the ancient and the traditional, he had also insisted on embracing every new technology, for he recognised that there could be no real progress without it. He thought about his fleet of cars, the state-of-the-art aircraft and the engineers he employed to search for ever more eco-friendly alternative travel.

'Now you insult my land,' he observed furiously. 'And thus my honour.'

'As you did mine!'

He met the rebellious gleam in her blue eyes. 'I said nothing which isn't true. Whereas you have just passed judgement on my homeland without knowing a single thing about it.'

'Well, that's tough. Deal with it. And now, if you wouldn't mind stepping out of the way, I'd like to leave.'

Hassan tensed. Was it her continuing defiance which made something inside him tighten? Something which had been tightening ever since he'd first started dancing with her and felt her soft and fragrant body in his arms.

Women never answered him back like this. They usually went out of their way to accommodate him. They didn't hurl champagne at him and then storm away, wiggling their silver bottom in a provocative movement which was designed to ensnare his fast-hardening body. For all her professed disdain of him and all he stood for, there was an undeniable sexual charge sparking through the air between them. It had been there from the outset and nothing they'd said or done had diminished it. He could read her hunger in the darkening of her eyes and in the flagrant thrust of her nipples as they pushed against the tiny silver beads of her dress.

He felt urgent sexual desire fire him up, heating his blood with its insistent throb. He'd barely been a week back from battle when he had flown here to Alex's party and the contrast between this glittering event and the months of arid hardship could not have been greater.

Warfare put many pressures on a man and perhaps the greatest of those was the absence of sex. For so long now he had sublimated his fierce sexual appetite in battle that it had become almost habitual. In some ways he welcomed it, for not only did it channel his energy into fighting, it also made him feel powerful. It gave him strength to know that he could subdue the weaknesses of the flesh. Yet how could he have forgotten what it felt like to be in thrall to his senses? And how could he not but thank a fate which had conspired to put him alone with a beautiful and eager young woman?

He looked around. The corridor was empty and bare of staff. Should he take her here and risk discovery? Or simply give her a taste of what would inevitably follow—the teasing brush of his lips over hers, the butterfly caress of his fingers over her jewel-covered breasts?

Yet he recognised that this tumble-haired brunette was a challenge, and that only fuelled his hunger, for he loved to conquer and to tame. That was his default mechanism. A way of inflicting control onto a life which had been filled with chaos.

Now that his anger had dissipated, there remained only desire. He remembered her defiance and the way she had struck him and his heart began to thunder. How it would please him to see her subdued. To hear her begging him to enter her, her fiery spirit temporarily silenced by her hunger for him!

His eyes were drawn downwards to see the way

she had wriggled a restless-looking foot and he gave a slow smile, for he could read women as well as he could read his beloved falcons when he raced them over the desert skies.

'Your feet are aching,' he observed softly.

Ella's eyes widened, momentarily disarmed by the lazy question in his. Had he read her mind? And what was it about this quiet corner of the palace which made her feel as if they had been suddenly cloaked in a quiet intimacy, so that she responded to him frankly? 'My shoes are killing me,' she admitted.

'Then take them off. Isn't that what Cinderella is supposed to do?'

The words were faintly erotic and Ella opened her mouth to protest, but when she thought about it, why not? Loads of women shed their shoes at parties. Some even secreted a pair of pumps in their bag. She made as if to bend but before she could move Hassan was there before her, crouching down to slide off both her high heels with a dexterity which made her think he might have done that kind of thing before. Briefly, he ran a thumb across her cramped toes and they gave an appreciative little wriggle before he put them down to meet the delicious coolness of the marble floor.

He straightened up, his black eyes mocking as they looked at her. 'Better?'

Ella nodded. Sure, her feet now felt comfortable and free, but stupidly she was missing his touch. Because hadn't it felt like some kind of delicious intimacy to have the sheikh's fingers on her toes? She forced a smile.

'Much better,' she said.

He handed her the shoes. 'Are you heading back to the party?'

Hooking her fingers through the glittery slingbacks, she shook her head. She couldn't possibly go back now, and not just because she had left the ballroom in such dramatic circumstances. She just couldn't face any more of this wretched partying, supposedly celebrating an engagement which nobody seemed happy about. Except for the happy couple, presumably.

'No. I think I'll call it a night. I need to organise a car to get back to my hotel.'

'I'll walk you back to the main entrance.'

Ella's heart raced as fear and desire fused into a molten ache at the base of her belly. It was something to do with the way he was looking at her, her sudden awareness of how close he was. Close enough for her to be able to inhale his distinctly masculine scent, just as he'd done on the dance floor. And to remember him sliding the shoes from her feet like some old-fashioned fairy tale, in reverse. Because wasn't the prince supposed to put the shoe *on*? She felt the rapid thunder of her heart. 'No, honestly. I'll be fine.'

His eyes narrowed. 'You know where you're going, do you?'

For the first time she became aware of her surroundings, of the dim silence of the cool corridor, in a network of passageways which all seemed to look exactly the same. She suddenly realised that there were no sounds of revelry drifting towards them and that they must be miles away from the other guests. But then she'd run like the wind, hadn't she? Running to escape him wearing too-high heels which explained her aching feet and why she now found herself in some unknown corner of a strange palace.

Should she brazen it out? Tell him that she'd find her own way back and she didn't need his help, thank you very much? That would be the most sensible thing. To walk away with her pride intact, and with some sort of uneasy truce having been reached between them. 'I'll be fine.'

'Are you sure? It's a bit of a maze. And I'd hate to think of you wandering around in circles for hours.'

'But a maze which you can negotiate with the ease of a born navigator, I suppose?'

He shrugged his shoulders. 'As it happens, I do have a superb sense of direction, but I also happen to know the palace well. I used to spend a lot of time here with Alex when we were children.'

Ella's fingers tightened around the straps of her shoes. It was strange to imagine this towering man with the cruel face ever having been a child. Had he told her that to emphasise his own royal credentials, reinforcing the fact that *her* family were simply arriviste social climbers?

Yet as she met the mockery in his black eyes, she realised that maybe she should do the grown-up thing and accept his offer. The last thing she wanted was to spend hours walking around this cavernous place and wandering into some part of the palace which was out of bounds.

She need never see him again—except, presumably, at the wedding, when her sister would marry his friend. And surely it would be better to part on cordial terms, particularly after she'd thrown champagne all over him. In fact, it was surprising and rather reassuring that he seemed to have forgotten all about that.

This time her smile was wider, even if it didn't feel exactly joyful. But then *joy* wasn't a word you really associated with a man whose eyes were so hard and so black they looked as if they'd been made from some rare, cold stone. 'In that case, yes, please. I wouldn't mind being pointed in the right direction.'

Hassan allowed a brief smile to curve the edges of his lips. 'Let's go,' he said softly, knowing instantly the route he was about to take.

They made no sound as they moved through the high-ceilinged passage, but Ella was so aware of him that she didn't take in any of the spectacular surroundings. For once, the ornate decor was completely overshadowed by Hassan himself. Without the added inches of her heels, his height and his breadth were almost intimidating. Did he always dominate his surroundings and the people in them? she wondered.

His question broke into her muddled thoughts. 'How long are you staying on the island?'

'I'm flying back to London tomorrow.'

'After lunch?'

Ella shrugged, dreading the thought of yet another formal meal while people looked down their noses at her and her family. She'd been hoping to escape and slip back to England straight after breakfast but from what she understood attendance at the lunch seemed to be mandatory. She was quickly learning that you weren't allowed to say no to royals. 'Yes.'

Hearing the note of heavy resignation in her voice, Hassan glanced down at her. She wasn't doing anything he had expected her to do. He'd expected a little more gratitude that he'd forgiven her for her shocking display of temper, and the seductive removal of her shoes would usually have guaranteed that by now she'd be glancing up at him from beneath her lashes and flirting like crazy. But she was doing no such thing. Instead her gaze seemed fixed firmly ahead of her, like a runner who had their eyes on the finish line. Like someone longing to reach their destination.

Was she?

Or was she just trying to dampen down the desire which had been so apparent since they'd first set eyes on each other? He let his eyes linger on her body as she moved. The shimmer of her silver dress was enhancing her willowy frame and the thick gleam of her dark hair made him want to run his fingers through it. And somehow her bare toes, with their gleam of silver polish, were much sexier without the stilt-like shoes he'd just removed. He felt a renewed stab of lust.

'So would you like a glass of champagne before you leave?' he questioned. 'Or is that just asking for trouble?'

'Champagne?' It was the hint of unexpected humour in his voice which made her waver, until she reminded herself of her dramatic exit from the ballroom. She stared up at him, her hair shimmying around her face. 'But I don't want to go back to the party.'

'I know. But since we're right by my own suite, I thought you might like to see it.' His lips curved into a smile. 'Especially as it happens to contain some fabulous paintings.'

It was ironic that he seemed unwittingly to have hit

on the one thing designed to make her heart beat faster and yet Ella's one feeling was one of disappointment. It seemed that all men were predictably similar, whether they were desert princes or hedge fund managers. 'As in, "Come up and see my etchings," I suppose?' she questioned sarcastically. 'Gosh, you really *do* need to take a refresher course when you're trying to chat up a woman!'

'I had no idea that I was dealing with such an expert in chat-up lines,' he murmured. 'Or perhaps you just don't like beautiful paintings?'

She heard the subtle put-down. There was that judgement of his all over again. Did he think she was too common to appreciate anything of beauty, that a Jackson would only ever enjoy some mindless pap on TV, or flicking through an undemanding glossy magazine? The anger which she'd thought had been extinguished now began to simmer once more. But infuriatingly, it was manifesting itself in the prickle of her breasts and a soft, melting feeling at the fork of her thighs. It was making her throat dry just to look at him, and her heart fluttered madly. 'Or perhaps I just don't like strange men coming on to me with sexual innuendo?'

'Ah, Cinders, Cinders,' he mocked as he watched the battle between her provocative words and her blossoming body. And wasn't it echoing the same battle which was taking place in his own? 'I was simply talking about art, yet all you seem to want to talk about is sex. And just what *is* your real name, by the way?'

'It's Ella,' she said, her head spinning. 'And will you

please stop twisting everything I say? I *don't* want to talk about sex!'

'Neither do I,' he agreed unexpectedly. 'Since talking about it is a complete waste of time.'

Before she properly realised what he was going to do, he had pulled her into his arms. Pulled her right up close to his aroused body and, with a thrill of shocked recognition, she was letting him. An urgent kind of hunger overwhelmed her as she felt the weight of his hands at her back. The touch of his fingers on her bare skin was as electric as it had been on the dance floor and it had precisely the same sizzling effect on her. Only this time they weren't in a crowd with the curious eyes of the other dancers on them. This time they were dangerously alone.

She opened her mouth to say something but by then his curiously empty eyes had begun to blaze into life as he lowered his head towards her. And then it was too late.

His lips came down to meet hers and Ella's mouth opened of its own volition, and she found herself unwillingly lost in the most sensational kiss of her life.

CHAPTER THREE

ELLA swayed as Hassan kissed her, his arms tightening around her so that every hard sinew of his powerful frame seemed to be imprinted indelibly on her body. She could feel the pricking of her breasts and their sudden aching heaviness as they pressed against him. And she could feel the coiling heat which was building inside her, pooling in an erotic, silken warmth at the juncture of her thighs.

The thunder of her heart played a backing-track as his lips explored hers and she sank against him. Yet even as his tongue slid inside her mouth and her eyelids fluttered to a close she knew that something wasn't right. Through a haze, she tried to remember just what that something was, but her greedy body seemed intent on pushing all sane thoughts from her mind. The blood pooling in her breasts and at her groin was denying her brain the vital fuel it needed in order to think clearly. But how could she think clearly when she was feeling like *this*?

She gasped as Hassan caught hold of her breast, his big hand splaying with arrogant possession over its hardening swell. Against the finely beaded surface, he teased the already-aching nipple with his finger, and at that split second she remembered the source of her discomfort.

She hated him.

And he hated her.

He was supposed to be showing her the way out of the palace…and instead he had her pressed up against some cool palace wall where he seemed intent on having hot and urgent sex with her.

So why wasn't she pushing him away and professing outrage at his seduction? Why was she winding the arm which wasn't holding her shoes around his neck and breathing urgent little sounds of encouragement?

Because she'd never felt like this before.

Never imagined that a woman could feel like this when a man kissed her. As if this was what her body had been invented for. Her one previous sexual experience now just seemed a mockingly bland rehearsal for this rapid awakening which was making her blood fizz.

But it was wrong. It was *very, very* wrong.

'Hassan.' With an effort, she tore her mouth away from his as her high heels nearly slipped from her fingers onto the floor. 'This is…absolutely…*crazy*….' She thought how weak her voice sounded. As if he had somehow sapped all her strength and resolve.

'Don't break the spell, Cinderella,' he warned unsteadily, pushing open the door to his suite. Pulling her inside, he kicked the door shut, before taking her into his arms and beginning to kiss her again, as if that might obliterate any objections she might have.

And it was working, wasn't it? It didn't seem to matter that she was in the bedroom of a man who was a virtual stranger—a dark and empty-eyed sheikh who had spoken about her family with the cruel lash of his tongue. Such was his skill that he melted away every single doubt beneath the practised caress of his lips. His hands stroked their way down over her body as he kissed her, until her nerve endings were raw with desire and she was moving restlessly in his arms.

Her skin felt heated, her body on fire. She groaned when he cupped her breast again, his thumb brushing negligently against the bead-covered nipple. Why couldn't he touch her bare skin instead, she wondered distractedly when, as if he'd read her thoughts again, he reached out and peeled down the flimsy bodice of her dress.

He leaned back a little to survey her, the way people did in art galleries when they wanted to get a better look at a painting. His eyes seemed to devour her breasts and she felt the skin tighten and tingle beneath that fierce black scrutiny.

'Do you always go braless?' he questioned unsteadily.

She wanted to tell him that the fashionable dress had made the wearing of a bra impossible but somehow the words seemed to have lodged in her throat.

'But then again, why would you ever cover up anything so beautiful as these pert little breasts?' he continued as he grazed a lazy thumb over one hardening nub. 'I like the fact that they are so instantly accessible. That they are within easy reach of the curl of my tongue.'

She wanted to protest at the outrageous mastery of his words but he leaned forward to suckle a taut nipple and the corresponding shaft of desire made her body shudder helplessly.

She could see the erotic contrast of his black head against her pale skin and could feel his tongue licking sensual pathways over the diamond-hard nub. And suddenly, the pleasure almost became too intense to bear. She felt her knees begin to sag and he responded by bending down to curl his arm beneath them to pick her up. He carried her across the glittering gilded room towards an arch beyond which she could see a massive, canopied bed. And the reality of what was about to happen hit home.

'Hassan?'

'That's my name.'

His teasing words momentarily distracted her. But not nearly as much as the warmth of his fingers as they pressed against her bare flesh. 'We…we shouldn't be doing this.'

'Shouldn't we? You don't sound very certain.'

That's because she wasn't. She'd never been carried by a man before and it was making her feel intensely *feminine*. As if for the first time in her life, she'd found someone strong enough to protect her. Her loosened dress was flapping against her bare breasts and she looked up to find his black eyes burning into her as if she was the most beautiful thing he'd ever seen. She had never felt quite so desired, nor so deliciously compliant.

He put her down on the bed and she lay there watching as he shrugged off his jacket and let it fall to the floor. His tie followed, and then his silk shirt. Shoes and socks were efficiently disposed of and then his

hand moved to the belt of his trousers, gingerly easing
them down over his formidable erection. Completely
absorbed by what was happening, Ella stared at him,
unable to tear her eyes away from his magnificent
body. Surely she should have felt shy at such a careless striptease, but she didn't feel a bit shy. Was that
because he knew that his hard, honed body was the
closest thing to perfection she had ever seen?

He moved to the bed, his face a dark mask as he bent
over her, his fingers moving to find the zip of her dress.
But the zip seemed to have been jammed by some errant beads and when he tugged at it, the whole thing
split, sending silver beads spilling all around them,
some rolling from the bed and others cascading onto
the floor. Ella heard someone laugh and realised that
someone was her, and that her arms were reaching up
to him and pulling him down to her.

He gave an unsteady laugh. 'So your sexual appetite matches your temper, does it, Cinders?'

'Does yours?' she murmured back, completely for-
getting her abysmal track record with men as she felt
the brush of his lips over her shoulder.

Her provocative reply fired him up even more.
Hassan had never felt quite so out of control before,
knowing that what he was about to do was sheer
madness and yet somehow powerless to stop himself.
Because hadn't he denied himself the comfort of a
woman for too long? He had forgotten how it felt to
touch silken skin, and the sweet contrast between the
hard male body and its yielding female counterpart.

Yet there were a hundred women more suitable as

lovers than she. Women back in that ballroom who had plenty of aristocratic credentials. Who knew how to behave and how not to behave. Who would never have doused him in champagne and then submitted to him so easily. He should go back right now. Renounce this insolent Jackson while he still had the strength left in him to do so.

But now her milky thighs were spreading wide, silently urging him into their secret, molten depths, and Hassan knew that it was too late. With fingers which weren't quite steady, he reached for a condom. Everything he wanted at that moment was centred on this woman and all he had to do was push his hard flesh into her silken sweetness to find that elusive peace.

Unable to wait any longer, he slithered her skimpy lace panties down, tossing them away before moving over her and positioning himself against her quivering heat. With an urgent moan he entered her, moving deep into her body with a trembling hunger he could barely restrain.

Ella gasped as she felt Hassan's intimate possession, momentarily dazed as his enormous length and power began to fill her. Surely he was too big for any woman? For a moment she tensed as she allowed her body to accommodate his and she could feel herself stretching and then settling, her blood pumping and her heart giving a little leap of joy. She made an instinctive sound of pleasure and he looked down at her, smoothing some of her tousled hair from her hot cheeks.

'Does that feel good?' he demanded.

'It feels f-fantastic,' she managed.

'Then let's see if I can make it even better, shall we?'

It sounded like an arrogant sexual boast, but somehow she didn't care. Especially as his words were true. He was making it *irresistible*. And somehow instinct made her respond to him in a way which relegated her relative inexperience to distant memory. Suddenly, she felt like the woman she had thought she could never be. Who could respond with passion and eagerness. No longer a miserable block of ice but a fiery equal who knew exactly what she wanted.

Her hips rose to meet his as she quickly became attuned to each powerful thrust. Clinging to his sweat-sheened back, she felt the powerful play of muscles moving beneath his silken skin as he thrust into her.

'Hassan!' she gasped.

'*Ladheedh!*' he ground out gutturally, in his native tongue

Helplessly, her head fell back as he kissed her neck and then her breasts, brushing his hungry lips against the tight buds of her nipples, increasing the urgent pleasure which was building inside her with every second.

Hassan groaned. She felt so *hot*. So *tight*. How many nights in the desert had he fantasised about being inside a woman's body like this, before spilling his warm, wet seed onto his own frustrated fingers?

He drove deep inside her before lifting her legs to wrap them around his back so that he could go deeper still. He could feel her fingers digging into his back, could hear her breathless little moans of pleasure as his own began to snowball. Was it because it had been so long that it felt this good? Or because it was so sudden and unexpected, and with none of the usual prerequisites demanded by even the most predatory of women? He felt as if he was clinging by his fingernails to the edge of a cliff, and at any minute he might simply lose control and slip away.

For a moment, he watched her. She looked lost in her own little world: her hair was splayed against the white of the pillow and her lips were parted so that he could see the gleam of her teeth. He watched as her lashes fluttered open so that their gazes locked but he quickly shut his eyes. For why would a man ever choose to let a woman look at him when he was at his most vulnerable?

Instead he began to concentrate on giving her pleasure, and thus taking back the control he had felt in danger of losing. Over and over again, he edged her to the very brink, like a man determined to showcase his repertoire of sensual skills. He heard her murmured little pleas, the entreaties she made, all warm and muffled against his ears.

'What?' he whispered. 'What is it, my fiery little beauty?'

'Please...' Her word trailed away as another wave of sensation swept over her.

He smiled, enjoying his habitual feel of dominance once more. She wasn't so defiant now, was she? 'I can't hear you,' he whispered.

Ella knew what he was doing. He was manipulating her. Playing with her as a cat would a mouse just before it moved in for the kill. She knew how she *should* respond—she should tell him to go to hell—but she was too desperate to hold back. Too eager to experience something which had always remained elusively just out of reach. 'Please, Hassan,' she whimpered. 'Oh, *please*.'

That breathless little plea was his undoing and with one final, powerful thrust he gave her the orgasm she had been begging for, as he had been determined she would do right from the start. But even Hassan could not fail to be carried along on the powerful tide as the spasms began to rack her body and he felt her contracting around him. And somehow, there was a quality in her shuddered little cry which he had never heard before. Something inexplicable which reached out and touched the very heart of him.

Unexpectedly, his own orgasm took him under. It hit him with a powerful force which was strangely bittersweet, so that afterwards he felt as empty as if she had drained him of all life. He heard the shudder of his breath as he sucked air deep into his lungs and felt the sheen of sweat drying on his body. For a few seconds, he felt as close to death as he had ever done in battle, while beneath him, he felt her warm body stir. Long seconds passed before she spoke. He'd been praying that she wouldn't, that instead she would just drift off into sleep and let some of this curious intensity he felt just ebb away. But it was not to be.

'Hassan?' she said drowsily.

'What?'

She swallowed. 'That was…*amazing*.'

'I know it was.'

'I can't believe it happened. It's never—'

'Shh,' he said, because her breathless words were

making him uncomfortable. Carefully, he pulled himself away from her body, his skin beginning to chill as reality slowly returned and he realised what he had done. What a hypocrite he had been! So full of proud words and certainties about the correct and proper way to behave. And yet how could he possibly pass judgement on his friend Alex, when he had proved to be just as weak as he? Despite all his contemptuous words on the subject of suitability, he had taken one of the Jackson sisters to his bed, had stripped her bare and made love to her.

Why the hell had he done *that*?

A cold self-contempt clenched at his heart as he lay there, wondering what he was going to say to her—what *could* he say to her, other than words of bitter regret? But when he turned his head, he saw that she'd fallen asleep, her head pillowed on her arm. She stirred and murmured something, the dark feathered arcs of her lashes fluttering a little. And he held his breath, unaccountably relieved when she turned over and snuggled down against the pillow.

He closed his eyes as he remembered their steamy moves on the dance floor, and then that very public row. She'd left, he'd followed and neither of them had returned. His jaw tightened. What on earth must the other party guests have thought of such behaviour?

And what the hell did he do now?

He *escaped*, that's what he did. Just as if he had been captured by the enemy in battle. He must get away from there before his weak body succumbed and made love to her all over again. Because while once might be regarded as regrettable, twice would be considered a serious error of judgement.

As if on cue, she gave a little moan and snuggled her face deeper into the pillow and, with the skill of the born hunter, he slid noiselessly from the bed. Silently, he collected his discarded clothes, but not before he noticed the silver beads from her ripped dress which lay scattered on the marble floor. With a shudder he imagined the reaction of the palace maids when they arrived to clean his room in the morning. But what was the alternative? That he should start crawling around on his hands and knees, trying to pick them up himself?

In the seclusion of the bathroom, he rapidly pulled on his clothes and from there he made a call to his aide.

Benedict picked up on the second ring. 'Highness?'

Hassan's voice was low. 'Prepare the plane for a flight back to Kashamak. I want to leave as soon as possible.'

'But, Highness, you're supposed to be attending the lunch tomorrow.'

'Well, I won't be,' said Hassan flatly. 'I'll email Alex when I get back. Oh, and Benedict, one more thing.'

'Highness?'

'Have someone bring some women's clothes to my suite first thing in the morning, will you? And before you make any wisecracks, no, I haven't suddenly acquired an appetite for cross-dressing.'

Benedict didn't miss a beat. 'Anything in particular you require, Highness?'

'Something which would be suitable for the lady in question to wear back to her hotel,' said Hassan, pausing as an inconveniently erotic stab of memory made him recall the naked body currently sprawled out on his rumpled sheets. 'American dress size six, I'd imagine.'

CHAPTER FOUR

ELLA stirred, lost in that disorientating split second between sleeping and waking. Where was she? Luxuriously, she stretched her arms above her head. Certainly not at her house in Tooting, that was for sure, because the thunder of lorries past the window was noticeably absent.

The trill of birdsong alerted her at exactly the same time as she registered the soft, moist ache between her legs. And the warm sunlight which bathed her skin. Giving a dreamy little murmur of contentment, she glanced down to see that she was completely naked, and that there were tiny blue marks blooming on her breasts, as if someone had been grazing at them with their teeth. And that was when her memory came rushing back.

Someone *had* been grazing them with their teeth! And a lot more besides.

Sheikh Hassan Al Abbas, to be precise.

With a sharp intake of breath, she grabbed the sheet and pulled it up to her chin. Lying perfectly still, she listened for the sound of movement. Her eyes stole to the other side of the enormous bed, to the rumpled indentation, where Hassan had lain.

So she hadn't imagined it.

Heat flared over her bare skin as vivid images clicked their way into her mind. The way she'd writhed beneath him and *begged* him to make love to her. The way she'd shuddered out his name as he'd made her climax.

She flushed with remembered pleasure. The first and only man ever to have brought her to orgasm and it had to have been *him*.

Her heart pounded. So where the hell was he now?

The bathroom, most probably. She raked her fingers through her tousled hair as she prepared herself for an embarrassing encounter with the man with whom she'd had wild sex the night before.

How *could* she? How could she have fallen into bed with a man who'd made no secret of his contempt for her and her family? Why, he'd barely had to try before she'd allowed him to practically rip her clothes off. Her eyes travelled to the silver dress which lay in a sad little heap on the floor, looking like last year's Christmas decoration, the tiny beads scattered in all directions.

And yet, hadn't he been the most fantastic and unselfish lover, hadn't he destroyed all her doubts and uncertainties along the way? Beneath his expert caresses and amazing lovemaking, he'd made her feel things she'd never felt before. Desire and hunger and *fulfilment*. Like a real woman instead of the frozen and uptight version she'd believed herself to be.

She glanced at the watch which was still on her wrist, appalled to see that it was gone nine. How ironic that the longest sleep she'd had in years should be on the morning when she wasn't even supposed to *be* in the royal palace. She was supposed to be tucked up in that fancy hotel with the rest of her family. What on earth would they say when she didn't turn up for a post-mortem of the party over their breakfast eggs?

Where *was* he?

But even as the true extent of the situation in which she now found herself sank in, Ella made a decision. It had happened and there was absolutely nothing she could do about it. It had been amazing and unexpected and she wasn't going to act all shame-faced and cowed. They had *both* been responsible for what had taken place last night.

And if he decided that he had enjoyed it so much that he wanted to do it all over again, what then? Ella stared at the ceiling, unable to prevent the rush of memories from flooding back. Wouldn't she be only too happy to start over, so they could prove to each other that first impressions needn't necessarily count?

'Hassan?' she called softly.

No answer.

She wondered if he was in the shower, perhaps lathering creamy soap over that honed, olive skin. Suddenly, she could imagine only too well what that might look like. The hard, flat planes of his body. The powerful legs, the taut stomach and the dark mass of hair which grew around his manhood. She closed her eyes. She wasn't going to take herself there. It had been…well, it had been absolutely fantastic. But she wasn't going to read too much into it, not at this stage. All she wanted was to get back to her family as soon as possible, and she needed his help to do that.

'Hassan!' Her voice was louder now but there was still no reply, when just at that moment came a rap at the door.

What should she do?

Ignore it? Wait for Hassan to come out of the bathroom and deal with it himself? Surely, the fewer people who saw her here, the better.

But the rap was repeated and there came the distinct and undeniable sound of someone saying *her* name.

'Miss Jackson?'

Ella screwed up her nose in confusion. That was her. No way on earth she could deny it. How the hell did they know she was here? Wrapping the sheet around her like a fancy-dress version of a Grecian goddess, she padded barefoot to the door, pulling it open and gazing suspiciously through the small crack. Outside stood a tall man she didn't recognise, with a polite smile on his face and what looked like some dry-cleaning hanging over his arm.

'Miss Jackson?' he said again.

Ella screwed her eyes up. 'Who are you?'

'You don't know me. My name is Benedict Austin and I work as an aide to Sheikh Hassan Al Abbas. He asked me to make sure that you got this.'

With this, he handed her the package and Ella blinked. 'What is it?'

'You'll find some clothes in there. The sheikh was most insistent that you have them, since I understand that you…' He hesitated. 'Spilt some wine down your dress last night.'

Ella could feel herself blushing since she suspected that this man knew very well what had *really* happened to her dress. And in that moment, she felt furious. Why couldn't Hassan have had the decency to hand over the clothes himself instead of sending one of his puppets to do the deed? She looked the aide straight in the eye. 'Do you have any idea where he is?'

'The sheikh?' The aide gave an apologetic shrug as if this was a question he had been asked by indignant women many times during his career. 'I'm afraid he had to fly back to Kashamak with some urgency. There were pressing affairs of state which he needed to attend to.'

Ella had thought it wasn't possible to feel any worse than she already did, but this new piece of information just went to show how wrong she could be. So he had done a runner. He had left without even bothering to say goodbye.

Humiliated, she wanted to tell this Benedict Austin just what he could do with his clothes, but pride told her that was a luxury she couldn't afford. What had happened was bad enough, but if she was seen slinking out of the palace wearing a tattered version of last night's dress then she might as well carry a banner, announcing to the world how she'd spent the night.

'Thank you,' she said with as much dignity as she could muster, before taking the proffered package and quietly closing the door on him.

Some women might have cried, but not Ella. She was a survivor. She wasn't about to waste her tears on someone as unworthy as Hassan Al Abbas. Instead she concentrated on making herself presentable enough to find her way out of the strange palace.

A shower and vigorous hair wash got rid of every

last trace of the sheikh's scent from her body, even if the memory of him wasn't quite so easy to shift.

She stared at herself in the mirror, reading the bewilderment which had darkened her blue eyes and wondering why she had behaved like that.

Hadn't she spent her whole life despairing at how easily her mother had capitulated to the whims of her straying ex-husband, allowing him back in her life whenever it pleased him? Time and time again she had begged her mum to grow a little backbone and stand up to the man who'd made such a fool of her. But once she'd realised that her mother would listen to nothing except the demands of her own heart, Ella had vowed that she would be different. *She* would always be cool-headed when it came to men. She would regard them with the same impartiality as she would a prospective business deal.

Up until now, she'd never had a problem with that strategy, but then, up until now she'd never met a man like Hassan Al Abbas. Nor ever felt as if she were a slave to her body. The only sexual experience she'd had prior to last night had been an unmitigated disaster, mainly consisting of her lying looking wide-eyed up at the ceiling, wondering what all the fuss was about.

Well, last night she'd found that out for herself. And suddenly she understood. Suddenly she could see why people took such huge risks when it came to sex. Why they made complete fools of themselves. She felt as if she had been initiated to a secret club, without having decided whether or not she really wanted to be a member.

With trembling fingers, she opened up the package which Hassan's aide had brought with him. Inside lay a cool white dress and a pair of panties nestling among sheets of tissue paper. But while the dress was a fairly respectable length, the panties were nothing but a peach-coloured thong, a sexy little garment which revealed more than it concealed. The thin, satin string made her bottom look almost bare and the filmy peach fabric at the front showed the dark fuzz of hair through which Hassan had hungrily tangled his fingers only hours before.

Her skin felt tainted as she put it on, yet what choice did she have but to wear it? Had *he* chosen it, she wondered, or did he usually leave that kind of thing to his aide?

Slapping on some makeup from her purse and a defiant slash of scarlet lipstick, she stuffed her ruined silver dress into the bathroom bin, sickeningly aware that there were tiny beads lying all over the floor. And then, having forced her feet into what was quite clearly a pair of evening shoes, she let herself out of the suite, momentarily trying to get her bearings.

Heading towards a wide corridor hung with lavish chandeliers she caught a glimpse of perfectly manicured grass in the distance and realised that she must be near the palace gardens. Could she find some passing member of staff and ask them to arrange a car to take her back to the hotel? Was that possible?

'Miss Jackson? Miss Jackson, isn't it?'

The icily cultured voice behind her made Ella freeze in horror because she couldn't fail to recognise those aristocratic tones. Oh, please don't let it be Queen Zoe, she prayed silently, her hopes crumbling as she turned round to stare into the cold features of her sister's future mother-in-law.

Awkwardly, Ella bobbed a curtsey, her cheeks burning with embarrassment. 'Er, good morning, Your Majesty.'

'It's Ella, isn't it?'

'That's right, Your Majesty.'

The queen raised her eyebrows. 'Forgive me for being a little surprised to see you here at such an hour. I thought that you and your family were staying at the hotel?'

Ella hoped her grimace resembled a smile. What could she do, other than be evasive? Tell the queen that she'd spent the night with the sheikh? Wasn't the fact that she was creeping around the corridors wearing new clothes which didn't match last night's shoes evidence enough? 'I...I fell asleep,' she said lamely.

There was a silence while Ella dared the queen to ask just *where* she'd fallen asleep. But fortunately, good breeding must have stopped her, for the older woman simply gave a disapproving look, as if she didn't believe a word of it.

'I see. And have you had breakfast?' asked the queen.

'Er, no. I'm not really very hungry, Your Majesty. In fact, I really ought to be getting back to the hotel. My mother will be wondering where I am.'

'Yes, I can imagine she will be,' answered the queen drily. 'Well, speak to one of the staff and they will arrange a car for you.'

'Thank you, Your Majesty.' Ella gave the deepest

curtsey she could manage and waited until the queen gave a brief nod before walking off.

It took her a while, but eventually she found someone and made herself understood well enough to order a car.

Minutes later she was being driven along a picturesque coastal road, grateful to put miles between herself and the Santina royal palace. But Ella's stomach was in knots and she barely noticed the deep sapphire of the sea or the perfect blue of the sky. For once, the island's scenic beauty left her cold.

All she could think about was the way she'd behaved. It was not only completely uncharacteristic, it was also shameful, because she had chosen the worst man in the world with whom to be sexually rampant. She'd been given the perfect opportunity to prove to Hassan Al Abbas that his bias against the Jackson family was unfair and unfounded. Yet instead, she had simply reinforced all those prejudices with her own behaviour. He'd accused the women in her family of behaving like cheap tramps and hadn't she gone ahead and done just that?

Ella bit her lip as the car began to snake down the road towards the hotel. She'd let everyone down. But most of all, she'd let herself down.

And she was the one who had to live with what she'd done.

CHAPTER FIVE

'I DON'T care how you do it. Just do it!' The woman's voice was shrill and insistent. 'It's my wedding day and I've dreamt about it for too long to make any kind of compromise.'

'I'll work something out,' promised Ella, replacing the phone with a heavy sigh, which wasn't entirely due to the latest unreasonable request from one of her high-profile clients. Since the earliest days of her thriving events company, Cinderella-Rockerfella, she'd been asked for many bizarre things, and usually she took them all in her stride. But usually she wasn't feeling a mixture of guilt and general queasiness, the way she'd been feeling nonstop since she'd returned from her sister's royal engagement party.

Nothing she did seemed to help. She found herself wishing she could forget the sheikh who had given her so much pleasure when he'd taken her to his bed. But what she wished even more was that she could rid herself of the nagging fear which was growing by the day. The fear which this morning had manifested itself in bringing up her breakfast only minutes after she'd eaten it.

With an effort, she forced the worrying thoughts

from her head and looked up at Daisy, her assistant, an efficient twenty-two-year-old whose high energy levels had recently made Ella feel as if she was about a hundred.

'What kind of couple wants to sit on matching thrones for their wedding ceremony, Daisy?' she asked wearily.

'A couple with massive egos?' suggested Daisy with a grin. 'But I guess that isn't so surprising. Two music stars that huge are bound to want to make a splash, especially as they've sold the photo rights to *Celebrity!* magazine. And anyway, you couldn't be better placed to organise something like that, could you, Ella, since your own sister is actually marrying a *real-life royal*!'

'Please don't remind me,' said Ella with a wince.

'Why not? Most people would be revelling in the reflected glory, yet you've hardly said a word about the engagement party since you got back and that was weeks ago,' grumbled Daisy. 'I had to read about it for myself in all the papers.'

'Well, there you go.' Ella realised that her fingers were trembling and she put down the black felt-tip pen with which she'd been doodling. She looked down and saw that she had actually drawn a *sword* by the side of her notes. What the hell did *that* mean? 'Daisy, will you try to organise two golden thrones for me? Ring up that theatrical props company we sometimes use and see if they can help out. I...well, I have to go out this afternoon.' She stood too quickly and her head spun like a merry-go-round. It had been doing a lot of that lately.

Daisy glanced at her. 'Ella, are you okay? You've gone a really funny colour.'

'No, I'm fine,' said Ella, swallowing down the increasingly familiar taste of nausea which was rising in her throat. 'I'll see you later.'

Blanking the concerned look of her assistant, she walked out into the busy London street where an unseasonal shower was in full pelt and she realised too late that she wasn't wearing her raincoat. But who cared about getting caught in the rain, or ostentatious last-minute additions to showbiz weddings, when there was something so big in your head it was beginning to dominate everything you did?

She was shivering as she took a bus to her house in Tooting. It wasn't the most fashionable post code in town but it was well served by public transport and had the added bonus of being cheap. Living there meant she didn't have to live in a shoebox and she'd been able to plough any spare cash into her thriving little business. The business she'd worked so hard to get off the ground, because she'd wanted to be an independent woman, determined that she would never have to rely on the whims of a man for her income or livelihood.

And the thought which was echoing round and round in her head was: *What's going to happen to your precious business now, if your worst fears are confirmed?*

The house felt cold when she entered and she went straight into the bathroom where the pregnancy testing kit she'd bought was still sitting unused next to the toothpaste. For a moment she just stared at it before pulling it off the shelf with hands which were shaking, knowing that she couldn't put off the moment of truth any longer.

Her heart was pounding as she tore open the cardboard box and as she crouched over the loo, attempting to pee onto the narrow little stick, she thought how surreal this felt. This is what millions of women all over the world have done, she told herself. Were probably doing even now. But she'd bet all the money in her purse that not one of them was doing it as the result of a one-night stand with an empty-eyed sheikh who'd left her without even bothering to say goodbye.

She didn't need to see the blue line on the stick to know that the test was positive. She'd known that in her heart all along. Forcing herself to make a cup of hot, sweet tea, she took it into the sitting room and sat drinking it as the light began to fade from the sky. One by one, the pinpoints of stars began to speckle the sky and all she could think about was the single fact which was going to change her life for ever.

She was pregnant.

Pregnant by the sheikh.

She was going to have an unplanned baby by a man who despised her and all she stood for. Ella put down her empty teacup and closed her eyes. It didn't really get much worse than that, did it?

Yet it was strange what tricks the mind could play. For a few weeks more, Ella pretended it wasn't happening. She let the secret grow inside her head as well as inside her belly and she was slim enough for it not to notice. It was as if, by not telling anyone else, she could almost convince herself that it wasn't happening. But aligned with this lack of logic was the overwhelming desire to tell *someone*, to unburden herself to someone who might understand.

Not her mother. Definitely not her weak, romantic mother. Not her sisters either—not if she didn't want word to get out. And definitely not her father. Ella shuddered. Her father would go *mental* if he found out.

Which left Ben, her brother. Brilliant Ben, who, for all his reputation as a control-freak tycoon, was fiercely protective when it came to the women in his family. He was currently living in some splendour in a beach house on the island of Santina while he worked on a charity project. Before she had time to change her mind, Ella picked up the phone and dialled his number.

'Ben Jackson.'

'Ben, it's Ella.'

The rather abrupt note in his voice gave way to one of softening affection. 'Ella,' he murmured. 'Who I still haven't quite forgiven for leaving the island in such dramatic fashion after the engagement party. Why the hell didn't you come to the lunch the next day? I was looking forward to a catch-up.'

'Actually, the reason I didn't come to the lunch is sort of the same reason why I'm ringing you now.'

His voice was teasing. 'Am I supposed to guess what that is, or are you going to cut to the chase?'

Ella swallowed, instinctively knowing that this was the kind of news no brother wanted to receive. And that there was no way of saying it which could possibly lessen its impact. 'Ben, I'm pregnant.'

There was a pause.

'But you don't have a boyfriend, Ella—or at least,

you didn't the last time I spoke to you. Which happened to be at the engagement party. What's going on?' His voice roughened in a way she hadn't heard it do for years. 'Who's the father?'

Ella felt stricken with shame, wishing that she'd never made this wretched call, knowing that she was about to fall off her sainted little-sister pedestal, big-time. But telling someone made it real, and that was the sorry truth of it—it *was* real. She couldn't hide from the reality any longer. And it was pointless trying to lie or to make the truth more palatable by putting some kind of gloss on it. Dreading her brother's reaction to her next piece of news, she licked her lips.

'His name is Hassan Al Abbas.'

There was another brief silence, and when he spoke, Ben's voice had taken on an entirely different tone. 'The sheikh?'

'That's the one.'

'You're having the baby of one of the most powerful men in the Middle East?'

Ella shivered. It sounded even more daunting when he put it like that. 'So it would seem.' She heard her brother utter a few terse expletives. 'Ben, don't swear!'

'What do you expect me to do?' he retorted savagely. 'Have you thought about what you're letting yourself in for? Don't you know what a reputation he has? Hell, Ella, I didn't even know you two were an item.'

'We're not!' she put in fiercely. 'We are most emphatically not. We…we met. We fought and then… then…'

'I think I can work out the rest for myself,' he said quickly. 'The question is what you're going to do about it?'

Ella's hand strayed to her stomach. A still-flat stomach, it was true, but not for much longer. Deep inside her was growing a tiny embryo which was half that black-eyed brute of a man, but also half *her*. Half Jackson. Bobby and Julie's first grandchild. A first nephew or niece for her brothers and sisters. A new life about to enter her crazy and dysfunctional family. A terrible pain clutched at her heart as she thought of the heavy burden of responsibility which now hung over her, but knowing, too, that there was only one thing she could do. And fast following on that pain came a powerful wave of protectiveness. A determination that something good would come out of this whole mess.

'I'm going to keep the baby,' she said fiercely.

'Good.' Ben let out a long and ragged sigh. 'That's good. And what about Al Abbas? What does he say about it all?'

'I haven't told him. And he won't want to be the father, Ben.' Her voice was flat as she remembered the way he'd snuck out of her bed, like a thief in the middle of the night. 'He doesn't even like me!'

There was a pause. 'So are you *going* to tell him?'

Again, she thought of Hassan. Not the man who had seduced her with such ease and shown her what true pleasure could be. But the other side of that same man. She remembered the strange, cold emptiness she'd seen in his eyes and a shiver rippled down her spine. 'I don't *know*,' she said desperately.

'You know that it'll be irrevocable once you do,

and that you'll have little control over what happens next?' he warned. 'That not only is he unimaginably wealthy, he is also an autocrat. Men like that are possessive about what is theirs, and he will see this baby as belonging to him. He's *ruthless*, sis—make no mistake about that.'

Ben's words told her nothing she didn't already know and part of her wanted to steer clear of Hassan in order to protect herself and her baby. Ella felt the drumming of her heart as she worked out what she wanted to do. If she could wave a magic wand, it would be to erase all memory of the heartless sheikh from her life. But this wasn't just about *her* any more, was it? There was a child involved and didn't Hassan have the right to know about the existence of that child, no matter what their feelings for each other were?

'I have no choice but to tell him,' she said quietly.

Ben's voice sounded gruff. 'Actually, you *do* have a choice. I just hope he appreciates the one you've made. Let me know if there's anything I can do. And I mean *anything*.'

'I will. Thanks, Ben.' Ella swallowed down the sudden lump which had risen in her throat. 'Oh, and Ben? You won't tell anyone else about this, will you?'

'Not unless you want me to. Let's hold off the hysterical reaction from the rest of the clan for as long as possible, shall we?'

Ella was thoughtful as she replaced the phone, realising that she couldn't put off telling Hassan a moment longer. Until she also realised that she knew very little about him, other than that he was a sheikh. She didn't even know where he lived! She frowned.

Hadn't his aide mentioned a country when he'd delivered her the dress and the insultingly sexy thong? Kasha-something. Kashamak?

She sat down at her computer and tapped the name into the search engine to discover that Kashamak was indeed a country, and that Hassan was its supreme ruler, although he had a younger brother.

She stared at a photo of him, clad in what was clearly his national dress, and thought how formidable he looked. His thick black hair was covered by a white headdress, held in place by a dark, knotted silk cord. It made him look more *foreign*. More unapproachable.

It was strange to stare at the sensual curve of his mouth and to remember how thoroughly it had explored her body. She remembered the powerful orgasm which had shaken her to the core, the first one she'd ever experienced. Was that what had made the sex seem so profound to her, or was that just the effect he had on all women?

With an effort, she dragged her eyes away from the photo. There were whole pages of facts about Kashamak's huge natural resources and the border disputes with one of the neighbouring countries, which Hassan had recently settled, but Ella barely took anything else in. She didn't *need* to know that to his country he was a hero, because the whole point of looking at all this stuff had a purpose. She now knew where he was based, but how did you go about contacting a man who was so obviously out of reach? His very position isolated him from people like her and he certainly hadn't left behind his mobile number and told her to be in touch, had he?

In the end, she summoned up the courage to ask her sister Allegra, who in turn asked Alex, who said, regretfully, that he couldn't really hand Hassan's number out to anyone, not even family. Security issues, he explained. But he would pass on her details to the sheikh and ask him to be in touch with her.

Ella felt mortified when this piece of information was relayed to her, though she supposed she should be grateful that her sister hadn't demanded to know *why* she wanted to contact Hassan. She guessed she was so bound up in her own impending marriage that she hadn't quizzed her about their smoochy dancing. Or mentioned the subsequent stand-up row on the dance floor....

A sense of frustration caught hold of her and she wondered what Hassan might think when he heard about her efforts to contact him. What if he failed to get in touch? What if he thought she was just a woman on the make who couldn't accept that he hadn't wanted to see her again?

At this, Ella brightened a little. That might be the best of all possible worlds. She would have appeased her conscience by trying to contact him, but there would then be no need to involve him in her baby's life.

Galvanised into action, she made an appointment with her doctor and went to see him the very next morning. Somehow it made her feel better to have done something really positive. Having her blood pressure taken and being checked out and told that she was perfectly healthy filled her with a feeling of hope for the future. She could do this. She *would* do this.

Lots of women brought up babies on their own, and some of them even ran their own businesses!

Later, she collected a cappuccino and an apple doughnut from the coffee shop near the headquarters of Cinderella-Rockerfella and realised that it was the first time she'd felt properly hungry in days. Swinging the brown paper bag from her fingers, she walked into the office and greeted Daisy with a smile, wondering why her assistant's face looked so peculiar.

'Are you all right, Daisy?'

Rather dramatically, Daisy started jerking her head in the direction of Ella's office. 'In *there*,' she said in a stage whisper.

'In where, what?' asked Ella, confused. But her confusion quickly morphed into something else, something she could never have put a name to but which felt like terror and excitement and a sudden cold dread all swirled together as she reached for the door handle.

Drawing a deep breath, she walked into her tiny office, shocked but somehow not surprised to see the towering form of Sheikh Hassan Al Abbas silhouetted against the window.

CHAPTER SIX

ELLA'S heart missed a beat as the sheikh's powerful body managed to block out most of the available light. And not just the light. It was as if he had sucked all the oxygen out of the atmosphere, making it suddenly very difficult for her to breathe. 'Wh-what are you doing here?' she whispered.

Hassan stared at the woman who had just walked into the cluttered office. The only colour in her pale face was the scarlet lipstick which coloured her un-smiling lips and he found himself thinking that she looked like a stranger. But she *was* a stranger, he re-minded himself grimly, one he'd only ever seen be-neath the false glittering light of chandeliers. Or naked, of course.

'You wanted to see me, Ella,' he said softly. 'So here I am.'

The shock of seeing him again felt like a physical blow and Ella put her doughnut and coffee down on the desk, afraid that her trembling fingers would spill the scalding liquid. 'I wanted to *speak* to you. There's a difference.' She met his black, empty eyes, furious with her body for the instinctive little tremble it gave. As if it was recognising that here was a man who had the power to turn her into a trembling mass of longing. Who could breathe danger into her heart. With an effort, she dragged her attention back to his sombre face. 'Do you always turn up in someone's office unannounced? It's certainly an unconventional approach.'

'Ah, but I'm an unconventional man in many ways. In others, of course, I can be rather more predictable.' His black eyes flicked over her, thinking how tired she looked. 'And since we didn't make any arrangement to hook up again, I'm curious to know what it is you want?'

Ella was finding it hard to cling onto her equilibrium. His appearance here had taken her by surprise, but that wasn't the only reason for the sudden racing of her heart. It was *him*. The effect he was having on her, no matter how hard she tried to remain immune to him. And seeing him in the flesh again was infinitely more powerful than studying a photograph on the Net.

The night they'd…met, he had been wearing a formal tuxedo, which flattered even the plainest-looking man. And this was a man who certainly had no need of flattery. Today he wore an expensive suit, the kind worn by successful businessmen the world over. And yet he did not seem to wear it comfortably. It seemed too constricting for the powerful lines of his body. Already, he had undone a button of his shirt and must have tugged impatiently at his tie. Ella suddenly became aware that beneath all the royal trappings lurked a very primitive man, and the enormity of what she was about to tell him filled her with dread.

But first it was important to establish some kind of

dialogue. There were a couple of things she needed to clear up, no matter what happened afterwards, because surely the answers to her questions would determine just how he viewed women in general, and her in particular.

'So tell me, Hassan,' she said in a low voice. 'Do you always leave a woman's bed in the middle of the night, without even bothering to say goodbye to her?'

He was surprised by her directness and more than a little irritated by her lack of remorse. Didn't she feel even a shred of shame over what had happened? he wondered. Or were one-night stands a regular occurrence in her life? His jaw tightened, unwilling to accept that he had chosen a woman who spread her favours freely, and yet, given her background, why was he so surprised?

'I decided that leaving when I did was the best form of damage limitation,' he said flatly.

'Excuse me? Did you say *damage* limitation?'

'Oh, come on. Let's not dress it up to be something it wasn't,' he said, shrugging off her outrage. 'It was great sex—we both know that—but under the circumstances, it was ill-advised. It wasn't going anywhere. It never could. So what would have been the point in prolonging it?'

'Surely good manners might have prompted you to say some sort of goodbye?'

He gave a short laugh. 'I think we abandoned good manners some time after you threw champagne in my face.'

'And they were certainly a distant memory by the time you ripped my dress off.'

Hassan's mouth hardened, because her defiant words were exciting him. And this was exactly what he hadn't wanted: to be reminded of just how completely he had fallen victim to her vixen charms. He remembered the soft yield of her bare breasts beneath his calloused fingers and felt a savage jerk of lust, along with a stab of self-contempt. For what use was a man who could defeat his enemies in battle if he then allowed himself to weaken in the arms of a woman he despised?

'You got the replacement dress and underwear I sent?'

'Yes, I got them,' she snapped. 'I happened to be wearing them when I bumped into Queen Zoe in the palace corridors on my way out.'

He winced. 'What did she say?'

'Oh, she's too polite to say anything much, although her face was a picture. Especially when I told her that I'd spent the night with you.'

Hassan looked at her in horror. 'You *told* her you spent the night with me?'

Briefly, Ella allowed herself to enjoy his discomfiture until she reminded herself that this was not about scoring points. 'No, of course I didn't tell her. But I wish I had. The high and mighty sheikh who'd made no secret of his contempt for the Jacksons, actually ending up in bed with one of them! That would have provided plenty of fuel for the gossips, wouldn't it?'

For a moment, Hassan almost smiled, because nobody could deny that she had spirit as well as beauty, and no woman had ever spoken to him in such a way before. If she was not who she was then he might have enjoyed a short and mutually satisfying affair with her, laying down his usual ground rules of no commitment before it commenced.

But that was not going to happen.

Not with Ella Jackson.

He looked around her office, his mouth flattening with distaste as he took in its garish appearance. It was as tacky as he'd imagined when the investigator he'd hired had told him that she ran an events company called Cinderella-Rockerfella.

The walls were covered with glossy photos of events she had presumably organised—ghastly montages of occasions which looked like the height of vulgarity. There was an enormous blown-up wedding photo of a couple he vaguely recognised, an international footballer and his bride. That the woman was wearing a gown which seemed to reveal most of her surgically enhanced breasts seemed to Hassan to mock at the very sanctity of marriage and respect for her groom. Why, she might as well have taken her vows naked, he thought in disgust, wondering how Ella could bear to work for such people.

Because she's a Jackson, that's why. She *is* one of these people.

'So why were you trying to contact me?' he questioned softly.

His question brought reality crashing back into her thoughts and Ella's heart began to pound. 'No ideas?'

'Plenty.' He looked into her eyes and remembered thrusting into her so deep that it felt as if he was in danger of losing himself in the process.

'Oh?'

'Maybe you decided your night with me was so hot that you wanted a repeat of it. I wouldn't blame you if you did.'

Ella was appalled at her answering stab of desire and even more appalled by his out-and-out arrogance. 'I try never to make the same mistake twice, Hassan. Any other suggestions?'

Dark clouds drifted into his mind. He made himself say it as a safeguard. In the same way that people often forced themselves to confront a worst-case scenario, thinking that if they did, it meant it would never come true.

'Or our ill-judged liaison has left us with something other than regrets.'

She stared at him, because didn't his words make what she was about to tell him even more difficult? 'That's the most cold-hearted description I've ever heard,' she whispered.

Her lack of denial unsettled him but Hassan kept his nerve, the same way he'd kept it when someone had once held the blade of a knife to his throat. In that moment, he had thought he was going to die. But he hadn't died, had he? He had defied the odds and lived to fight another day. 'That's because I am a cold-hearted man, Ella. Be in no doubt of that. And I haven't come here to play guessing games. What is it that you want to say to me?'

'That you're right!' She swallowed as she forced out the bitter truth. 'That we have been left with something—or rather, I have.' She looked into the narrowed black eyes and spoke in a low voice. 'I'm having a baby, Hassan.'

Hassan swallowed, remembering the way that the knife blade had nicked against his skin, a wound made to warn him rather than to slay him. But the flesh had healed, hadn't it? While this…*this*…

This would not heal!

He took a step towards her, his voice low and urgent, his eyes locking on hers as if looking for the essential flaw in her argument. 'But not necessarily my baby?'

'Of course it's your baby!'

'There's no *of course* about it,' he denied as the rush of blood to his head threatened to deafen him. 'You fell into my bed with a speed which is unequalled—even in my experience. How am I to know that you don't do that with a different man every night of the week?'

His words hurt, as no doubt he intended them to, but Ella didn't show it. She forced herself to be logical rather than emotional, the way she'd had to be for most of her life. Because could she really blame him for jumping to such a conclusion, when all he had was the evidence of how she'd behaved?

She realised that he was lashing out at her because of what she'd just told him. That he was scared. Because what man would jump for joy at being informed that a total stranger was having their baby? He probably thought she was trying to railroad him into marriage or commitment—he was certainly arrogant enough for that. Well, maybe it was time to reassure him that she could manage perfectly well on her own.

'Because actually, I don't sleep around, though of course you're perfectly at liberty not to believe me,' she said quietly.

'You made an exception just for me, did you?'

'There's no need for false modesty, Hassan. I'm sure plenty of women have made an exception for you in the past.' But stupidly, that hurt too. Why on earth should it hurt to think of him in bed with other women? She sucked in a deep breath. 'I realise this has come as a shock to you—'

'Oh, the mistress of all understatement!' he mocked, because somehow mockery was easier than having to acknowledge that what she said was true. And that even as she stood there in her blue silk dress, with her scarlet lips trembling, his child was growing deep inside her.

'But I want you to know that I am planning to have this baby and to keep it and to...to love it.' She saw his mouth twist with derision and she guessed what he thought was about to follow. 'And I'm not asking you for anything.'

He gave a cynical laugh. 'That really would be a first. So why bother telling me?'

'Because you're the father and I felt it was my duty to let you know.'

Hassan stilled as he plucked one word from her breathless sentence.

Duty.

It was a word which had made him the man he was. A word his own mother had rejected, causing irreparable damage to their royal house and wrecking three lives in the process. Wasn't it now his duty to stand by and support this woman, no matter how much he abhorred the idea?

'This is like some bad dream,' he said suddenly.

Ella nodded. Because hadn't she thought exactly the same? 'It came as a shock to me too,' she admitted.

He shook his head. 'But I made sure that I was careful.'

'I know you did.'

He wondered how it could have happened and then remembered the way his hands had trembled as he had pulled on the protection.... 'Just not careful enough,' he said bitterly as he looked into her ice-blue eyes. 'Call it weakness—yes, why *don't* we call it weakness?—but having you writhing all over my bed made my attention to detail a little lacking! I'd been away fighting a war and it was a long time since I'd been with a woman. What's your excuse?'

'My *excuse* is that I had a momentary lapse of judgement,' she said, not wanting to tell him that he had blown her away. Because wouldn't that make him even more arrogant and unreasonable? 'As it happens, I'm pretty much a novice when it comes to sex—'

'You weren't acting much like a novice that night.'

'Maybe that has more to do with your breadth of experience rather than my lack of it,' she answered. 'There's no point in us arguing about it. I just felt you had a right to know that you'd fathered a child. And now you do. I've discharged my duty. So if you wouldn't mind leaving, I really do have work to get on with.'

He read defiance in her eyes. It was not an emotion he encountered very often and, to his surprise, he realised that she meant it. That she was not posturing or making empty threats in order to impress him—that she *actually wanted him to leave*!

The contrary side of his nature made him want to rebel against a woman trying to dictate what his behaviour should be. But so did something else. He felt the sudden twisting of his gut as a rush of unwanted emotion hit him. For a moment, the pain of it took him back to a time he had buried deeper than the most precious artifacts which surrounded his father's tomb. The time when his mother had walked away to be with the man she 'loved.' Leaving behind a small and confused little boy who had vowed fiercely never to allow himself to be hurt as his father had been...

And then the dark mist of memory cleared and he found himself staring into the ice-blue eyes of Ella Jackson.

She was having his baby, he realised incredulously. And therefore this was not just any baby. The child she carried was the son or daughter of the sheikh. And it was *his. His.*

He had once vowed never to marry. He had told his younger brother that one day the sheikhdom would be his—for no child would ever spring from the loins of Hassan Al Abbas. Blighted by the pain he had felt at his mother's desertion, he had known that fatherhood would never be on his agenda, but now suddenly it was.

His mouth hardened and the hands which had hung by the sides of his powerful thighs now clenched into fists, because he recognised in that instant that what Ella Jackson had told him had changed his life irrevocably. In that moment, all his plans and certainties underwent a dramatic transformation and he knew what he must do. More importantly, what he must *not* do. He would not do as his own mother had done. He would not turn his back on his own flesh and blood.

He leaned towards her. 'I'm not going anywhere. We need to talk,' he said grimly.

She eyed him warily, his disturbing proximity reminding her that he was dangerous in more ways than one. 'I thought we'd said everything there was to say.'

'Are you kidding? We haven't even touched the surface, Ella. Or did you think you could get away with telling me that you're having my child and I would just walk away and leave you to get on with it?'

Yes, maybe she had. Maybe she had been that stupid and naive. Maybe she'd hoped that fate, or his reluctance to acknowledge his baby, would have taken him out of her life for good. But not any more. There was no mistaking the dark determination which had made his face look even more intimidating and something about his stance made her realise there was trouble ahead. The phone on her desk began to ring and automatically Ella reached out her hand to answer it.

'Leave it,' he bit out.

'I can't leave it. It's my—'

'I said, *leave* it. Let the other girl answer it.'

Their eyes met in silent combat as the phone rang six times before Daisy picked it up in the outer office and Ella knew this was a fight she would not win. Because how could she possibly conduct a business conversation with one of her clients under the grim gaze of the sheikh? She wouldn't trust him not to snatch the phone right out of her hand and slam it down. And what if Daisy heard them arguing through the thin walls? 'Okay, I'll talk to you,' she conceded wearily. 'But not now and not here. I'll meet you later, when I've finished work.'

'Good.' He held her gaze for a moment. 'Come and have dinner in my hotel suite.'

She shook her head. 'There's no way I'm coming to your hotel.'

'No?' He saw the parting of her luscious scarlet lips and felt an unwilling kick of lust. But wouldn't bedding her only be counterproductive to the idea which was slowly forming in his mind? An idea he would need to broach very carefully in order to get her to accept it...

'Then where else do you suggest?' he continued. 'If we have what will inevitably be a difficult conversation in a crowded restaurant, we risk being overheard by waiters or other diners. And I don't want to find our meeting making headlines in tomorrow's newspapers.'

Ella heard the undeniable command in his voice and part of her wanted to rebel against it. He was so unashamedly autocratic, she thought. So completely used to getting his own way. If she went to his hotel suite then wouldn't that allow him to call the shots? She didn't know what he was going to say but she knew she needed all her wits about her, and maybe the best way of ensuring that was to be on home territory.

'You can come to my house instead,' she said. 'Get the address from Daisy on your way out. I'll see you there at nine, but you'd better have eaten something first. I'm not planning on making you dinner.'

He paused for a moment as he went to pass her, studying the dark spill of her silken hair and the scarlet tremble of her lips. The desire to kiss her was over-

whelming. But he fought it as he had fought so much
else in his life.

'I'll be there,' he said softly, ignoring the dark dilatation of her eyes as he walked out of the office without another word.

CHAPTER SEVEN

WITH his bodyguards sitting grim-faced in two waiting cars, Hassan rang the doorbell, briefly wondering if he'd got the wrong address. He frowned. This neighbourhood was like no other he'd ever seen and Ella's house was in a row of other small houses which looked directly onto a busy main road.

He didn't know anyone who lived in a place like this—the kind of place you lived in when you didn't have a lot of money to splash around. And yet Ella Jackson had blended in perfectly at the royal engagement party in her sparkling silver dress, her sky-high heels and those gleaming scarlet lips. He'd thought she'd be living somewhere trashy and flashy, displaying the complete lack of taste which had been on show in her office today. Not in this rather ordinary little house which was situated on the wrong side of town.

The door opened and Ella stood there, confounding yet another of his preconceptions. Gone was the silk and the gloss. With her shiny hair tugged into a ponytail, she was wearing a plain white T-shirt and faded blue jeans which emphasised the blueness of her eyes. He frowned. Gone too was that shiny red lipstick which drew attention to the luscious mouth which made a man have sinful thoughts, no matter how hard he tried not to. She was scarcely recognisable from the slick party girl he'd met, and for a moment, he felt disorientated, as if she had suddenly produced some low-key twin sister.

'This is where you live?' he questioned slowly.

'No, I thought I'd rent the place out in order to impress you, but I can see that I've failed.' She pulled the door open and ushered him in, stupidly unprepared for the tingling response of her body as she looked up at him. 'Yes, it's where I live, Hassan. Why, did you think I'd be living in some over-the-top boudoir, all gilt and ceiling mirrors and shaggy fur rugs lying all over the place?'

Actually, this was so close to what he *had* been thinking that for a moment he didn't answer. Instead he stepped into the small hallway, shutting the door behind him. From there he followed the blue-jeaned sway of her bottom into what should have been the sitting room.

Except that this wasn't what it seemed either. The surprisingly large space contained a sofa and a couple of chairs, but these were all bunched up at one end, as if they were nothing but an afterthought. Pride of place had been given instead to an easel, on which stood a half-finished painting of a naked man. It looked pretty good from where Hassan stood but his critical judgment was suspended as he made the inevitable comparison. He emerged from that with his ego satisfied but his morals outraged by the thought that she must have spent time studying another man's genitals.

'Who is this?' he demanded furiously.

'That's none of your business.'

'On the contrary.' His eyes glittered. 'You carry the child of the sheikh and that *makes* it my business! Who is he?'

Ella heard the control-freak quality in his voice and it set off more warning bells in her head. She'd been wondering how this meeting was going to proceed and now she had her first indication. Was he going to play high-handed and possessive with all that 'child of the sheikh' stuff? Her first instinct was to tell him to go to hell but some deep-rooted protectiveness told her not to inflame him. That he was not a man to make an enemy of, especially in these circumstances.

'He's an architectural student who poses in my life-drawing class.'

'You have had sex with him?'

'Of course I haven't had sex with him! I hardly know—' Too late she stopped herself as she realised the irony of her words, but not before a look of bitter triumph had filled his empty eyes with a dark light.

'You hardly know him?' he finished acidly. 'You hardly knew me either, but that didn't stop you opening up your milky-pale thighs for me, did it, Ella?'

Ella bit back the angry retort which hovered on her lips, telling herself that it didn't matter. He was here to talk about the baby and that was the only thing which mattered.

'We could waste a lot of time insulting each other, but I'm too tired to want to. And that's not why you're here, is it?' She flashed him a polite smile. 'So in the spirit of trying to conduct this conversation in a ci-vilised way, perhaps you'd like to sit down?'

'No, I'll stand, thanks.' For the first time in a long while, he realised that he had no game plan to follow, and no idea of how to get what he wanted from this woman. Although ironically, he still wasn't quite sure *what* he wanted.

Restlessly, he went to look out of the window, just as a large red bus lumbered to a halt and discharged a group of teenagers who stood in noisy conversation right outside. When he turned back to face her, his expression was as perplexed as the grim faces of his waiting bodyguards. 'Why do you live in a place like this, Ella?'

'Why do you think? Because I like the sound of the traffic?' She met his grim expression and shrugged. 'It's what I can afford, Hassan, that's why. Any available money I have goes straight back into the business, rather than being wasted on paying a high rent.'

'Your father doesn't give you an allowance?'

Ella almost laughed out loud, wondering what kind of planet he was on. Or maybe it was a mark of her father's chameleon-like qualities that he could still manage to convince the world that there was money in the family.

'No. I don't get anything from my father.'

He heard the acid note which had tinged her voice and for the second time that day he noticed the faint blue shadows beneath her eyes. *Didn't pregnant women suffer excessively from fatigue?* A sudden pang of guilt washed over him. 'Perhaps we will sit after all,' he said unexpectedly, putting his hand on the small of her back and guiding her towards one of the chairs. 'You look a little tired.'

Ella didn't have the energy to object, but the small act of kindness left her feeling dangerously vulnerable. And she *was* tired. All the emotions which had accumulated over the past few weeks had left her so wrung out that it was as much as she could do not to put her head in her hands and weep.

She thought about all the plans she'd made for the future. All her strategies for exploiting a gap in the market and making a success of herself. Her determination that she should earn a decent living for herself and never have to rely on a faithless man, the way her mother had done.

Where were all those plans now?

Up in the air, that's where. Because every woman knew that a baby meant a major career juggle, whether you were single or not. And now she had to deal with a powerful and dauntingly sexy man who she suspected was going to try to outwit her. *And she still didn't know what it was he wanted.*

He waited until she was settled before he sat on the sofa opposite her, his long legs stretched out in front of him, his black eyes enigmatic and watchful.

'So when is the baby due?'

'Well, it's been fourteen weeks since the party, which means the baby's due in January.' She looked at him steadily. 'January 8, to be precise.'

Hassan tensed, because having an actual *date* to focus on changed everything. It transformed her pregnancy from a dark and unknown spectre into something real. Something which was happening. To her and to *him*. For a moment there was silence while he tried to make sense of her words. That early in the new year, as the snows were falling onto the highest peaks of the Samaltyn Mountains, he would become a father.

'This is momentous news,' he said slowly.

'Yes.'

'Who else have you told?'

She hesitated. 'Only my brother, Ben.'

'He is discreet?'

She heard the doubt in his voice and bristled. 'Actually, there's nobody as discreet as Ben, though you probably find that difficult to believe as he happens to be a dreaded *Jackson*.'

'Actually, I happen to know that in the business world your brother has a formidable reputation,' conceded Hassan drily. 'But this is something very different.'

The nod to Ben's undoubted talent should have pleased her but Ella was too concerned with the implication behind Hassan's question to do anything but stare at him in growing horror. 'Why are you so concerned who knows about this? You think…you think…' She sucked in a deep and unsteady breath and expelled it again on a horrified shudder. 'Listen to me, Hassan Al Abbas. I am *having* this baby, no matter what. And nothing you can ever say will change my mind.'

The fierce look on her face was unmistakable and for a moment he admired her passion and integrity before indignation reared its head and his face darkened. 'You think that I am suggesting—'

'Don't even say it!' she warned.

Hassan gave an impatient wave of his hand. 'I am not used to being interrupted.'

'Well, I'm not used to having insults hurled at me.

So if you can manage to keep a civil tongue in your head, I promise I won't interrupt you and then we should be fine, shouldn't we?'

His eyes narrowed as he remembered her determination to remove him from her office so that she could continue working and suddenly a solution came to him. Suddenly, he realised exactly how he should handle this. 'We need to decide what we're going to do,' he said.

The use of the word *we* made Ella faintly uneasy. 'I told you, the decision has already been made. I'm having the baby, and I'm perfectly prepared to bring her or him up on my own.'

'But you can't make decisions like that because it isn't just *your* baby,' he said softly. 'This child has royal blood in its veins. Do you have any idea what that means, Ella?'

'How can I? The world of sheikhdom is a mystery to me. Actually, come to think of it, so are you.'

'Oh, I don't think so.' His voice dipped as he ran his eyes over her body. 'I think there are plenty of things about me which are no mystery whatsoever.'

The sensual allusion was obvious and, she suspected, intentional. To Ella's fury, she felt her face grow hot, despite all her best intentions. She'd vowed not to react to him in any way other than a strictly business-like one, and now here she was, colouring up like a naive schoolgirl. 'I don't want to talk about that.'

A mixture of emotions he didn't even want to acknowledge made him want to hurt her. To make her pay for having trapped him, because wasn't that easier than admitting that he had walked right into it? 'What, the sex you couldn't get enough of?'

'But it was the same for you!' she flashed back. 'Wasn't it?'

He met the challenge in her eyes and had to fight down an urgent desire to kiss her. He had been wondering just what it was about her which had made him lose his head—and his body—so completely. Her own amazing body coupled with his own frustration had been obvious contenders, but he realised that her fearlessness was a turn-on too. He'd seen it in the way she'd turned on him in the darkened corridor of the palace at Santina and faced him down. And she was demonstrating it now—her clear blue eyes wide and unafraid, despite the enormity of her situation. 'Yes,' he admitted harshly. 'It was the same for me.'

His words ignited memories she was trying her best to forget. The feeling of being in his arms. The crush of his mouth on hers and the instant flaring of her body in response. Ella tried to ignore the sudden yearning to have him make love to her all over again. *Concentrate on what is real*, she thought as she forced herself to confront her greatest fear and most foolish hope. 'Are you saying you want a hands-on role as father?'

For a moment, Hassan didn't answer. 'I'm saying that's a possibility. But I think it's important that we discuss your needs first.'

Ella blinked in surprise. Was that genuine concern she heard in his voice? 'My needs?' she echoed.

'Well, you have your own business, don't you? I don't know very much about party-planning, but I imagine it must require a lot of hard work and dedication, especially as you're the boss.'

Cautiously, Ella nodded. 'Yes, it does.'

'And some pretty unsociable hours?'

'That's one of the drawbacks,' she agreed, softening in spite of herself, because she would never have believed that he could be quite so understanding.

'And a baby might get in the way of that?'

'Well, ye—' The words died on her lips as she looked into his face and saw that it wasn't concern but calculation she saw in his black eyes. And suddenly, she realised just where this was leading. Suddenly, she realised what a sucker she was for just a few kind words. Was that what her mother had done, over and over again? Fallen under the spell of a man who had treated her like dirt just because he'd uttered a few sweet nothings along the way? The shock of realising that she had very nearly done the same thing made the blood drain from her face.

'My God,' she breathed. 'You are completely and utterly ruthless! I see exactly what you're doing. You're trying to get me to admit that I won't be able to cope with this baby, aren't you?'

'And isn't that the truth?' he challenged, his vow to tread carefully forgotten in his determination to get his own way. 'Have you actually stopped to think about it, about what it might mean to you?'

'Are you crazy? I've thought of nothing else for weeks!'

'But you're planning to carry on working?'

'Of course I am!' Did he have no idea how real people lived their lives? She supposed he didn't. 'It's how I earn my living, Hassan. We weren't all born in palaces and given trust funds while we lay around like pampered princes!'

He gave a short laugh. Oh, the famous myth that all princes were pampered simply because they were princes. If he told her what the reality was, she would never believe it. Instead he leaned forward to emphasise his point, slamming his forefinger into the palm of his hand. 'And while you're "working," Ella, while you're dealing with all the mindless Z-list celebrities and their attendant problems, what will you be doing with our baby? Farming it out to some underqualified child-minder who has no vested interest in its future?'

Heart racing, Ella stared at him. 'That's such an ignorant comment, it doesn't even deserve the dignity of a reply.'

'You think so? Well, how about coming up with an answer to this one? How about when the baby is ill. Who's going to cover for you then? Or are you planning to bring a carrycot into that cramped excuse for a room which you call an office?'

His words were crowding into her mind like a flock of dark birds flapping their demented wings and Ella shook her head as she tried to shake them off. 'I'm not the first woman in the history of the world to contemplate bringing up a child on my own! These are things which can all be worked out.'

'How?' he shot back.

The question caught her off-guard because in truth she hadn't sat down to work out the day-to-day practicalities. 'Okay, so what's the alternative?' she questioned hotly. 'Are you saying you want to take the child off to your desert palace and bring it up as a baby sheikh or whatever it is they call the girl version?'

'It's a sheika, and yes, I can bring up a baby,' he said. 'The way my father brought me up. A child doesn't need a mother in order to survive.'

Ella heard the strange bitterness which had distorted his words and suddenly she realised just where this was leading. She could read the ruthless intent which had darkened his face just as easily as if he'd said the words out loud.

He would take her baby away without a qualm. Take it away to live in some remote desert kingdom and she would never see it again.

Her stomach lurched and pinpricks of sweat broke out on her forehead. 'I think I'm going to be sick,' she croaked.

CHAPTER EIGHT

HASSAN had dealt with sickness before. He'd seen men spill their guts up after battle and afterwards lie grey-faced and sweating. But he'd never witnessed it in a beautiful young woman in her prime and he thought how tiny and frail she suddenly looked. Overwhelmed with remorse at the harshness of his words, he carried her to the tiny bathroom and then held back her hair from her face as she retched. Eventually, she stopped and slumped against his chest, exhausted, her eyes closed.

'I'm sorry,' she said eventually.

Stricken with remorse, he shook his head. 'It is not you who should be sorry, it is me,' he grated. 'I am responsible for your sickness. I should not have said those things to you.'

At this, her eyelashes fluttered open to reveal ice-blue eyes which were slightly bloodshot, and to his astonishment, a faint smile was lifting the corners of her lips.

'Your words *were* rather wounding,' she conceded. 'But not quite powerful enough to induce nausea, Hassan. That's something which happens to lots of pregnant women, no matter what their circumstances.'

'You have been sick before this?' he demanded.

Ella swallowed, feeling much too weak to be able to maintain a stoic attitude. 'Most days.'

'Most days? But this is not good! This is why you are looking so thin and so pale.'

'The doctor says the baby will be fine.'

There was a pause. 'You have seen a doctor?'

Ella knew that she ought to move. That it was bizarre, ridiculous and inappropriate to be lying slumped against the man who had said such cruel things to her. But the stupid thing was that she didn't want to go anywhere. He felt warm and he felt strong. Most important of all, he felt *safe*. 'Seeing a doctor is what normally happens when a woman gets pregnant, Hassan.'

'And who is this doctor?'

'He's my GP from the local health centre and he's very good.'

Hassan tensed, his apprehension eclipsing the sudden realisation that her back was pressing against his groin.

'A local GP cannot be charged with caring for the progeny of the sheikh,' he said, and then saw her eyelids flutter to a close again. 'But this is not the time to talk about it. For now, you need to rest.'

Her protest died on her lips as once again he picked her up and carried her through to her bedroom, though she couldn't miss his faint double take when he saw a series of charcoal drawings she'd done of Izzy lining the walls. They were entitled 'Izzy Dressing' and they showed her sister pulling on various items of clothing. They were less shocking than most things you'd see in a municipal art gallery, but that didn't stop Hassan's mouth from flattening critically.

He put her down on the bed, banking the pillows up behind her, his black eyes raking over her.

'What can I do for you?' he demanded. 'What can I get you to make you feel better?'

Stupidly, she felt like asking him to hold her again. To cradle her in his arms where, for just a brief while, she had felt safe and cosseted. And how pathetic was *that*? She struggled to sit up. 'I don't want anything.'

'Sure?'

The unexpected softness in his voice made her hesitate, especially as her throat felt scorched and dry from all that vomiting. 'There's some flat cola in the fridge.'

His eyes narrowed. 'Flat cola?'

'It helps the sickness.'

'Right.' Grimly, he made his way to her refrigerator, an ancient-looking beast of a thing which contained a lump of cheese, some wilting salad and a bottle of cola, minus the top. His expression was no less thunderous when he took the unappetising brown liquid back to her, and held the glass up to her lips while she sipped from it.

It was an unexpectedly considerate gesture, powerfully intimate, and Ella felt some of her strength returning. 'You make a good nurse,' she joked.

'And you make an appalling patient,' he retorted. 'If you think that you can sustain yourself and a growing baby on that pitiful *excuse* for food in your kitchen.'

'I don't have a lot of time to go shopping,' she defended, and then realised that she had walked into a trap of her own making. 'But all that will change, of course.'

'How?' he demanded. 'Where's the magic wand you're going to wave? Who's going to help you, Ella?'

'My family.' But even to her own ears, the words sounded unconvincing. She knew that Ben would help her in a moment and yet she baulked at the thought of running to him, terrified of disappointing her beloved big brother and becoming a burden to him. Besides, Ben lived on an island which was miles away.

And what of her business—how *was* she going to cope with the day-to-day running of it? Her celebrity clients expected a super-willowy boss, with smiling lips covered in her trademark scarlet gloss. Not some tired and lumbering pregnant woman who wasn't even with the father of her baby, a pregnant woman who was finding it increasingly difficult to stay upright without wanting to fall asleep. Or be sick.

'No, most definitely *not* your family. I am not having this baby influenced by the Jackson family,' said Hassan unequivocally.

Her hackles began to rise. 'You can't stop me.'

No, he couldn't, and he recognised that to try to push her would only make her stubbornly stand her ground. Far better, surely, to appeal to the innate sense of greed which lay at the heart of every woman? Greed which he had seen in many forms ever since his powerful body had reached adulthood and the vast resources of his inheritance had become available to him. He put the half-empty glass of cola on the bedside table and leaned forward by a fraction, seeing her ice-blue eyes widen automatically.

'But what if *I* were to wave the magic wand instead?' he questioned slowly.

'By making yourself disappear from my life? Now that really *would* be a wish come true!'

How indomitable she was, he thought. And what remarkable spirit she would pass on to their child! Unexpectedly, he smiled. 'By listening to reason.'

'Are you trying to tell me that you're a reasonable man?'

'I can be.' He paused. 'What if I arranged for someone to stand in for you at work while you're pregnant? Someone who would ably assist the woman who was staring at me so intently when I came to see you today.'

'Daisy,' she said automatically. 'And I can't afford to just hire someone in.'

'Maybe not, but I can. And not just anyone. The very best in the business—someone of your choosing, of course—can be yours for the taking.'

She stared at him, her heart beginning to race, unable to deny that she was tempted by his offer. How easy it was for him, she thought. He could just chuck money at a problem and the problem would go away. What must it be like, to be that powerful? 'And what's the catch?'

'The catch is that you let me look after you.'

'I know I just said you'd make a good nurse, but I wasn't being serious.'

But even as she attempted the poor joke, Hassan could hear the lack of conviction in her voice. Sensing weakness, he moved in for the kill. 'Think about it, Ella. You can spend your days doing exactly as you please. You can read books you never have time for.

You can relax and watch movies.' His eyes strayed upwards to the drawings of her sister and, again, his mouth flattened. 'You could even do some drawing, if you wanted. Maybe it would be good to have time to do those kinds of things for a change?'

Ella felt temptation grow as she considered his offer. Time to paint? Or to do nothing at all? To lie in bed in the morning until this wretched sickness had passed? She imagined not having to dress for work, to slip on the high heels and slap on the makeup. She'd worked since the age of sixteen and she couldn't imagine *not* working, and yet there was no denying that the idea appealed to her.

But she felt like a bit like a starving stray cat who was too scared to reach out to take the morsels of delicious food which were being offered to her.

'It's very generous of you,' she said slowly.

Hassan allowed himself a charitable smile. 'I can afford to be generous.'

She swallowed. 'And what…you'd come and see me from time to time, would you? Whenever you're in London?'

His eyes narrowed. Surely she had understood the main thrust behind his offer—that in return for rescuing her, she would come under his control? He looked at the question in her eyes. It seemed not. 'But that is not my plan,' he said softly. 'I have a country to run and many pressing matters. We have only just finished fighting a war. I won't be in London and neither will you, for you will fly back to Kashamak with me, just as soon as your replacement can be appointed.'

Ella looked at him blankly. 'Kashamak?' she said faintly.

'The land that I rule which produces fine warriors and great poets,' he said proudly. 'And the child that you carry must know all about their heritage, Ella.' There was a pause. 'And so must you.'

Yet deep down, he suspected she would find his land much too harsh for her Western sensibilities. What if prolonged exposure to Kashamak made her want to escape from its restrictions and return to the freedoms of her old life? What if she discovered that motherhood was not for her?

A sudden and audacious thought occurred to him. *She could leave the child behind. Leave him to care for that child, as his own father had cared for him. Because didn't he know better than anyone that you didn't need a mother in order to survive?*

Hassan's heart began to beat with an exultant kind of excitement as he realised what lay within his grasp. That perhaps this was the answer to his prayers. The heir he knew his people wanted and yet which, so far, he had been unwilling to provide, because the idea of marriage had been abhorrent to him. But now he was being forced to marry, wasn't he? And that completely changed the playing field.

Ella watched as his body tensed and wondered what had caused his face to darken like that. 'But I might not want to go and live in Kashamak,' she objected. 'And then what?'

'I think you'll find that you don't really have any choice in the matter,' he snapped, because the alternative was unthinkable, especially now that he had glimpsed the possibilities. The idea of his child being tutored in the ways of the world by the Jackson family would simply not be allowed to happen. He forced his voice to soften as he looked down at her. 'Your welfare is my number-one concern, Ella, and I cannot monitor it if you are thousands of miles away.'

She heard words which sounded as empty as the look in his eyes and a shiver of trepidation whispered its way over her skin. Her welfare was his 'number-one concern,' was it? Sure it was! She didn't believe him. Not for a minute. This felt more about possession than anything else. *His* child and therefore *his* woman.

His hawk-like features looked cruel in that moment, almost triumphant. How she wished she could just pull the bedcovers over her head and make him and all her problems go away.

But he was right. She didn't have a choice. Not really. She was pregnant with the sheikh's baby and she was going to have to accommodate that fact, as were other people. For the first time she thought how this piece of news would go down in Hassan's homeland and she looked up into his flinty eyes.

'Won't your people find it odd if you just turn up with a Western woman who's so obviously pregnant?'

'They would find it completely unacceptable,' he agreed silkily, realising that there was only one solution to their predicament. One which would inevitably mean a deeper association with the outrageous Jackson clan. Instinctively, he baulked against it, but what choice did he have other than to accept it? He looked down into her ice-blue eyes. 'Which is why we must be married immediately.'

Married? Ella stared at him, her heart beginning to beat very fast. 'Are you out of your mind?'

'Not last time I looked.' He saw the tension in her face. 'What's the matter, Ella, were you holding out for Mr Right?'

She thought of her father's multiple marriages and the women whose hearts he had trampled along the way and she shook her head. 'I'm too old to believe in fairy tales,' she said.

His cynical smile mirrored hers. 'Me too. So you see, maybe we are more alike than you think, since neither of us have any illusions to destroy. Maybe that makes us the ideal couple to get married, if the purpose of marriage is to legitimise children. And my country tends to be rather liberal about divorce. If you find living in Kashamak to be unbearable, I will give you your freedom, once the child is born.'

Ella's teeth dug into the fleshy cushion of her bottom lip, because his offer of an easy divorce seemed to make a complete mockery of his marriage proposal. Yet wasn't his suggestion the only thing which made sense in this whole crazy situation? That there was an escape route all mapped out if she chose to take it—and frankly, she couldn't imagine *not* taking it.

It was just his arrogant *certainty* that he could just snap his fingers and she'd fall in with his plans which made her want to rebel. And so did something else—the very real fear that going to a faraway country to live with Hassan would throw up all kinds of new problems. Alone with a man who seemed to despise her… How on earth could she feel comfortable about something like that?

'And what if I refuse?' she challenged quietly. 'What then?'

Hassan stared at her. Was she seriously pitting her will against *his*? It seemed that she was, judging by the sudden determined tilt of her chin, and he forced himself to remember that she was pregnant, and volatile. 'Don't make it hard on yourself, Ella,' he said silkily. 'Why not sit back and let me take care of you?'

His words were like soft but very effective weapons aimed straight at the most vulnerable part of her and Ella felt temptation wash over her. Someone to take care of her. Because when had *that* ever happened before? She thought about the struggle of doing this pregnancy on her own. Of lumbering into work every day on the train and worrying like crazy about money.

And then she thought about this man who had put her in this predicament. She saw the glitter of his black eyes as they observed her. Would it be so terrible to let him take over, to use the abundant power at his fingertips to make her life a little easier? A wave of nausea washed over her and briefly she closed her eyes to let it pass. But it had the effect of emphasising her general weakness and, with a heavy sigh, she nodded. 'Okay,' she said. 'I'll marry you.'

Hassan looked down into her ashen face as he registered her grudging tone and the briefest of smiles glimmered on his lips. Whoever would have predicted it?

That after years of women plotting and scheming to get him to commit, his eventual bride should consent to marry him with such obvious reluctance.

CHAPTER NINE

'So you really *are* called Cinderella?'

Ella had been staring out of the car window at the stark beauty of the desert speeding by, but she turned now to look at the robed figure by her side. *Her new husband.* She might have thought she was in the middle of a particularly bizarre dream were it not for the faint weakness and queasiness she was still experiencing from her pregnancy. But she dredged up a rueful smile from somewhere as she turned to answer Hassan's question. 'I'm afraid I am. Apparently, my father told my mother that giving me such a name meant I'd be bound to marry a prince.'

'Then for once, your father was right,' commented Hassan drily. 'I am rarely surprised, but I certainly was when the registrar read out your full name during the marriage ceremony.'

'I wasn't planning on announcing it,' she admitted, giving a little shrug of her shoulders. 'It's something I tend to keep quiet about, but the registrar insisted that I declare it.'

'You must have been teased about it a lot at school,' he observed.

'Oh, being a Jackson was enough to ensure *that*.

Having a ridiculous Christian name didn't really make any difference.'

But her airy assertion didn't quite ring true and Hassan surveyed her with thoughtful eyes. He'd dismissed her as nothing but a playful flirt when she'd first introduced herself with the storybook name. He'd never have dreamt in a million years that she was telling the truth. And yet it had fitted his stereotypical views of women to think of her as a sexy and teasing minx, rather than this rather solemn mother-to-be who now wore his wedding band. He let his gaze drift over the paleness of her skin and felt a sudden beat of anxiety. 'The car is not too bumpy for you? You don't feel sick?'

'No sicker than I was feeling back in London, and it's nothing to do with the car, or the road. Why, it's so smooth that you'd hardly believe we were speeding along in the middle of a desert!'

'Probably because you imagined the roads of Kashamak would be primitive dirt tracks, potted with holes and barely passable because of camels? Didn't you once say something predictable about camels?'

'Maybe I was a little guilty of that,' she said as she stared down at the shiny new wedding ring on her finger, still dazed by the speed of everything that had happened. Still unable to believe that the dark-faced man sitting at her side really *was* her husband, as well as the father of her child.

Had she been out of her mind to agree to their hasty marriage, or simply too dazed by sickness and general worries to protest about the future? And hadn't her decision to wed him been made easier by his offer of an 'easy' divorce, should she want one?

She sat back against the soft leather of the car seat. 'I wasn't sure what to expect when I got here, but so far everything has defied all my expectations.'

The insights as to how her new life would be had begun the moment she'd boarded the luxury jet on a private airfield just north of London. The flight had been seamless and further than she'd ever flown before. With mainland Europe far behind them, they'd skirted the edges of the beautiful Caspian Sea before coming in to land at the airport in Samaltyn, the capital city of Kashamak.

Protocol had been discreet on the plane, which had been empty save for them and the crew members who outnumbered them. But the moment they'd landed and Ella had heard the national anthem being played, she had realised that she was actually in the company of a real-live king.

While she—unbelievable as it seemed—was his new queen. A queen kitted out in lavish silks which covered every bit of available flesh, except for her face and hands.

Their marriage had taken place in the Kashamak Embassy in central London, with only two diplomats as their witnesses and no advance publicity given out, not even to their respective families. Hassan had been adamant he didn't want an international frenzy with swarms of paparazzi clustering around to take photos of the sheikh's new Western queen.

But Ella knew this wasn't the only reason he had insisted on no fuss and why a quiet statement about their union had been issued only this morning, just as they were about to board their jet. She suspected he was terrified of all the negative publicity which always surrounded the Jackson family. And if that *was* the case, then she was forced to concede that he might be right.

She could just imagine how her family might have sabotaged their wedding day. Her father boasting that his daughter was marrying one of the most powerful men in the Middle East. Her mother playing her habitual doormat role beside him. And Izzy—heaven forbid—trying to sing her congratulations.

But Ella was also afraid that one of her sisters might have discovered the truth behind her bright smile and realised the heavy burden she was carrying. That Hassan was only marrying her to stamp his mark of possession on their unborn baby.

And now they were travelling in a sleek air-conditioned car towards Hassan's palace, on roads which were as flat as millponds. She felt…well, she felt as displaced as most women would feel if they were newly pregnant and leaving behind everything they knew. *But most women in her position would have the comfort of knowing that they were loved and desired, instead of regarded as some sort of royal incubator.*

Her actions instinctively mirroring her turbulent emotions, she moved her hand to let it rest on her stomach.

'You are experiencing discomfort?' questioned Hassan instantly. 'Some kind of pain?'

She shook her head, because she had decided that she was going to be strong. She wasn't going to start whingeing every time she had a little ache or wave of sickness. 'Hassan, I'm fine.'

He stared at the fingers which were curled protectively over her stomach, wondering when this would all start to feel real. As if it was happening to him and not to someone else. He stared at the unfamiliar bump and tried to make sense of it. 'The baby is kicking?'

'No, not yet.'

'When?'

Her fingers tightened around the still unfamiliar swell. 'Any day now, I hope.'

'How can you know all these things?'

His dark, gleaming eyes were curious and Ella thought at that moment how gorgeous he looked, and yet how unreachable too. His traditional Kashmakian robes made him look so darkly foreign and yet the flowing silk emphasised the honed body beneath, mocking her with memories of that snatched and forbidden night they'd spent together. The first and only time they'd made love...

Blocking out the sudden flare of desire which shimmered over her skin and the inevitable questions that raised, she attempted to answer his question.

'There's a chart which you can download from the internet and it tells you all the things you can expect,' she explained carefully. 'Movement starts around sixteen weeks.'

'And will you let me feel my child when it kicks, Ella?' he questioned suddenly. 'Will you let me lay my hand on your belly so that I can feel it move?'

Despite the cool of the air conditioning, Ella's cheeks grew heated at the intimacy of his question.

Their night of passion had happened so long ago that sometimes it seemed as if it was nothing but a distant dream. And the more time passed, the more unreal it seemed. Because there had been no revisiting of that passion since that night. No sense that he wanted to touch her in any way at all.

So if he laid his hand on her stomach, would that start her yearning for a greater intimacy altogether? Did he still want her in that way? she wondered.

'Yes, of course you can,' she answered quietly, knowing that she couldn't possibly refuse him. Not just because he was the baby's father, but because he'd done so much to help her. And for once in her life she had just sat back and let him help with a passivity which she put down to her pregnancy and to the accompanying nausea which still hit her in waves.

Somehow, Hassan had produced a clutch of women who were eager to step into her shoes at work and Ella had interviewed every one of them. And right now, back in England, Daisy was working quite happily alongside her replacement, while the business was ticking along just fine.

But there were more things to occupy her mind other than the business she'd left behind. Ahead she could see an enormous and elaborate pair of golden gates dazzling in the sunshine and, beyond those, neat lines of palm trees bordering a bright rectangle of water. A vast creamy-gold building rose up in the distance—a structure so wide and so grand that, once again, she wanted to pinch herself to convince herself she wasn't dreaming.

They had reached the royal palace at last, and suddenly all her doubts came skimming to the surface, making her stomach churn with fear. Had she forgotten who she was? Just one of the notorious Jacksons whose father had kept the British press entertained for years. How could she go from being mocked and ridiculed to wearing a crown on her head and carrying it off with any degree of confidence?

'Hassan, I can't do this,' she croaked. 'What if your people won't accept me?'

Hearing the crack in her voice, Hassan turned, trying to see her as others would see her for the first time. She was wearing an exquisite Kashamak robe in bridal colours of deep scarlet and ornamental gold. Her hair was covered by a golden veil and her eyes were ringed heavily with kohl pencil. Even her scarlet lipstick had been replaced by a glimmering rose-pink, which made her mouth look so much softer.

She had told him that she wanted her first appearance in his land to be as traditional as possible and he respected her for her thoughtfulness. And she looked, he thought with a sudden wrench of longing, absolutely beautiful. A delectable mixture of East and West, she seemed to represent the very best of both their cultures.

'Your appearance is faultless,' he said slowly. 'You need not concern yourself on that score. And as king, my people will accept what I tell them to accept.'

His reassuring words gave her a moment of comfort and she clung to it, as a child would to a security blanket. 'And what about your brother, Kamal?'

He flicked her a glance. 'What about him?'

'I'm…looking forward to meeting him.'

His smile was bland. 'That won't be happening immediately, I'm afraid, since he has decided to ride off into the desert in order to escape the rigours of court life.'

Ella swallowed. Or to escape from having to meet *her*? she wondered. 'Didn't you say that he's been running the country while you were away fighting the war? Won't he mind handing back the reins to you?' She hesitated. 'Power can be addictive stuff.'

He gave a hard smile. 'Kamal is going to have to get used to a lot of changes,' he said. 'And to build a new role for himself. Because, of course, of much greater significance to him than my returning to rule is the fact that you are carrying my child.' *And hadn't he always led his brother to believe that he had no desire to procreate? Would Kamal think that he had broken his word and thus changed both their destinies?*

Ella's voice broke into his troubled thoughts.

'And that child will one day inherit?' she asked.

'Only if it is a son.' His black eyes bored into her. '*Is* it a son, Ella? Do you know that already?'

She felt colour rising in her cheeks as his gaze washed over her. 'No, no, I don't. They couldn't tell on the first scan and I...'

'What?'

She shook her head, hating the way that he made her feel like a butterfly pinned onto a piece of cardboard. 'I don't want to know!' she said fiercely. 'I don't want that kind of pressure spoiling the pregnancy in any way. I don't want you being pleased if it's a boy and your brother being pleased if it's a girl, so that I'll end up feeling tugged both ways. I want the surprise of *not* knowing. Otherwise it will be like knowing what all your Christmas presents are before you actually get around to unwrapping them.'

For a moment, he smiled. 'I'm afraid we don't celebrate Christmas in Kashamak,' he offered drily.

'Well, your birthday presents, then.'

'I wouldn't really know about that either.'

She stared at him in disbelief. 'You're not trying to tell me you never had any birthday presents?'

'So what if I didn't?' He shrugged. 'My father was too busy for that kind of thing. Sometimes he remembered, sometimes not. It wasn't important.'

Ella's heart gave a funny little flip. Of course it was important, especially to a child. It was the one day a year when you could guarantee that all the attention would be focused on you. You got the feeling that you were loved and cared for. Even when money was at its tightest her mother had always managed to pull together *some* sort of celebration. And it couldn't have been easy for her, she realised suddenly. Not easy at all.

'And what about your mother, didn't she want a birthday cake for her little boy?'

Silently, he cursed her overemotional use of language. Was that deliberate? Was she trying to get under his skin, in the way that women always did? 'My mother wasn't around,' he clipped out.

'What happened to her?' Ella's voice softened. 'You never mention her, Hassan. Did she...did she die?'

The knuckles of his fists gleamed white as Hassan clenched his hands over his silk-clad thighs. 'No, she didn't die—at least, not then. She left us to find a different kind of life, and I don't particularly want to talk about it. Especially not now at such a significant moment. Look, here are my advisers and staff come out to greet us. Prepare yourself, Ella, for I am sure you know how important first impressions are.'

Hearing the finality in his voice as he halted the discussion about his childhood, Ella straightened her golden veil with trembling fingers. She certainly remembered her first impression of *him*. How his dark and proudly arrogant beauty had seemed to call out to something deep inside her. How for one blissful night she thought she'd found it, only to have it swept away by his callous desertion of her. Had that been just an illusion? she wondered. And had she been guilty of imagining a special bond where none existed, as a way of justifying her own wanton behaviour?

The powerful car drew to a halt and her memories melted away in the presence of a practical dilemma. Because how on earth did you prepare yourself to face people as their brand-new queen?

'Do they know I'm pregnant?' she asked.

At this he gave an odd kind of smile. 'Of course not, though it is fairly obvious to all but the most careless observer. But you need not concern yourself with that, Ella. Don't you know what they say about royalty? Never complain and never explain. There will be no need for any kind of announcement. Many of my people will not realise the good news until a child is presented to them, for you will largely be hidden from view.'

Hidden from view?

What the hell did *that* mean?

His words sent feelings of alarm skittering over her

skin but there wasn't time to demand further explanation because the door to the car was being opened and a warm blast of fragrant air hit her. Ella exited the car as gracefully as she could—not an easy move, given that her beautiful gown was so jewel-encrusted that it weighed a ton.

Slowly, she walked along two lines of assembled people, where the advisers were exclusively male and wore subdued versions of Hassan's robes. The only women present were servants and they lowered their eyes deferentially as she walked along the line, shyly uttering the Kashamak greeting she'd been practising for days.

There was so much to take in. High ceilings and marble floors, the glimmer of gold and the glitter of crystal. Was this how her sister Allegra had felt when she'd first arrived in Alex's royal palace? Blown away by the sense of history and tradition? And the wealth, of course. Only this was the real thing. Not the kind she'd known when she was growing up, when one minute they'd all be driving around in a gold limousine and the next hiding from the bailiffs.

This was rock-solid wealth. Enduring and sustaining. Money like this could totally influence your thinking and behaviour. And yet, this was their child's heritage, she realised. All this splendour and beauty was his or hers by birth—and she did not have the right to deny their baby that.

'Clearly you approve?' Hassan had watched with interest the movement of her ice-blue eyes as they quickly assessed her surroundings. Was she silently adding up his worth and realising that never again would she want for money?

'It's beautiful,' she breathed. 'Absolutely beautiful.'

Briefly, he found himself wondering whether he should have taken his lawyer's advice and made her sign a prenuptial agreement. But something about that action had made him baulk. It had seemed inherently wrong to ask that of the mother of his child. No matter how outrageous her demands for any divorce settlement, he could easily afford it. And a woman who was satisfied with her pay-out would be less likely to cause trouble in the future....

'So...you must be tired after the long journey,' he said. 'Would you like to see your quarters?'

'My...*quarters*?' Ella's smile was uncertain. 'Um, you've left the army now, Hassan.'

'Forgive me.' His answering smile concealed a faint confusion, an unknown feeling of being out of his depth. Who cared *what* he called it, the detail was surely insignificant? Usually, he would have gone straight off to long meetings with aides and ministers, followed by a hard ride on one of his horses. But now the comforting familiarity of his routine had been broken by a woman with rose-pink lips and ice-blue eyes.

His wife.

If it was anyone else, he would have assigned a servant to show her around. But because it was Ella and she was pregnant and therefore vulnerable, he found himself in the unheard-of position of being her guide. *And for the first time in his life, he felt out of his depth.*

'I will show you to your suite of rooms. Does that sound better?'

'*My* suite?' She looked at him in surprise. For weeks, she'd been psyching herself up for married life. She'd vacillated between wondering if she was crazy to go through with it, or whether it was the only sane choice. But once she'd decided to marry Hassan, one comforting thought had remained to sustain her. At least sex with her new husband was guaranteed to be amazing. He'd shown her that she could experience pleasure in his arms, and the truth was that she couldn't wait to sample it again. She edged him a tentative smile. 'But surely we'll be sharing a suite, as a married couple?'

Hassan shook his head, wiping out the tempting thoughts provoked by the soft curve of her lips. 'It is not the tradition, no, not here. It dates back from the days when a monarch always had to be ready to go to war and did not want to disturb his wife if he left for battle in the middle of the night. So his isolation was a necessity, rather than a luxury.'

Ella's heart missed a beat. 'You're joking?'

'No, I am not. I am simply abiding by tradition, as well as giving you the opportunity to have some private space of your own.' He saw the way her blue eyes had clouded, but for the hundredth time, he told himself it was better this way. Better for both of them. For a divorce would be far simpler if there had been no intimacy. His voice gentled by a fraction. 'My culture is very different from the one you've grown up in, Ella, and you'll need to accept that if you want to find any kind of contentment here.'

Contentment? Did he think she was going to be

content if she was going to be locked away like a nun
without even the warm comfort of her new husband
by her side? She stared at him, daring herself to voice
the truth. 'So we aren't going to be a proper married
couple?'

Almost reluctantly, Hassan let his eyes drift over
her. With the golden veil framing her pale face he
thought how lovely she looked, like some fragile, shimmering statue. In that moment, he could have pulled
her close to him and drunk in her exquisite beauty
with a passionate kiss. But something stopped him
and that something was logic. This was nothing but a
marriage of convenience, made with the sole purpose
of legitimising their baby. Much better by far to keep
their relationship on a formal footing.

'But we aren't a proper married couple, are we,
Ella?' he questioned, his harsh tone subduing the sexual hunger which had flared inside him. 'We were
never intended to be. And I think it best if we don't
complicate this already difficult situation by pretend-
ing to be something we're not.'

Ella felt his words rip through her like a chill wind
and she stared at him in dismay, realising how isolated
her life was going to be if Hassan was planning on distancing himself from her.

Well, she certainly wasn't going to *beg* him to sleep
with her! Biting back her hurt, she accompanied him
along the wide expanse of marble corridor, wanting to
ask him why the hell he hadn't told her all this *before*
he'd made her his bride.

Because he *couldn't* have told her, that was why. If
he'd given her any intimation of how constricted her

life would be in his country then she would have refused to come. No amount of money or the promise of a quick divorce would have tempted her to a life of virtual imprisonment. She would have found some other way to support herself because she would have *had* to.

To all intents and purposes, Hassan had deceived her. But that was now irrelevant. She couldn't change what had happened. All she could do was react to it. And she would do what she had done all her life, no matter what fate had thrown at her. She would adapt to circumstances and she would make the best of them.

But her determination wavered as Hassan informed her that dinner would be at eight and that a servant would come to collect her.

The door closed behind him and she was left alone in the gilded suite. She looked up at the glitter of the crystal chandelier and breathed in the deep scent of the roses which had been crammed into beautiful golden vases. It all looked so perfect, but so unreal. And it *felt* unreal too. As if someone had put her down in the middle of a film set and if she pushed too hard she might discover that the walls were made of cardboard.

Another wave of sickness washed over her and quickly she lay down on the bed, clutching one of the brocade cushions to her stomach as she tried to fight against a tide of tears.

CHAPTER TEN

ANOTHER day in paradise.

Ella stared out of the window which had just been unshuttered by one of the sweet maids whose job it was to attend her. The early-morning scent of flowers wafted fragrance into the room and vied with the perfume of the jasmine tea which stood on the filigree cabinet beside her large bed.

Leaning back against the feathery plumpness of the pillows, she contemplated what the new day might bring. Outside, there was a vast swimming pool which she could use any time she wanted. The beautiful gardens were enormous and varied, with plenty of shaded paths for her to walk along. Benches were positioned at eye-catching vantage points where she could stop to read a book from the palace's vast and comprehensive library. Anything Ella wanted, she could have.

Except it wasn't quite like that.

The one thing she really wanted constantly eluded her.

She wanted her husband.

She wanted to relive the passion they'd shared that night back in Santina, when she'd tasted pleasure for the first time in her life. And surely as his wife she was entitled to that?

The sickness she'd experienced had now passed and she realised that she hadn't been herself when she'd agreed to this marriage. He had asked her—or rather, *told* her—that she would be his wife when she had been at her most vulnerable. Still reeling from the discovery of the baby and weakened by nausea, she had allowed Hassan to take command.

But something had changed. Now that she felt better, it seemed as if she had got some of the old Ella back, and then some. She was filled with a new vigour, buzzing with energy and life. And not only was she growing increasingly frustrated at the celibate state of her marriage, she was determined to do something about it. So what if she was only destined to be here for months. Couldn't they at least be *pleasurable* months?

Had the desire Hassan felt for her disappeared? Ella didn't think so. She may not have been the most experienced woman in the world, but she had definitely seen the hard gleam of his eyes sometimes when they were alone at dinner. Hadn't she once noticed his big body tense when she reached forward to pluck a ripe damson from the heap of fruit piled in a shallow dish? And sit there perfectly still for a moment or two afterwards, as if he was composing himself? No, Hassan certainly wasn't immune to her, no matter how much he'd like to be.

The strangest thing was that once she had allowed herself to acknowledge that what she was feeling was sexual frustration, the feeling just grew and grew. It became so that it dominated her thoughts. So that every time she looked into Hassan's hawk-like features, all she could remember was his helpless look of abandon as he plunged deep inside her body.

She wanted him.

She wanted him badly.

And she realised that nobody was going to make it happen except her.

Quietening the voice in her head which asked if she wasn't crazy to consider seducing such a proud and worldly man as Hassan, she set about her plan.

Piecing together fragments of things she'd read in magazines and books back home in England, she waited until Saturday evening, because she'd learnt that Saturday was one of her husband's lightest days, in terms of royal duties. And that he often lay in bed late on a Sunday...

Dressing carefully in a filmy azure gown which made her eyes look intensely blue, she spent ages on her hair and her makeup. Not too much makeup, because she'd also learnt that where Hassan was concerned, less was more. The ebony sweep of her lashes and rose-pink glimmer of her mouth was flattering but very natural, so that she might almost have been born that way.

As she joined him in the dining room, she was filled with a nervous kind of excitement, and a sudden realisation of what she was about to do made her momentarily reconsider whether she was being sensible. What if he rejected her?

As he rose to greet her, she heard the soft swish of his silken robes and once again she remembered the magnificent body which lay beneath. Swallowing down her fears, she quickly replaced them with determination. She would not *let* him reject her!

A servant poured iced water into her goblet and began to serve the meal, but Ella barely paid it any attention. She pushed various delicious slithers of neglected food around her golden plate and tried not to stare at her husband's dark and thoughtful face.

'You're not eating much,' Hassan observed suddenly.

'Aren't I?' she questioned innocently.

'No.' He studied her through the flickering light of the countless candles which illuminated the gilded room and thought how much she bloomed as every day passed. And what hell it was to resist the temptation of taking her to his bed...

With an effort, he forced his attention back to her lacklustre appetite. 'Are you displeased with the fare which my chefs have slaved over all day in order to impress the sheikh's new bride?'

'The food is delicious. As always.'

'So why haven't you touched it?'

'Because I'm not...' Her words tailed off as nerves began to get the better of her. How could she possibly seduce a man who showed no sign of wanting to be seduced, despite the fact that they were newlyweds?

She wondered what had happened to the hungry hunter who had dragged her to bed on the night of the engagement party. Maybe he was one of those men who only enjoyed sex with a woman he didn't know. Maybe he shied away from that whole intimacy thing. Or was turned off by the fact she was pregnant.

Or maybe he just didn't fancy her any more.

Her pulse rocketed at the thought of tackling such a daunting mission. That she, who had never seduced anyone, should be taking on one of the world's great lovers. Yet Ella wasn't easily defeated. There were many disadvantages to being a Jackson, but one thing it gave you was determination—and grit.

'Not what?' he prompted.

She pushed away her dish more heavily than she'd intended and leaned back against the brocade cushions. 'I'm not very hungry,' she said.

Hassan felt a pulse began to flicker at his temple. 'You need to…eat,' he said unsteadily, trying to ignore the fact that the position she'd now adopted meant that her breasts were looking especially lush and inviting. And hadn't he been resolutely trying to avoid thinking about her breasts, or her lips, or indeed any part of her which reminded him of thrusting deep into her body?

Ella shifted her position a little, pleased to see that the blue silk of her robe was now clinging to her thighs like melted butter. And that Hassan seemed transfixed by the movement. She slanted him a smile, telling herself there was nothing to be gained from a lack of courage. 'I keep thinking of you, asleep nearby.'

'Do you?' He wondered what she'd say if he told her that he had been getting precious little sleep of late. That oblivion stayed tantalisingly out of reach as he lay there imagining the silken touch of her skin and the enticing curves of her body.

'Mmm. And sometimes it gets so hot.'

Did that mean she slept naked? An unstoppable image of her milky thighs and rose-tipped breasts crys-

tallised in his mind and Hassan almost sliced the top
of his thumb with the knife he had been using to peel
a peach. With trembling fingers, he put both down.
'The palace is air-conditioned,' he growled.

'I know it is, but sometimes I turn it off because
it's noisy. And…' Oh, for heaven's sake! Ella winced.
What kind of a seduction was *this* if all they were doing
was talking about the wretched air conditioning? 'And
I wish you were there with me. I'd like that.' She hesitated as she looked straight into his eyes and drew a
deep breath. 'In fact, I'd like that very much.'

Hassan tensed as the innocent longing of her words
cut through him in a way that the most seasoned seduction could never have done. He felt the tight, hard
spring of an erection and silently cursed her. 'That isn't
a good idea,' he said thickly.

'Why not? What's stopping us?'

He shook his head. A fear of intimacy, that was what
was stopping them. Or rather, stopping *him*. And a very
real fear of how such intimacy could complicate this
strange marriage of theirs. Should he tell her that he
saw nothing but danger if they succumbed, that sex
could sometimes cast a dark and distorting spell? But
how could he tell her anything when she was pushing back her dark, glossy hair and he was imagining
it tumbling down over her naked breasts?

'Ella,' he ground out.

'What?' she whispered, thrilled to see his formidable mask drop for once, to reveal the man beneath.
To suddenly see the hard-faced desert sheikh with all
the vulnerabilities and doubts of any other person.

With an effort of will which seemed only a little

easier than the time he'd had to endure a full day's ride without fresh water to sustain him, Hassan stood.

'It has been a long day for both of us,' he bit out. 'Come, I will escort you to your room.'

Ella could have wept with disappointment as she realised that the formidable mask was back in place. It hadn't worked and she had no one to blame but herself. All she'd done was to stumble out her pathetic little desire to have him sleep with her. Shouldn't she have been a bit bolder than that? Reached out and *touched* him maybe? Wasn't that what women usually did when they were trying to seduce a man?

What had seemed like a brilliant idea at the time now seemed like complete madness. Once again, she had simply reinforced all his awful prejudices about her and her family with her attempt at seduction, only she couldn't even do *that* properly.

'Very well,' she said stiffly, rising to her feet and waving away the hand he extended to assist her. Did he think she was some kind of invalid?

In smouldering silence she walked alongside him through marbled corridors which were open on one side to the scented courtyard gardens. She heard the soft movement of their flowing robes and the sweet, high trill of a bird she thought might be a nightingale. It seemed almost painfully beautiful and yet she could take no pleasure in it. All she could feel was a terrible emptiness inside, and an underlying ache that he no longer seemed to find her attractive as a woman.

The journey to her room seemed to take forever and she found herself wondering how she was going to be able to endure such an empty and lonely existence, knowing that there was no hope it would ever change.

'Here we are,' he said abruptly as he stopped outside the door to her suite. 'I'll leave you here.'

'Yes.' She looked up at him, surprised by the ravaged look on his face. What had put that terrible bleakness in those eyes of his? she wondered. Had *she*? Had her failed attempt to seduce him reminded him that she shouldn't even *be* here? That she wouldn't be here were it not for the baby? 'Hassan, those things I said at dinner…I, well, I shouldn't have said them. I shouldn't have come on to you like that.'

There was silence for a moment, and when he spoke, his voice sounded as if it was being half strangled out of him.

'I don't want to hurt you, Ella,' he ground out.

She looked at him in confusion. How could he hurt her any more than she was already hurting from him pushing her away? 'I don't understand,' she whispered.

At that moment she looked so damned soft that Hassan felt the unfamiliar prickle of guilt. Usually he used women before they could use him and he had no compunction about doing so. But Ella was different. Even putting her fragility aside, what if deep down she had expectations of him which he could never honour? What if she expected him to be like other men, to feel the things which women wanted men to feel? Could he really bear to crush her hopes and her dreams when she realised that his words had been true. That his heart *was* cold. That it would be easier to facilitate an end to this marriage if they had not grown close through sex.

He made one last appeal as he looked down into the

rose-pink gleam of her lips. 'Don't you realise that this is going to complicate everything?'

'What is?'

'This is,' he ground out. *'This!'*

She honestly didn't realise it was coming until he pulled her into his arms and started kissing her with a fierce urgency which instantly set her on fire. Her arms snaked up round his neck and she clung to him, almost wanting to sob aloud with joy. So he *did* want her—and judging by the tension in his powerful body, he wanted her as badly as she wanted him.

She wondered whether this wasn't a bit public, standing, making out in the corridor of the darkened palace, until she remembered that they were newly-weds. This is exactly what they were *supposed* to be doing, she thought exultantly as he pushed open the door to her suite and pulled her inside.

His hands were shaking and so was his voice as he pulled his mouth away from hers and cradled her face in his palms. 'I don't know how gentle I can be.'

'You don't have to be *gentle*.'

'You're carrying my baby, Ella.'

She turned her head so that her lips brushed against his fingers. 'Well, unless you were planning to tie me up and suspend me from the ceiling...'

'Stop it.' For a moment he bit back unexpected laughter as he ran his fingers through her hair so that the glorious waves of her red-brown hair tumbled free. 'How about if we take it very slowly this time?'

'I'm not sure that I can,' she whispered.

He wasn't sure that he could either, but he would make sure that he was careful. He led her over to the bed and slowly peeled the silken robe from her body. And this was a first too. He'd never undressed a woman who was wearing his own traditional robes and it seemed to add another dimension to the surreal aspect of what was taking place. It was as if all his certainties had been shaken up and scattered haphazardly, like a handful of dice thrown onto a gaming table. And everything was up for grabs. Including his blushing wife.

Clad in exquisite lingerie, her lashes half shaded her blue eyes as she watched his reaction. The cami-knickers clung to her slender hips and the silk bra caressed the curve of her breasts. Eyes narrowing, he studied the pale, creamy colour of the garments which looked distinctly bridal.

'Did you choose this especially for me?' he questioned unevenly, curving his finger around the lace edge of her bra.

'Of course I did. I went out shopping especially.' Hadn't she slunk out almost shamefacedly to buy it in the few hours available before their rushed wedding? Wondering if she was being a hypocrite by purchasing brand-new underwear for a wedding which felt distinctly empty. Yet now Ella was pleased she'd done it. It had been worth all those doubts just to see the dark fire which had shifted the emptiness from his eyes. 'It's called a trousseau. It's what every bride should wear on her honeymoon. I know that, traditionally, it's supposed to be white, but I don't really qualify for white, do I?'

'Who cares about that?' he questioned roughly.

'You mean you don't?'

He shook his head. He hadn't seen her body since the night of the party and it had changed. Of course it had. The breasts were fuller and her belly curved over the edge of her lace panties. He gave a groan which was part lust and part admiration as he let his fingers curl over the gentle swell, because beneath her silken robes, he hadn't realised how big she was getting. Did all men experience a rush of possessive pride when they witnessed their child growing in a woman's belly? he wondered.

'You look beautiful,' he husked as he pushed her down onto the bed, quickly removing his own robes before joining her and pulling a throw over them both.

'I'm not cold,' she murmured as they were cocooned in the light concealment of silk.

'No?' He kissed the soft flesh of her shoulder. 'Then why are you shivering?'

'You know very well why,' she whispered as she curled her hand around his neck and brought his head down to kiss her. It was the second assertive thing she'd done that evening and it seemed to liberate Hassan from his porcelain-like treatment of her as he opened her lips with the thrust of his tongue.

Ella could feel the warmth of his breath mingling with hers. His kiss was like a drug—one taste and she was hooked. Deeply and passionately she kissed him back, her fingers kneading at the silken skin which played over the muscles of his back. And then he began to touch her.

Everywhere.

She closed her eyes. This was unbelievable. Even better than last time. She could feel the relentless heat building inside her as he unclipped her bra to free her aching breasts, capturing first one and then the other in the hot, moist cavern of his mouth. She was restless and gasping by the time he slid her panties off. She knew he'd said he was going to take it slowly, but *really*...

'Keep still,' he urged her mockingly.

'I *can't*!'

Concerned that his weight might press on the baby, he brought her instead to sit on top of him, positioning the tip of his erection against her slick, moist folds. But even as he gripped her hips to slowly guide himself inside her, he was aware of a sudden sense of discovery. Of something unfamiliar happening to him. He felt the warmth of her thighs as they pressed into his sides and he shuddered as she pushed her hips forward to make him go even deeper. And then he realised what it was. That this was the first time he'd ever had sex with a pregnant woman, and the first time he'd never worn protection.

And it felt...

He closed his eyes. It felt *unbelievable.* He'd overheard men talking about the joys of 'riding bareback' while knowing that, for him, it would never be an option. Because royal seed was too precious to squander by careless lust or an inability to wait. But now he was experiencing it for the first time in his life, and it felt almost unbearably intimate as he thrust deep inside her. Skin on skin. Her slick heat against his hard heat.

'I'm not hurting you?' he managed.

Ella shook her head, barely able to speak, realising that she had wanted this so much. To feel this close to him again. To experience the pleasure which only he had ever given her. 'I'm going to…going to…'

'I can see that for myself,' he murmured, watching as her head tipped back with helpless joy. She made a moaning sound as she came, a low note of uninhibited pleasure which initiated the beginning of his own orgasm. Holding tightly onto her hips, he felt the powerful spasms which swept him up in a mindless spill he never wanted to end.

Afterwards, his head fell back against the pillow and he felt as drained and as elated as a battle-weary soldier. Yet even as his hand encircled her waist to draw her closer and he found himself breathing in the raw scent of sex, he found himself thinking that this could get addictive. Dangerously addictive. The combined warmth of their damp skin made their bodies seemed glued together and he found himself absently kissing the tangle of her hair as long, silent minutes ticked by.

He must have slept more deeply than usual because when he opened his eyes, sunlight was filtering through the open shutters and the early-morning scent of roses was powerfully intoxicating. For a moment he didn't remember where he was, but as he turned to see the sleeping form of Ella beside him, it all came back. Her shy and stumbled entreaty at dinner. A hesitant seduction which had proved inordinately irresistible.

Yawning, he thought that his senses had never felt so finely tuned, nor so richly satiated. Last night had been, he realised, the most erotic experience of his life.

More than that, he felt a rare moment of contentment which allowed him to push away the nagging questions which were hovering at the back of his mind.

He knew that there were a million things he should be doing. He should rouse himself and move away from the warm comfort of this bed....

But instead, he picked up a handful of Ella's hair, watching as it fell in satin tendrils across his chest before bending his lips to her ear. 'Awake?' he questioned lazily.

She wriggled and smiled against the pillow. 'I am now.'

He guided her hand towards his aching groin. 'You are the most amazing lover, do you know that?'

Ella froze as her fingers encountered the steely shaft of his erection, and in the cold light of day, fear began to run through her veins. What if he now expected her to run through a repertoire of sexual skills—skills she didn't have, and which would leave him sorely disappointed?

Before, she had not cared about his good opinion of her but suddenly it became vital that he should know the truth. 'I'm not the person you think I am,' she said, pulling her hand away from him. Even though she saw his eyes narrow with disappointment, he needed to realise that she wasn't the sexual expert he imagined her to be. Not some uber-experienced party girl with dozens of men in her past and a long list of lovers she could barely remember.

Hassan winced, wondering why women always chose precisely the wrong moment to pour out their feelings. But he was in no position to move. He registered the heavy aching at his groin and realised he was in no position to do anything except... 'And what kind of person is that?' he questioned unsteadily.

She drew in a deep breath. 'I don't make a habit of seducing men.'

'I'd kind of worked that out for myself, Ella.'

'You had?'

'Mmm.' He moved his hand between her legs. 'Last night you came over as sweet, rather than seasoned.'

She wondered if that was a good thing or a bad thing. In fact, it was difficult to wonder anything when he was stroking her like that. 'Up…up until that night of the party, I'd…well, I'd never behaved like that before.'

'I'm very pleased to hear it,' he replied gravely.

'I'd only ever had a relationship with one other person. And I went out with him for ages before we had sex.' Through her growing waves of pleasure, she met the question in his eyes, admitting to herself for the first time that she'd been scared of sex. She'd seen from the example set by her own parents what fools men and women could make of themselves in its pursuit. 'When eventually we did it, I…well, I tried my best. But I never…never…' She shook her head, the words sticking in her throat.

'You never had an orgasm before me?' he guessed as he remembered the way she'd clung to him that first time. And suddenly it all made sense. The breathless little words which had sounded almost like gratitude as she had bucked wildly in his arms.

'Right.' She looked into his eyes, wary now that she had given too much away. Wouldn't a man like him hate such transparency? 'So I misled you. I'm not the woman you thought I was. Are you angry with me, Hassan?'

His mouth twitched. 'Absolutely furious,' he said.
'Seriously?'

His laugh was low as his fingertip thrummed
against her heated flesh. 'Oh, Ella,' he murmured.
'Don't you know that it's every man's fantasy to be
the first person to awaken a woman in that way? I *like*
the fact that I am the only man to have shown you true
pleasure. That everything you learn will spring from
my lips and my loins.' His voice dipped into a throaty
murmur. 'Shall I show you how good it feels when a
man tastes a woman?'

Shyly, she nodded, her cheeks growing warm as
he began to move his lips slowly down over her body.
And in that moment she thought she'd just discovered
the *real* danger of sex. Because when a man made her
feel this good… When his tongue was licking her in
places where she'd never imagined being licked… It
was easy to start imagining what it might be like if
Hassan loved her.

And that was *never* going to happen.

CHAPTER ELEVEN

'HASSAN.' Ella paused long enough to ensure that she had her husband's complete attention. 'I can't spend much more time doing this.'

Hassan looked up from his newspaper. The light was flooding into the breakfast room and glimmering off the red-brown curls which spilled over Ella's shoulders. The silk robe she wore was loose and flowing but the unmistakable swell of her belly drew the eye like nothing else. And the by-now familiar sense of wonder settled over him as he surveyed the blossoming body of his wife.

The passing weeks had made obvious the unspoken secret within the palace—that the queen was with child. And Hassan couldn't help but question if that was the reason for his brother's continuing absence from court life. It was unlike Kamal to be away from Kashamak for so long but attempts to contact him had proved fruitless and Hassan had been forced to accept that his nonappearance was deliberate.

Was his younger brother hurt that his position as heir apparent might soon be assumed by a newborn baby? Or just angry that Hassan had done what he had vowed he would never do: marry and procreate?

Yet maybe it was better that Kamal wasn't here, demanding to know what his position would be once the baby was born. Leaving Hassan to admit for the first time in his life that he just *didn't know.* That nothing was as it seemed, or as he had thought it would be. That he had been lulled into a curious state of contentment by the sweet nights he now shared with his wife. A false contentment, he reminded himself grimly, and nothing but a pleasurable distraction while they awaited the birth of their child.

Because hadn't there always been the underlying certainty that they would divorce soon afterwards? Hadn't the thought that she might go back to England leaving their baby for him to raise been his secret desire?

But he had come to realise that was never going to happen. Sex taught you much about a woman beyond how she liked you to play with her breasts, and Hassan had discovered a dangerously sweet and soft side to Ella which had defied all his expectations.

Shaking his head to clear his thoughts, he looked at Ella's faintly disgruntled expression. 'What did you say?'

'That I can't carry on doing nothing all day!'

'You are bored?' he questioned.

'Not bored, exactly. More a little restless.' She shrugged her shoulders, aware of the heavy swell of the baby as she moved. 'The gardens are wonderful and so are all the books in the library, but I…'

'What?'

She met his black gaze. What would he say if she told him that she wanted to spend more time with *him*?

Quality time which involved finding out more about him as a person. That seeing him only at breakfast, dinner and when they were in bed at night was proving oddly frustrating. Or maybe the source of her frustration was Hassan's ability to keep her at an emotional distance. She felt as if she could never actually get *through* to him. That after the confidences she'd shared with him during their first night together at the palace, the shutters had come slamming down again. Why did he *do* that? she wondered. Why did he guard his feelings so that she never really knew what was going on in his head?

Oh, he played the part of attentive husband to perfection. He fussed around and made sure she was comfortable, sometimes causing the servants to smile as he positioned a cushion behind her back, like some overzealous nursemaid. Sometimes he even did cute things, like picking her the sweetest pomegranate from the bowl and having the chef prepare it just the way she liked it. And things like that got to her every time.

But somehow it all felt like some sort of displacement therapy. She still felt as if he was pushing her away from him. She fixed him with a steady look. 'I need to get my teeth into something.'

He put the paper down and gave her his undivided attention. 'By doing what, exactly?'

'I want to paint you, Hassan.'

He slanted her a reflective look. 'Run that past me again?'

She took a deep breath, her well-rehearsed words coming out in a rush. 'In London, you promised that I could paint out here if I wanted—and I do. When…

when the baby arrives...' She met his eyes, acutely aware of his sudden watchfulness. 'Well, I certainly won't have time to paint then, will I? So I'd like to do it now, while I can.'

Hassan drummed his fingers against the table, but could see instantly that her idea had merit. His aversion to sitting still was legendary. So wouldn't his people be pleased to have a new portrait of him, as well as giving her something to do?

'I suppose it's a possibility,' he conceded slowly. 'As long as you're aware that my schedule is packed and my time is very precious. I can't sit for hours on end.'

'I know that. I'm not expecting you to. Please, Hassan?' Ella made no attempt to hide her eagerness because she wanted this. She didn't care how snatched their sessions were; she needed to do something other than *wait*. To focus on something other than the baby and her uncertain future, and the sense that her feelings for Hassan were growing stronger than she'd ever intended them to be.

Was that what happened when a man made love to you every night, so beautifully that sometimes it was as much as she could do to prevent tears of joy spilling from her eyes afterwards? Was nature a cunning as well as a random mistress, making a woman form a strong attachment to the man whose child she carried, no matter how emotionally distant that man was?

Well, painters always learned masses about their sitters during portrait sessions—everyone knew that. Maybe this was the only way to get through to him and to find out what really made him tick.

She looked at him enquiringly. 'So can I?'

'How can I possibly deny you when you ask so sweetly?' He picked up his newspaper to resume reading. 'Tell Benedict what it is you need and he'll make sure you get it.'

'I will. And, Hassan?'

'Mmm?'

'Thank you.'

'Just go away and let me read my newspaper, will you?' he growled.

Ella was smiling happily to herself as she went off to find Benedict and, as always, the English aide was surprisingly friendly towards her. Surprising considering he'd delivered the replacement dress and underwear the morning after Alex and Allegra's party. At the time Ella had wondered what he must think of women like her, and how many he had to deal with in the course of a year. Women who fell into bed with a powerful man without really knowing them. Was it strange for Benedict Austin to see that same woman now installed as queen?

But he was nothing if not efficient and had soon allocated her an airy, north-facing room at the far end of the palace, close to the perfumed garden. Deliberately, she left the shutters open so that drifts of sweet scent could waft inside. As a place to paint, it took some beating.

Ella prepared the room thoroughly before the first sitting, intending to make rough sketches in charcoal before attempting to put oil to canvas. She positioned a chair against a completely plain background and decided that she would depict Hassan in his everyday robes. She'd taken the opportunity to study existing portraits in the palace and the few of her husband showed him looking resplendent in his various military uniforms and his more formal sheikh regalia. But she found herself wanting to show the person behind the position, the man not the king. As if by doing that, she might discover more about the man herself.

She sat down to wait for him, realising just how little she really knew about him. He'd still never mentioned his mother, and hadn't said much about his father either. She remembered the day she'd arrived here, when he'd resolutely silenced her questions about his upbringing. And she had let him silence her, determined to maintain a precarious kind of peace no matter what the cost.

But pregnancy was changing more than just her body; it was changing the way she viewed the world. Hassan's mother was not just a person whose name had caused the face of her elder son to darken with pain. She was also a part of the child whose daily kicking inside her belly grew stronger each day. And impending motherhood had also forced Ella to re-examine her views on her own family. She'd recognised that while she might not always approve of the way they behaved, she loved them all very dearly and could never deny their influence on her and the child she carried.

Why, this baby might be a boy who would grow up to be the spitting image of her father! And so what? She let her hand drift to lie on the hard swell of her belly. Was this what her own mother had felt, this powerful bond connecting her to her child? For the first time in her life, she acknowledged how difficult it must have been for her mother to have reared Bobby's children and also the children he'd had with another woman. He'd been unfaithful for much of their marriage and she had simply turned a blind eye to what was going on.

And yet Julie Jackson had somehow managed to keep it together. Ella and her brothers and sisters may not have had much money, but their messy home had been full of laughter, hadn't it? Not like this great, silent palace where Hassan had grown up. She tried to imagine him and his brother playing in the wide corridors and thought how lonely it must have been for them.

'Ella?'

Still lost in her thoughts, she looked up to see that Hassan had arrived at the 'studio,' his dark brows raised in mocking question.

'Sorry.' She smiled at him. 'I was miles away.'

'I can see that for myself. Are you ready for me?'

'Absolutely. Come and sit over here. That's right, just here.'

He sat where she'd asked him to and as she smoothed the headdress which covered his black hair, she resisted the urge to lean over and kiss him. It was one of their rules—or rather, it was one of *his* rules—no physical intimacy outside the bedroom. He'd told her that protocol demanded it, that the aides and ministers who moved with such silent deference around the palace would not approve of their king fooling around with his new bride. Because kisses tended to get out of hand and lead on to other, deeper intimacies. And Ella understood that. Just as she understood that it was yet another way for her husband to keep her at arm's length.

He glanced up at her. 'What must I do?' he asked.

She laughed. 'You know exactly what you must do. You've sat for paintings before.'

'Ah, but it was always with a man, never with the woman who just a few hours ago was lying in my arms.'

'Can you please not talk about sex?' She began to make rapid sweeps on the paper with her stick of charcoal.

'Why not?'

'Because it changes the look on your face. It makes your eyes turn smoky and your mouth grow tense.'

And not just his mouth, Hassan thought wryly, shifting his position slightly. He studied the sweeping movements of her hand and remembered the sketches he'd seen of her sister back in her house in London. The subject matter may have been a little *outré* for his taste, but there was no doubt that she had talent. 'You've never had any formal training?' he questioned.

'Nope.'

'Why not?'

'Because money was too tight to send me to art school.'

'I thought your father made a fortune.'

'He made several fortunes, and then lost them again. Plus, there were his many alimony payments.'

'He is known for his liking of women,' he observed.

'Understatement of the century,' she answered acidly. 'He is also known for his love of grand schemes and the temptation to make a quick buck, which is why there's never been any real money in our family. Everything we owned was only ever temporary.'

His eyes narrowed. 'I see.'

'I wonder if you do,' she said as she put a finger to her lips to indicate that he should stop talking. He'd certainly never known what it was like to worry about paying the gas bill, or to hunt in the cupboard to find nothing but a long-forgotten tin of caviar and to wonder whether slimy fish eggs could possibly fill you up.

For a while she worked in silence and once again Hassan used the opportunity to watch her. Her movements were economical and the studio was completely quiet apart from the scrape of the charcoal and the occasional song of a bird outside. Yet beneath the calm surface of their life, he was aware of a dark kind of uncertainty. A time bomb which was ticking away inexorably. Both of them waiting for something which had the potential to change their lives in ways he couldn't quite imagine. And didn't want to imagine…

He had seen her patting her growing bump, her face growing almost dreamy as she did so. He'd watched her drawing little circles on the tight drum of her belly, as if she was playing some secret game with the child inside her, and his heart had given a painful wrench. He felt jealous, he realised—because his own mother could never have felt a bond like that if she'd been able to just walk away from him and his brother…?

'Hassan, stop frowning.'

'I wasn't.'

'Yes, you were.' She stopped drawing, wondering what had caused that terrible bleakness to enter his eyes. 'What is it, Hassan?' she questioned softly. 'What on earth was making you look that way?'

He saw the understanding on her face and instinct

made him want to push her away. She wanted to probe into his past, as all women did. But with Ella he wasn't in a position to terminate the discussion and then make a cool exit. With Ella there was no escape; the fact that she carried his child had made her a constant in his life. So why not tell her the truth and wipe all that sweet understanding from her face? Why not make her understand where he was coming from, so she'd learn why he could never really love a woman, nor she him?

'I was remembering my mother,' he said.

Something about the silky venom in his voice made the hairs on the back of Ella's neck prickle with apprehension. 'You never talk about her.'

'No. Haven't you ever stopped to wonder why?'

'Of course I have.'

His mouth flattened into a grim line. He'd never told anyone, he realised suddenly. Even he and his brother had never discussed it. They'd locked the memory away in a dark place which was never allowed to see the light of day. As if such a rejection had been too painful to acknowledge, even to themselves. 'Maybe you *should* know, Ella. Maybe it will help explain properly the man that I am.'

Something in his voice was alarming her, and the cold, dark look on his face was scaring her even more.

'Don't tell me if you don't want to,' she whispered, but his face looked so frozen and forbidding that she wondered if he'd actually heard her.

He shook his head as the dark memories bubbled up from the deepest recesses of his mind. 'My mother was a princess from the neighbouring country of Bakamurat,' he said. 'And she was betrothed to my father from an early age—as was the custom at the time. They married when she was just eighteen, and not long after that, I was born. Two years later, Kamal came along.'

'But the marriage wasn't happy?' Ella saw the clenching of his jaw and bit her lip, appalled at her own naivety. 'I'm sorry. That's a stupid question. It can't have been happy if she…left.'

'In those days there was not such a realistic expectation of *happiness* as there is today,' he bit out. 'But, for a while at least, we had a contented family life, the four of us. Or at least, that's how it seemed to me.'

She heard some odd, metallic quality enter his tone. 'But something happened?' she guessed.

'Something most certainly did,' he agreed, his voice bitter. 'My mother went home to visit her sister in Bakamurat, leaving Kamal and me behind. She was gone longer than my father had anticipated, and when she returned, she was…different.'

'How do you mean, *different*?'

For a moment he didn't speak. He had buried this as deeply as he could, but even now he could vividly recall the distracted air which had made it seem as if his mother barely noticed him. The way she'd looked right through him and Kamal as if they hadn't been there. She'd gone off her food, so that the weight had dropped away from her and her beautiful face had seemed to be all large, confused dark eyes. In a way, she had never looked more lovely, and yet even at that early age, Hassan had sensed his father's increasing concern. He remembered the sound of their raised voices when he and Kamal lay in bed at night and the terrible silences at breakfast in the mornings.

'She had fallen in love with a nobleman from Bakamurat.' He heard the distorted sound of his own voice. 'She said she could not live without him. That he was the only man she'd ever loved. My father was as patient as I had ever seen him but eventually his patience wore thin. He told her she must choose between them.'

Ella broke the awful silence with a question she already knew the answer to. 'And she chose *him*?'

'Yes. She chose her lover over her husband and she left behind her two little boys while she went off to find what she described as the only man who had ever really understood her.'

'Who told you that?'

'My father.'

Ella nodded, her heart going out to him, cursing the loose tongues of broken-hearted adults. 'Sometimes parents tell their children too much,' she said falteringly. 'I remember my own mother sobbing and telling me things about my father I wish she hadn't said. I think she forgot who was the parent and who was the child. Sometimes people act inappropriately when their emotions get the better of them.'

'Exactly! Which is why I don't *do* emotion—or "love."' His lips curved into a cynical half-smile, thinking that she couldn't have given him a better platform for the truth if she'd tried. 'Why embrace something which makes people act shamefully?' he demanded. 'Which eats into what is good and what is true. And it changes—that's the truth of it. Love is as inconstant as the wind. My mother vowed to spend her life with my father and she broke that vow. So how can anyone ever put their trust in it?'

Ella put the charcoal down, afraid that he would see the sudden trembling of her fingers. The warning in his voice was implicit; she heard it loud and clear. But she wanted to know the ending. Whether any happiness had been squeezed from the sour story he was telling her.

'What happened to your mother?' she questioned softly.

He shook his head, because the supposed retribution which had been heaped upon the woman who had given birth to him had brought him no comfort. 'The shame of her desertion went with her. Her nobleman would not marry a woman who was tainted in such a way. I don't think he'd ever intended to marry her in the first place. She'd just built up the fantasy in her head. And of course, my father refused to take her back.'

'Did she want to come back?' breathed Ella.

'Oh, yes. It seemed that she realised just what she had lost—two little children and a man who loved her. But it was too late and his pride would not countenance it. He had been made a fool of once and would not risk it happening again. She began to neglect herself. She wasn't eating properly. She went to Switzerland and it was there, in the cold of the winter snows, that she caught pneumonia.'

Ella didn't need to hear the words to know that his mother had died; she could read it from the bleak look on his face. 'And you never...you never saw her again?'

'No.'

'Hassan—'

'No!' he said again, shaking away the soft hand which had reached out towards him. Standing, he moved away from the chair and her tantalising proximity.

But Ella went after him because the look of bleakness on his ravaged face was more than she could bear. She moved up to his tensed, hunched body and, rising up on tiptoes, she put her arms around him.

'Hassan,' she breathed into his ear. 'Darling, darling Hassan.'

His heart was thumping and he could feel the contrasting softness of her cheek against his. He should have pushed her away, but how could he do that when the hard curve of her baby bump was pressing against him and her welcoming arms were enfolding him. And that was the moment that his long-suppressed emotions ruptured. When anger and hurt and shame and resentment all came swimming darkly to the surface and threatened to swamp him.

He opened his mouth to groan but her lips were reaching towards his and somehow he was kissing her, kissing her with an urgent kind of hunger he'd never felt before. His hands splayed over her breasts and her muffled little cries urged him on, and as he felt the nipples harden beneath his palms, a primitive hunger began to rise in him.

With a low moan like the sound of a wounded animal, he pulled away from her before locking the door and, when he turned back, Ella could see from the look of dark intent on his face just what he was going to do.

His embrace was hard and his lips heated, but she matched him kiss for kiss. Greedily, she scrabbled at the silk of his robes as he slithered hers up over her thighs, his fingers skating over the cool skin there until he found the molten heat which awaited him.

She did not dare cry out, not even when he thrust deep inside her, taking her from behind because it was more comfortable that way, before beginning his inexorable rhythm. Ella swallowed as he caught hold of her shoulders, his lips on her hair as he whispered to her, strange, fractured words in his native tongue. It had never felt quite like this: with all her senses heightened by the emotion of what he'd told her and the fact that Hassan was breaking his own rules by making love to her in the makeshift studio.

Her orgasm happened quickly—almost too quickly, it seemed—and it was as if she had given him everything she had to give. She felt his own, final thrust. Heard the little choking sound he made as he clung to her, spilling his seed deep inside her.

'Hassan,' she whispered.

For a moment he couldn't speak as he sucked in gulps of air, sanity returning to cool his ardour like a summer rainstorm. Against the rumpled spill of her hair, Hassan briefly closed his eyes, a wave of guilt washing over him as he realised just what he had done. He had used her, as he used all women. He had taken the sweet comfort she was offering him and had turned it into the only commodity he was familiar with. Sex.

'That should never have happened,' he said hoarsely.

'But I'm *glad* it happened!' came her fierce reply.

Biting back his remorse, he withdrew from her, adjusting himself before turning her around to cup her face in his hands. 'So now do you understand why I am the man I am?' he demanded. 'Why I can't love. Do you understand that, Ella?'

She looked at him, her heart twisting with pain, wanting to tell him that his mother's rejection didn't mean that *all* women were going to do the same. That she would love him and cherish him if only he would give her the chance.

'I understand perfectly,' she said softly. 'But these things aren't set in stone, Hassan. There's no reason why you can't change.' *I can help you change.*

He saw the hope and understanding written on her face and a bitter wave of recrimination washed over him. She didn't have a clue, did she? How horrified she would be if she knew how ruthless he had been. If she discovered that he'd brought her out here hoping that she would leave him. And leave their baby too.

He shook his head as he unlocked the door and wrenched it open. 'I think we'd better call it a day. This session is over and I have work to do.'

And he swept from the room. Just like that. Leaving Ella watching him, blinking away the sudden shimmer of tears which had sprung to her eyes.

She glanced down at the start she'd made on the drawing which now bore the outline of Hassan's face. But it was strange how a few black lines had somehow managed to capture a true likeness of the man she had married. The hawk-like nose and the shadowed jut of his jaw. The autocratic cheekbones and the empty black eyes.

A proud man who had told her he could never love.

Closing the door quietly behind her, Ella left the studio and walked in silence along the scented marble corridor towards her suite.

CHAPTER TWELVE

So THIS was how it was going to be. Everything had changed, yet nothing had changed, and Ella felt as if she was living in a strange kind of limbo. She moved around the beautiful palace feeling like a gatecrasher who the benign host had allowed to remain at the party.

The stupid thing was that, at first, Hassan's emotional outpouring had given her hope. She'd thought that once he'd given himself time to reflect on her words that he might come around to her way of thinking. To realise that change *was* possible. That anything was possible if you wanted it enough.

And maybe the simple truth of it was that he just didn't want it. Maybe the thought of allowing himself to *feel* stuff secretly repulsed him. That his childhood experiences had scarred him too deeply for him ever to contemplate living his life in a different way.

Because he behaved as if nothing had happened. As if he hadn't torn open the blackness which seemed to envelop his heart and allowed her to glimpse the bitter pain which lay beneath.

Once again, the barriers came crashing down, only this time it was worse than before. Because now she had something with which to compare it. She'd felt a snatch of real closeness when he'd opened up to her about his past. When she'd felt as though they'd discovered a new honesty...and when she'd realised how easy it would be to love this proud and tortured man.

But that was all now a distant memory; the hot passion which had flared between them now mocked her, because Hassan had told her that sex was no longer on the agenda.

Her hands had trembled when he'd dropped *that* particular bombshell. 'You're saying that you no longer find me attractive?'

He had shaken his head, still not quite believing that he had opened up to her. Still dazed by the powerful and very basic sex which had followed, which had left him feeling...what? As if she'd laid him bare on every level. As if she could see right into his soul. 'I'm saying that your pregnancy is getting too advanced,' he responded. 'And I don't think sex is a good idea.'

Ella had turned away to hide her distress. And so the pleasure she'd found in his arms became nothing but a taunting series of memories. The nights were nothing but long, lonely hours to be endured. Her enormous bed allowed them both to lie there without touching, and the longer this went on, the more impossible it became to return to what they'd had before.

Ella would hold her breath as she felt the mattress dip beneath Hassan's weight, and perhaps if she hadn't been so pregnant, she might have attempted some form of seduction. As it was, even sitting up was a big, lumbering effort. She didn't even want to think of how clumsy it would look if she tried to launch herself at him. Anyway, such plans were pretty pointless since

Hassan would fall asleep almost as soon as his head touched the pillow, while she was left staring at the moon shadows flickering over the ceiling.

One morning she awoke to find him leaning over her, his dark face creased with concern, and for one crazy moment, she thought he was going to kiss her. Her lips parted as eagerly as a young chick on the nest, but his face became shuttered as he drew back from her.

'You look exhausted,' he observed quietly. 'Can't you sleep?'

'No.' She waited for him to ask him why and wondered if she dared tell him the reason. *Because I miss you. I miss you touching me. Kissing me. Making love to me. Because I'm scared of the future...and I'm only just beginning to realise the heartache which lies ahead if we're living these separate lives.* But she wasn't going to beg. Or whine. She hadn't quite sunk to *that*. She kept her voice light. 'Nobody ever died from lack of sleep.'

'No, but it isn't fair to you or the baby to see you looking so exhausted,' he said harshly. 'I will move back into my own rooms and sleep there from now on.'

Her eyes beseeched him to reconsider even if her pride stopped her from asking him outright, but he was true to his word. It didn't take long for one of his valets to move his few possessions out of her suite, and after that night, Ella slept alone.

As the days passed, so her loneliness increased. With her sickness firmly in the past and without the diversion of long and erotic nights with Hassan, Ella's life in the palace seemed empty and pointless. Only continuing with her husband's portrait, into which she poured all her thwarted passion and despair, helped fill the long, waiting days.

But that was her only distraction. The constant heat and lack of seasonal change were having a disorientating effect on her. She felt like someone who had awoken from a long sleep and found themselves in an unknown place. The flowers in the garden looked fake; the sky seemed too blue to be real. The beautiful, gilded palace began to feel like a glittering cage.

Hard to believe that it was early December and, back home, everyone would be gearing up to Christmas. She thought about the glittering lights which twinkled along Regent Street and the supermarkets which would be stuffed to the gills with chocolate. She thought about those tacky paper chains her father used to insist on, because no matter what his faults were, he absolutely loved Christmas and had passed on that love to his children.

And crazily, she began to miss her family. *All* her family. Her mother might be a walkover where her father was concerned, but she had always been there when you needed her. The email correspondence they'd been sharing suddenly seemed woefully inadequate, especially the last one which had expressed a wistful desire to 'see my little girl looking pregnant.'

She even missed her sisters. She hadn't had a chance to talk to Allegra about her engagement. And while Izzy might be erratic at times, she was filled with an energy and enthusiasm which Ella missed.

Now that all the Jacksons knew she was pregnant, would there really be any shame in admitting defeat and going home and accepting help from her family instead of from Hassan? Because his help came with a price tag which was beginning to seem way too high. She didn't *have* to be some sort of passive wimp who just took whatever type of behaviour the sheikh doled out to her.

Her troubled thoughts wouldn't leave her and eventually it dawned on her that she wanted to go home. And that she would have to tell Hassan. She would emphasise that her trip out here hadn't been wasted because at least it had enabled them to get to know each other and to establish a degree of civility. And she wouldn't be unreasonable over access either. In fact, she would make sure that he had as much of it as he liked. Because she would never allow a man who had been neglected by his mother to be kept at a distance by his son or daughter.

Once she had psyched herself up enough, she sat down to breakfast, her manner curiously calm as she took her place opposite her husband.

She went through the ritual of drizzling honey onto her bowl of yoghurt. She could sense him watching her, so suddenly she put her spoon down and looked up to meet the dark fire of his eyes.

'You're still not sleeping?' he questioned before she could say a word. 'Even though you now have the bed to yourself?'

'No.' She shook her head. 'It's getting much too uncomfortable to sleep.'

'Is there anything I can do?' he questioned.

For a moment she was tempted to say yes. To tell him to come back to her bed and get close to her. And despite her determination not to, she allowed herself a brief glimpse of how it *could* have been. She imagined a scenario where joys and problems could have been discussed, and shared. And then she thought about what it *was*: an empty relationship with a man who was cold and unloving towards her. Who had told her emphatically that he *couldn't* love. What woman in her right mind would settle for something like that?

'Yes.' She hesitated, clasping her fingers together just in case they started trembling. 'Actually, there is.'

Something in the tone of her voice made his eyes narrow. 'And what might that be, Ella?'

There was a pause. 'I want to go home.'

Hassan nodded as a terrible tearing sense of inevitability twisted his gut. 'Home?' he questioned.

'Yes, home. I want to see my family.'

'But I thought your family drove you mad?'

'And they do—frequently!' Her gaze was very steady as she looked at him. 'But at least they *feel* stuff. At least their hearts are in the right place, even if they often get it wrong!'

Her implication was crystal clear and suddenly Hassan was forced to accept what he would have once considered impossible. That, for all their faults, at least the Jacksons had the courage to face up to their own emotions. Their lives might be chaotic at times, but they didn't run away and hide from their feelings. And yet didn't he despise that kind of messy emotion? Surely that wasn't a brief pang of *envy* he was experiencing? His mouth hardened. 'And you miss them?'

'I do.' She nodded, steeling her heart. 'I feel like a shadow here, Hassan. As if I'm invisible. I want to fly home so that I can see a few friendly and familiar faces and eat some mince pies and listen to c-c-carols….'

To her horror, she realised that tears had sprung to her eyes and when Hassan made to move towards her she waved him away. 'D-don't!' she stumbled, knowing that if he touched her she would be lost. 'Please don't. You've made it very clear you don't want me near you, so please don't let a few tears tempt you from your chosen path. My life has telescoped down to this beautiful place which now feels like a prison, though I'm starting to wonder if that's how you wanted it to be all along.'

Hassan sucked in a breath. He felt as if he had wandered into a maze of his own making, where darkness had suddenly fallen. He had pushed her away in order to protect himself. Pushed her and pushed her until she had decided that she could take no more. Now she wanted out, and he had no one to blame but himself. He looked at her pale face, at the swollen curve of her belly, and was overcome with a terrible wave of regret.

'But you're nearly thirty-six weeks pregnant,' he pointed out.

'So?'

'So the airlines won't allow you to fly.'

'You've got your own plane, Hassan, so I can't see *that* will be a problem.'

In silence, he got up from the table and walked over to the window, his mind teeming with conflicting thoughts. What if he asked her to stay, what then? What did she really want from him? he wondered. Deep in his heart he knew. She wanted the *impossible*!

She wanted the man he could never be, the close and loving partner all women were programmed to want.

He turned away from the window to see her looking at him, her blue eyes wary, her arms folded defensively across her breasts. And suddenly he realised that this was the one area of his life where he had consistently shown a complete lack of courage. Was he so afraid of reliving the pain of his childhood that he wouldn't take any risks for a chance of happiness? Couldn't he at least *try* to be what she wanted?

'Maybe you're right,' he said slowly. 'I *have* been guilty of neglecting you. But if it's any consolation, I thought I was doing it for the best.'

'For the best for who? For you? Or for me?' she shot back. 'And meanwhile, you mooch around being all king-like and solitary, while I've been cooped up inside this wretched palace for weeks!'

'I realise that.' He drew a breath, unused to this new-found role of mediator in his own marriage. 'Which is why I wondered if you'd like to go on a trip?'

'That's what I'm proposing, Hassan—a trip back home to England.'

'No, not that.' He shook his head. 'My brother has a traditional Bedouin tent situated on the edge of the Serhetabat Desert. It's not far from here, although it feels like a different world. We could go and stay there for a couple of nights.' His black eyes narrowed. 'It would give you a break. Give you a complete change of scenery. Wouldn't you like that, Ella?'

Despite all that had happened between them, Ella felt tempted. Surely two nights in a Bedouin tent meant that they'd connect again—and wasn't that something she still wanted even though her aching heart told her that she was crazy to want it? She wondered what his offer represented. Whether it was his way of saying that he understood her frustrations and wanted to make some amends. Or whether it was simply a sweetener to get her to do what he wanted and stay in Kashamak.

'I don't know,' she prevaricated.

Her reluctance didn't surprise him and neither did the fierce light which sparked from her blue eyes. Hassan realised that he *admired* her defiance and her determination to stand up to him. All the things which he'd once claimed not to like in a woman, he found amazingly attractive in Ella. And yet didn't nature ensure that what attracted also repelled? Didn't what drew him to her also drive him away, with a feeling which was the closest he'd known to fear?

'It is a very beautiful place,' he said steadily. 'Which you really ought to see for yourself. The desert sky when it's washed in moonlight is a sight not to be missed.'

'And afterwards, Hassan? What then?'

He felt an aching dryness in his throat as he met the question in her eyes and knew he couldn't offer her empty promises. He could take this first step and see where it led, but he wasn't in the habit of dishing out false hope. 'If you decide that you're missing England so much, then of course you must go back. I won't stop you, and I will support you and our child in whatever way I can.'

Her heart pounding, Ella stared at him. He was offering her freedom, and never had an offer seemed like such a poisoned chalice. 'And you wouldn't mind?'

He shrugged. 'Naturally, it would be easier to keep you and the baby here,' he said heavily. 'But I don't intend to force you to stay. Ultimately, it has to be your decision.'

Ella shook her head in frustration. With his burnished skin and magnificent body, he might look like every woman's fantasy come to life, but inside he was frozen. *Frozen.* It was like dealing with some sort of robot, one who was conditioned to move but never to feel! *He doesn't care whether you go or stay! Nothing has changed in all the weeks you've been here.*

The voice inside her head mocked her hesitation and yet something inside her made her want this trip. Some illogical little hope which refused to die, despite all the odds which were stacked up against it.

'Then let's go,' she said as she stared into his black eyes. 'Maybe seeing the desert sky washed with moonlight is exactly what I need.'

CHAPTER THIRTEEN

THEY left the next morning in a four-wheel drive which Hassan drove himself, the powerful car eating up the miles of straight, desert roads. Ella was determined to make the most of what might be her one and only desert trip, but her excitement was tempered by the niggling backache she'd developed during the night and which seemed to be preventing her from getting comfortable.

She felt *edgy*. Wondering why was she was going to the bother of putting herself through all this—the newlywed queen being shown the desert by her sheikh king—when it was nothing but a sham. Hassan had probably only offered to take her in order to placate her. To keep the little lady quiet. Restlessly, she wriggled in her seat.

Hassan shot her a glance as he saw her tug impatiently at the seat belt which was straining over her swollen belly. 'Are you okay?'

'I'm absolutely fine,' she said. 'So will you please keep your eyes off me and look at the road instead?'

She had been in an irritable mood all morning, he acknowledged, but he did as she asked, silence falling as they drove along until he saw a familiar marking on the horizon.

'Look,' he said. 'Straight ahead and a little to the left. Can you see it?'

Ella screwed up her eyes to see a small blot on the stark landscape. As they grew closer, she could see that it was a tent, but nothing like as glamorous as she'd been expecting. Apart from its dense, black colour, it just seemed like a much bigger version of the tents you saw at music festivals.

'Does it stand empty all the time?' she asked.

'This one does. Kamal uses it only infrequently. I sent some servants here earlier to make it habitable for us, but they will have returned to the palace by now.'

He stopped the car in a spray of sand and went round to the passenger door. The pure, clean air filled his lungs as he inhaled deeply and he looked up into the deep cobalt of the sky before helping his wife down. It had been a long time since he'd been in the desert for the purpose of pleasure, rather than war, and inevitably he felt the fizz of exhilaration. Stealing a glance at Ella's face, he helped her down from the car. Maybe not quite pleasure, he amended wryly—at least, not for her. Endurance might be a more accurate description, judging by her expression.

'Welcome,' he said. 'To a genuine Bedouin tent. For the weary traveller, the sight of one of these is like stumbling across an oasis.'

Ella dredged up a smile from somewhere. She was feeling very weary herself, and it was much hotter out here than she'd imagined. But she recognised that Hassan was trying hard to please her, so shouldn't she just try to enjoy the experience? Fanning her hand across her face, she made her way over to the entrance of the tent, but as she pulled back the flap and stepped inside the surprisingly cool interior, she sucked in a breath of amazement.

Lit by intricate metal lamps, the canopied ceiling was hung with rich fabrics of scarlet and bronze, all shot with shimmering gold. Rose and turquoise wall hangings glimmered with a soft intensity, and on the woven rugs stood low sofas, cushions and bronze tables. The air was scented with something spicy and evocative and for a moment Ella's niggling backache was forgotten.

'Oh, wow,' she said softly, because it was exactly like stepping into an illustration from the *Arabian Nights*. 'It's beautiful.'

But Hassan's attention wasn't on the decor. He was momentarily transfixed by the look on his wife's face. By the parting of her rose-petal lips and the widening of her ice-blue eyes. *She* was beautiful, he thought suddenly. Her face bare of makeup and her body swollen with his child, he thought he'd never seen anyone look quite so lovely in his life. *And she wants to leave you. She wants to leave you, and you have no one to blame but yourself.*

'Shall we sit down?' he questioned unsteadily. 'And I'll make you some of the tea for which the Bedouin are famous.'

A wave of dizziness swept over her as Ella nodded, cumbersomely lowering herself onto one of the cushions. 'If you like,' she said.

He set about boiling water and measuring out herbs

and sugar before adding them to the heavy pot in which the tea was made. But he turned round when he heard the ragged little sigh she made and saw her eyes momentarily close.

'Are you okay?'

Her lids flew open again. 'I would be if you'd just stop fussing!' She sounded as if she was spoiling for a fight but Hassan didn't react. She's just emotional, he told himself. And she has every right to be. He carried over a tray bearing tiny cups and the steaming tea.

'What's that funny smell?' she questioned suspiciously.

'It's probably the habak and marmaraya. They're the desert herbs which gives the tea its distinct flavour. The habak tastes a little like mint.'

Ella swallowed. 'I think I'm going to be sick.'

'It isn't *that* bad.'

But his attempt at humour was forgotten as Ella suddenly realised that something momentous was happening to her.

'Hassan, I feel weird.'

'What kind of weird?'

She swallowed. 'I think I'm going to have the baby.'

'Don't be silly.'

'Don't you dare tell me I'm silly!' she flared back. 'How the hell would you know? You've suddenly gained a qualification in obstetrics, have you?'

'You've got another four weeks to go.'

'I know exactly how long I've got to go and I don't *care*! This baby's coming *now*!' Staggering to her feet, she felt the unexpected warm rush of liquid cascading down her leg and she stared down in numb horror as realisation began to dawn on her. 'Hassan!' she gasped, raising her head to meet the disbelief in his eyes. 'My waters have just broken!'

Hassan froze. He thought of the clean, bright interior of the labour ward at the hospital in Samaltyn, of the fully trained teams of doctors and nurses who could be summoned at a moment's notice, and denial washed over him. 'They can't have done!'

'They have! Look! *Look!*' Reaching out, she caught hold of his hand, her nails digging roughly into his flesh. 'Hassan, that was a definitely a contraction!'

'Are you sure?'

'Of course I'm sure! Oh, heavens! The baby's coming and we're stuck out in the middle of the bloody desert!'

One glance at her was enough to convince him that she was speaking the truth and his instinct was to panic like never before. Desperately, his thoughts whirled as he thought about the options which lay open to them. Was there time to get her back to Samaltyn? He heard her gasp and clutch at her stomach with her free hand and he knew there was not. Sweet flower of the desert, why ever had he brought her out here at such a time?

But her blue eyes were dark with fear and Hassan knew he had to quash his own spiralling terror and get a grip. He had to be there for her. He had let her down so many ways in the past but this time she was relying on him like never before.

Carefully, he laid her back down on the cushions, barely noticing the nails which were digging into his hands so hard he could feel them drawing blood. His heart was pounding frantically as he leaned over her and squeezed her hand. 'Stay here!' he commanded.

'What else do you think I'm going to do?' She clung onto his hand as she felt him pulling away. 'Hassan! Where are you going?'

He cursed as he stared down at the flat line on his cellphone. 'I'll have to go outside, to ring the hospital. There's no damned signal in here!'

'Don't leave me!' she whispered.

'Sweetheart. I'll be right back.'

Ella felt as if this was all happening to someone else and the unfamiliar *sweetheart* only compounded it. As if the woman lying back against a pile of cushions, gasping with pain, was someone she'd once met but didn't really know. Dimly, she could hear Hassan outside the tent barking out a series of instructions in his native tongue. Hurry up, she thought faintly. Just hurry *up*!

She had never been so glad to see anyone as when he came running back into the tent and crouched down beside her. But then another contraction rocked right through her and she clung to him, panting for breath.

'It's okay,' he said, closing his eyes briefly against her damp hair as he held her. 'The hospital is sending a helicopter with a full obstetric crew on board. They say that you've probably got plenty of time before you deliver, especially as this is a first baby.'

She shook her head as another contraction racked through her body, feeling as if someone had sent a red-hot poker slicing up inside her. 'No!' she croaked.

Helplessly, his gaze raked over her ashen face. No,

what? 'Just hang on in there,' he urged from between gritted teeth. 'They'll be here soon.'

'Hassan,' she gasped, sweat breaking out on her brow as another contraction came. Her nails dug into him even more. 'They're wrong.'

'Who is?'

'The hospital. I—' She gasped as the pain made speech momentarily impossible. 'I think this baby's coming now!'

His heart pounded. 'It can't be.'

'Yes, it *can*.'

'How can you be sure?'

'I just *am*!'

Desperately, he looked out into the starkness of the empty desert which could be seen through the flaps of the tent. How long would the helicopter take, he wondered distractedly, and would it be able to pinpoint their position? 'I'll go outside and get a signal. Speak to the doctor—'

'Hassan, there isn't time!' She gripped even tighter as another contraction tightened its vice-like grip around her. 'Just stay!' she gasped. 'Hassan, I need you here with me. I need *you*. Please.'

He saw the change in her and realised that she was speaking the truth. That their baby was about to be born. Here. Now. And that he was the only person who could help her. He was going to have to deliver the baby. *His* baby.

He felt a brief roaring in his ears before his head cleared and he suddenly became calm. It was like being in battle, when the sounds of melee all around him suddenly blurred into silence and he could see nothing but the task which lay ahead.

'I'm here,' he said softly, injecting calm into his voice as he began to loosen her clothing. 'I'm here for you and everything is going to be fine. Shh, Ella. Just take it easy. Breathe very slowly. That's right. Very slowly. Nature knows what to do.'

She looked up at him. 'I'm scared.'

So was he—more scared than he'd ever been. But Hassan had had a lifetime of experience in hiding the way he felt. Right now, he'd never been so glad of that. Gripping her hands tightly, he looked deep into her eyes. 'Trust me, Ella,' he said softly. 'I am here for you, and believe me when I tell you that it's going to be okay.'

Ella nodded and, despite the pain and fear, her trust in him at that moment was total and complete.

He found a soft blanket, remembering the first time he'd seen a foal being born and recalling what the stable boy had told him: that mares were like humans, that every birth was different and that most of what happened did so without the need for intervention. Please let that be the case this time, he prayed silently as he brushed her sweat-soaked hair away from her face.

'Hassan!'

'I'm here. Keep breathing. Go on, breathe.'

The vice-like contractions were increasing in frequency and intensity. She began to anticipate the next one, wondering if it could possibly be as bad as the one before, only to discover that it was worse. Was this what every woman who'd ever given birth had experienced?

'I can't bear it!' she cried.

'Yes, you can. You can, Ella. You can do anything you want to do because you're strong. The strongest woman I ever met.'

At any other time such words would have moved her but now they were nudged onto the periphery of her mind as another great contraction racked through her. Ella bit hard down on her lip as something in her body changed and she looked up into Hassan's black eyes, saw the question written in them and realised that something very powerful was happening. 'I think the baby's coming right now,' she gritted out. 'Oh, Hassan! Hassan, please help me!'

He moved just in time to see the slick crown of a head appear. 'You're doing fine,' he said unsteadily. 'You're amazing. You're nearly there.'

Dimly she remembered what she'd been taught: not to push until the need to push was unbearable. Guided by that and governed by an instinct as old as time itself, she held on to that thought. 'Yes,' she breathed, her face contorted with effort. 'Yes.'

He heard the keening sound she made and his heart began to race. Every sense intensified, he moved as if he was on some sort of autopilot. 'That's perfect,' he said roughly. Suddenly, he was aware that he was looking down at the baby's matted black hair and a great lump rose in his throat. 'Just one more push, Ella. Do you think you can do that?'

Yes! No! I don't know!

'Yes, you can. Ella, you can.'

The moan she made sounded as if it had been torn from some unimaginably deep place inside her and

Hassan stretched out his palms to form a miniature cradle just as his baby was born into them.

His baby.

He felt the slippery unfamiliarity of new life in his hands and his heart clenched with terror as nothing else happened. The whole world seemed suspended in that moment of absolute silence before a lusty cry split the air.

His eyes blurred with tears and he looked down to see the wriggling form of a tiny yet perfect human being in his hands, which he quickly wrapped in the soft blanket before laying the child gently on Ella's stomach.

Her voice seemed to come from a long way off. 'Is…is everything okay?'

'She's perfect, my darling. Perfect. Just like you.'

Ella's hand was trembling as she reached out to touch her baby, amazement and relief compounded by the realisation that Hassan was crying. And that he had been there for her.

He had been there for her when she most needed him. On every level he had delivered. He *could* be the man she wanted him to be: emotional and strong and equal.

She gave a ragged breath as she heard helicopter propellers descending from out of the desert sky, and even while she was glad that help was arriving, she wanted to hold on to that private moment for ever. Just the three of them in their own little world. With none of the fears that once they stepped outside that tent, Hassan would go back to being the cool and distant man of the past.

CHAPTER FOURTEEN

HASSAN shut the door of the studio behind him and began to walk down the wide marble corridor towards the nursery suite. His heart was heavy but he knew he could not put off this moment any longer. It was time to accept and face up to the truth.

He'd been waiting for the right moment. For Ella to properly recover from the birth. For the doctors to give both mother and daughter the thumbs-up. And for this terrible sense of remorse to leave him.

Yet it wouldn't leave him. It clung to him like glue. Deep down he knew there was only one thing which would make him feel better—ironically, the very thing which would bring his world crashing down about him.

He found Ella standing by the window in the main salon, looking out onto one of the smaller fountains where a plume of water formed a graceful curve. Barefooted beneath her cream silk robe, her hair was hanging loose down her back and she turned round when she heard him enter. Her blue eyes were as bright as usual but he saw darkness in their depths, as if she, too, had recognised that the moment of truth was here.

'Your father has been on the phone,' he said heavily.

'Oh? What did he say?'

He saw the faint lines crisscrossing her pale brow and realised that she must have lived much of her life like this. On a kind of knife edge, never knowing what her father was going to do or say next. His mouth hardened. And hadn't it been exactly the same when she'd met him? Hadn't he brought that same element of uncertainty into her life? He wondered why he had never seen that before, but the answer came to him almost immediately. He'd never seen it because he'd never allowed himself to see it.

'He wants to know whether we are planning to go to Alex and Allegra's wedding.'

She looked at him. 'And what did you tell him?'

'I said that we hadn't decided. Because that's the truth of it, isn't it, Ella? We haven't decided so many things, and I don't think attending your sister's wedding is top of the list of things we need to resolve.'

Ella nodded, but his words made her heart plummet. She knew they couldn't keep putting off the inevitable, yet she was afraid to face up to it. Afraid of what lay ahead—of a cold and empty future without her husband by her side.

Hadn't she hoped that they could just forget the past and move on? Capitalise on the love—yes, love—which had pulsed through the air between them after their baby had been born. That moment of pure and unfettered joy when their eyes had met and they had silently acknowledged the new life they had created.

She looked at Hassan now, wondering whether they should postpone any decisions for a few days longer. He still looked slightly shell-shocked, even though it had been a week since they had returned from the desert. The longest seven days of her life, and easily the most eventful.

They'd been dazed and disorientated as they had entered the celebrating city of Samaltyn, cradling their newborn daughter with pride. They'd called her Rihana because they both liked the name, and when Ella had discovered it meant 'sweet herb,' that had clinched it. Because hadn't Hassan been making sweet, herbal tea when she'd gone into labour? For a while she'd been on such a high of hormones and emotion that it was all too easy to pretend they were like any normal couple who'd just had a baby.

But now the intensely intimate memories of the birth had started to fade, leaving a couple who had resolved nothing. Who had begun to eye each other warily, as if each waiting for the other to make a move. She found herself wishing that she was back in that simple Bedouin tent again, where she had felt so incredibly close to Hassan. But she couldn't keep getting herself into medical emergencies just to get him to show some *feelings*, could she?

'You said you wanted to go home,' Hassan said roughly, his words breaking into her thoughts and sounding almost like an accusation. 'Have you thought any more about that?'

Ella winced as his stark words brought reality crashing in. During the ecstatic days following Rihana's birth, it had been all too easy to forget about her insecurities, but Hassan's question brought it into such sharp focus that she could no longer ignore it. Her insecurity was all bound up in her marriage, she realised, in her relationship with him. And nothing had changed.

Yes, during those heightened and unbelievable moments in the desert, she'd felt as close to him as she'd imagined it was possible for a man and woman to feel. When the helicopter had landed and the obstetricians had rushed in and taken over, before leaving the two—no, three—of them alone again for a few minutes, it had seemed a very precious time indeed.

Their eyes had met over the dark head of the baby who had latched so eagerly onto her breast and she thought she'd read something other than dazed pride in Hassan's expression. She'd clung to the hope that he might now want to forge a new and closer future. A future for *all* of them.

But all those hopes had evaporated by the time they returned to the palace, where it seemed that normal procedure was to be renewed almost immediately. Hassan had done what he did best and occupied himself with the practicalities. Making sure that she had the best after-care. Issuing statements to the world media and declining to the give them the full and dramatic story of Rihana's birth. Filling the nursery with a department-store quota of soft, fluffy toys.

Yet the subsequently smooth transition from pregnant queen to new mother seemed to have left Ella feeling just as displaced as before. *And nothing would ever change so long as she was with Hassan,* she realised. Why would it, when he didn't seem to want anything more than this?

Now she focused on his words and realised that it

was worse than she'd thought. That he actively *wanted* her to go.

'I'd thought I'd wait—'

'For what, Ella?' he interrupted bitterly. 'For me to bond even more with Rihana so that I'll find it unbearable when you take her away from me?'

'You want me to go,' she stated dully.

Hassan flinched. Was she determined to twist the knife, to make this even more painful than it already was? And could he really blame her, if that was the case, for surely he deserved everything she chose to heap upon his head?

'I can't see any alternative.' His voice was harsh. 'Surely you can't wait to get away from a man who forced you to come here even though you wanted to stay in London. A man who doesn't have a heart, nor any compassion. Because I now have looked at myself through your eyes, Ella, and I do not like what I see.'

'What on earth are you talking about?' she whispered.

He shook his head as the memory swam into his mind, like dark, distorting smoke. 'That portrait!' he grated. 'I have just been into the studio and seen the man that you have painted. A ravaged man—'

'Hassan—'

'Isn't there some novel where the man agrees a trade-off with the devil for eternal youth?' he demanded. 'And meanwhile there's a portrait in the attic which shows the growing darkness inside him?'

'It's called *The Picture of Dorian Gray*,' she said automatically.

'Well, the darkness is right there on that canvas

you've done of me, only I haven't even had the eternal youth in exchange,' he said bitterly, until he realised that wasn't quite true. Because in a way, every man who ever had a child was given the gift of eternal youth. Only he would never see the daily miracle of his daughter's developing life. He would be resigned to meeting her on high days and holidays, their precious time eaten into by the initial adjustment of having to reacquaint themselves every time they met. He would grow older never really knowing his child, and he would have no one to blame but himself.

Ella stared at him. 'What are you trying to say, Hassan?'

He knew that he had to tell her. Everything. Every damned thing. She had to know the terrible lengths to which he had been prepared to go—and that would be the end of their marriage, once and for all.

'Do you want to know the real reason why I was so insistent you came out to Kashamak when I discovered you were pregnant?' he demanded.

She remembered the way he had expressed it at the time—as concern for her morning sickness and the need for someone to look after her. But she hadn't been naive enough to think they were the real reasons. 'It was about control, wasn't it? About making sure that I conducted the pregnancy in a way you approved of.'

'Yes, it was. But deep down, it was even more manipulative than that,' he said quietly. 'I thought you'd have trouble adjusting, you see. That motherhood would cramp your style.'

'Cramp my style?' she repeated blankly.

'That was when I was still labouring under the illusion that you were a good-time girl. A social butterfly. I thought you'd hate your life here and you'd want to be free again. And that's what I wanted too.'

Ella saw the muscle which was working frantically at his cheek and the expression in his black eyes. But for once, they were not empty. Instead they were filled with the most terrible look of *bleakness* she had ever seen. Even worse than the time he'd told her about his mother.

'You wanted me to leave?' she guessed slowly. 'And to leave the baby behind, with you?'

He winced, but he did not look away from her. The truth was painful but he could not deny it—and didn't he deserve this pain? Didn't he deserve all the recriminations she chose to hurl at his head? 'Yes.'

'To bring her up as your father once did, without a mother?'

'Yes.' He shook his head, as if he was coming out of a deep sleep. 'It's only been during the past few weeks that I realised I couldn't possibly go through with it. That I couldn't inflict on my own child what I had suffered myself. But for a while, the intention was there.' He met the question which blazed from her eyes. 'How you must hate me, Ella.'

For a second she thought that perhaps it would be easier if she did, because the man who stood before her was the most complex individual she'd ever met. And didn't she suspect that the dark and complicated side of him *wanted* her to hate him? That it would be easier for him if she did, if she pushed him away and thus reinforced all his prejudices against women.

But Ella realised that nobody had ever been there

for Hassan, not emotionally. After his mother had left, he'd never let anyone get close enough to try, and she wondered if she had the courage to do that. To risk being rejected by him all over again.

Yet what choice did she have? To live a life blighted by regret because she hadn't had the guts to put her pride aside and reach out for a man who badly needed love. *Her* love—and their daughter's love. Couldn't she and Rihana help his damaged heart to heal?

'I don't hate you, Hassan,' she said softly. 'In fact, I love you. Even though you didn't want me to love you. And even though you did your best to make me turn my heart against you. I have to tell you that it hasn't worked. And that if you were to ask me to stay here, with Rihana, and to be a proper wife in every sense of the word, then I would do it in a heartbeat. But I will only do it on one condition.'

Her soft and powerful words had momentarily stilled him, but now he stirred because conditions were familiar territory to him. His eyes were wary as they looked at her. 'Which is?'

She swallowed. 'I need to know that you care for *me* in some small way. That there's a small seed of affection in your heart which maybe we can nurture and grow. And that you *will* nurture it, because while I've grown rather fond of the sand which surrounds us, I can't live my life in an emotional desert.'

For long, silent seconds he stared at her, recognising the courage it had taken to lay open her feelings like that. How she humbled him with her courage! His eyes began blinking rapidly and when eventually he could bring himself to speak, his voice sounded strangely hoarse to his ears—the way it had done when he'd had his tonsils removed as a boy. 'Not a seed,' he said brokenly.

'Not a seed?' she repeated in confusion.

He shook his head. 'Not a seed, no, but an eager young plant in its first rapid flush of life. For that is the strength of my "affection" for you, Ella!' A rush of emotion surged through his veins as he reached out and pulled her in his arms. 'But I do not know it by such a mediocre word as *affection*, because for days now I have been realising that it is called something else. Something I have never known before, nor dared to acknowledge.'

'Could you perhaps try acknowledging it now?' she suggested gently, knowing instantly what he meant because she could see it written all over his face. But she needed badly to hear it. She had bared her heart to him and now Hassan needed to redress the balance. To be her equal in every way there was.

He took both her hands in his. 'Ella, I…love you. You hear how my voice falters on these words, but that does not mean you should doubt them. With all my heart and body and mind, I love you. You are everything a woman should be and I do not know why a generous fate should have brought you into my life. You have offered me your heart when I do not deserve—'

'No!' Her fierce word cut him short but her hands were trembling as she reached up to cup his dark and beloved face between her palms. 'You didn't *deserve* the childhood you had and maybe I didn't either. But I think it's time we had some lovely things in our life together, and they are right here at our fingertips. We can reach out and take them any time we want, start-ing right now. Not palaces or privileges or some flashy lifestyle with *stuff*, but you, me and Rihana.'

'And our marriage will not fail,' he declared softly.

'No, it won't—because we won't let it fail,' she agreed shakily. 'We will learn from all the mistakes our parents made and we will give Rihana the kind of childhood that neither of us knew.'

His lips were passionate as he claimed hers in a kiss far deeper than any kiss he'd ever known. It was about more than passion and maybe about even more than love. It was about understanding and forgiving. About commitment and sharing. About making a happy home for the little girl who lay sleeping in her crib.

Bobby Jackson had christened his daughter Cinderella because he'd wanted her to marry a prince and somehow his rather ambitious dream had come true.

But Ella and Hassan had very different aspirations for their little girl, and that was why Rihana's middle name was Hope.

* * * * *

LET'S TALK
Romance

For exclusive extracts, competitions
and special offers, find us online:

f facebook.com/millsandboon

⦿ @millsandboonuk

🐦 @millsandboon

Or get in touch on 0844 844 1351*

For all the latest titles coming soon, visit
millsandboon.co.uk/nextmonth